I0763452

Horrified over her mother's treason,
desperate to redeem her family's honor,
a Japanese-American girl infiltrates a
World War II Japanese prisoner-of-war camp
to free victims of medical experiments.
That's the plan, anyway . . . .

A rare glimpse into civilian life in wartime Japan.

"This is a gem . . . a well written story that explores different perspectives during World War II."
a taleflick *"Top Pick"*

- taleflick.com

"This novel was filled with drama, action, and well-researched information that made this an intense yet entertaining read. Very impressive."

- Readers' Favorite Book Reviews

- Killer Nashville Writers Conference, "Thriller" category

$29.95

RIPPLE IN THE SEA

by Charley Pearson

CEP Books

Printed by Ingram-Spark

This book is a work of fiction. Except as discussed in the Historical Notes at the end, names, characters, places, and incidents either are products of the author's imagination or are used fictitiously. Any resemblance to actual persons, living or dead, events, or locales is entirely coincidental, except as indicated in the Historical Notes.

RIPPLE IN THE SEA

ISBN-13: 978-0-997299-3-5-9

Publication Date: 15 August 2020
(the 75th anniversary of the end of the Pacific War)

Second printing:
10 9 8 7 6 5 4 3 2

Dedication

This book is dedicated to Chiune and Yukiko Sugihara. As Japanese Consul-General in Lithuania in 1940, Chiune and his wife defied their government, risking life and career, to give transit visas to over 6000 Jews, allowing them to cross the Soviet Union and pass through Japan to safety before the Nazis invaded.

And

This book is also dedicated to Helene Deschamps, who served in the World War II French resistance, and to all the other young women who, without training, became spies and risked all.

Acknowledgments

I need to express gratitude to many who helped along the way. Fellow writers provided needed input on the various stages of this project from its original incarnation as a screenplay (Part I only) through its evolution into a novel. Critique partners included Cindy Rinaldi, Pat Charles, Merry Elrick, JC Walkup, and Sonja Contois.

Following writers conferences and charity auctions, several agents and editors provided great suggestions, from pacing to scene sequencing to redrafting the whole thing in first person instead of third.

Finally, beta-reader Taketo Ohtani provided invaluable advice on Japanese language and culture.

Much thanks to all.

An Introductory Thought

This is a story I had to write, thanks to my father's experiences in the Pacific Theater during World War II, after which he suffered from PTSD. It's been 75 years since the end of that war, and in all that time very little has been published regarding civilian life in wartime Japan (the Historical Notes at the end list a few examples; they tend to be at least somewhat autobiographical). A more wide-ranging accounting of this era, in a fictional format that could appeal to readers, appeared worthwhile. Part I of the following tale sets the stage for it, balancing the things done to Japan with the things Japan had done earlier in the war (which are also addressed in many other works).

This novel does not address details of the internment of Japanese-Americans living in the western United States during the war years, since the characters in the story would have been unaware of these issues. Readers are encouraged to explore other sources in that regard.

To those who consider it inappropriate that a person of a given ethnicity should write from the perspective of another, I apologize. "Own voices" may be optimal, but it would seem wrong to suppress a story simply because no one from the relevant culture has chosen to tell it. (As you might expect, at this point few are still alive who experienced the culture of wartime Japan, so I am fortunate to have found one to help as a beta-reader.)

In addition to readers interested in the history of the era, it is my hope that teachers might find this an acceptable way to present details of the period in a manner that intrigues students.

RIPPLE IN THE SEA

"War chews up people and spits them out,
mangled and broken.
But some it swallows whole,
and there's no telling what may emerge."

- Kristy Hara

Part 1: The Isle

"This, indeed, is not the Japan
that we have known and loved."

- Joseph Grew, U.S. Ambassador to Japan

Chapter 1

Face it, girl, you're a coward. Frisco sat there right across the bay, rich, vibrant, and tempting. Too close to home, of course; someone would recognize me. But it glistened like a beacon of independence, chastising me for sticking around. I could have picked among a hundred other places no more than a day down the road.

I placed the last piece of silverware and gazed out the window. This weekend, tomorrow, it would happen. I'd finally mustered some spirit. Now I just had to go through with it.

"Wake up, you lazy thing. Where is that aircraft carrier?" My mother surveyed the dinner table, tapping a ruler against her palm, but I'd laid it out perfectly for her party tonight. She had nothing to complain about.

My father gave me a sympathetic eye and hid behind the newspaper. A great guy for some things—last night he helped me build a dollhouse for the cutie two houses down—but the one time I questioned my mother's habits, all I got was 'raising daughters is a mother's business.' I could swear it wasn't like this with Maxine, or anyone else in high school.

I dug out my sketchbook and touched up the stern of the carrier I'd seen the other day. They rarely came into San Francisco

Bay, mostly they stayed around San Diego and Puget Sound, so I'd leapt at the chance to draw one. Didn't like what I'd done with its island; they kept changing the design of their new radar towers and it was hard remembering what the different ships had. Easier for my favorite kinds of boats, submarines, as they rarely put up their masts in port and I didn't have to draw them.

"Hurry up."

My mother stuffed a letter and another of my sketches into the envelope she was sending to my cousin in Osaka. She claimed he made the best ship models in Japan and needed accuracy to outsell competitors. I finished the carrier drawing, tore it out of the book, folded it where creases wouldn't hurt the lines of the ship, and handed it to my mother. She snatched it without a word.

Well, she didn't rap my knuckles. That was something.

"I'm going out." I grabbed my jacket and went to the door. Middle of the day, Saturday, homework done, so my mother had no reason to keep me. I guess she agreed, since all she did was sniff at her reflection in the glass-fronted china cabinet and mumble something about turning grey before my father.

I went out the back way, blowing a kiss to the freshly-turned mound of soil along the fence, and the small wooden cross laying beside it. My mother had knocked it over twice already, and I'd only put it up to spite her, so I left it where it was.

By the time I got to the knoll, the only decent park in Alameda, Maxine was already nestled between the roots of her favorite Pacific willow, buried in her own sketchpad, resplendent in the pleats and ruffles of the latest fashion. I waded through a maelstrom of cacophonous sea gulls dive-bombing the leavings of careless picnickers, found a shady spot, and plopped down beside her. Then bounced up to recover a wayward ball and toss it to one of the squealing cherubs who seemed to need a turn.

Floating strands, shiny and black, whipped into my mouth as I sat back down. The misbehaving stuff was always escaping my ponytail. I shoved it around the purple ribbon and retied it. "Stupid hair."

Oops, too loud. Maxine didn't bother looking up, she just

singsonged. "The prettiest thing from your Japanese genes." Like that was supposed to shut me up. I'd never figured why she was jealous. I preferred her ginger Sicilian curls; call it a greener-grass thing.

I turned to my latest drawing, a half-finished cruiser, and brushed a stray leaf off my skirt, exposing the high school mascot embroidered along the hem.

Maxine snickered. "Anybody tell you that's the world's ugliest beaver?"

"You and half the school."

"Only half?"

"Oh, cork it." Who was I kidding? That wouldn't stop her.

"Your mom's weird. You shouldn't let her decorate your clothes."

Not a conversation worth repeating, so I reached over and adjusted the chrysanthemum perched among her tresses. She smiled, lost in her art, and the wilting flower sagged again.

In the harbor below, U.S. Navy ships lined the piers, transports and World War I-vintage flush deck destroyers, plus one of the newer *Gridley* class, fresh off the ways around 1937. My mind sailed back four years. Eighth grade, that would have been, when I was first getting interested in such things. Not that anyone else cared. I mean, here I was, living in a port; why didn't more people share my passion? I was so tired of hearing 'you are really strange.' I should probably learn to control myself and stop regurgitating tidbits about ships.

Oh, well.

Along the waterfront, one of many cranes lifted a five-inch gun turret. Clangs rang across the waves, and strands of white and grey rose from scattered industrial smokestacks. Naval Base Alameda was busier than I'd ever seen it, with more ships and more bustle surrounding every one of them. Maybe they were sending some to the Atlantic to defend against U-boats.

Maxine frowned in concentration. I leaned over and took a gander. Yup, horses. I tried to recall her ever drawing anything else, but there were no fish on that hook. She was so content I didn't tell her what they looked like. This latest one had a mane that resembled antlers.

And she says I have no sense of humor.

Hmm, my own pad held aircraft carriers, cruisers, and submarines, all in intricate detail, but not a single horse. Or much of anything else. Maybe I shouldn't make fun of Maxine.

I filled in a radio antenna and added signature and date to the bottom right corner, Navy style: 6 DEC 41. A titmouse scolded an overfed squirrel above our heads and flittered off into the leaves. So lovely, days like this. The down side was it made stalling way too easy, and I'd been putting it off for weeks. Or days. Or however long it was since I'd made up my mind.

I couldn't delay any more.

"I'm doing it."

"Doing wha—wait, really?" Maxine's pencil hovered over a hairy fetlock. "Now?"

"Benjamin Franklin died."

"Oh Kristy, sweetie, you loved that dog."

I held it in. Anyone else would be cracking along about now. She was right, that pooch had been a delight for as long as I could remember.

I smoothed my skirt from thigh to calf. "You know how old he was. Mother called it mercy killing. She made me watch."

"Goodness!"

"Said it builds character. Anyway, it's perfect timing. I've got some money. Rosita returned part of what I lent her. And I . . ."

I fidgeted, wondering why my mouth kept running when it was time to stop. Hoping Maxine wouldn't pick up on those last two words.

A doomed hope, a chimerical desire. Maxine glanced at the scar on my ankle, then moved on to my face and arms. Here it came. She squished my last two words, expelling their meaning.

"And you don't have any bruises. That are visible. At the moment."

I pulled my foot out of sight. "You promised not to notice."

"That was years ago." Maxine kept studying me, biting her lip.

"You know how it is. I'm tired of cringing every time I open the front door. I could file for emancipation, though why bother with the paperwork?"

Maxine set down her pencil. Picked it up, stroked it, set it down. "You could stay in my sister's old room."

A nonstarter if I ever heard one. This wasn't temporary, and what would her parents think?

Maxine's eyes shimmered. "You keep in touch, you hear me?" She shook a fist at my nose and wiped droplets off her cheek.

I wanted them to be angry droplets. I wanted the fist to be real. It would be easier if she were enraged. But that wasn't how Maxine was wired.

I handed her my handkerchief. "I'll write as soon as I can."

Tears for Maxine, arid desert for me. Why couldn't I act like a normal person? Why did I have to entomb every emotion before others found me out? It was my parents' fault. Their culture, my upbringing. Or it was the teasing at school for being an outsider. Or some unremembered trauma. There had to be something to blame it on. It couldn't just be who I was, acting the way I did, for that would mean something was wrong with me.

Dang, I hate being spot-on. Wrong, indeed. Two weeks ago I could barely scribble a sappy 'best friends' line in Maxine's birthday card. I had to pry every word from the pencil and nail it to the paper before it got away. Kristy the ice fish, don'tcha know. Maybe I'd feel less frigid if I could bring myself to tell Maxine about my cubbyhole in the toolshed, what my parents called a kid's fort. My haven of old mattresses and thick blankets. The place I went to scream.

"Where did you decide? You ruled out Frisco a thousand times. And how will you live?"

Thank you, Maxine. You always drag me from the dank holes. "There's a morning bus to L.A. They're hiring people who look like me for propaganda films. I can finish school there."

"They better have art class or you'll go crazy."

I shrugged, and there it was again, me brushing aside the chance for any deeper connection. Why did she put up with me?

"Come on, we're getting ice cream." Maxine snapped her pad shut and drew me to my feet. She was such a light bulb, mad to sad to glad in the swipe of a switch. "You really expect you can pull this off?"

The chrysanthemum fell out of her hair and I kicked it into a thorn bush. "My parents think I go to church. I'll have hours to get away."

~~~~

Yeah, that's what I got for being cocky.

An hour and a half since I sashayed out of the house, pretending everything was normal, eager for my grand getaway. Ninety minutes spent sneaking to the bus depot and perching on a warped wooden bench as soft as Mount Rushmore. I'd never considered the sort of character likely to inhabit places like this, even on a Sunday morning. The putrid rot, tobacco smoke, and diesel exhaust were nothing compared to the aroma wafting off the bum panhandling his way through the waiting room.

"Here," I said, "get something to eat."

The bum shuffled off, but two nuns across the room scowled at me. Did they begrudge my handout? Nuns, of all people? I twisted on my seat and caught a man eyeing me, the guy who'd shoved the bum away earlier. It grew into a leer. Could be the nuns thought I was flirting. I moved to another bench, facing the other way.

An hour and a half, and it turned out to be for nothing. My bus hadn't even shown up yet when the policeman strutted in, scanned the room, and came straight at me.

"Come along, Miss Hara. Don't make me drag you."

The jerk grinned like it was all a joke. He could have at least pretended to be annoyed, so I wouldn't feel so fatuous. Here I was, cultivating the image of respectability in school blouse and skirt, quite appropriate traveling clothes, and I had my book bag, and . . . well, I guess seventeen-year-old girls stood out, especially when alone.

He led me to the police station a few blocks away. Four cops
~~~~

occupied the congested office. A dozen desks were crammed into three rows, surrounded by walls full of mug shots, a Rita Hayworth pinup, and a dingy calendar. The patrolman escorting me into the room hadn't looked at me since he'd arrested me. Or whatever he'd done, bringing me here.

"See what I rounded up? Name's Kristy Hara," said the patrolman.

"They oughta shoot people like that."

I whisked my head around. The cop who spoke wasn't talking about me. He was with a third at a water cooler. A secretary set a cup of coffee on one desk and a folder on another. A fourth policeman swore as the patrolman sat on a table and parked me in front of them both.

"Bus station, as usual," said the patrolman. "Her friend Maxine couldn't keep her mouth shut. The mom called us."

Maxine? So that was it. I tried to get upset, but the fire wouldn't stay lit. Why had I told Maxine of my plans to leave? To keep my only real friend from worrying, was the thought at the time. In hindsight, could it be I had wanted to be stopped? I knew Maxine was prone to panic-blabbing, and a tip-off from her mom welded the coffin. Which meant I clung to the shame of deserting my home. Which meant, in turn, what? That a fragment of me still believed I deserved my contusions? That I should have been grateful my mother let me wear make-up to hide them? Disgusting.

The fourth policeman finished writing something. "Japs don't run away. It's craven."

"I'm not Japanese." I let the other part hang in the air.

"What about her parents?"

I may as well have been a stray dog, for all the attention they paid me.

"They're probably Nips," said the patrolman.

"No, did you call? Tell them we found their daughter?"

The secretary stopped by the table, dumped a folder, and winked at me.

A commotion erupted at the front door and a supervisor

bulled in, shouting.

"The Japs attacked Pearl Harbor!"

"What?" One of the cops at the water cooler dropped his cup. "How?" Others leapt to their feet.

"Hundreds of planes. Must be off a carrier."

"Wait, Pearl is hours earlier. Were they even awake?" "Goddamn sneaks." "How much damage?"

"Sank a battleship. Fires everywhere."

Two more cops charged in. I couldn't keep them straight. They scurried around, knocked files off desks, turned on a console radio, made calls. One ran out the back, another came in the front.

"Did you hear?" said the new cop.

The secretary leaned near me. "You better go, kid."

I gaped at the radio, lost in the news. The secretary poked my finger with the corner of a folder.

"Yo, kid."

I ran.

"Hey, isn't that girl Japanese?"

I hit the door and ran faster.

Not away. Home.

Japan had done it. They'd attacked America. All the threats, all the posturing, and I'd been letting it glide over my head for months. Nothing bad could really happen. The fighting in Europe would never make it to our shores. History class had made it clear, we'd already had the 'war to end all wars,' why pay attention to the news?

The bliss of ignorance ripped away, searing my skin, leaving me raw. How could this be? My parents were first generation immigrants. Maybe they could explain.

I took the roundabout way. Something told me to stay out of sight. People would be getting ready for church or listening to the news, so the streets were pretty empty, but that was no reason to take a chance. I snugged a knot into my waist-length ponytail and stuffed it down the collar of my blouse—this wasn't the day to broadcast my Asian background—and followed the abandoned rail line toward the poorer side of town. My father teaching at Berkeley didn't qualify us to rent in the nicer neighborhoods, or so he said. That suddenly felt like more of a slap than usual.

"Now, now," I could hear my father say, when I complained about such things. "Be fair. They let us into their country. They gave me a great job that would otherwise go to a white man." He loved relating how much better off we were than we'd be in Japan. Mother never agreed and said he was too tolerant, especially toward his inferiors. How many times had I lived through their arguments? And why was I thinking about such things on a day like this?

A trio of the tougher boys from school hung out on one corner, flicking switchblades and smoking. I almost popped out in plain sight. I caught myself and backed up. I'd had run-ins with them before, but they'd always let me go. Today, I couldn't tell; if they'd heard the news, it might be different. I took the long way around toward the rear of my house. It would force me to cut through the park, but that should be empty this time of day.

It wasn't. An old man leaned on a cane, inching his way across the knoll. I waited, out of sight, half glad for the delay, half willing the man to move faster. Yesterday, here with Maxine, I basked in the sun. Today I crouched in undergrowth. The old man swung his cane, batted a piece of trash out of his path, and hobbled out of sight. I popped up and raced over the knoll before anyone else appeared.

I cut through the shell of a burned-out restaurant and reached a fenced lot filled with decaying automobiles. A hundred yards off, beyond the lot, on the other side of a cinder-paved alley, my backyard teemed with people barking commands. Hard to see through all the bushes, but something was wrong.

I tore at the fence, scrabbled up a loose section of chain link, and squirmed through, tearing a hole in my short-sleeved blouse. I dashed across the junk car lot and reached the next line of fence, across the alley from my backyard.

Shapes resolved themselves through gaps in the foliage. A man with an FBI jacket and a shotgun stood guard in my backyard, and two more agents wielded pistols.

FBI? They chased criminals. Why would they be here?

"Mother?" The sound scarcely made it past my lips. My lungs were clogged with wool, and I could hardly breathe.

Other agents searched in the toolshed and under the house. A senior agent heaved my father out the back door and threw him down.

"It is only a radio," said my father.

Something about all the guns penetrated my mind. I crouched lower behind the shrubbery.

Three more agents came from the house and dumped large radio transmitting equipment on the ground. The kind of thing no amateur needed. Professional quality, long-range apparatus, like I had seen in a navy magazine.

"What is that?" said my father.

Another agent hauled out my mother. She planted her feet, stood as straight as she could, and jabbed a finger at the radio gear. In English, slow and nearly uninterpretable, she announced, "That is mine."

My fingers wove through the fencing. "Mother?" I whispered. No, my mother hated English. "*Okaasan*?"

My father slumped. "How could you? Our daughter was born here."

"That is not my fault," said my mother, back to Japanese.

"Get them out of here." The senior agent pointed toward the front yard. "Hurry up. We got three more raids today."

"Boss, that's—"

"Stow it. Now a war's on, the judge cut loose every search warrant we ever wanted."

The agents led my parents around the side of the house and into a black Ford sedan. Another agent came out of the house with an open ledger and my sketchpad. "Port information. Ship movements." He held out the pad. "And some damn fine pictures."

The senior agent took the pad and flipped through it. I knew exactly what he was seeing. Modern warships gave way to schooners, three-masters, and a lighthouse, the things I used to draw before my mother hooked me on military vessels. The old stuff was romantic, why . . . oh, right, she raised my allowance when I switched. Then, admit it, I had fallen in love with the streamlined steel beasts.

Either that or I was the standard issue, Mark One, Mod Zero teenage girl, drooling over sailors. That would certainly fit with my vacuous mentality, and the timidity of hiding.

The agent grunted. "Leave someone to pick up the girl. These chumps don't even know what church their daughter attends."

I shrank down behind a dead Chevy and grasped a greasy wheel well, watching everyone leave. Watching my world dissolve. "*Okaasan*?"

FBI agents got into three more black Fords beyond my house and the cars pulled away. Neighbors ventured out, slowly, one after another. "I knew they were spies." "I vote we shoot 'em." "I got a nephew at Pearl." "Damn Japs. We should round 'em all up."

I soaked in the anger, the fear, the sheer loathing. Was this the war, or was this how they had always seen my family? Had every greeting, every wave, every sign of goodwill been a lie?

And what had my mother done? Or rather, why? She laid claim to duplicity like she was some kind of Mata Hari. I could see bitterness at leaving Japan, but this? I floundered for a memory to explain it, some sign I had missed, some closet never opened.

Nothing.

This was the person who drilled me on *otemae*, Japanese tea ceremonies, telling me to quiet my mind. Teaching me a *shin* bow, leaning deeply forward, palms on the floor, fingertips inward and nearly touching. Contemplative and serene. My cheek prickled, the one she cuffed if I wasn't serene enough.

How dare she be a spy? I found a jagged piece of metal and sawed off the embroidery on my hem—the high school mascot she had put there. I dug out every single thread.

The ranting of the neighbors continued. They weren't merely castigating my mother for treason, they censured all Japanese. Tarred with the same brush, one put it. I bit my lip, watching the last few neighbors spit on the ground and return to their homes.

The unthinkable had happened. The inconceivable. It couldn't be true, it couldn't have happened, but it had, and it was true, and it couldn't be. Somebody needed to fix reality, for it was seriously broken.

Why did my finger sting? I looked down. The side window of the car beside me lay shattered. I'd beaten it with a rock and cut myself. The blood tasted metallic, but it stopped leaking soon enough. Careless, drifting like that.

I rubbed the scar on my ankle and spent the rest of the day hiding among the ruined vehicles. No one was around except a sleepy, half-deaf watchman who played the radio at full blast. I listened to one report after another: assaults in the Philippines, updated damage reports from Pearl, calls for retaliation from every side. Occasionally they mentioned my parents' arrest and the fact I was still at large. The police would be livid when they figured out they'd let me slip through their mitts.

I tried to absorb what I'd seen. Something ached so far down I didn't know where it came from. One fact surfaced, though, shiny and hard. For the rest of my life, I would never be able to forget what my mother had done. After everything my father had worked toward, everything the entire Japanese-American community had done to fit in and gain acceptance in this new country, my mother had ruined it all.

Of course, Japan hadn't helped. Declaring war, and for what? I still didn't understand how tensions had grown so high.

Focus. What should I do? My home was gone, for now. Perhaps things would settle down and I could resume my old life, eventually. My father hadn't done anything wrong, had he? Did the FBI think he helped my mother?

They pegged me as helping. They had my drawings. My attempt to run away made me look even more guilty. Kristy the traitor, that's what they were sure of. What did that mean? What would they do if they caught me? They shot spies, didn't they?

Forget that. And stop the pointless trembling. What did I want to do?

Ah, that led to a peculiar thought. A bold idea. Wouldn't it be fitting if maybe, someday, I could find a way to compensate for my mother's betrayal?

As if I'd ever have the nerve. I had the guts of a month-old cucumber. Atonement for my mother's crime, redemption of my family's honor, wasn't much of a plan when there was nothing I could imagine myself doing. On top of which, it wasn't logical. I ran away from home, striking out on my own in a reckless, daring act of independence. A Western way of thinking, my mother would call it, and the height of disloyalty. Now I worried about my family's name, and making up for my mother's crime, which sounded like an Eastern honor issue. How could both make sense?

Overanalyzing again. Bogus thoughts. Western, Eastern—just call me mongrel.

I needed water. Someday I would need food, when I felt like eating again. And most of all, I needed a place to go. Not Maxine's. She could never keep a secret, and I could never again put her in the position of having to try. Perhaps I could ask that Chicano woman I had helped once. Rosita knew something about smuggling Mexicans. She might have an idea what I could do, if she was willing to talk, if it wasn't too dangerous for her.

I waited for dusk, then dodged around, staying out of sight. A few people were out and about, but they seemed lost in their own thoughts, reflecting on all that had happened, most likely, and calculating its impact. A barking dog and one nosy homeless man later, I made it to the alley behind Rosita's store, and hid for nearly an hour until she came out to dump trash.

"Hello?" No response. Whispers were all well and good, but not when garbage cans were rattling about. I tried again. "Rosita?"

Rosita jumped six inches, saw my shrinking form, and took charge like a drill sergeant with a green recruit. She rushed me inside and down one aisle after another in the stockroom of her small grocery store, stuffing things in my book bag. Shelves of goods, canned and dry, whizzed by faster than I could read the labels. Rosita put an apple in my hand and clucked at my torn blouse. Whirlwinds would have been easier to follow.

I dropped the apple in my satchel. Rosita took a fifteen-second break, made a phone call, and went back to the shelves. In the background, a radio burbled out 1940s boogie hits when it wasn't spouting war news and warnings.

"I can't leave again, Rosita. If I wait, I could—"

"You heard the radio. There's no other way. They're searching for you everywhere." A sack of dried fruit and a pair of yams went into my satchel.

"Like when you left Mexico and came here."

"Younger than you are now. They called this place the melting pot."

I nodded. A wonderful concept, a phrase I'd always loved.

Rosita snagged a box of sanitary napkins. "They were right. America is the melting pot, and we are the slag."

"No!"

Rosita paused. I pushed aside a copy of *Hamlet* in my satchel.

"Even the American Dream has wake-up calls." Rosita fit in the napkins. "I don't know what you'll do when these run out." She hustled me to the alley door and guided me into the reeking dark—urine overlying rot.

I stumbled. A cat stalked by and a trash can crashed.

"My cousin Carlos is sailing tonight," said Rosita. "Good thing Siam is neutral."

"Right now? Tonight?"

Rosita chuckled. "Seventeen cousins, four brothers. All different ships. That's what you get, living here. One's always going out." Rosita hurried me along.

I shook my head. "Why are you doing this?"

"After all the help you gave me? I almost lost the store."

"Yes, but, I mean, I just borrowed that from my parents."

Borrowed, hell. She'd be horrified if I told her what I'd done, snitching a good twelve hundred dollars from a pile of bills my mother kept hidden in the false bottom of a cedar chest. It was, wow, over ten years since I'd found the cache, poking around when my parents weren't home. Maybe now I could guess why my mother didn't use a bank. Maybe I had a feeling where it came from. Either she never missed the loss, or she'd been waiting to see if I would have the honor to admit it, or . . . or she dare not say anything, because it was money my father knew nothing about. Money from my mother's masters in Japan.

And I would never be owning up to the theft. Never be making it right.

Several blocks later, Rosita and I skulked alongside warehouses to the commercial docks of Alameda. We wriggled between piles of stacked crates, hiding until we saw a figure under a buzzing arc light.

Carlos leaned on a quay piling, smoking the stub of a cigarette. A sea gull huddled on a box near him. He flicked ashes at the bird as Rosita forced me out to meet him. The gull squawked and flew off.

"Stop that," said Rosita. "You'll attract attention."

Carlos ignored her and ogled me, his eyes sweeping across my long black hair and floating along my skinny body.

I pulled back. "Couldn't I—"

"You can't stay here," said Rosita. "It'd never work."

Carlos stubbed out his cigarette.

"Do what you have to," said Rosita. "Survive." She gave me a hug.

"Hurry," said Carlos.

Rosita ducked into shadows and was gone. Carlos and I sped toward the nearest gangplank. We dashed up, jumped onto an Argentinean freighter, and hid behind a pile of cartons. Carlos lifted the corner of a tarp and shoved me underneath.

"Stay here. I'll get you below soon."

His footsteps faded and I peeked out a slit. I'd been peeking all day, slithering around like the snake the authorities considered me. But I had to accept the situation for what it was. As Rosita said, the heat would not abate, and innocent or not, I could never go home.

It wasn't long before Carlos returned, snuck me below, and hid me outboard of some shipping containers in the bilge. Vibrations kicked in a few hours later, massive engines and propellers, signaling departure.

It was too late to change my mind. California had become a thing of the past.

Chapter 2

Blinding sunlight glittered off two-foot waves in the restless Pacific Ocean. Acrid engine fumes and the whimper of rusty rivets spiced every moment of my existence these days, and I treasured the rare glimpse out a porthole.

Far behind, a low curving wake from the mid-sized freighter said we were changing course again. Evading another storm, if I was lucky. Sea gulls cried, wheeling around the Argentinean flag on the stern, waiting for handouts. Not likely, from this crew.

Clanking came from the side. A sailor backed into the passageway thirty feet off, lugging a chain with fatter links than I had ever seen except on anchors. I ducked behind a roped-down crate and slid through a chink toward the nearest ladder. I shouldn't be here. Too far aft and too high up. A peep down the hole revealed no sign of humans and only one rat. I headed below, continuing to listen. Despite how few manned a ship this size, I could still be caught.

I went deeper into the hold, paused, listened, and darted through a hatch and along the next bulkhead. A scraping sound, another crewman. I scrambled around more cartons. My skirt ripped on a nail, matching the tear in my blouse. So much for proper attire. But then, suitability for a California high school did not correspond with practicality for climbing through a ship. I tightened the knot in my ponytail—oh golly, someday I'd have to sort out that tangled mess—and moved on.

Beyond the next box, sunshine poured through a hatch, swamping the glow from a few bare bulbs. I reached a dead end, heard a sound from behind, and tried to squeeze between the last two crates, heart beating faster.

A head poked out. I gasped.

And relaxed.

"Told you to stay put, Kristy." Carlos held out a small loaf of bread.

I retraced my steps. "Thank you." I took the bread and fondled it. I hadn't eaten since he brought a piece of sailfish the day before. I should be tearing into it, starving, but somehow I couldn't when he looked at me like this.

Carlos reached out and caressed my hair. I pulled back.

"You don't like my food."

"It's all right." Considering where I was, it was great. I just wished the water didn't come with a charred flesh aftertaste.

"Too plain for you?"

"No."

Carlos reached again. I twisted my head aside.

"You only like your own kind?"

I went still. I hadn't expected that from Rosita's cousin. The last time I heard it was in the basement of my high school. I cowered from two blond boys, trapped between old desks, blackboards, and packing crates, as brave as a bag of jelly.

One boy shoved me to the floor and took a boxer's pose. "C'mon, samurai. Show some honor."

I tried to rise.

The second boy knocked away my feet. "Her kind love it."

I glared and leapt up, clawing my fingers at their faces. The boys laughed and dodged, letting me go.

Would Carlos let me go? Dare I resist him if he didn't? How far was I willing to go to survive?

And why did I never think of such things in advance? God, I'd never even kissed a boy. How much did Carlos want?

I avoided another caress. "No," I said. "I've . . . never been hungry."

"Whoa, you've led a sheltered life."

"That's one way to put it."

Somewhere overhead came a yell from the second mate. "Carlos, where'd you go?"

Carlos whipped his head upward. The mate knelt at the sunlit hatch.

"Checking the hold-downs," said Carlos.

I backed into darkness.

The mate saw Carlos. "Get your butt on deck."

"Yes, sir."

Carlos muttered something and left. I slunk to the passageway, glanced around, and crept out.

I wove between boxes to another niche, more secluded, and padded with rags for sleeping. I sat, brushed off the loaf, and took a bite. Not too stale; I ought to thank Carlos, even if I couldn't show him the type of gratitude he craved.

Or . . . could I? If he persisted? I really didn't want to answer that question.

I leaned back, closing my eyes.

~~~~

Days went by. Weeks. I lost track. Storms, and long stretches of peace. A port call in New Zealand where I tried to sneak off the boat three times without a prayer of success. I didn't think Carlos wanted to help me debark. He was probably hoping to wear me down, get me to let him pet me. In that, I had no interest, with him or anyone else. If his cousin Rosita hadn't made him promise to take care of me, heaven knew what he'd have done.

Ah, Rosita, my would-be savior. Why had I let her railroad me into this? Was I too reliant on authority figures? Was my brain even working the day she set me on this path? And yet, she must have been right. If I hadn't left, I'd long since have been spotted. Captured or, like as not, shot on sight. Carlos' spotty war news
~~~~

made it clear how incensed America was.

Some days held all the excitement of watching rust grow. I spent my time lost in reminiscence. What should I have done differently, what could I have avoided if I paid the slightest attention to the world around me, and what were to be the consequences? To think I had once been frightened at the notion of moving to Los Angeles on my own. That seemed so petty, now.

Another storm, wind howling through steel cables, waves crashing, and lights flickering in the wheelhouse visible through a cracked-open hatch far above. A sideways lurch tore my grip off a crate, landing me in a bilge pocket full of oily water. I lay dazed for a second, got to my knees, and wiped at the slime on my blouse. Scents assailed me. It always got smellier during squalls, spills or leaks, paints or solvents or fuel oil. Not at all what I'd once envisioned, sailing the ocean blue.

My nose grew dull and back I slid into memories.

~~~~

Carlos found me some coal and I filled the side of a large box with drawings. Far better than trying to read *Hamlet* for the fifth time in eye-squinting shadow. I touched up the hull of a submarine. I always came back to subs, the most intriguing things afloat. It wasn't seemly, not for a girl, but I nursed a whim of one day diving in one. Except now, much as I hated to admit it, I was getting tired of ships. When was the last time I saw a flower? I used my piece of coal to sketch a tulip, but it didn't come out right.

An unwelcome thought broke in. I was in my family's modern kitchen, surrounded by flower motifs on curtains and cabinets. My mother put cans in the cupboard while I washed dishes in the first double-basin sink on our block.

"Those American friends make you wild," said my mother. "Spelunking, of all things. And dating is not our way."

"But he's nice. Half Irish and—"

"Speak Japanese!"

She threw a plate. It shattered across my feet, slicing open one ankle.
~~~~

The slivers of porcelain morphed into chips of black. My hunk of coal lay broken in my hand. What had the FBI done with my mother? Had they tried her? Was she dead? And why did I care? I shouldn't. I ought to be done with her.

Why couldn't I stop thinking about her?

I pulled my knees to my chest, leaned against the hull of the freighter, and gazed down through the deck grating. Shimmering oil-rainbows danced across the bilge water, pretending beauty could emerge from filth.

~~~~

One night, weeks after it left the latest port, the freighter plowed through phosphorescent plankton. A glowing wake stretched far behind, tangoing under the stars. Carlos described every sparkle, saying he was no good at art, yet painting with words that filled my imagination, and framing his image with jokes about the crew. Who knew he could be so charming, when he wasn't trying to seduce me?

He agreed to help me go ashore in Siam, as I first intended, ribbing me about those abortive attempts in Auckland. Siam was neutral, and I could fit in well enough. Make a new life for myself, at least until the war was over.

Unless, that is, I ever found a way to make up for my mother's betrayal. Measures a milquetoast like me could handle.

~~~~

I felt a pressure. My eyes flew open. I'd fallen asleep against the hull, the cool metal pleasant in the roasting hold, while Carlos pulled a duty rotation. Now he knelt beside me, stroking my cheek, holding out a half-full bottle of rum.

I drew back and wrinkled my nose. "I cannot."

He whammed down the bottle, too hard. It splintered, glass shooting everywhere, missing me, but Carlos rubbed a cut on his arm, smearing the blood.

He reached for me again. "You owe me a drink."

I grabbed his wrist. "I know. I'm sorry I'm dry." The cut

wasn't deep. I pressed, even though the bleeding was slow.

Carlos pondered my words, then appeared to understand what I meant. "Rosita's fault. It would be one thing if a girl looked like week-old fish bait, but she gave me you. Said you'd be appreciative, and I—"

A horn blared three times, followed by squealing feedback from a loudspeaker. The first mate's commands scratched through the circuits.

"All hands on deck. Attention. On deck."

"Diablos." Carlos pointed aft. "Hide. Fast."

The ever-present groan of overstressed metal and the thudding of propellers faded away.

Carlos hastened up a ladder. What did a three-alarm warning mean? I stood, hopped across the broken glass, and crawled over several hull frames to my special container, the one I usually slept in. I rotated the loose pair of slats in the side, each held by a single nail, revealing a hollow in the packing. Where had Carlos hidden the goods he removed? Had they been found? If that was the alarm, it was a short step from finding them to finding me.

Through the hatch overhead, a searchlight played across the bridge of the freighter. A voice boomed, English with a heavy Japanese accent. "Siam is now a member of the Greater East Asia Co-Prosperity Sphere."

High-pitched engines revved. A Japanese patrol boat must have pulled alongside. The Japanese official's orders grew strident.

"Neutral shipping is being diverted. You will proceed to Fukuoka."

I stared through the hatch at the glow from the searchlight. "Japan."

My knees folded and I collapsed into the crate. Oh God, Japan.

My hands shook like a palsied ninety-year-old. It was hopeless. So much worse than the crew finding me. I was so petrified I couldn't think. Or was it despair? Why did the term seem important?

I'd meant to flee, evaporate into neutrality, never to emerge.

But now? I tried to focus while noises continued.

The official came on again. “You will communicate on this frequency. You have no options.”

I blinked. Options? No, obviously not. I never had—

Options?

An idea trickled past. The same thought I’d had before. Wouldn’t it be apropos if maybe, someday, I could compensate for what my mother had done?

Yeah, right. It wasn’t really a choice. I couldn’t admit who I was, when we got to Japan. It was spy or die. But I could survive, possibly, and do something. A pretty weak excuse for a plan, but it was a start.

The official went on and on about obedience, punishments, and rewards. I peered upward, out the hatch. A Japanese crewman with a rifle appeared and I withdrew into the open crate, watching. High above, the patrol boat’s searchlight played across the freighter’s bridge again, backlighting the crewman. He slung his rifle over his shoulder and moved from the hatch.

I heard more sounds—the crewman, leaping from the freighter to his boat. Another horn blast, and the Japanese official yelling at the freighter’s captain to make all haste.

The patrol boat chuffed away, the freighter’s lumbering engines pounded to life, and the hull shuddered as the propellers dug in.

Chapter 3

Another day, another billion gallons of water left riled behind the freighter. Black clouds invaded the blue dome overhead. Carlos and other sailors slathered paint on a bulkhead with wide brushes, while the second mate prowled around, glowering at the clouds, at the crewmen, at the squeak of a rat in the bilges.

I crouched in a dark corner of the hold, watching the topside drama when it was visible. I pulled on coarse, whitish sailor's pants and tucked in a matching shirt. A gift from Carlos. Not sure why he'd made me beg for them; he knew darn well I'd not blend in wearing the rags my school clothes had turned into. It would pay him back if he got embarrassed when I gave him the leftover sanitary napkins to dispose of. I didn't feel sick, but I hadn't had a period in forever. No idea what was wrong with my body.

Blending in. Uh-huh. I found a splinter and picked at my purple ribbon until it came free. No idea if hair ribbons were common in Japan, so I'd not take a chance. Man, what was I getting myself into? This was going to be a disaster.

The square hatch framed the outside world.

~~~~

LIEUTENANT JEREMY MAISON studied a square of white, the
~~~~

only light in a darkened conference room. The clack of a slide projector echoed off bare wooden walls, showing a picture of Mr. Hara, Mrs. Hara, and Kristy in front of their home.

"And here they are again, our featured spies this week," said a Navy security officer. "There's no sign of Kristy Hara—the FBI was slow to stake out docks and rail yards—but we've got her drawings." The commander waved Kristy's sketchpad, fluttering the pages. "You know what they say. Loose lips sink ships, and a picture is a thousand words. Put 'em together."

Twenty Navy officers in the audience watched him, representing twenty different ships. Maison glanced around. Several wore the dolphin breast insignia of the submarine service, same as him. Others were surface boys or airedales, the new nickname for flyers. The security officer rapped a yardstick against the projection screen.

"You can bet there are more enemy agents. Four in Alameda, one right here in Point Loma. So far. Stay alert." The commander didn't bother to consult any notes. He'd likely memorized the spiel and delivered the same briefing at bases from Puget Sound to Mare Island to San Diego.

Overhead lights snapped on. Maison waved off someone's offer of a cigarette. Like everyone else in the audience, he imprinted the picture of Kristy's family.

~~~~

From deep in the freighter's hold, I stared up at the hatch, wondering what had happened to my parents, wondering if anyone was still looking for me.

A tortured cry came from a shaft bearing back aft. Moans, metallic squeals, and vibrations from the ship were never-ending. I was living inside a tooth being constantly drilled for cavities.

Clouds darkened the sky and a drop of rain hit me in the face. I let it flow along my cheek, nearly to my chin, before I bothered to wipe it off.
~~~~

Chapter 4

Time dragged itself from one day to the next. One night, silent, star-laden seas surrounded the freighter, and the faintest of breezes sent ruffles gliding over the surface. I smiled at Carlos' eloquent description.

"And then that cretin of a second mate says, 'The moon looks like a potato chip.'"

I broke up laughing. Carlos slapped a palm over my mouth, muffling the sound. He segued into another tale.

A topside hatch smacked open. Carlos broke off mid-sentence and dashed up a ladder. I finished my stub of salt pork, worrying that his nerves were fraying. Mine already had. He returned, took my arm, and led me along a passageway. A light bulb sputtered as we passed.

"We get to Chosen, you be careful."

I tripped over a pipe. "Chosen?"

Carlos steadied me. "Korea. Some island. They changed us again."

I splashed through a puddle. They needed to pump the bilges. "Any idea why?"

We rounded the edge of my half-hollow sleeping crate. Carlos reached in and showed me a package of syringes.

"This medical shit? Some kind of research hospital out there. Guess they need this."

I took the package. Carlos helped me into the cavity.

"You get caught, we never met."

"Thanks for not stopping me."

"Well, you had to get off somewhere. Good luck, whatever you're up to."

I touched his elbow. "It'll be okay."

I crouched down into the crate. He hesitated, pulled off a necklace with a crucifix, and slipped it over my head.

I bowed thanks. "I'm not actually, um . . ."

"Not Christian? With a name like Christine?"

"My father's idea. He converted. Mother refused to use it. I made up 'Kristy' after I was old enough to realize how demeaning 'girl' and 'you' sounded."

"Damn!"

He stole one last stroke of my hair. I couldn't begrudge it, and for a change, it didn't feel sexual. It felt comforting.

He twisted the two loose slats over the hole and padded away. I slid one plank aside and watched until he was gone, chewing my lip. I shoved the syringes into the crate, tugged up my school satchel, and pulled out an apple core. The remains of a present from Carlos a few days ago. It reminded me of the apple Rosita had given me months before.

I nibbled a bit, uncertain at the smell, and laid back, contemplating what was left of it. Contemplating my past. Dare I wonder about my future? Would it do any good?

~~~~

I jolted awake. One arm trailed out the opening of my hollow crate, past one of the loose planks, and the apple core lay by my outstretched hand.

A bilge rat poked at the core. It sniffed my finger and I jerked my arm back. The rat filched the core and darted off a few feet.

I stretched, rubbed my eyes, and massaged dream-memories back into my head. I'd been at one of my father's office picnics. He
~~~~

was surrounded by other professors, praising American technical ingenuity, lauding the generosity of the United States in donating relief after disasters like the Kanto earthquake near Tokyo, and extolling the increasing educational prospects for girls in the U.S., as if his audience needed convincing. Well, it was a dream; maybe the audience was me. He clearly adored his new country. Did I harbor any doubts that America deserved my own loyalty?

Perhaps I did, lying here in the bowels of a freighter. But if I was honest, they were small ones. Every country had its bad apples, its overreactions, its need to recenter when it got off-kilter. With a war, America would be off-kilter for quite a while. No matter. A nation that could produce Maxine, that could accept, however reluctantly, someone like Rosita, was a place I could still admire.

Besides, even if I wasn't awash in patriotism, my mother's crime remained an issue. A debt I had to pay.

The rat squeaked at me. My finger tingled where it had sniffed. I sat up, flexed bare feet, and pouted at the four-legged thief.

"That was my last one."

The rat chewed on a seed.

"In case you didn't notice, it's rotten."

The rat took another bite.

"Sort of like my plan. But I have one, now."

The rat's nose went up.

"What, you want to hear it?"

The rat twitched. It dropped the core and scampered away.

"Gee, thanks for the support." Seriously, though, what had gotten into the creature? I looked around.

Carlos leaned against the outer hull fifty feet along, smoking. I smiled. It must have been so hard for him to keep his hands off me, when it was always clear what he wanted, and none around to stop him. But here we were, nearing our destination, and he'd shown me as much respect as I could have desired.

Strange. What was that drone?

Sweet heaven, a vibration that scared a rat? Getting louder?

Please no, it couldn't be. Get away from the hull. It might—

An explosion flung me into a bulkhead.

The blast ripped out the side of the ship. Right where Carlos had stood.

I flopped onto a crate and ricocheted into the bilge. Shards of wooden containers, syringe needles, shrapnel from distorted pieces of hull, shattered glassware, bomb fragments—so much debris rained around me I couldn't move. I huddled in the bilge, hiding under the deck grating where I'd been thrown, until water covered my head. The ocean gushed in from a gaping ten-foot hole, but oddly, it didn't roar. It all happened in silence. Who turned off the sound?

The ship listed. I felt it when I dragged my head above water. I reached for a stanchion. No! The wreckage. Everything was sharp. Crates, wiring, and piping lay in mangled heaps. I had to get out, and I had to be careful. And fast. A conflagration was gutting the other end of the hold where a fuel line must have burst, and the ship had to be sinking fast.

Purring now. Sound was returning. How odd that a roaring fire was merely a tinny hiss. And why hadn't Carlos come for me?

Stop it. Think. Carlos was gone. Get out, and do it now.

But which way?

~~~~

INSIDE *USS BARRACUDA*, Lieutenant Maison yielded the periscope to his commanding officer and edged past to check the sonar station. The CO pulled his eye from the periscope a minute later and surveyed the cramped conning tower. Electronics gear lined the bulkheads, and the plotting table and periscope well ate up much of the deck area. The rest of the ship was packed just as densely. The U.S. Navy wasn't about to waste space on a boat designed to sneak beneath the waves. Every member of the crew garnered a fresh bruise every couple of weeks, one way or another. Maison tried to warn new sailors, but they insisted on learning the hard way.

"Good shot, ex-oh," said the commander.
~~~~

"Thank you, sir." If he did things right, Maison hoped his stint as executive officer might be short-lived, what with all the new submarines the Navy was churning out. "At least the old fish work."

"Wish they'd fix the new torpedoes," the navigator said. He leaned over his plotting table, making a notation on a chart. Maison was glad they had the man aboard, for training. Normally the XO got that job. He watched the navigator rap out a cigarette and turned away.

The commander wagged his finger from the navigator to Maison. "How can you be in the Navy and not smoke?"

"Same way I can be in submarines and not drink coffee."

The chief-of-the-boat barked a laugh, spitting coffee past the rim of his mug. Maison brushed droplets off his khaki pants.

The navigator patted his pockets. "I keep telling you he's an infiltrator. No army brat could drive pigboats."

Maison swiped the chief's matches and tossed them at the navigator. "And no one who can't find their lights should be navigator."

The others laughed easily, and Maison grinned. Thank Wotan they weren't teasing him about his likeness to a Nazi war poster anymore, the 'Aryan ideal.'

The navigator struck a match. It blazed.

~~~~

Flames spurted up the side of the Argentinean freighter. I grappled my way from the hold and lay on the deck, gulping in cleaner air, beating at the tongues of hysteria licking my mind. Black clouds billowed out behind.

Huh, I wasn't even cut. I was the undamaged lamp in a house destroyed by hurricane. Freaky.

Across the deck, barely visible, a dozen sailors swarmed into two lifeboats. The first boat filled and took off. One sailor helped another to the second boat. The mate pointed toward a distant glow on the horizon.

The sailor's lips moved. "Hell, they couldn't put it off another
~~~~

hour?"

Or that's what I thought he said. "Wait. I'm coming." My voice was nothing but a vibration in my jaw.

The men went down a rope ladder, got in the second boat, and began rowing. Metal screeched, crying in agony as compartments buckled.

The sailors hadn't seen me. There was no way they could hear. I pulled my aching body to the rail, panting. The smoke thickened. It grew so hot my cloths began steaming. I removed Carlos' necklace, kissed the crucifix, and tossed it down a hatch. It felt right, somehow. In any case, it wouldn't be wise to carry such a thing into Japanese territory.

The freighter heeled over further, going down by the bow, and I lost my grip on the rail. I flailed across the deck and caught the raised edge of the hatch, the coaming, to stop my slide. Fire licked up the superstructure and the bow went under. Rats floundered through a sheen of oil spreading across the ocean.

The deck was nearing a forty-five degree angle. I put a foot on the coaming, made it back to the rail, and hauled myself along—along and upwards—to the stern. The ship quaked from blasts and collapsing bulkheads, and the firestorm kept getting closer. I climbed over the railing and stood on the outer hull, calves against the lower rail, fighting for balance. Island lights twinkled in the distance. The lifeboats were out of sight.

Now or never, as they said. I dove past the rudder, leaping as far as I could.

Chapter 5

MAISON SWIVELED *BARRACUDA*'S periscope a fraction of a degree and dialed a higher magnification. His knuckles whitened on the handles: someone was still on the ship. A woman teetered on the railing, crouching.

She dove, arms spread like wings, long hair streaming out, silhouetted by the flames.

"Good God." He turned to the commander. "A girl just took a swan off the stern. The boats are away."

The commander manned the 'scope. "Currents?"

"Strong. Out to sea."

The commander walked the periscope all the way around. He backed away, slapped up the handles, and the periscope lowered.

"Gone," said the commander. "Sonar, any contacts?"

The sonarman raised one earphone. "No sir. Only the ship breaking up."

"What time is it?"

"Oh-dark-thirty," mumbled the navigator, eyeing the chronometer. "That is, almost zero-two-hundred."

The commander tapped his shoe against a stanchion, his standard thinking pose. He ran a finger along the navigator's plotting table, checking their position. "I'm not a fan of these new unrestricted warfare rules. Guess I'm old school."

"Nothing honorable in supporting the enemy's economy," said Maison. "But I know what you mean."

"I don't, sir," said the navigator.

"You're too young," said the CO. "A few years back, we'd be required to notify before sinking, give their sailors a chance to get off. Maybe even rescue the odd stray. Not anymore. Nowadays everyone has radios to call in our position and attack planes to chase us down."

"Doubt they radioed this time," Maison said. "No real risk at this point."

"I suppose not." The CO tapped again. Maison gave him a nod.

The commander spun around. "Chief, come to bearing two-eight-zero."

The chief called down to the control room. "Two-eight-zero, aye. Helmsman, left five degrees rudder."

"Left five degrees rudder, aye."

"Prepare to surface," said the commander.

"Prepare to surface, aye," said the chief.

Maison signaled for the periscope to be raised again.

~~~~

I popped up, gagging and coughing. Atop the dusky ocean, water curled in a dying whirlpool. Boxes and debris appeared sporadically, but all the rats were gone. So was most of the oil sheen. A few patches burned, but they wouldn't last long.

I fought my way to a crate, pulled myself up, and draped myself across the top, shivering. I must look like a drowned rat, and smell worse. A quick dip in the ocean wasn't enough to wash off months of oil fumes and sweat. Poor Carlos had no taste at all if he thought I was pretty.

After a moment, I looked up. No shore lights were visible, not from this low. The moon shone through a break in the clouds, but which direction would it be, this time of night?

"Compass. Next time, bring a compass."

I struggled to my knees, trying to stand and check for lights
~~~~

from higher up, but the crate was bobbing too much. I sat down, rubbed my arms, and crossed myself. Who cared if I wasn't Catholic? It couldn't hurt. On the bright side, my hearing was nearly back to normal.

A bulge formed on the ocean off to the side, catching a glint of moonlight. I twisted around. Shark? Whale?

A huge vertical fin broke the waves. No, not a fin, the sail of a submarine, rising up fifteen feet, and followed by the hull. So the noise I'd heard had not been the scrape of a tethering line along the side of the freighter. It had been a tiny propeller. The ship hadn't hit a mine, we'd been torpedoed. From all my reading, all my drawing, I recognized the class of ship, although the hull number was painted out for wartime. It coasted to a halt not far off, showing me a starboard broadside, and a head materialized on the bridge atop the sail, scanning with binoculars.

A hatch opened in the hull aft of the sail, two men came up, and one of them yelled. "Over there."

The binoculars swept toward me. "I see her."

American English, confirming what I already knew. A U.S. submarine. Getting rescued at sea was supposed to be a good thing, but not now, not here, not by these people.

It wasn't like I had an alternative.

Several minutes later, a petty officer took my arm, guiding me as I stepped off the ladder aft of the submarine's sail. We were in a narrow passageway filled with the odors of diesel fuel, battery acid, and urine. The petty officer put a blanket around me and we headed forward past the mess decks.

I saw a basket of rolls. A small whine escaped me.

"Go ahead," said the man.

I tore into one as we scaled a ladder into the conning tower.

"Is this *Bass*?" I said. "*Barracuda*?"

"*USS Barracuda*. How'd you know?"

"Quiet, sailor," said an officer. His name tag read Maison. "You can't trust her kind."

That again. He was an older version of the blond boys who once trapped me in the high school basement. But where they had been derisive and superior, this guy took it fifty stories higher. Contempt beyond that of my former neighbors, clutching at his belt like he thought a holster should be there. I briefly imagined a growl, until I realized it came from a piece of equipment overhead.

I tried to defuse him. "I am not Japanese."

"You don't say." He crossed his arms. I tried to think of it as an improvement over reaching for a non-existent gun. "What's your name?"

I hesitated. I didn't have to tell the truth. Who would know? I'd meant to spy when I got to Japan, and spying meant lying, so I was already effectively a liar, so why not make something up?

But no. My mother had dishonored the family enough, and I could not compound that disgrace. Besides, they wouldn't likely know of me clear out here, so what difference would it make?

I took a breath. "Kristy Hara."

Maison's nostrils flared. "Hara? From Alameda?"

I backed half a step, banging my head on the handle of a valve. So much for not recognizing my name. The submarine force was a small world, and subs made occasional port calls in Alameda. Was that where he heard?

The commander joined us. "You know her, Mister Maison?"

"She's a spy." He uncrossed his arms and removed a foot-long wrench from a toolbox strapped to the periscope well housing. "Security briefed us before the squadron deployed to Pearl. Her family was the highlight."

"That's not—" Control, I told myself. Don't sound so scared. Don't sound guilty. "Would a spy tell you who she is?"

Maison loomed over me. I'd never been loomed at before. Some deformed part of me found it funny, which had to be the most out-of-place reaction I'd ever experienced, which made it even worse, until I understood what the feeling really meant.

Pure, undiluted fear.

I turned to the commander. "May I speak with you, sir?"

"Very well." The commander sent the petty officer on an errand. "Maison, you come too. Sneider, you have the conn."

The navigator threw him a salute and rose from his plotting

table. Maison returned the wrench to its box—I wanted to take that as a good sign—and the commander led Maison and me down the ladder and along a passageway to his stateroom.

Maison followed the commander and me inside and shut the door. A photograph on the wall showed a task force glowing in moonlight. Warlike, yet peaceful. Below it was a hand-made sign:

'There are two kinds of ships: Submarines and Targets.'

I couldn't help it. I laughed. God, I was in so much trouble, and I laughed right in front of these men. How stupid could I be?

The commander sprawled in his chair and steepled his fingers. Maison remained stiff. I fidgeted.

"Okay, XO," said the commander, "what do you have?"

"She draws ships. Our latest radar, newest anti-aircraft guns. That kind of information isn't published. Then war breaks out and she's here."

My flawless pictures, the precise features of every vessel, the glory of getting it right.

The accuracy my mother demanded. And now I knew why.

"The ship was Argentinean," the commander said. "The Japs are pulling in all the merchantmen. If not for that, we wouldn't have to sink it and she'd be headed somewhere else."

"Yes, sir, but what's her story?" Maison pointed at me. "Were you helping your mother?"

That was not a question I wanted to answer. Because the answer was yes. I'd never known it, but that wouldn't matter. I shook my head, a half-hearted denial, and bowed to the commander. "Please, sir. I cannot stay."

"Why not?" said the commander.

"A hull full of men?" I said. "For what, months?"

"We'll manage."

"What do you have in mind?" said Maison. "You proposing to go somewhere?"

Ignore the tone of voice, I told myself. Control your damned face.

"Dump me here. You've got a dinghy."

The commander frowned.

"What happens if you take me home?" I jutted my chin at Maison. "He thinks I'm a traitor."

"You'd have to be American for that."

I fought myself, holding back, when I wanted to scream.

The commander waved Maison silent. "What were you planning?"

"If the *raiju* eats your road, make a new path."

"Come again?"

"Call it a dragon." Time to open the spigot, let the words flow, while he was willing to listen. "I was led here for a purpose. How many could get into Japanese lands? I speak the language, know the customs."

"You know nothing of espionage."

"Neither did anyone in Norway until the Nazis marched in. Or France. Now they have resistance groups." I pinched my roll. I should have gobbled it when I still had an appetite. But with Maison knowing who I was, I could barely think straight, much less eat. "I can learn things. I heard there's a research hospital on that island outside, in the middle of nowhere. Why would that be?"

The commander and Maison looked at each other. What were they thinking?

"I'll get something useful. Ferret out some intelligence. Prove what I am, show you what I am not, and sneak out on a neutral ship."

"Like the one we sank?" said the commander. "It's a war zone."

"Fine, pick me up next patrol, in six months or so."

The commander made a dubious noise.

"So," Maison said, "you admit you were in Japanese territory by design, after all. I think the FBI would like to hear that."

I went blank, every wisp of expression gone. I swayed and held onto a chair.

"So . . . that's what you wanted."

Maison wasn't offering me an opening to explain my innocence, to propose a course of action of any kind at all. He was cataloguing my reactions to their questions, for their inevitable reports, for what he would call my confession. No matter what the commander thought, Maison had already finished with me. I slowly placed the rest of my roll on the commander's desk.

"Yes, the FBI will believe me. With my history, and my parents in prison."

The commander kept frowning.

"Why do you think I ran?" I said. "I had a good life. Friends."

"Then you caught a freighter to Japan," said Maison.

"Like I had so many options."

"Look," said the commander, "if you're not lying, you're asking me to send an untrained girl into enemy territory. Not a chance."

"Especially with inside info," said Maison.

"What could I possibly know?"

"The fact we're here."

"You sank a ship! Of course you're here."

"Enough," said the commander. "I have work to do. You're not a prisoner, but stay out of the way. We'll figure out where to bunk you tomorrow." He pulled a microphone off the wall and thumbed a switch to '1MC,' the master circuit for ship-wide announcements. "This is the captain. As you have undoubtedly heard, we have a guest onboard. You will treat her with respect, but keep an eye out. She is not to touch anything." He replaced the mike and pushed past me. "Lieutenant Maison, bring her to con for now. We'll check out that island."

After he left, I put a hand on the bulkhead to steady myself. I swallowed before I could speak. But I had one more thing to say.

"You're right, you know."

Maison blocked the doorway.

"Some of 'my kind' do what you suspect." I fingering a strand of long black hair. "There's no way you could know if I'm one of them."

So grim, this lieutenant, like it was all more of my confession. But when I reached for the door, he stepped aside.

I leaned against the jamb, my voice as dull as the background hum of machinery.

"So hate us all."

Maison's scowl drilled into me all the way to the conning tower. He headed for sonar. I lingered near an aft door, or rather, hatch. There was no place truly 'out of the way,' and someone might want the hatch, so I squeezed behind the ladder that led up the sail to the bridge.

And recalled my last California night, in the grocery store stockroom, where I wedged around a ladder and held my satchel open for Rosita.

"You can't trust them," said Rosita.

"That's not their fault."

Rosita rammed sweet rolls into the satchel. "Such loyalty to the land of your birth. Just like your mother."

I winced, gripping the side rails of the bridge ladder. The chief had been keeping me in view since I got back to the conning tower. He probably wondered why I was twitching. I didn't dare smile. He might share Maison's opinion of me.

The commander and navigator leaned over the plotting table. After twenty minutes and some muffled communications with the topside watch, the commander tapped his chart and came over to me.

"You're right, Miss Hara. There's a facility on that island. We're getting pictures."

The sonarman raised a fountain pen. "Commander, contact, bearing zero-two-three."

"Range? ID?"

"Not clear. Near ten thousand yards. Could be a warship."

"Prepare to dive."

The diving klaxon went off. The chief barked orders; a sailor rushed in with a note for the commander; Maison donned a headset and fired off commands. Smooth professionalism snapped into calm urgency—paradoxical, I would have thought, before seeing it. As sharp as the cocking of a gun.

"Set your trim," said the chief.

"Flood main ballast," said the commander.

I drank in the flurry of activity. Diving in a submarine. Heady.

The fulfillment of my inappropriate dream.

Rosita's hazel eyes appeared out of nowhere and impaled me. "Wake up," they seemed to say. She guided me to the alley door of the grocery stockroom and peeped into the mist. A cat meowed.

"You know what they think," said Rosita. "If you go home, you're dead."

I stumbled after Rosita into the dim, foul-smelling alley. A trash can crashed nearby.

Trash can? No, the clang from the conning tower hatch above me. My head shot up. Diving in a submarine. Something that had now become a nightmare. A conviction for treason when they got me to the States.

Feet clattered down the bridge ladder, and a seaman wearing a sound-powered phone headed aft. Commands for rudder angle, diving planes, and valve positions crackled all around. They might attack, they might run, but they would not be on the surface for long.

The officer-of-the-deck descended through the lower hatch, right above me, and leaned down. "Bridge secure."

"Dive," said the commander.

"Dive, aye," said the chief.

The officer-of-the-deck reached up to lower the hatch.

I dropped my blanket, sprang up, and grabbed his belt. I hauled him off the ladder and charged up through the hatch.

"Ow. Hey!"

"Sorry." I yanked a lever and released the bottom hatch. Maison glared up at me.

The hatch fell. I clawed up the ladder to the one above. Pitch black, but you couldn't get lost in ten feet. All you could do was hit your head if you moved too fast.

I did.

It took forever to twist the upper hatch handle and push it up, but they wouldn't chase me, not with the submarine slipping down into the waves. They'd be too busy dogging the lower hatch, in case I left the upper one open. Protect the ship at all costs, the one rule every sailor knew.

I clambered out atop the submarine's sail, dropped the hatch, and knelt on the tiny bridge as water rose halfway up. I dogged this hatch as well; they really needed both. Whether I made it or not, the sub would be safe. I tightened it, mounted the coaming around the bridge, and prepared to dive.

The hatch behind me banged open and the water level fell as the ship resurfaced. I slammed against a radio mast. Maison stuck up his head.

"You won't stop me," I said.

"You jump now and the screws will chew you to bits."

I glanced aft toward the propellers. "I'll risk it. I can't go home."

"You still call it that?"

I turned and crouched.

"Wait."

I paused. He was climbing out of the hatch, but he couldn't move fast enough to stop me.

"Please. That water is cold."

I nodded at lights on the island, a half mile off the port beam. "Not cold enough."

Maison leaned over the ladder to the conning tower. "Yes, sir. Right away." He looked at me. "Miss, you don't need to do this."

It was almost humorous, in a black sort of way. Maison hated my guts. He wanted to take me home, for trial. For execution. Yet here, now, he wanted to protect me?

"I'll watch," I said, "every new moon. If you ever come back, I'll have something for you."

My legs gave launch and I soared, arching into the sea.

"Crap." Maison yelled down the ladder. "All Stop! Man Overboard, Port."

I swam straight to the side, as hard as I could. I was a strong swimmer, but oddly, I couldn't make any progress. I drifted closer to the hull as the stern approached. The propellers churned, sucking, sucking. I cast a panicked look and kept swimming.

Atop the sail, Maison yelled down the hatch again.

~~~~

KRISTY DISAPPEARED. MAISON stared at the water through binoculars. The propellers stopped, the water settled, and the stern swung starboard, away from where she'd been.

Nothing. Not a sign. It was too dark to see blood in the water, and too soon for sharks. If the damn girl had just—

Kristy popped up, coughing and spitting. Maison lowered the binoculars and released the breath he must have been holding. She treaded water a few seconds, watching him, then swam toward the island lights a few hundred yards off.

When she was clear of the props, Maison descended and closed the hatch. Orders flew, the screws started up, and the boat submerged.

Maison leaned against the plotting table, watching the navigator scribe a line. It was very strange, the more he thought about it. Kristy hadn't acted right. She didn't fit the image. A kid that age shouldn't be able to sound so convincing, not if she was lying. To come across as if she weren't, impossible as it had to be, guilty.

Damn the girl, anyway.
~~~~

Chapter 6

Dawn broke behind me as I pulled myself onto the rocky shore of the island, well north of the lights I had seen. Halfway here from the submarine, a concern had bubbled up. Maybe I shouldn't barge in like I expected the locals to welcome a stranger, especially when the crew of the sunken ship didn't even know I existed. I needed a story. I'd come from somewhere else. A fishing boat, sunk in the storm that pounded through the area two days ago on its way to my freighter. And that log floating offshore, that's what I rode in on, but only if anyone asked.

I lay on the stones, wheezing in exhaustion. Simple. Keep it simple.

My shivering slowed, and I sat up and gazed east over the water toward where the submarine had been. Maison had let me go. After all he said, he'd saved my life. And the shimmering golds of a brilliant sunrise framed his act. I kissed the fingertips of my right hand, touched my heart and forehead, and held my open palm toward the empty sea.

A crunch of gravel told me someone had come up behind. Uncertain steps. Civilian.

"Who are you?" The raspy words of an old Japanese woman.

I lowered my hand.

"Have you sea gull brains?"

Sea gull? Keep it simple? I fought down the upward tic at the corner of my mouth.

"I haven't seen a youngster honor the rising sun for decades."

Okay, girl, do it. Soften every facial muscle. I was certain my Japanese was up to the task, but if I limited myself to broken speech, playing simple, it would be even easier.

I rose, turned, and bowed to the old woman. Only a small bow, to an unknown like this. "Sun is good."

The old woman scratched her leg with a spatula. "You mocking me, girl?"

"I was cold. Boat sank. Now I am warm." I bowed again, uncertain how much respect a feeble-minded girl should pay to a shabbily-dressed vagabond of a woman, even if much my elder.

The old woman studied me a moment. "Come on, child. Let's get you dry."

So far, so good. I would develop a better story, if necessary. Infiltrate, that was the word. I could do this.

I'd better.

The old woman led me toward a fisher's hut. Two steps inland, the ground started weaving. I swayed and the old woman took my elbow.

"Why is ground moving?"

The woman laughed. "You've been on the water too long. It'll pass."

Another step, and I caught a movement at the edge of my vision. Amongst the boulders and surf arose a wizened, ancient man, who stood there, mute, staring at me. My toe caught a rock.

"Steady, I said." The old woman followed my eyes. "That's our local hermit. Don't mind him."

A quiver took me. From his angle, the hermit would have seen my face as I looked to sea. He would have seen my expressions. He would have seen me wipe them off. And now, he kept staring at me. I forced myself to walk.

Yeah, right, infiltrate. Could I really do this? Or was it already too late?

Inside the old woman's hut, the crone kindled a fire in an open pit in the middle of the room. I huddled near it, watching smoke dissipate through a hole in the roof while the old woman puttered behind me, chattering with ten times the energy she put into her work. After a time, she gave me a bowl of rice.

"Thank you, um, what I call you?"

"Don't you go asking me that. I left my name in Japan. Don't ask that hermit, either; he'd likely swat you."

Left in Japan? Strange. I filed it away and shoveled grains into my mouth with a pair of chopsticks, thankful for all the training my mother had given me in Japanese customs.

I had a feeling audiences must be rare for this old woman. She regaled me with whatever came to mind. "That brainless second cousin never did make crab stew right, no matter how many times she was shown. And her foul-mouthed brother—mercy, he was piece of day-old tripe. Then my third cousin married the village idiot. Laziest legs I ever saw." She sat, picked up a bowl, and waved it around. "But she can't handle money, so she goes to my uncle. Those shoes fit?"

I patted the worn shoes beside me, the woman's cast-offs, and kept chewing.

"The old souse. She brings him sake, but he throws her out."

I didn't try to absorb it all. It wouldn't have been in character even if I could.

~~~~

I hoed in the old woman's vegetable garden, upslope from her hut and along the southern edge of a forest. I had no idea what was in the trees to the north, or up the rocky escarpment to the west. Unclimbable, that hill, as far as I was concerned. The forest had a couple of openings that might be paths, and a northern breeze carried hints of mold and blossoms, briefly chasing off the bouquet of dead crab.

The south, on the other hand, was pretty barren for a half mile to the edge of a military encampment of some kind. A high fence, barbed wire along the top, led from the escarpment to the ocean,
~~~~

with one truck-wide gate I could see. If there was knowledge to be gained on this island, that's where it would be. How in the phooey did I think I was going to learn anything, like I'd bragged to Maison? What could have possessed me to think I could get into an army compound?

Patience, patience. I'd just arrived. Three days, so far. Stay cool.

I put my back into the hoe. My sailor shirt and pants were clean, for a pleasant change of pace. I also wore a tattered jacket against the lingering chill of spring, and the old shoes were more than welcome. I needed to show thanks for the gifts, and hard chores were hardly new. Not to the real me, nor the weak-minded girl I was playing.

Near mid-morning, a Japanese army private appeared from behind a boulder, casually patrolling the shore, rifle slung over his shoulder. I had to ignore him. Soldiers would be normal to real Japanese. He wandered along until he got closer and noticed me, or realized I wasn't the old woman he expected to see. He came toward me.

"Who are you?"

"Kira. I hoe." I gave him a polite bow and kept working.

"That's a Russian name."

"No, it mine. Two many Keiko in village. I pick new one."

"What village?" He grabbed my arm. "How did you get here?"

The old woman came out of her hut, wringing water from a dishrag. "Leave her alone, you *gaijin*."

"How dare you." The private let go of me and pulled himself up straight. "I am Takijiro Terauchi, Imperial Japanese Army."

"With round-eye boots, round-eye clothes, and round-eye gun."

"We make these."

"From German plans."

Terauchi glared at the old woman and took my arm again. He shook me so hard I dropped my hoe. "No one is allowed on the island."

"Not even us?" said the old woman.

"You know what I mean."

"I'd better. You're not clear."

Terauchi threw me to the ground, unlimbered his rifle, and pointed it at my nose.

"Tell me, or you are a spy."

I shuddered. No, I was trembling like an aspen in an earthquake. It couldn't end. Not yet. I hadn't accomplished a thing.

Think. Interrogation was logical. Trembling fit my role, though I hadn't expected to be so utterly terrified. Worse than when Maison identified me.

I needed to respond.

"Kira spy? Why Kira spy?"

The old woman shoved Terauchi aside. "You're not a spy, child. A little confused, is all."

Terauchi jerked his rifle from me to the old woman and back. I took off a shoe and picked at a blister, the archetype of reassured innocence. I hoped.

"What's wrong with her?" said Terauchi.

"Her boat sank. Family drowned."

I rubbed my foot and put the shoe on.

"She may have been under too long herself." The old woman helped me stand. "Tell your commandant he's got a new local."

Terauchi slowly re-slung his weapon. "He won't like this."

"True. Such a menace. Works like a boy."

She handed me the hoe and made hoeing motions. I beamed and dug in.

"You never know what a child could do."

Terauchi ground his teeth and plodded off to the beach and north. The old woman watched me a moment, and went into her hut.

I stopped scraping and leaned into the hoe, letting the tension drip down the handle and soak into the soil. If I dared relax, I'd go limp. I had to get a better grip on myself. I lifted the blade and heard a cough.

The hermit peered out from the forest to the north. The same man who had seen me that first day on the coast.

I faltered. Had I looked tired, taking a rest, or had I looked relieved, which wouldn't do at all? And why would he spy on me, yet say nothing? He must be suspicious. Was he up to something himself? He was a danger, but I couldn't think what to do about it, except pray it would be all right. Head thrust deeply in the sand. A brilliant strategy, yet the only option I had.

I buried my eyes in the dirt, digging furiously with the hoe.

~~~~

Days passed. Guards patrolled the shore at random intervals, but no one bothered me or spoke to the old woman. I hoped this meant I was blending in, though how you did that on a lonely island with an army outpost wasn't plain.

The next afternoon, the local army commandant rode his mare north along the sand. A daunting sight—uniform spotless, medals gleaming, samurai blade at his side. The old woman and I stopped gutting fish when we heard a neigh. The woman frowned.

The commandant reined in near us. "You the new girl?"

I dropped my fish, stood, and bowed awkwardly. "Not so new, general-sama. I am almost eighteen."

He beat a riding crop against his boot. Twice.

"She means naught, Colonel Ushijima," said the old woman. "She is damaged."

"Has she contacted anyone?"

"How? Anyway, there's no one she knows. Orphan, so she says."

He grunted.

The old woman tapped the basket of fish. "Back to work."

I knelt, picked up a long, skinny, largehead hairtail, and slapped it on a rock. I gutted it neatly.

"Fisher folk?" said the commandant.

"Perhaps."

"Where you from, girl? What's your name?"

"Kira, sir. Kira Hara. Village Sake."

"Sake?"
~~~~

I bowed confirmation.

"Never heard of it."

"You'd never heard of this island, either," said the old woman.

The commandant growled his contempt. He kicked his mare and continued his ride to the north.

I stood and watched him enter the forest. The pale green of spring adorned the branches, new leaves waiting to open.

"Pretty."

"You stay away," said the old woman. "He'd as soon stick his sword in your hide as smell you."

I kept looking.

The woman pushed me down and made a rude gesture at the commandant's back. "You don't understand. That man is the epitome of everything wrong in the world. Half the honor of Japan evaporated when my country invaded China. Or before that, when government by assassination became the rule of the day."

"Assassination?"

"I abandoned the motherland in protest. Pointless. The army followed me, and now travel is banned."

"When did the hermit—"

"That useless, love-sick goose? Gave up his professorship and fine house, copied my protest. Ha. He's left me alone ever since I broke a ladle over his head."

"Really?"

"If only I could break a ladle over the head of the Imperial Japanese Army. Now get to work."

I lowered my eyes and deboned the hairtail. The vaguest notion of an idea was sprouting into a half-baked plan. If I fertilized it a little, it might mushroom into a full-grown weed. Ah, and what would my high school English teacher say if he ever got ahold of that messed-up phraseology? He'd flunk me sure.

~~~~

Early one morning, I stole some free time. I broke a slender branch threatening to block the entrance to one of the woods paths, rubbed the tip against a stone to sharpen it, and strolled
~~~~

along the beach until I found a patch of moist mud above the tide line. I knelt and scratched with the stick, sketching the sunrise, lining in clouds and rays of light. It was a lovely picture, considering the medium.

The old woman's footsteps squelched up behind me and stopped. I pretended not to hear, and tried to fit some gulls between the clouds. I hadn't drawn since the freighter, and every muscle from jaw to little toe loosened up the longer I was at it. At some point, the woman left.

She returned from the army base that evening, loaded with rice and a few spices that stung the nose when she walked past. I washed my face and hands in a tub beside her door and dried off with half a faded old shirt, the color of sea-diluted blood.

She came back out and handed me three pencils and a fistful of paper, crinkling it like she was embarrassed by her generosity. "Here."

The old woman went inside before I could react. I held the paper and pencils like fine porcelain, fragile and priceless. Such a gift. Shoes, jacket, and now this. Kindness, when all I dreamt of was undermining them all.

"Thank you," I whispered.

I smoothed the paper, thoughts skittering from the pleasure of art to the potential for something more. Something that could help that submarine commander, and Maison, if I ever saw them again.

"*Sumimasen,*" I said again, louder, and rushed inside.

~~~~

The next day, I raced through some quick pot-scrubbing and seed planting, and obtained the old woman's reluctant permission to explore. I hiked north into the forest, following the easternmost path between stunted maples, taller chestnuts, and musty, moss-covered boulders. A black woodpecker with a white belly composed its version of music, a percussion solo, on the gnarly trunk of a laurel. Mosquitoes and metallic-blue butterflies clogged the air until I emerged beside a rocky beach where a Japanese
~~~~

patrol boat cruised offshore, doodling along like a fishing boat. When I saw a sailor trolling off the stern with a bamboo pole, I almost laughed.

I checked trees and shoreline and saw no one, so I knelt, half-concealed, and brushed off the top of a flattish grey rock. I laid out a sheet of paper and drew the boat, squinting against the glare and sketching quickly. It had no apparent radar, and the only anti-submarine warfare capability was a single depth charge launcher. ASW details could be useful someday, if I could ever get them home. I lost myself in the image.

A voice came over my shoulder. "Smart," said the hermit. "Nature abounds, and you draw military hardware."

I leapt up, breaking the point on my pencil and almost losing my paper to a gust of wind. He'd spoken in the polished Japanese of an educated man, syllables flowing like melted gold. I checked the woods, the beach.

"No soldiers," said the hermit. "Most fortuitous."

I rubbed the drawing, smearing the lines, and wadded it. "Pretty boat. Kira bad. Won't draw boats again."

The hermit chuckled. "Do not play sham, girl. You know right well what you are doing." He headed through the forest.

I hesitated. He wasn't suspicious, he was certain. From seeing my face a couple of times? What else had I done wrong? And he didn't seem to care, like it meant nada to hold my life in his hands.

I folded my papers, sped after him, and caught up before he entered a cave. I touched his arm and he turned, clearly annoyed.

"Why haven't you reported me?"

"For lying about your wits? After showing up with no credible explanation?"

"Yes."

"Well, if you want me to."

"No!"

He laughed and started to go inside.

"Thank you, sir. I am in your debt."

The hermit stopped, and came back a step. "You have a streak of honesty. Not like that sow-spawn running the POW camp."

"POW?"

He considered me. "Prisoners of war. Americans, from the Philippines."

That once, I didn't hold a poker face.

"Of course, if you are mining for information—" He pointed at my eyes. "—that is a bit too honest."

The hermit swiped my drawing and led me into the cave. A small fire glowed in the center of the large chamber. Smoke flittered and drifted into cracks in the ceiling. Statues of piled varicolored stones decked out the room: a matched pair of leopards and a zebra. No mortar. He had interwoven longer and wider rocks, and counter-balanced others, to anchor each creation in a moment of frozen action. I gazed at them in awe.

The hermit flipped my paper into the fire. I let out a squeak.

"Sit down," he said, throwing me an Asian pear.

I sat and took a bite, and the hermit launched into a cryptic, abbreviated version of recent island history. Deporting healthy Koreans and establishing a leper colony fifteen years earlier. Importing Japanese immigrants opposed to the government's expansionist policies, too old and respected to kill off but welcome to leave the Home Islands. Declining population in the leper colony as health care dried up, thanks to the drive on China. Invading the Philippines and setting up a new POW camp, blocking access to exiles on the other side of the island.

The hermit had taken to splitting branches while he talked, feeding pieces to the fire. "Two weeks after they brought in the new doctor, they moved out what was left of the leper colony and expanded the POW camp."

"So no Koreans are left. Only . . ."

"Misfits, loners, and outcasts. And the army."

"I'm sorry. I didn't mean that."

"You should have."

I wiped sweet pear juice off my chin, sucked my finger, and tossed the core into the flames. "And now you have told me this?"

He stood and drew me up. I gathered my papers and pencils, and he shoved me toward the entrance.

"Now you keep away from that commandant. Keep away from everyone, especially that doctor if you ever see him. He's pumping one and all, chronicling the island for some god-awful reason, and you'd likely slip up." He pushed me out the opening.

I turned to bow, but he flicked his hand and went to the fire.

He hadn't said a word about why he was on the island himself, what personal beliefs or political dissent had led him to depart his prior life.

Or why he'd taken the time to explain anything.

~~~~

A few days of rain bottled me up in the hut, where I failed to absorb yet more of the old woman's endless supply of complaints about relatives, authorities, and ill fortune. If I had bothered to remember any of the tales, I could have spoken up and avoided some repetition. Maybe. I tried to imagine living amid an extended Japanese family, with this woman for an aunt. Oh, my.

When the sky dried, and only the leaves continued dripping, I went for a walk along the inland forest trail, this one heavy with oak and pine. They didn't do as well near the coast, or the soil was different. Or it was chance. Giant fan-shaped orange mushrooms decorated the oak trunks, and a hint of cedar tinted the air. I came to a fork, looked down both paths, and took a few steps on the left one. A pile of decaying horse dung proved I'd found the commandant's route. Good enough.

The track ascended, curving west. Interesting how the escarpment receded and grew more gentle north of the old woman's hut. The broader area didn't last long, though. Further north, near the hermit's cave, the cliffs were back to being steep, with a goodly spread of sylvan tranquility between them and the sea.

After a while, I reached a village. Abandoned, as the hermit had said. Seven unpainted shacks and a larger structure surrounded the remnants of a stone well. One hovel had a rotting porch, and fallen fruit from a nearby tree was several months past the ripe stage. It gave me a sour feeling in my stomach. Where had
~~~~

they taken everyone? What did people do, when forced from their homes?

Bamboo wind chimes clanked in the breeze, sending me back to Alameda.

In the kitchen of my California home, metal wind chimes tinkled in the breeze from an open window. My mother and I sorted laundry on the kitchen table.

"Propellers helped," she said in her ever-present Japanese. "But your cousin needs the fine points of radar masts. He wants to make the best ship models in Japan."

I answered in my mother's tongue. "I'll work on it. Is he still in Osaka?"

"Yes. When you graduate, you should visit your homeland."

I switched to English. "I live in my homeland."

She cuffed me, a backhanded blow that bent me over the stove.

I flinched, and fell against the stone well in the Korean village. The hollow music of the bamboo wind chimes pulled me back, and a thought formed in my mind, growing like a cancer, swelling into a sudden, horrid realization.

Did I even have a cousin, someone who made ship models? My mother was mailing my sketches, two or three a week. With all the animosity building between Japan and America, why had I never considered what they could do with accurate ship descriptions? I was an adult, for heaven's sake, or close enough. Responsible for my actions. And I had been helping all along, drafting exactly what my mother's homeland wanted. One reckless, blind, unforgivable picture after another.

A shudder rippled through me. It wasn't just my mother, after all. It was me. I really was a spy, a traitor, giving aid if not comfort to the enemy. I wanted to shrivel. Maison had been right all along. I should have been shot.

I bit back a sob, sinking to the ground. Why had it taken so long for me to recognize the truth? How could I live with what I had done? What kind of simple-minded denial had I wrapped myself in, claiming virtue, denying guilt, when my actions were plain to the blindest fool? And was there even a hope of redemption, some way I could make up for treason?

Another tremor shook my body. Redemption. Not likely. Not even remotely. But I couldn't wither away and do nothing, not after what I had already done. I could try. I could scour every foot of this island, every inch, until I learned something of value to match my sketches. To redress the sin, as much as fate would allow. To make amends for all my family had done.

I had to.

~~~~

Finches were daring to approach before I could move again. I replaced fallen stones around the lip of the well and straightened its wooden cover, in case anyone came back someday, and passed on through the village.

Another hour, gradually climbing, and I stopped near some heavy bushes. Two parallel barbed wire fences stretched left and right, ten feet high and twenty feet apart. A guard manned a machine gun in a tower on the left, outside the fence lines, aiming inward at what must be the POW camp: rows of low buildings, all white, all quiet. A tall, skeletal doctor in a lab coat hurried past a Shinto shrine.

I raised a hand to slap a mosquito, but stopped in time and stabbed it with a pine needle. No noise.

It occurred to me that all the buildings were to the left. Straight ahead, another fence, a single one eight feet high, went perpendicular to the other two and disappeared in the distance. To the right, inside the double fence, were only trees. Why had they fenced a bunch of woods?

I inspected the ground. Hoofprints and dung followed the fence line to the left, south, toward the built-up portion of the camp.

I headed right.

Several hundred yards on, the double fence ended, jutting into the air beyond the edge of a cliff. I went to the rim and peered down. It fell sixty feet to a narrow band of wave-beaten rocks.
~~~~

No buildings, no guard towers, not this far north. Strange.

I retraced my steps.

~~~~

Next afternoon, I knelt before a gently-curved boulder on the beach and sketched on one of my precious sheets of paper. The old woman finished brewing her latest version of fish stew in a cauldron swinging from a tripod in the hut, and produced her typical "*hai.*" I pictured her dispersing the coals beneath it, reducing the heat to a simmer. The crone may look like a witch, and paddle her concoctions like a witch, and cackle like a witch over mumbled memories, but I couldn't fault her products. Everything she cooked put to shame anything I had eaten back home. I savored the smells, lost in my drawing.

"I told you to find crabs."

I gave a start. I hadn't heard the old woman coming. I pointed to a basket and kept sketching.

She went to the basket and poked around inside. It was full of small crabs, healthy enough to try pinching her. She said something on the order of "Hmph," walked behind me to see the drawing, and took on a harsher tone. "I never would have gotten that paper if I had known you would use it this way."

I kept at it, hurrying when I saw the commandant riding in from the south along the open shoreline. His usual time, his usual day. I'd been counting on it.

"Stop that now."

I disregarded the old woman and shaded in a few more lines as the commandant got close. I finished up, dropped my pencil, and raced toward him.

His mare shied and he raised his crop at me. "What are you doing?"

I bowed and held up my picture.

"I'm supposed to be interested in that?"

I bobbed my head again and kept holding the sketch toward him. After a moment, he took it, threw a glance at it, then spread it out and examined it.
~~~~

It was a picture of himself, mounted proudly on his steed. "This is good, girl. What was your name?"

"Kira, general."

"Kira." He rolled up the paper and tucked it in his jacket. "Treat yourself like a picture. You may like the results."

He rode off north, into the forest, and I trailed him a few feet, imitating rapt adoration. Step One, carried out. Contact had been made.

The old woman whacked me over the shoulder with a stick. "I told you to leave him alone." She snatched up my papers.

"No!" I grabbed them. "Mine. Present."

"You wretch. I will not consort with poison." She picked up the basket of crabs. "Go live with the commandant." She stomped into her hut.

I looked down at my papers. So long, fish stew, or having a place to lie down at night. I hadn't thought it through. If I had, would I have predicted the old woman would react so harshly?

Well, nothing for it now. Time to leave. I headed into the forest.

Chapter 7

I spent the night huddled in the hollow trunk of an aging oak. Not comfortable, but it drained well and was merely damp from all the rain. Damp meant buggy, though, and a cloying scent teased my nose. I cradled my papers, afraid to sleep for fear I'd wrinkle them or lose them to the wet. Thankfully, the old woman hadn't demanded I return the old jacket or shoes. I could have died of exposure otherwise.

The animal calls should have been scarier, perhaps. A couple of high-pitched howls, a lot of scratching, and an owl or two. But I was too busy pondering what to do next to be scared of the dark. Imaginary perils would have to wait their turn. Besides, I was on a small island that used to have a settlement, and now housed an army. I hoped that meant no dangerous predators, other than the human kind.

A dollop of homesickness hit me. How was Maxine doing? And Rosita? Did that toddler down the street still play with the dollhouse I'd made her, or had her parents thrown it out, a tainted gift from an evil spy?

This wasn't the time. I could pine my losses some other day. I wrested myself back to the present.

Near sunup, the sharp point of a crescent moon tore a hole in the clouds, and a few stars poured through the gap. By then, I knew I needed help. It was too soon to approach the POW camp and expect a welcome. I likely couldn't survive on my own, much less accomplish anything, and with the old woman alienated, but one option presented itself.

I sought the hermit's cave when dawn fought its way through baby leaves bursting open all around. I stood outside, twenty feet from the entrance and off the path, looking at my few remaining papers. At my pencils. At the cave. Was he awake? Did I dare to knock? How did you knock on a cave, anyway?

Smoke appeared from crevices high up, and I watched it curl around a vine. The rock must be riddled with cracks and nooks, or even passages. Lava tubes and stress fractures, I thought that's what they were called.

"How long will you be blocking the light?" The hermit peeked out the entrance.

I gave a nervous bow. "Sorry. Do you buy supplies from the army? Rice and things?"

"Only store in town. Best prices."

"Do they buy anything?"

"What, like native crafts?"

"I was thinking, more like pictures."

He laughed at me. "Soldiers? Sure. Art lovers, every one."

So much for help. I turned away.

"Hold on, girl. What have you got? Anything as good as that boat?"

I went back and handed him the top sheet. He came out in the light and gave it sober contemplation: a classic Japanese rising sun over the ocean, with delicate shading.

"Not bad. A bit weak on color."

I fingered my pencils and rolled my eyes.

"Don't be so serious. I'll keep this one. For my commission."

"Then you think I could sell?"

"Not this. Wrong audience. Try samurai. Battles, weapons. Or portraits."

He withdrew into his cave. I followed.

The hermit held the picture against the solid rock. “No nails. No hammer, for that matter.” He laid the picture on a half-built statue of an ox and weighted the corners with rocks. His zebra was gone. The distinctive striated stones that had given the zebra its coloring were now scattered among a hawk and three swans.

“I’ll need more paper,” I said. “And food.”

“What happened to the hag you were helping? She finally die?”

“She asked me to leave.”

“I see. Couldn’t take her chatter?”

“She was fine. My fault.”

He frowned, but I said nothing more.

“Thought I told you to stay away from that commandant.”

Had he been watching again, or was he overly perceptive? “So did she. I guess she meant it.”

“You think I did not?”

“I haven’t any choice.”

He tugged on a lip, and headed to the side of the cave. “Of course you don’t.” He rummaged in some sacks. “I will give you rice. Sell you matches.”

“Thank you.”

“You cannot stay here. Find your own cave.”

“There are more?”

“Whole island is hollow. Army will figure it out sooner or later.” He handed me an iron bowl and two canvas pouches. “Bring me something good. I will get you a blanket and knife.”

I held his gifts. “Thank you.”

“Now scram before I forget what it’s like having a little peace and quiet.”

I smiled, bowed, and left.

He’d done it. Helped me again. And once again, chased me off before I could ask why. But now I had the means to get what I needed, and my pictures would ease my name into the camp. Getting the soldiers used to me was a prerequisite if I expected to pick up anything. Though what I could learn from a POW camp, even one with a hospital for some reason, I wasn’t certain.

Information on where they were invading next? Plans would be useful. Or the low-down on that research they were supposed to be doing.

One step at a time. Next job, find a cave.

I went north through the forest for quite a ways, along the base of the steep rock face, without seeing anything at ground level. Flickers of shadows and vines obscured the surface higher up, but there were no obvious openings there, either. Just as well, I could never have reached anything that high. I ran my tongue along my teeth, studying the wall, and kept walking.

Near the base of one escarpment I found an opening and ducked through it, but came out after a minute, shaking my head. Stubby, dank, and reminiscent of rotten meat.

Many failures later, sun long past its prime, I found one possibility, if nothing else turned up. But it was cramped and didn't have any good cracks to vent smoke.

I kept searching. Had to be near the north end of the island by now.

A trick of light caught my eye. I studied the rock more closely, stepped to the side, moved a bit more, and climbed a few feet. I pulled aside a pair of vines and found a cleft, not wide, but decent. I slipped through.

And stopped, gawking. I was in the perfect cave. Light filtered in through slits in the rock overhead, illuminating a large, level—and more important, death-dry—cavern. A breeze from the interior cooled my face and wafted a strand of hair toward the main opening. I looked toward the back, but it was locked in darkness. I did a complete revolution, and another, looking up. Blue stripes, the crevices high above, made skylights like I'd never seen, with an overhang to keep out rain.

Heavenly.

~~~~

A fire burned brightly in the center of my new cave that night. An open bag of rice lay beside it, as did my iron bowl, which I probably should have washed before the leftover rice converted
~~~~

itself to cement.

I leaned over a thin board, a piece of driftwood, and scrubbed it with a rock. I dribbled more sand and kept rubbing. I switched to my left hand. My right was too close to cramping, and I needed to save it for later.

After another half hour, several checks, and the finest sand I'd found, I stopped and felt the board again. I shook off all the sand, brushed away dust, and stroked with the tips of my fingers. Excellent.

I laid a piece of paper on the board and picked up a pencil. Now came the right-hand stuff. Supposedly.

I tapped the pencil on my lower lip, waiting for inspiration.

~~~~

I decided to check on the old woman the next morning. It was possible one of us had overreacted, and there might be room for rapprochement. Fresh horse dung coated the breeze before I left the shelter of the forest, which could only mean the commandant, so I held up in the deep shadows. I lifted a branch aside, and there he sat, perched on his mare outside the old woman's hut, glaring at her. He held a small bundle.

The old woman beat laundry on a rock. "No clothes. No food. So what?"

"She was under your protection."

"She prefers yours, the ungrateful ninny."

"You, widow, are a spiteful witch."

"Thank you, Commandant. Coming from a morally upstanding person like yourself, I am fairly judged."

She kept whapping a kimono on the rock. The commandant snarled and headed south.

I went back north. Question answered. No chance of repairing relations where she was concerned.

~~~~

Standing a short way inside his cave, the hermit loaded my arms with several packages. His stone ox statue was finished. A candle fluttered in an angle of the cavern, revealing a spray of flowers, a *tatami* for kneeling, and a teapot. I wondered if he would ever invite me for a tea ceremony, or if it would be appropriate to offer myself as *Teishu* and host one for him. But no, it could be too intimate, too forward of me to suggest such a thing, and quieting my mind was beyond me these days, anyway.

"Socks; two blankets, they were thin; a knife; more matches; a comb. Come back for your rice, I am not carrying it any farther."

"Did you get—"

"Certainly. Paper. Pencils." He laid a slender box on top of the pile.

"Thank you. It's more than I expected."

"You don't know your talent. How you got firelight to scintillate off armor I cannot understand."

"It just sort of came to me."

"You have a gift. Why in the name of Fuji don't you take a ship home?"

"Why don't you?"

"Ah, a voice with edge." He gave me the tiniest of bows. "Congratulations."

"Sorry."

"Don't spoil it. Now get out of here before you stink the place up."

I bowed twice, once deeply, and left. I saved my smile for after I was in the trees.

~~~~

Two days later, I reached a conclusion. I was sick of rain. It never did this in California. Well, it did, but I could overlook it. I'd never been locked inside with nothing to do but watch it fall so consistently, perpetually, repeatedly. So darn much. But today I caught a break, a cloud-free sky that reminded me of summers at home. A good day to reconnoiter.

North, naturally. Find the end of the island.

I reached it near noon. The gap between sea and escarpment narrowed to a point, made a sharp left turn, and continued west a
~~~~

few dozen feet before petering out. When I could walk no further, I found myself at the foot of a sixty-foot cliff stretching off to the west, rising straight up from a medley of rocks being punished by the waves. Up at the top, way up there, the POW camp ten-foot fences jutted out directly overhead.

I scanned the rock. Ledges, dark crevices, and fronds littered the surface. I kicked off my shoes and stepped out into the sucking, frigid, calf-deep water. Birds flew into the rock face and disappeared. Crevices, for sure. Lots of them, all the way up.

Something grabbed at my ankle. I looked down, expecting seaweed.

It was hair.

I screamed and stumbled back. The corpse of an American soldier lay mangled in the foam, manacles on his wrists, brown bandages on stubs where his feet should be. The surf bounced him off a boulder and swept him out to deeper water. I crumpled into the froth, hands over my mouth, muffling a puling sound that bleated through my fingers. Far above, the fence became fangs reaching out to disembowel me. What had I gotten myself into? What was this place?

A camp with a research hospital?

~~~~

Early morning brought the most light into my cave. The sun was practically due east. I tugged a vine tighter, tying a mass of thick twigs to a larger stick, every twig smeared with pine sap collected the afternoon before. No matter how careful I'd been, no matter how much I scrubbed my hands with saltwater and sand, my left little finger would be tacky for days.

I lit the makeshift torch from my small fire and headed to the rear of the cave. A vertical slit beckoned, blowing sparks from my torch. Not exactly the equipment I used that time I went spelunking back home. Hopefully it would last awhile. I skipped inside, holding the flame away from my face, waving off smoke.

A path led steeply upward. I shoved my hair behind my ears and followed it.
~~~~

I hunted passageways as long as I dared. At one among many intersections, I knelt and drew lines on a paper, moved my torch, and peered down a side tunnel. Rising, and much steeper. I touched up my map, blew off dust, and checked the torch.

Sputtering, and I only had a few matches for emergency light. Time to stop. I needed better, if I wanted to keep up the explorations. And if the hermit was correct, if the island was hollow and the Japanese didn't realize it, maybe there was a way into the camp.

Or maybe not. But it would be interesting to find out.

I headed downhill.

~~~~

Next time I visited him, the hermit dragged me in, sat me on a boulder, and said, "How solid is your background."

"I'm not sure what you mean."

"The commandant had me brought to his office last time I was in the camp. Wanted to know where you were staying now the old woman kicked you out. When I got there, his aide was pushing him to sign a form, an inquiry about you. If they forward it to headquarters, what will happen?"

My mouth made some vain attempt to frame an answer, but nothing came out.

"Well, you are lucky. The commandant was too busy fiddling with an origami flower. He accused the aide of acting like a German, called you inconsequential, and said headquarters had a war to concentrate on."

"Oh. Um, thank you."

"Not my doing. The aide also gave him a framed portrait, the commandant on his mare. Your work?" The hermit sounded truly disgusted with me.

"Probably."

"You have made an impression. Foolish girl. I hope you do not come to rue it." The hermit scraped up some things. He dumped a packet of paper in my arms and added a hand-held lamp and can of oil. "On top of which, you waste your money," he said. "Draw in
~~~~

daylight."

"Too many shadows."

"Not in my world. And you cannot have used up your paper."

"First drafts are pretty bad."

"That boat was not."

I scuffed my toe. Was that more suspicion? "Some things need to be burned."

"Assuredly." He didn't sound convinced.

"Were you able to find watercolors? I think they'd sell better."

"On order," he said. "Do not know why you need them. Your pictures are getting darker. You mad at somebody?"

"Good point." I couldn't tell him what I'd seen on the northern shore. "I'll lighten them up."

"Do that."

His eyes bored into me as I walked away. He helped me. He questioned me. He kept his silence. What was his own agenda? How far could I trust him not to betray what he knew?

Not that there was a blessed thing I could do about it.

Chapter 8

Starlight glittered off the ocean. No moon was visible. I paced the beach a few hundred yards from my cave, clenching my arms, shivering in the chill, gazing out to sea.

New moon, I'd told Maison, so I had to be out here, just in case, the three nights surrounding that time. Every month.

It was too soon. If the Navy ever came back, it wouldn't be for ages. But I couldn't take the chance of missing them, so here I was, tonight and tomorrow and the night after.

So quiescent, so still the night.

So deceiving.

~~~~

LIEUTENANT MAISON PACED in a small, cluttered office in one of the larger buildings on Submarine Base Pearl. The squadron had been permanently relocated to Pearl Harbor with the outbreak of war. Now that Maison was back from patrol, he found himself intrigued by the unusual girl who'd taken a dive off his sub, so he'd looked up the security officer who'd given a long-ago briefing on the Hara family. The commander had been transferred to Pearl as well, attached to CINCPAC.

The security officer hung a plaque behind his cheap metal
~~~~

desk: 'Office of Naval Intelligence.' "Not guilty," he said, wrapping up a description of the Hara case. "Not her."

"You're certain?" said Maison.

"They searched the house. Grilled both parents. The father's loyal, the girl knew nothing, and the mother is certifiable."

"But a spy?"

The security officer clicked his tongue. "You know how many Japanese we've rounded up?"

Maison shook his head.

"I won't white-wash 'em. A few are agents. But if we did the same to Russians, we'd get ten times the spies. And they're allies."

Maison didn't like it. Security briefings were supposed to identify real threats, not waste time scaring people. But they had to act on what they knew at the moment, and this guy changed his melody when the facts came in. That much Maison could respect.

The security officer took photos from a box and arranged them on his desk.

"If the girl didn't do anything, why did she run?" said Maison.

"Kristy? Maybe she didn't trust us. Or herself. We deal in labels. Hard to know who people are."

Maison scowled.

"But if you or I were spies, they wouldn't arrest our wives. Or children." The security officer set down a photograph of his family, smiling around a Thanksgiving feast on an eight-foot mahogany table.

Maison tried to picture Kristy in a similar setting. Not half-starved, filthy, and desperate. It was harder than he imagined.

What was she doing right now?

~~~~

I paced along the beach, arms clenched, gazing out to the starlit sea. Nothing appeared. Of course it didn't.

Would Maison ever think of me again? Or would he get home and confirm anew what a traitor I was, drawing my awful pictures?

Either way, he wouldn't return. No one would ever come.

But I would be here. Just in case.
~~~~

Chapter 9

High in one of the tunnels that branched out behind my cave, I hefted a stone. It was a good size, comfortable, like a well-balanced hammer. I leaned against a side wall and bashed rocks from a crevice, widening it. The last thin, sharp piece broke off. I picked up my oil lamp and inspected the opening. Good enough.

A week now, and I'd mapped a whole slew of passages. Explorations were so much faster with steady light. And more fun. I couldn't believe I'd bothered trying pine sap torches. I made a note on my papers and passed through.

A short while later I crouched on the floor of a tunnel and examined my map. Myriad lines laced across the page. I tapped the end of one track and looked up. The passageway bent left and continued rising.

I held up my lamp and checked the oil level. A quarter full. It didn't take much heading downhill along known pathways, and I really wanted to continue, and . . . and actually, the level was below the quarter mark. Who knew how far the tunnels went?

"Rats."

Well, in the 'phooey' sense. Fortunately, I hadn't run across any actual rats. Nothing for them to eat in pitch-black tunnels, apparently. I folded my map, stood, and turned downward.

A muffled cry came from behind. I whirled. Very brief, and quickly gone. An injured bird? But it meant an opening, somewhere ahead. Darkness beckoned, beyond the reach of my light. I checked my lamp again, bit my lip, and crept upward.

At another sharp bend, the tunnel angled right, and sunlight trickled in. A happy guess, I'd found the opening. I blew out my lamp and knelt, filling in my map.

Birds cried and wind rustled the leaves. I went to the mouth of the tunnel, brushed aside a flower-studded vine, and leaned out over the ocean far below. I hadn't realized my survey had climbed so high. A stunning vista added detail after detail the longer I looked, from a hundred different green and blue and turquoise ocean shades to the bright yellow flash of a long-tailed bird.

I inhaled, partaking deeply of the fresh buds on the vines. Peace, at last.

A scream erupted in front of my face. I jerked back. Arms flapped before me, a boot flew off a foot, and everything was gone in a fraction of a second.

I went stiff. The howling faded away.

~~~~

Blackout. I must have blanked for a second, sitting there. I came to as another screaming form passed before me. I dropped pencil and paper, scrunched my eyes shut, and covered my ears. Why did the flowers smell so sweet? It wasn't right. And the birds far off kept singing. Couldn't they tell what was happening?

Voices came from outside the opening and above. Chattering in Japanese, laughing, good-natured bantering. "My turn, Endo." "You did one after Ijuin, Terauchi." "Silence. I'll do it." "*Hai*, Sergeant Sakonju."

I opened my eyes and forced down my hands. Terauchi, he was the private who threatened me on the beach. And voices from above meant I was beneath that northern portion of the POW camp, the woods with a fence jutting out over the rocks. The rocks where I'd found the footless body.

I slunk to the opening of the cave and peeked out past the
~~~~

vines.

Another prisoner fell, this time yelling, not screaming. “Nip bastards!”

I recoiled, falling on my fists, shaking so hard my knuckles leaked red over the rough stone.

“Well done.” “I hate these blind ones.” “Grab those other three. Let’s finish this.” “*Hai*, Sergeant.”

Raucous laughter drowned the next few moments. Two more bodies sailed past, two more screams trailed off. But a different kind of sound broke the pattern. A thud landed outside the cave entrance. I stared at the opening.

The laughter faded, with a stomp of boots and the snap of broken twigs. I waited, unsure what had happened.

A man groaned.

I beat down my panic and snaked aside a vine. One prisoner lay on a ledge. A leg slipped off and he grasped at the wet, slimy rock, sightless from wrappings over his eyes.

I stuck out a hand and gripped the man’s arm. He gasped. I gasped at the same time and glanced upward. The edge of the cliff was ten feet up, but no one was there. I whispered at the man.

“Hush.”

I snuck out, got both hands on him, and pulled until he lifted his knee to the ledge.

“This way.” I hadn’t noticed before, but now I did. I’d reverted to English. If that was an instinct, it could be lethal. Careful, careful.

I drew the man into the cave.

“Rest,” I said. As if he might do anything else. Except he might. “Don’t move. It’s hazardous.”

I crawled out the opening, smoothed the moss, and went rigid. A sound. Had the soldiers come back? Were they going to check? Look over the edge and see me? I should back up. No, remain immobile, and hope they didn’t look. I twisted my head to see the cliff edge, and heard it again. A scrape. I felt for the cave with my foot.

Movement on the cliff. I almost shrieked, and had a saving

thought. They wouldn't know a prisoner had survived. If the man was quiet, I could pretend to be out exploring. Harmless. Or better yet, delighted to watch their work, hating Americans as much as they. I could—

A face came over the edge. A thin peep blurted past my lips.

And then I relaxed, relief flooding through me. A raccoon, or the local version of one. Possibly a fox, now I could see it better. An inquisitive visitor, out to check on the ruckus himself. I sagged against the rock, limp as overcooked *soba* noodles. If the animals were out, the army was gone. I was safe.

This time, I was safe. But what on earth was I up to? Acting without thinking. Playing hero, for goodness sake. I had no resources for that. Stupid. So why didn't I regret what I had done? Not even a little bit?

Stupid.

I backed into the cave, arranging vines to cover the hole. When I returned to the man, he'd passed out.

"Wake up. Sit up." I pulled the man to his knees and dabbed at a knot on his forehead. "Take off your blindfold."

The man touched the wrapping. "No. They ruined my eyes."

I had to control my breathing. Seek serenity, regardless of provocation. Missing feet, bloody eyes, and screaming executions. This wasn't what I had bargained for. This wasn't the Japan my mother always talked about. And this wasn't military information that could redeem me from Maison's point of view. This was, what? So much more than I could deal with.

Except I had to. Who else was there?

"Wait," I said. Wait for what? I didn't know, but I needed time to think. And there wasn't any time. The soldiers could still come, with more prisoners, perhaps. They might hear the man if he groaned at the wrong time.

I dug a match from a pocket and picked at a dirty thumbnail. Where could I take him? I lit the lamp. There was one place. It might do, for now. I took the man's elbow.

"Come." We headed down the tunnel.

I deposited my soldier in a cavern, the best of many I had

charted. Twenty feet around with a sandy floor, so not only flat, but more comfortable for lying down. Best of all, it had a built-in ledge for sitting. I set my lamp on the floor, spread my map on the ledge, and marked a spot.

"Where are we?" he said.

"You are safe." I guided him to one end of the ledge. How could he still be sane? I'd be flying on fumes if I'd been a prisoner, expecting to be killed. Must be nice to be tough.

"Safe. That's debatable. I'm Sergeant Anders, U.S. Army. And you?"

"Kristy. My light is almost gone. Make no noise."

"Damn, girl, tell me what—"

"I can't stay. Don't move around, there's a drop-off nearby. I'll bring food."

I inched backwards. He felt around himself, muttering soft curses. Of all the times to be short on oil, this was worst. He needed comfort, explanations, something to make him trust me. I had nothing to offer.

"I'm sorry. I promise I'll return when I can."

He swore again, louder, then tapered off. I think my name was in there. Could be I was hearing things, feeling guilty at abandoning him, however much it had to be done.

I picked up my lamp and map, and darted away.

~~~~

I rushed into my cavern from the rear tunnel as my lamp sputtered out. Lucky again—no breeze today. My oil would not have lasted in the typical draft through the caverns, where it burned brighter and faster. I dumped lamp and map behind a rock, hastened to the fire, and hoisted a sack. I pulled out a crab, jiggled the bag, and nodded. Enough food for now. Almost. I dropped the crab in and added a bowl of cooked rice.

"I thought I saw a path," said the commandant.

I spun around. The colonel stood inside the entrance to my cave. He had found me. Sought me out and tracked me down. Alone. Why?
~~~~

Don't be naive, I knew why. The hermit had been right to worry. But how could I make him go away without spoiling my chances to get into the camp someday?

He pointed at my sack with his riding crop. "Going somewhere?"

Japanese. 'Pay attention' raced through my mind.

"No," I said. "I clean up."

He stepped forward, grabbed the bag, and opened it. "This is rubbish?"

"I cannot leave it loose."

He tossed down the bag and snooped around one side of my cave. I shivered.

"You're getting friendly with the hermit." The commandant kicked a stone and peered in a crevice.

"He helps me."

"And you help him." He eyed me up and down, slowly, in a way no man had looked at me before. No, that wasn't entirely accurate; Carlos had been similar. Except this was worse. Cruder. There was no admiration in this appraisal, merely cool assessment of my value as an afternoon's diversion.

He headed for the back of my cave.

My eyes flicked to the rock hiding my map. "I not understand."

He kept wandering, picking up half-done pictures, poking around on ledges. "No? I'll bet you can be a real helpful girl."

He ogled me again, moved toward the other side of my chamber, and rapped the bamboo wind chimes dangling from a niche. They gave up their hollow notes to the stagnant air.

"Sir?"

He neared the map. I shuddered.

"You don't think so?"

I held out my hand. "Please."

The commandant stopped and regarded me. He was five feet from the rock, from seeing my lamp, my map. One tread from finding everything.

"Show me?"

"Show you what?"

"How to help?"

A leer grew large, and he took a step. Not toward the map, toward me. This was the moment I was supposed to feel thankful that my ruse had worked.

I didn't feel thankful at all.

~~~~

Not very long, only a lifetime later, the commandant stood and adjusted his trousers. I knelt, clasping my shirt around me.

"I am honored to be your first," he said.

"Thank you."

He buttoned his coat and pulled it straight. Precise and martial, everything I had once admired, back in the park above the Navy piers of Alameda. Would I ever be able to respect such neatness again?

"But you could use training."

I concentrated on the sand. Training. I would be getting more. His eyes beat that lesson home. Sour sweat and pungent sex fought for dominance, sharp, biting, mixing with the coppery scent of my blood. My mother had taught me about periods, but neglected to mention the agony of a first encounter. "You'll bleed a little. It will be fine," she had said. I could hardly move.

But pain was the least of it. Worse was the fact he'd been gentle, wanting me to enjoy it. And some wicked, treacherous portions of my body had wanted to respond, so I let them. All part of the act. Reality and fiction and wretchedness and horror at every part of myself, blended and scrambled and mutated into the most nauseating hash I had ever tasted.

The commandant went to the entrance of my cave. He stopped and picked up a bundle. "I almost forgot." He tossed it at my knees. "A present. For your picture."

A bundle. He had been carrying a package like this when I'd seen him with the old woman several days ago. Was this . . . ? I slowly picked it up.

"Thank you, general."
~~~~

"Flattering, but I'm a colonel. Time you learned that."

I opened the package. A shirt and skirt, not fancy but in good shape.

"Burn those seaman's rags."

"Yes, sir. Thank you."

He left. I closed my eyes, and the mare clopped away.

Oh, God, he had done it. I had done it. It was over, and something had vanished forever.

I dropped his gift, pushed to my feet, and reeled to the entrance. I leaned against the opening, listening to the crash of distant surf, staring into the forest. This was not what I had meant to do when I got up this morning. It seemed an important point. It was not what I had planned.

A bird cried, wrenching me back to the world. I was grimy, yes, in many ways, and desperately needed to bathe. To scrub with sand and salt till my skin came raw. But I had no time for the ocean. I had work to do.

I pulled myself around and entered the cave. I stuffed a canteen into the bag with crab and rice, and added my map. I picked up the oil tin, crouched, and refilled my lamp. My fingers slipped. Hands shook, and arms, and oil splashed over everything. I barely set the tin aside before I dumped it all.

I bowed my head and clutched my mutinous belly. My whole body trembled. It just went on, and on, and on.

Chapter 10

I begrudged the time it took me to feel like moving again. Anders was waiting. Who was I to wallow in self-pity?

When I reached his part of the cave, I unbuckled the leather strap on my Japanese army canteen, pulled out the cap, and wrapped Anders's hand around the canvas webbing. My oil flame scarcely lit up the cavern. Anders shifted his fingers on the unfamiliar shape and spilled a little. He brushed water off his chest, paused, and stabbed inside his shirt.

"Oh, right. They took our dog tags."

"Your what?"

"Identification."

I took his hand and put a crab in it. "Eat this."

He fiddled with the creature and produced an "ah," like he'd figured out what it was. Probably mean of me, not telling him up front, but I wasn't used to dealing with the blind. I told myself the challenge was good for him.

He pulled off a leg. "Look, who are you?"

"No one." No one, indeed. I would not give my full name again. What if he had heard of my family, as Maison had? I would never be able to help him. "Can I see your eyes?"

"Sure, if you want to get sick."

I carefully unwound the bandage. Anders' left eye was gone; the gaping pit seeped blood. His right eye was bruised, but as I held up the lamp, it appeared otherwise healthy. I stayed silent, not making him feel worse with sympathy.

"I can, um, yes, there's something," said Anders. "A glow."

"It may get better. You may recover sight. Keep it covered."

"Right. You another doctor?"

"No."

I wound on his bandage, took a paper, and sketched his face without it, darkening his missing eye.

"Are you American?"

I stopped drawing. A memory sharp as a paper cut stifled my breath.

My father, replacing a hinge on the front door of our California home. I left Maxine at the sidewalk and headed toward him. He waved over his shoulder to Maxine as I walked up the steps, leaned against the doorway, and removed a muddy shoe.

My father hissed at me in Japanese. "We are American. Do not embarrass us." He glanced at a neighbor and pointed indoors.

My mother stood in the foyer, watching my feet, face tight with anger.

I crossed the threshold, wearing one shoe and carrying the other.

The memory bled out; I'd have thought it scarred over by now. I resumed sketching Anders in the cavern, and drew his shoeless feet. "I'm sorry. What?"

"Are you American?"

"What difference does it make?"

"A hell of a lot."

I kept sketching, my pencil digging harder into the paper. "If you can't tell, what could I say that you'd believe?"

I leaned the bag with its bowl of rice against his leg and kept drawing. He listened to my scratching, undoubtedly exasperated at my evasiveness, and cracked the crab shell with a loud pop.

~~~~
~~~~

A week dribbled past. I wrestled to find a pattern to my life. Food and water for Anders, explore more of the caverns, clean out Anders' cave, finish charting what I could reach on the island, keep Anders company. Check his eye. He claimed he was in solitary confinement, and complained that was worse than death. It could have been the fever talking. It was like taking care of a baby.

One day a merchant ship came to the wharf on the south end of the POW camp's small island. I had watched it approach that morning. There was so much yelling by soldiers during the docking, I could hear them half a mile off. Curious.

I cleaned myself up, combed my hair while longing for a brush, and headed south. When I crossed the beach in front of the old woman's hut, the crone came to the door and watched me. I gave a bow, but the woman didn't reciprocate, unless slamming the door counted.

Near the docks, Japanese guards were herding a column of new prisoners along a fenced corridor from the pier to the main entrance of the camp. More guards patrolled outside the fence. I mounted boulders to the side to see better. The first of the prisoners reached the entrance just as Colonel Ushijima showed up, reviewing the operation.

The commandant was my target audience. Time to act.

"Trash!" I yelled in Japanese. "Slime of diseased mussels."

I picked up a couple of rocks and threw them at the prisoners. One rolled past Superior Private Ijuin's foot. The other sailed over everyone's heads.

"I hope you rot in moldy cells."

Sergeant Sakonju hooked my arms. I paid no heed, lost in my diatribe.

"Food is wasted on your scrawny bodies."

Sakonju hauled me off the boulders and carried me to the commandant. I went quiet.

The commandant signaled to put me down. "You dislike our guests?"

"They kill our soldiers."

He snorted. "Not as many as they'd like."

I tried to put on a sulky expression.

"Run back to your cave, silly child."

"I want to help."

"No thanks."

I blushed. "I mean, to work."

The commandant examined me. I was wearing his gift clothes, and my hair was washed and straight. "Corporal Akiyama?"

"We could use a cleanup girl," said his aide. "I suppose."

"Take care of it." The commandant strolled off, inspecting the prisoners.

I bowed to the aide. I'd rarely seen such an absence of enthusiasm. Was it distrust? Disgust?

I followed him to the gate of the camp. Step Two, infiltrate, now underway.

~~~~

In the dimly lit cavern, much later, I swapped canteens with Anders and put a roll in his hands.

He felt it, squeezed it, embraced it. "Bread? Real bread?" He tore into it.

I smiled. A clerk at the camp store said they'd traded with a visiting Italian submarine, but Western bread wasn't popular. I had volunteered to try the 'novelty.'

I sat behind Anders. "It's been several days. Can we try again?"

The sergeant's shoulders sagged. I think my optimism annoyed him, but he gave me permission. I gently unwrapped his eyes.

The light from my oil lamp glistened across his right eye. Anders blinked, swore, and blinked some more.

"I can see. Shit, I can even focus." He turned toward me. "Thank you, sweet—"

White glowed around his eye. He leapt at me and pinned me to the ground.

"You lying Nip! What's next?"

He pressed my throat.
~~~~

"You blind me, damn near kill me, and now you want to play? Where's the doctor?"

He looked around wildly and hopped up. I coughed and backed away.

"You messed up this time. You should have brought help."

He grabbed the canteen and lamp and took off down a tunnel. I lurched after him. Him and the only source of light.

Anders hesitated at an intersection and I caught up. I gripped his leg from behind. He spun, but I hung on.

"Please," I said. "You'll get us lost. I don't have that much mapped."

Anders batted at my arms. "Where are the guards? Which way out?"

"No guards, only me. They think you are dead."

Anders ripped my hands off his leg. He waved the lamp around, flashing it into one branch and the other.

The silence of a million tons of frozen lava squashed every dream of liberation.

"Please," I said. "I could not save the others. You landed on a ledge. Remember?"

He frowned. "I think so. But I won't put up with more Jap games. Who are you?"

"I am not Japanese."

"What? Korean? That's better?"

"I was born in California."

He raised the lamp and thrust it at my face.

"I just want to help," I said.

Anders scanned the tunnels again and lowered the lamp. "Not good enough. How'd you get here?"

"I was going to visit Japan. The war . . . my ship sank. I swam here."

"So you've no way to rescue anyone?"

"I can keep you alive. Maybe I can sneak you out on a boat someday."

Air sucked through his teeth. He locked me in place with silent accusations, analyzing, watching for my response. I held still, devoid of ammunition to convince him I meant well.

"Blasted naivety." He waved me toward the cavern. "I suppose you think I have no choice."

I rose, rubbed my leg, and led the way.

Choices. Or lack of same. It always came back to that. I quivered once, but that was the cold. Purely the cold.

Chapter 11

Lightning slashed the sea out beyond the coastline. Thunder boomed and massive waves crashed ashore.

I stood in the forest, drenched in rain, contemplating the fury. Another new moon was coming. Another three-night wait. It was still too soon to expect Maison, or anyone else. And who would surface a submarine in this maelstrom?

I waited and watched. So pointless. So necessary, just in case.

~~~~

MAISON BRUSHED A spot of lint off his new lieutenant commander stripes. He wasn't in his normal work-day khakis today. It was full-dress blues out in the civilian world.

He sat on top of a picnic table in a park high above Pearl Harbor, fresh from a long-distance, scratchy, radio-telephone talk with Maxine in Alameda, California. Maxine, that friend of Kristy Hara's who'd made a scene at the police station when Kristy's family was arrested. Maxine had graduated from high school, furious that Kristy wasn't with her, and Maison couldn't tell her why. What he knew was reserved for military intelligence until further notice. All he could say was that Kristy was fine, last time he saw her.
~~~~

Far down the hill, beyond the fence of the Naval base, a new destroyer was being loaded out with five-inch shells and enough canned meat and vegetables to last a couple of months. A rail-mounted crane moved along the pier beside it.

Maison tried to imagine he was sitting in the park Maxine had told him about. The place where she and Kristy drew their pictures, where Kristy fostered her love of the sea. And where the two girls compared notes on the angst of growing up. In Kristy's case, he was beginning to believe it was serious. Maxine had perhaps seen more than Kristy knew.

If he'd had the chance, he'd have liked to talk to that Mexican woman Rosita. A friend of Kristy's, according to Maxine, with connections in the merchant marine. He had a feeling she had something to do with Kristy being on an Argentinean freighter. But he'd used up all the favors he had, getting that one overseas call to Maxine, in his drive to learn more about the strange girl who wanted to be a spy. Besides, there seemed to be a war on, and he had to get to Subase Pearl. His boss was expecting him soon.

A half hour later, Maison bounded up the steps into his squadron commander's office. He came to attention and snapped a salute. "You wanted to see me, sir?"

Big band music played on a radio. A Navy captain turned it down, came around his desk, and handed Maison a green folder. "Congratulations."

Maison opened the folder and read a line. New orders. He looked up, and the captain shook his hand.

"Thank you, sir," said Maison. "I didn't expect my own boat so soon."

The captain poured himself a cup of coffee and Maison stood at ease.

"Promotions come fast in war," said the captain. "Coffee?"

The coffeepot steamed on a side table, daring Maison to imbibe. He was beginning to think it was a rite of passage. "Yes," he said, forcing out the word. "Please."

The captain smiled. "Good for you. We'll wean you into submarines yet." He scrounged another mug and filled it. "You don't mind staying with *Barracuda*?"

"No, sir. Good ship. Good crew."

"True, but you'll have a lot of replacements. We're pulling a bunch for training on the new subs."

"Yes, sir."

The captain handed him the mug. Maison sipped and made a face.

The captain chuckled. "You'll get used to it." He raised his own cup. "May your targets be plentiful."

Maison grinned. They clinked their mugs together.

~~~~

Lightning cracked again, a quarter mile off, and stones rattled in the surf. And the trees leaked badly. I brushed soggy hair off my forehead.

What had become of my parents? Poor Rosita, she deserved to know about Carlos and how much help he'd been. And what would Maxine be doing now? Had she graduated? I'd lost track of the date. I'd check, next time I had cleanup duty in the POW camp.

The rain picked up again. It was too late for a submarine. Dawn would be here soon. But forget any golden rays of light. Today, morning wouldn't be discernable.

I turned away from the moonless sea.
~~~~

Chapter 12

I dumped leaves and trash in a rusty, dented bin in the middle of the prison camp compound, and resumed raking. One more pointless task out of the way, but not so many as yesterday. I'd done the right thing, buying these nondescript tan trousers and jacket, saving the commandant's gift clothes for his visits. Not only did it cut down on the leers, but fewer soldiers were seeking me out to give me orders. I knew a feeble excuse to flirt when I saw one.

Thank heaven I'd remembered to tie the jacket sash—no, *obi*—behind me. Among Japanese women, only whores tied it in front. Doing that wrong would have been worse than wearing the skirt.

I missed underwear, though. One of those things I never reflected on, until a different custom jarred me awake.

Late in the afternoon, no one was around. I scraped my way over to the main hospital building and peeped in a window. First time I'd managed to get over this way unspotted.

Sergeant Sakonju and Superior Private Endo chatted as they emerged from the dark-leaved trees north of camp. I jumped at the sound and hurried from the window. I hadn't seen a thing, darn it.

Endo opened the back fence gate. From the other direction,

Private Terauchi hauled a manacled, dazed corporal out of a hospital annex and through the compound. Corporal Saunders, that's what someone had called him earlier in the day, on the way to the hospital. He hadn't been limping then, but he wove and staggered now.

"Wait," said Terauchi. "They gave me another."

My breath stuck in my throat. Endo and Sakonju came from the north, from the woods, from where prisoners were thrown off a cliff. And Terauchi had another one. Oh, God.

"Take care of it yourself," said Endo. "We've got liberty, and we're not missing the boat."

"But I'm . . . I was . . . ."

Endo laughed.

"Private," said Sakonju.

Endo cut it off, bowing an apology to the sergeant, though not to Terauchi. A show of condescension? Endo and Sakonju headed through the compound, leaving the gate open for Terauchi.

Terauchi stared after them, angry or jealous. It didn't matter. I had to move. Shake off my useless dread, and move. I raked my way near him.

"You want I throw him out?"

Terauchi startled.

"I am good at trash." I sent a piercing whistle into the corporal's ear. He didn't react.

"You are not a soldier," Terauchi said. "Last I saw, you were beach dross."

I shrugged and went back to raking. Terauchi looked from the corporal to me to the departing guards.

"I haven't been to the mainland in weeks," he mumbled.

I spat at the corporal. No response. Terauchi clicked the bolt on his rifle, open and lock, open and lock. Endo and Sakonju disappeared around a corner.

"You know where he goes?" said Terauchi.

"*Hai.* A life is but a ripple in the sea."

Terauchi studied me a moment longer, and shoved the corporal at me.

"Oh, wait." He ripped off the corporal's dog tags. "Lock the gate."

He took off after the other guards. When he was out of sight, I leaned my rake against the fence. I closed my eyes, quelling a shiver, hiding any trace of the terror or relief or anxiety fighting for control of my brain. Whatever it was, I didn't have time for it. Once again, I had leapt at an opportunity without thought. Done the only thing I could, at a moment's notice. At least, it seemed the only option.

I dragged the unresisting corporal toward the gate—

—and out of the north woods to the barren, rocky, flat area along the top of the cliff. I stopped and considered the pink flowers of spring, trailing through moss-covered rocks, scenting the air with innocence. If I could, I'd have ripped every one of them out of the ground.

"Can you hear me? Can you climb?"

The corporal kept weaving, his face glazed.

"Damn."

I knelt at the rim and peered over, shifting right until I located the ledge where Sergeant Anders had landed, not too far from the double line of ten-foot fencing. At the ledge's widest point, I rose, noting the position of every tree and rock, locking the spot in my mind. Then I fetched the corporal, turned him around, and fought him to his knees, facing me. I held his manacles and knocked his feet over the edge. Leaning back, easing forward, more, until I was flat on my belly, I lowered him as far as I could.

I blinked sweat from my eyes. The corporal's feet dangled above the ledge. Ledge? It was a ribbon, a string, a mere scratch from above.

"Sweet Mother."

I swung him side to side.

"Wake up."

Nothing. I stopped swinging him. The manacles were getting wet from perspiration. I tightened my fists.

"I have to drop you. Two feet."

His forehead wrinkled, the first sign of awareness.

He fell six inches. I shot forward, dragged by the chains. My head jutted over the cliff. I let out a cry, flailed with one hand at the rock face, and kept sliding. The manacles slipped from my other hand and the corporal fell.

"No!"

He flopped on the ledge as I teetered off the cliff. I caught myself, hanging over the rim from hands and one foot. I heard sounds below me, but had the—

The corporal groaned. He hadn't gone down. I bowed my head briefly.

"Thank You."

The corporal tried to rise. Moss broke away and his hands skidded off the ledge.

"No!" I dropped my foot and scrambled down the cliff, landing beside the corporal and grabbing his belt before he slid off.

I heaved him up, panting, crying, swearing words I wasn't supposed to know, until I could grab his manacles and lug him the rest of the way onto the ledge. That got his own adrenaline flowing, and he was able to crawl with me to the cave opening. I drew him inside and got him to nod about staying put.

I came back out, telling myself it didn't matter how high I was. Or how dark it was getting. It wasn't far to the top. There was a trick to this, or so I'd heard. Don't look down.

I only slipped and had one heart attack before I made it up.

Black surrounded my return to the prison compound. The glow of distant spotlights guided me, but they didn't reveal slapping branches, thorns, or nasty roots. I entered the gate, locked it, and pried a splinter from an elbow.

Doctor Kawabe seized my wrist, spun me around, and waved a flashlight in my face. I managed to swallow a squeal and not leap over the fence. I faked it into a wince and pulled at my arm.

"Where have you been?" said the doctor.

Calm down. I was supposed to be uncaring. "I dispose of trash."

He pointed to the rusty bin as tall as I was. "That's for trash."

I was heartless. And confused. That was it. "They said he went over cliff."

The doctor cocked his head. "You threw a man over the cliff?"

"He American. Trash. Yes?"

The doctor laughed, let go of me, and sauntered off.

I grasped my rake, closing my eyes in relief.

The doctor seized me again, still laughing. This time I did jump.

"Come. I've something you'd like to see."

I dropped the rake and stumbled after him. He was leading me to the hospital. I would be seeing inside after all, where they did their experiments. Where men were slaughtered.

Be careful what you wish for, my father had always said. The phrase reverberated in my memory as the doctor opened the door.

~~~~

Doctor Kawabe led me down a hall and into a room filled with rows of beds occupied by American prisoners. Each man was handcuffed to a bedframe, which in turn was bolted to the floor. Every prisoner wore bandages on head, torso, or legs. The doctor pushed me into a recess and told me to watch, maybe I'd learn something.

Colonel Ushijima entered from the far door and the doctor rushed to meet him. The commandant's boots clomped across the thick timber flooring. He rubbed his nose at what the doctor called a medicinal aroma: iodine, ether, and rotting flesh. The colonel gave one amputee a disdainful look.

The doctor scurried behind the commandant, flipping pages on a clipboard, leaning over so he didn't tower above his superior. He stopped by one bed with a major in head bandages.

"Here, sir," said the doctor. "Major Donnerty is our prize."

The commandant halted. "Oh?"

"Second highest pain tolerance, and fastest healing. I'm culturing tissue samples to see if I can discover anything."

The commandant didn't appear impressed. Just another American, his expression said. Major Donnerty ignored him, but the commandant didn't respond to the lack of respect.
~~~~

"Quite special. He surrendered like all the rest."

The doctor shrugged. "Their culture does not fight to the death."

"Their culture is inferior."

The doctor bowed at this 'wisdom' and led the commandant off to observe another prisoner. Except the doctor never called them that. They were patients, or test subjects. He varied, as if he couldn't make up his mind. Either way, he kept using terms derived from Western words. The commandant called him out on it, telling him to use the government-approved Japanese replacements.

The doctor was right. I did learn something. I learned how not to throw up when I really, really wanted to.

~~~~

It took a couple of hours, once I got to my cave, but eventually Anders and I guided the corporal through the convoluted rock passageways to the dim cavern where I'd first secreted Anders. We maneuvered him onto a blanket, laying him down.

"Thank you," I said.

Anders put a rolled shirt under the corporal's head. "How long will he be like this?"

"He'll keep the limp. Most of their drugs wear off quickly."

"I need more water."

"And food. Are you warm enough?"

"Not really."

"I'll see what I can get."

I handed him an eye patch. He fingered it, and tied it on.

"Thanks."

I looked at his feet. "I'll try to make some moccasins. They're not stealing boots so much anymore, but you . . ."

"Yeah, that'd help."

I started to leave.

Anders grabbed my arm. "Are you for real? You either play a dangerous game, or you are worse than the doctor."

I ripped my arm free. "As long as you don't find out, that's a
~~~~

good sign. Yes?" I snatched up my map and lamp.

"I want a map of my own," said Anders. "And light."

I paused. "You wish the ability to get us both killed very, very slowly."

"I'll be careful. Don't worry."

"Don't you say that! I worry. I worry all the damn time. You better, too."

Chapter 13

Anders and the corporal sat on the ledge in their cavern, an oil lamp between them. The corporal sawed at a wrist manacle with a file I had found in the scrap the day before. Dull, but I'd thought it would help. Anders held a shard of stone near the flame, playing with reflections. He let it slip to the ground. The model of boredom.

I watched from a tunnel. I couldn't do much about the boredom, but I could improve their living conditions. When I was ready to face their abuse.

Yeah, well, no way to help that. I wet my lower lip and entered. "Get your stuff. We're moving."

The men rose and circled to either side of me. Suspicious? Threatening?

"Where?" said Anders.

"Why?" said the corporal.

"It stinks in here. And you're wasting oil. I found a better cave."

Anders snapped his fingers. Why would—

At the second pop, they assaulted me.

"What are you doing?" I struggled briefly. A waste of energy. They were stronger than I expected.

"Shut up," said Anders. He took my ankle knife and they released me. "I'll go with you and check it out."

I pointed at the knife. "I need that."

Anders waggled it at me. "So do we. We're not about to go quietly into another trap."

I glared at him a moment, and tramped away. I didn't know why it made me so mad, their lack of trust. It was perfectly logical. I'd seen some of the psychological games the doctor played, and heard of others. But it pricked me, deeper than it should.

Anders followed me into the tunnel and gripped my shoulder. "Slow down."

I did, concentrating on every step. I mustn't waver, must not misstep, not with the knife a half inch from my back. Not with Anders in this kind of mood.

I led him through a series of winding passages, past a few branchings, and made him hug the left once where a crevice on the opposite side dropped straight down. A bit of climbing, but mostly descending, and then we were there.

Anders released me as we entered the roomy cavern, and I set down my lamp. Light sifted through cracks in one wall. I twisted vines aside, letting in more.

Anders lingered at the entrance before joining me and looking at the ocean twenty-five feet below. "Room with a view. Cost extra?"

"I hope we never see the bill."

"Neighbors noisy?"

"Not so far."

One streak of light highlighted a crevice that cut out a section of floor. "Rest room. I'll clean up the old cave."

Anders poked at a vine near the hole. I pulled out a piece of paper and handed it to him.

"This is a route to the outside. Don't use it unless I don't come back."

Anders took it, slowly, evaluating me.

He watched me so long I generated a whole nest of bats in my gut. Big ones. He had the knife and map. He might believe he didn't need me anymore, in which case . . . .

I crossed the chamber to where a thin line of water dribbled down and outside.

Anders folded the map, tapped it on his thigh, and slipped it in a pocket. He walked up behind me.

"I know it's not enough," I said.

He put a hand on my shoulder again. I cringed, facing him. He tilted his head, as if he didn't expect my apprehension.

He held out the knife, hilt first. "You probably do need this."

I reached, slow, uncertain, and accepted the blade. A sign of trust? Not likely. More like covering his bases, being practical, on the off chance I was truly helping.

"But we need weapons."

I nodded, and Anders waved toward the tunnel, to go fetch the corporal. I put away the knife, picked up my lamp, and led him out.

All in all, I supposed that had gone as well as I should have expected.

~~~~

I was playing silent observer again as Doctor Kawabe dimmed the bare overhead bulb in an office in the hospital, and went to one of a half dozen small discs of one-way glass in the side wall. He pried off the cover, and the commandant did the same at another disc. I copied their actions. We peered into a shadowy room as John Philip Sousa marches played on a 78 rpm gramophone behind us.

"It speaks of their ethos," said the doctor. "Even the major fell for the 'sympathetic orderly' gambit, telling them how to get out."

Inside the storeroom we watched so intently, Major Donnerty and a Philippine soldier pushed wooden boxes aside and removed concrete blocks at the bottom of the far wall, exposing the forest beyond.

"I find it insulting," said the commandant. "They think us so imprudent?"

The major and soldier shook hands, got on their bellies, and
~~~~

slithered through the opening.

"This is my favorite test," said the doctor. "Their fear clashes with their initiative to escape. The woods, of course, are fenced."

An explosion rocked the building.

"And mined."

The doctor laughed. Machine gun fire accompanied a second explosion.

Major Donnerty crawled back into the storeroom, uniform torn, left arm bleeding.

The doctor made a note on his clipboard. "I thought he'd make it farther."

"Waste of mines," said the commandant, pulling away from his window. "Find a cheaper test." He stalked out, switching off the gramophone on his way. I replaced the covers on all three windows.

Doctor Kawabe grimaced. I wondered if the commandant knew how much the doctor despised him. Or if he cared.

~~~~

A week later, I found Anders doing push-ups in the new POW cave. Again. His morning routine. The corporal and newly-retrieved Private Zeiss lay on blankets, as if they could sleep through Anders' grunting. Zeiss wore a bandage over a missing ear, but it didn't need changing yet. Good thing. I didn't have much in the way of medical supplies. The doctor kept those locked up.

I entered and set down canteens, bags of food, and extra lamp oil. The corporal got to his feet and flanked Anders, as if a bodyguard were in order. Zeiss arose more slowly and circled around behind me. This was going to get old, if they kept this up every time I appeared.

I reached in a pocket and gave Anders a metal file.

"Here is another, Sergeant. Newer."

Zeiss raised his manacled hands. "Oh, swell."

"A key would be preferable," said Anders.

Gee, I must not have thought of that. I didn't say it out loud.
~~~~

I was trying to help these men, not badger them, but they sure made the latter tempting.

I slapped a knife at his feet. “They would only sell me one. I told them I lost the other.”

Anders picked up the blade and spun it. “Yes. An excuse. Thanks for the one.”

“Damn it, what do you expect me to do?”

“I don’t expect anything. If I ever see home again, I’ll be shocked as hell.”

And there it was. The crux of the problem. I needed to encourage these guys, give them a reason to endure, a belief in some kind of future, when all they had was me, the slimmest excuse for reassurance in the whole Pacific theater.

So I gave them the little I had, knowing it wouldn’t inspire a rock to roll down a hill.

“You don’t expect anything. Fine. But is hope—” I tripped on the word. “Is hope so terribly bad?”

Chapter 14

Summer came early in this part of the world, or we were having a heat wave. I wasn't sure and didn't particularly care. All I knew, walking past the hermit's cave on my way north, arms full of blankets and clothes and rice and oil tins, was that I wished I had a hand free to swat mosquitoes and wipe sweat from my eyes.

The hermit sprang from behind a tree, two feet in front of me. I yelped and stopped.

"What are you doing?" said the hermit, needles in his speech.

"Don't do that!"

"You bought rice yesterday."

"It had bugs. I threw it out."

"I got you more blankets last week."

"They fell in the fire."

"How do you justify clothes?"

"I'm a girl. I need variety."

The hermit tossed a dark red rock back and forth. "You try that tale at the store?"

"No one asked."

He clenched the rock. "A handful of civilians on this island, and a grand total, all told, of one pretty girl. You are right. No one will pay attention to what you do."

He stumped into his cave.

Okay, he had a point. I followed him in.

The hermit's stone ox was gone. In its place was a nearly-complete giant pelican, with striped wings folded along its back and the ugliest short, stubby legs I'd ever seen. Well, it was made out of balanced stones, what did I expect? The hermit set his rock on the pelican's head, creating an eye, and rooted in a pile of junk.

Sunlight broke through the trees and bounced inside, lighting up the walls. I stopped cold. The hermit had seven of my pictures mounted on stone statues around his cave—several landscapes, plus a samurai and a sword fight.

"You bought all these?"

"No. I stole them from the Imperial Japanese Army."

I bowed as low as my loaded arms allowed. "Thank you."

"What, you think it a compliment? I only bought them so you would not starve."

"I see." One of the pictures was framed by seashells. "That's why you hide them."

He sniffed. "Now that you are working for them, see if I buy any more."

"As you wish."

He stood up, dangling a snare and length of fishing line, and shoved past me to the entrance.

"Don't go meek on *me*. Benighted mouthy teenagers. Girls. Whole world would be better off without teenage girls."

I hid a smile.

"You coming?"

I looked up. "Really? I mean, sure."

We hiked north at the hermit's rapid pace. He veered off the trail that led toward my cave and headed into the woods. I dumped my supplies on the path and raced to catch up.

The hermit glanced over his shoulder. "Yes?"

~~~~

Deep in the forest, the hermit and I knelt over a snare. I touched a stick. A branch whipped up and a vine noose snugged
~~~~

around my hand.

"Yes," I said. I freed my hand and reset the snare.

~~~~

I knelt beside a sparkling spring, filling a nautilus shell I was using as a spare canteen. It was amazing what you could acquire on a deserted beach, unlike crowded California. Beautiful shells like the one I now held, glass ball floats from fishing nets, even the odd coin from a shipwreck.

"Yes," I said, sipping from the spring, "it's much closer."

I set down the shell and a green snake dropped on my palm. I jerked back my hand.

"Avoid those," said the hermit. "Kind of poisonous."

I shuddered as the snake slithered away. "I lead a charmed life."

I picked up another nautilus shell and shook it. I peered inside, and the hermit tittered. I gave him a dirty look and dipped the shell in the spring.

~~~~

Along the edge of a forest glen, the hermit dug up a fat lavender-colored root and handed it to me. He pointed beyond a young mimosa tree, leaves so pale they were almost yellow, and I dug up a different root.

"Cook those," said the hermit. "These are best raw."

"Got it."

"Remember your fruit?"

"Yes."

"And that over there is ginseng. Do not harvest more than one plant in twenty. Too rare."

"Medicinal, yes? How do you—"

"Later. We are still on vegetables."

~~~~

That night the weather held good, so we went to the coast. The hermit sat on a boulder, holding a thumb-thick branch with a line
~~~~

trailing into the ocean. I bent over and removed a hook from the mouth of a fat fish.

I giggled. "I would never have used crickets for bait."

The hermit looked daggers at two other fish beside me. He picked up his single small one when he thought I was fussing with the hook, and flung it back in. I pretended not to notice.

Dawn broke as we returned to the hermit's cave. He walked to the entrance and turned to me. Two fish dangled from my *obi*; I held out another, which he snubbed.

"Now you can get all the food you want."

"Yes," I said. "*Sumimasen.*" I bowed deeply in thanks.

"Get home before dawn. Patrol boats."

"I shall."

"Unless you want to get caught. Then make sure whoever you are feeding is as loud as you are."

He went inside.

I gaped at him. "Please, how, I mean, don't you want the fish?"

The hermit's voice floated out of the cavern. "I will catch my own cursed fish."

I felt the tug of a smile.

I wrapped one fish in a large leaf and laid it by the entrance. I pulled a tuber from my pocket, balanced it atop the leaf, and headed north toward my own cave.

The hermit came out as I passed a rhododendron bush encroaching on the path, scarlet flowers in full bloom. He picked up the fish and tuber, and yelled after me.

"Adolescent! Female!"

I looked back in time to see him go inside. There was no possibility I would respond, not after all he had done for me. He would always be the one deserving the last word.

~~~~

That night I charged into the POW cave and kicked out a fire they'd built from strips of vines. The corporal, Zeiss, and Anders sat on one side of the fire, and two newer men sat across from them playing with rocks. Checkers, maybe, though all the pebbles
~~~~

looked the same. The big guy, Brutus, scratched his bald head and grinned up at me. He was the only one who took me at face value. I hoped it didn't mean he'd suffered a head injury. I kicked the fire again, stamping on the worst of it.

The slender man, Taffin, recoiled from the burning sticks. He crossed himself and finger-combed his beard over a scar on his chin.

I rounded on Anders. "No fire. A glow at night, smoke in the day, either will bring them."

"Who?" said the corporal. "Your Jap friends?"

"We know who you are," said Zeiss.

Taffin retreated farther from a smoldering stick. "Foul harlot."

"You damn near brained me with a rock," said Zeiss.

"I brought you here. I keep you safe."

"For how long?"

The corporal's words echoed through the chamber, robbing me of breath. There was no answer to that question, or none I dared to name. The feeble chance of a submarine one day was not a story they'd believe, not if they couldn't even take food without hatred dripping from every pore in their bodies.

Brutus stood up and moved beside me like a guard dog. I'd brought him down yesterday, and he had yet to say a word. Christ, I hoped he was all right.

"Japs play games," said Anders. "It's hard to trust when you keep us captive and feed us rice."

What did they expect, apple pie? Would that convince them of anything? But today I could offer them something different. I reached into the tunnel, picked up a home-made reed basket, and dumped fish, tubers, and fresh fruit at their feet.

"We don't eat raw fish," said Zeiss.

"Learn how."

"Right," said the corporal. "That'll be a delightful pastime."

"We need fresh air," said Anders. "And if you are who you say you are, you shouldn't have to baby us. Let us hunt."

"Very well." I couldn't have asked for a better setup. "Not hunt, that would never be safe. But you have a map, you have a lamp. Tonight there is no moon. We'll go fishing. Perhaps you can even cook it."

Zeiss and the corporal smirked. Taffin was more in the leery category.

"And you will keep absolutely silent, and you will come back when I tell you."

"Naturally," said Anders. "We were soldiers before we were prisoners."

After a second, I realized I was in a glaring contest with him. I hated those. I never won. I stomped an ember and whirled away.

It took several minutes to lead the men through tunnels unfamiliar to them, zigzagging downward toward my cave. A light ahead indicated our arrival.

I entered my cave and stopped short. I put one hand behind me, fingers spread, halting Anders and the other four soldiers in the tunnel behind.

"Commandant," I said in Japanese. "Welcome."

I stuttered forward and blew out my lamp. Anders blew out his own, and the men backed further into the tunnel. I rustled my basket to cover their sounds.

The commandant stood a foot inside my cave, scanning the surroundings. My fire, my blankets, my scattered colorful drawings. He lifted a fancy lantern. "Nice decor, Kira. Simplicity, with beauty ever-changing."

"I not understand. You want picture?"

"I thought you might want another lesson in being helpful."

I hesitated.

The commandant frowned and moved forward. "What's wrong?"

"Nothing. I am so honored, I not know what to say."

I set down my lamp and basket, and opened my arms.

The commandant stepped around me and went to the tunnel entrance. I watched as he flashed his light inside. I knelt and unsnapped the loop on my ankle sheath, hidden by my skirt. I loosened the knife.

The commandant blew out his lantern. "Nice closet."

I let go of my knife, brushed dirt off the blankets beside me, and patted them. I suppressed any reaction to my deliverance. Nothing could I show. The commandant came over and sat down.

~~~~

At one point, I think I cried out, and once I tried a moan, but it didn't sound very convincing so I gave it up. As before, the Colonel took his time, and it all went on forever.

~~~~

When the commandant was through, I huddled on my blankets, clothes awry, holding a delicate origami crane. I stroked a crease in its beak, trying to bury the experience, trying to ignore the stench of sex and sweat. Trying not to wince from the bruises, from the raw patch where sand had dug a hole in my shoulder. Nothing must reveal my feelings. Nothing must blemish the colonel's satisfaction.

Why did he have to come tonight?

"Thank you," I said, rubbing the crane. "I practice."

The commandant granted me the slimmest of bows, and left. Leather creaked and his muffled commands filtered in. "Easy, girl."

His mare clopped over the stony path, and a heartbeat later, Anders and the others appeared from the tunnel.

"We'll help you too, Kristy," Zeiss said. "Or is it Kira?"

My head snapped up. "What?"

Taffin made the sign of a cross. "The Lord shall see your every sin."

"Surely you won't refuse us what you give the enemy," said Zeiss.

"If he is your enemy," said the corporal.

I jabbed a finger at the entrance, hissing, not daring to release the scream welling up inside. "How do you think I get in the camp? How do you think I save your lives?"

Zeiss oozed derision. "And at such a bargain price."

I flinched. My anger fizzled away, faster than it had come. For he was right. The crane rolled from my hand.

Taffin knelt. "Jesus, guide her."

"Enough," said Anders.

"We know what kinda dame she is," said the corporal. "It's just a question of who she does it with."

"I said enough."

"No, let them." I huddled, letting my hair fall forward to obscure my shame. "It's cheap enough. I abandoned my family. I prostitute myself. I can't get much lower." I clutched my arms. "Do what you like." For some reason, I couldn't add treason to the list of my wrongs. What strange denial kept that admission inside me? But punishment—yes, that I could accept.

Zeiss took a step. Brutus shouldered him aside. Taffin reared up and blocked the corporal.

Anders came to me, bent down, and lifted my chin. "We're American," he said. "We know what's right."

I jerked free. "Damn you, I am not Japanese. And they know 'right' as well as you."

"'They'? 'You'?" said the corporal.

"Which are you?" said Anders.

I couldn't meet his eyes.

Anders stood. "As you say. We'll find our way back. We can fish another night."

"No." I yanked my shirt together and stood. "We'll do it now. The commandant won't have patrols out to see what he does." I grabbed my lamp and pointed to the side. "Hooks and lines are there."

I limped to the entrance, crushing the paper crane underfoot, adjusting my skirt.

The men looked at each other. The corporal shrugged, and Anders nodded. Brutus got the tackle, and they followed me out.

~~~~

A few stars gleamed above the beach, but the sea was too roiled to reflect them. I sat on a rock and studied the horizon, or the line where the stars ceased to exist, while my five soldiers
~~~~

waded farther out, splashing and enjoying their first whiff of freedom.

Five. So far. How many could I save, feed, keep hidden, and for how long? What would happen when one broke down and made a run for it? Or attacked me? Or got in a fight? Thank goodness they were soldiers; they had a predisposition for discipline, for now. But how many more could I add?

More to the point, how could I ever *not* save another, if I had the chance?

I leaned back on my boulder. The middle of my three-night submarine vigil. No moon. Not a sliver would arise.

~~~~

IN THE CONNING tower of *Barracuda*, Maison slapped up the periscope handles. "Goddamn it." The periscope lowered.

The navigator rose from his table. "Another dud?"

"Lousy depth gauge. I ought to shoot pictures. I might hit something."

"High speed screws," said the sonarman. "Destroyer. Closing."

"Hard left rudder," said Maison. "Come to one-eight-zero feet."

A muffled rumble shook the conning tower. Depth charge.

The navigator monitored a row of overhead gauges for symptoms of damage. "These guys could be good."

Maison scowled at him.

~~~~

I sat on my beach rock and studied the eastern horizon. A few new stars joined the parade as time passed. Older ones would be diving below the hill behind me. The world moved on, oblivious of my tiny island, and no submarine would break that isolation.

Off to the side, Anders and the other four had settled on their own rocks, fishing. Anders checked on me now and then. I'd like to think someday, somehow, they'd start to trust me. But that would be poor judgment on their part, wouldn't it? From their perspective, that could be deadly.

I sighed.

Chapter 15

As always, I pulled up under the trees before continuing south past the old woman's hut, on my way to the POW camp. She got annoyed if she caught me crossing 'her property,' but I hated having to scramble over the western hills.

Today she was out surveying the garden along the side of her hut, hacking at a weed, then resting. It would take her all day at this rate, but she'd not thank me to offer help.

She stuck her spade into the ground, stretched her back, and looked to sea. Private Terauchi was patrolling the shore again. That got the old woman moving. She attacked the weeds with the spade as if she thought that would make the private leave her alone.

It didn't work. He came straight on.

"Old one," said Terauchi, "your beach dross is getting famous."

"Sluts don't get famous." The old woman kept spading.

Terauchi strolled north. "She's our Bloody Angel. Exterminates the leftovers."

The old woman pulled herself upright. "You lie like a round-eye."

Terauchi laughed.

"Have you seen it?" said the old woman.

Terauchi stopped laughing. He headed into the trees.

The old woman brandished her spade. "She would never help you. Kira may have the morals of a she-goat, but no woman of my culture could do as you claim." She jammed her spade in the ground.

I waited until she entered her hut, and continued toward the camp. So, I was the bloody angel. And in this woman's eyes, I wasn't acting like a normal Japanese girl.

Yep, I was definitely keeping the low profile appropriate for a good spy.

~~~~

I followed Doctor Kawabe, Colonel Ushijima, and a technician into one of the more expansive hospital laboratories on the grounds of the POW camp. A guard manned the laboratory door, and a second stood in the middle of the room, outside a small chamber. The technician continued on into the chamber and strapped a groggy prisoner to a chair. Wires trailed from the prisoner to various devices with lights, dials, and yet more wires.

I hovered behind the doctor, bearing file folders, hiding the expression that tried to invade my face. The doctor's labs were the sickest things I'd ever seen, up to and including the screams. Garish banners draped the walls, bright-colored silk in clashing colors, with gold thread exhortations to sacrifice for the emperor, obey authority, and win glory for Japan. One even proscribed admiration for things of the West, while the doctor's ubiquitous Sousa marches blared over a speaker.

Major Donnerty stood shackled to a file cabinet. The doctor seemed to enjoy making him watch what happened to others. Perhaps it was supposed to be an honor, a favor to an officer.

"This should prove my skill to those elitists in Unit 731, and earn me a transfer to headquarters," said the doctor. "I'm testing response to cold. Note the refrigeration units, and thermocouples on his skin."

"Yes, yes," said the commandant. "All this cost how much? I
~~~~

don't care who your father is, we have a war to win. And will you turn that down?"

The doctor pouted—I didn't think I'd ever seen a grown man pout—and lowered the volume on the gramophone. "I'll get you the figures."

"Are you still using my pet to get rid of your failures."

"Your little geisha is bloodthirsty."

The commandant gave me a speculative look.

"She likes it." The doctor gurgled with glee. He repeated what they'd said in English, for the major's benefit.

The commandant turned his attention to the technician sealing the small chamber. The major's attention was all on me. I kept blank.

"Waste of resources," muttered the commandant.

~~~~

I sat on a mossy tree trunk outside the hermit's cave, waiting on his assessment. Daydreaming. Or daymaring. Was that a word?

Summer was well advanced, and I'd logged more hours with the camp doctor than I cared to remember, not one of them pleasant. He kept interrupting my chores, dragging me to his hospital to boast about some new device, some clever test, some peculiar result. My feigned incomprehension didn't faze him. Worst was when he invited me to help with something. I hid my repulsion and did as I was told. Nothing else would have been acceptable from such as I.

And I could never lose the appalling incongruity of it all. They ran their tests on 'inferior' races, yet understood all they learned about pain, cold, disease, and healing to apply equally to Japanese because, well, people were all the same.

The hermit shifted atop the boulder beside his cave entrance. He held my latest paintings, the record of all I had witnessed working with the doctor. What I called my medical sketches, a euphemism that made me ill just thinking about it.

He thumbed from one picture to another, faster and faster, shaking with irritation.
~~~~

"I help you because the commandant has betrayed our nation's honor. The whole government is corrupt. But our people, these pictures. You exaggerate."

"No," I said.

"You believe rumor."

"This is only what I saw."

The hermit flipped past two more pictures, and pointed at a third. "No one could survive this mutilation."

"None of them survive. That's not the kind of research they do."

He chose another picture from the stack. "The soldiers will rebel. We are Japanese."

"I'm sorry." I almost put a hand on his arm, but stopped myself in time. Too Western. "There is nothing of Japan on this island. They will not rebel."

The hermit wadded the sketch and threw it at my feet. He hopped up, dumping the rest of the pictures, and his face went so rigid the wrinkles disappeared.

"These are not real. You are a mean and spiteful girl. You would not go there if this is what you saw."

He stormed into his cave.

I slowly rose and gathered up my pictures. I wasn't sure what I had expected. Support of some kind? Help collecting food? He knew I was collecting people.

I hadn't expected rejection of the truth. Although, why not? When did anyone ever believe me?

I folded the pictures, rose, and trudged north to my own cave.

~~~~

A couple of days later, I found the corporal grappling with Anders in the POW cave, while Zeiss bored holes in a length of bamboo with their knife. Brutus scratched at his manacles with a file; he paused, picked up a nautilus shell, and drank, prompting me to count the shells along the far wall. Several full ones, so water was fine for now.

Taffin and the two newest men stood near one of the wider
~~~~

cracks, studying the sky. Nearby, piled tree branches hid the gap in the floor, their rest room.

Taffin pointed up. "No, altocumulus. See, they're smaller."

Anders and the corporal got up and crouched, facing off. The corporal leapt past Anders, but Anders caught up and tackled him as I entered with a couple of my poorly-made reed baskets. I evaded their rolling bodies.

Anders got up and brushed himself off. "Sorry. Football."

I eyed their bruises—absurd, the chances they took—and scanned beyond. "Careful, Private Zeiss."

Zeiss sniggered. He twirled the knife on his fingers.

"No, your flute," I said. "Sound carries over water."

I set down one of my baskets and pulled off a towel, revealing several packages. The smells shanghaied their attention before I could speak.

"There is cooked fish. Cooked tubers. And squirrel, with wild onions. Hot."

"Squirrel?" said the corporal.

"Something like that."

The men descended on the packages. Anders restored order and shared them around, snapping tubers and ripping apart the meat so they could all try a little of everything. I tapped Taffin on the arm and gave him a crude wooden cross.

"Oh, my," he said, "you made, for me . . . ?"

I almost risked a smile. Almost. If only I had been brave enough to keep the necklace from Carlos, the crucifix, I could have given Taffin that instead.

I handed a narrow package to Anders.

He raised an eyebrow before opening it. "Scissors. A whetstone, a razor. I can shave." He beamed at me.

I set down my other basket and pulled out three more packages. "You say you don't like games. But they got some in. Here are German cards, Italian chess, and Japanese Go. I translated the Go rules."

It was like flipping a switch. The men dropped the food and tore into the games. The two newest men grabbed chess, the corporal and Zeiss held up the rules to Go in a sunbeam, and Brutus opened a deck. They chattered, comparing their presents, animated as kids at recess.

I watched a moment. A wistful air chased across my face, quickly gone. I'd done something right. It was time to leave.

Anders looked from the games to the men to me. And again. He jumped up and took my arm before I got out the opening.

"Thank you."

My eyes darted to his hand.

He let go. "Really. Thank you."

I turned. This time I couldn't stop it. An uncertain smile flicked my mouth. The men were so content, shuffling cards and sorting game pieces. I bowed my head, acknowledging his gratitude.

"I should have thought of it long ago." I backed a step.

"Stay. Join us."

I stopped, and the men went quiet. Why would Anders say that? A cruel jest? He couldn't possibly mean it. Could he? Brutus and Taffin scooted away from each other on the floor, making room, and Brutus waved cards at me.

"Come on," said Anders. "They might even let you win."

I tried again to smile. Oh, dear, he was serious. They weren't playing mind games of their own, this was a real invitation. I couldn't absorb it. And I couldn't bring myself to check Zeiss or the corporal, to see if they agreed.

Anders led me over to Brutus and Taffin, crouching on the floor. "You know many games?"

"Old maid, hearts, euchre."

"Right," said Anders. "Canasta? Bridge?"

"What's that?" said Taffin. "Why not poker?"

Brutus tapped me and wrote in the dust.

I made out the fat, overlapping letters. "Whist?"

"Brutus!" said Taffin.

Anders and Brutus laughed, a rather airy thing for Brutus.

I looked at Anders. "Is he—" No, that was rude. Talk to Brutus. "Are you okay?"

"Lost his vocal cords," said Anders.

It was long past the time such things should shock me, yet still, and still. Brutus shrugged and shuffled the cards. Nothing wrong with his mind, though. Good news, at last. I'd bring him pencil and paper to communicate next time I visited.

"How about five card draw?" said Anders. "You old enough to gamble, Kristy?"

"I will be in three days. Will you tell on me?"

Anders' expression was priceless. How old did he think I was? He looked like he'd meant it as a compliment for my youthful appearance, not imagining I could be only seventeen. I cut the deck.

"Tell us about yourself, instead," said Anders.

I stopped myself from getting lost in another memory of pictures and parents. Brutus dealt the cards, Taffin fiddled with the wrapping on a case of chips, and Anders kept looking at me funny. It occurred to me that 'telling on someone' was an American idiom, that my speech was peppered with Americanisms. That Anders might be getting suspicious about his suspicions, so to speak. That he might be coming to believe in me.

"Go on, tell us," said Anders. "All the gory details."

"You really want to know?"

"Call us a captive audience."

Anders grinned as if he expected me to be impressed with his humor. Taffin opened the case of chips and dumped them out before Brutus could restrain him. They scattered like leaves, to the first general amusement I had seen in the POW cave.

Chapter 16

Leaves scattered from my rake in the middle of the prison camp compound. The ground was spotless except for the leaves; they were hard to keep up with. Shadows lengthened as I neared the back gate, singing softly, three-day-old memories of poker chips and pleasure fresh in my mind. How long had it been since I felt like singing? I'd been doing it all day. In fact, three days, ever since that glorious evening of cards.

I'd learned where the men all came from. I really had led a sheltered life. Anders' North Carolina mountain accent was the first southern drawl I'd heard, and I had a hard time following Taffin's Brooklynese. Unfortunately, no matter where they were from, they all smelled the same. Occasional fishing runs were poor substitutes for showers, with or without my small supply of odoriferous soap.

Terauchi, Endo, and Ijuin rounded the edge of the hospital wing, chatting, dragging Major Donnerty and two GIs in wrist and—this was new—ankle chains. Three more for the cliffs, while the Japanese yakked about food and family and days off. Just another day in the trenches.

And I could do nothing about it. They never gave me more than one prisoner at a time, always well-drugged. When they had groups like this, the guards took them all, and they disappeared forever. I went silent and bent my head, raking harder, trying to get away from the gate before they arrived, before I had to see the faces of the doomed. Bad enough when they were groggy, but the major was aware.

I failed.

"There she is," said Ijuin.

Endo left the squad and cut me off, pointing at the gate. "Hey, slut. We got more for you."

For me? Multiples? What was going on? I followed his instructions and waited as they approached.

"I will show you," said Terauchi, apparently continuing some mundane argument. "I have pictures. My own little girls."

"And your own very big wife." Endo cackled.

Ijuin glowered and chugged from a bottle.

"You are jealous," said Terauchi. "She has good family."

"Very big family, I bet," said Endo.

Blood on the two GIs, under their ankle bracelets. Not worth anyone's time to treat. They'd be dead soon. I stiffened my frame. Just another day.

When they got near the gate, Terauchi slipped his picture in a pocket. The major growled at me, wordless loathing.

"You not drug them," I said. "I cannot handle three."

"He's the only one awake," said Endo. "We'll help."

Terauchi sneered. "We want to watch the Bloody Angel." Endo and Terauchi laughed.

I froze. Watch me? They couldn't do that. How would I . . . . The thought skittered away. I couldn't follow where it led. I didn't dare. Yet it latched on, steering me toward an abyss, an underworld that would scorch away every vestige of my spirit.

The major lunged to the side and bashed Endo with his chain. Ijuin clubbed the major with the bottle, knocking him to his knees.

"Don't break it." Endo kicked the major in the ribs and hauled him up.

Terauchi pushed the two GIs toward the gate. Their chains rattled when they bounced off the barbed wire, bleeding in several new spots, unresponsive to the injuries. “Open it.”

“I have no key,” I said.

Ijuin tossed me a small key ring. I opened the padlock on the gate and the Japanese shoved the prisoners through.

A brief hike through the woods, climbing from the level of the camp, led us to the barren area at the top of the cliff. I tailed along after them. I had no alternative.

“This is improper,” said Ijuin.

“What?” said Endo.

I lagged behind. Would Ijuin stop them? Were they not supposed to do this? Maybe there was hope, to save the men, or get me out of here. The Japanese forced the prisoners into the open area.

“Waste of good soldiers,” Ijuin said.

“Them?” Terauchi pointed at the GIs.

“Us, you simpleton. We belong in combat.”

My body quavered. I tried to get my face under control.

“Why?” said Endo.

Terauchi nodded. “My wife is happy I am here.”

Ijuin looked disgusted. I wished some of it was for their actions, but I knew better. He fancied himself a modern samurai, and shepherding POWs was beneath him, a demeaning duty that offended his sense of *Bushido*, of military honor. Neither he nor any other in this camp had shown the smallest sign of regret for the fate of their prisoners. Morality didn’t apply. Was that the mentality the army sought, when picking people for duty on this island?

The Japanese cast the Americans to the ground a few feet from the edge of the cliff, adding random kicks here and there.

I went taut. No hope, then. There never had been. Foolish thoughts, by a foolish girl. I had set myself up for this moment from the day I volunteered to dispose of the corporal, yet hadn’t the common sense to see where my actions would lead. To see there would be a Step Three—proving myself, surviving suspicion. Never conceived it could happen, never prepared myself, never planned.

"Come on, killer," said Terauchi. "Get over here. Show us your tricks."

Endo leered, grabbed the bottle, and drank. I stepped closer. I wasn't tall. Today, though, I towered above the prisoners. The Japanese had given me the power of life and death. No, that was incorrect; it was only the power of death. A power that made some people heady. A power that made me sick to my toes.

Terauchi got an ugly look. "Why do you dawdle? You dumped the others, didn't you?"

"Of course," I said, gripping my emotions and stuffing them in the tiniest box I could find. Searing over every feeling. Quelling what was left of my humanity. "But they not fight."

"Jap bitch." The major spat at me. "You haven't got a soul to send to hell."

I didn't answer. I wasn't supposed to know English. I pointed at Major Donnerty. "He healthy. I save him for last."

Endo chortled. Ijuin watched sourly.

I pulled up the bloodiest GI, covered in dirty bandages, and supported him, making him stagger to the edge, left of the spot with the ledge below.

I hesitated, closing my eyes, praying to every god in every religion I could think of to stop this now. Daring the Pacific to rise up and wash the island clean.

"Now what is it?" said Terauchi.

No, there would be no cleansing today. Today was solely about filth. I faced Terauchi. "It seem a waste."

He raised his rifle and slammed home the bolt. "I knew something was wrong with you."

He pointed it at my forehead, hands steady, not the slightest hesitation in his aim. I stared down the barrel. The long, murky, hollow shaft. I fancied I saw the tip of a bullet. Impossible, it was too dark. Everything was black. The trees should have been ebony, the birds should have been crows. If ever I saw a glimmer of light, it would be nothing more than a spark, powder going off behind a slug.

Terauchi's finger slid inside the trigger guard and closed on the trigger. "What did you do with the rest?"

Yet until I saw that spark, until that inevitable day, I had work to do.

"I mean, all these good manacles. Should you not take them off before we throw out trash?"

Stunned silence met me straight-on. But only for a moment.

Endo bent over, howling with laughter.

Terauchi slowly lowered his rifle. "Manacles?"

Endo pulled out a key and flung it at my feet. "Go ahead, Angel. Save the chains." He kept chuckling.

I picked up the key and bent to remove the iron cuffs from the bloody GI. He feebly attacked me, so I punched him on a bandage. He gasped. Stay impervious, I kept telling myself. No humanity.

I leaned over, put my hands on the sides of his neck, and pressed. After a few moments, he went limp, and I finished removing his shackles.

I rose, stepped sideways, and stood behind the prone soldier, looking out to sea. Clenching a fist. Fighting back tears.

And then I kicked him off.

And rubbed my eyes, pretending to wipe sweat off my brow.

Endo leaned over the edge.

"Why knock him out?" said Terauchi. "More fun to see a round-eye scream."

"Fun?" I said. "He merely trash. Drag me down if he could."

Ijuin rubbed his neck. "Where'd you learn that?"

"What?" I said. "Oh. Doctor made me practice. He show me many things."

The guards didn't seem to know how to react. What had they expected to see me do? I went to the second GI, with splints on arm and leg, and drew him forward. Terauchi guzzled from the bottle.

The GI tried to hit me, so I chopped him in the head. No emotion. I wrestled him to the edge.

He grabbed at me. Weak, frail motions. I batted his arms aside and pressed his neck until he, too, went limp. I removed his chains, stood, and hooked a foot under his waist.

And sent him over the edge.

"Not angel," said Endo, gaping at me in awe. Or respect. "Goddess. *Yuki-Onne.*"

Ijuin peered over the cliff. The soldier smashed onto the rocks and waves washed over him.

Endo backed from me. "Snow Queen. Numbs her victims to ease death." He drained the bottle, dropped it, and headed into the woods, toward the camp. Ijuin squinted at the lowering sun and joined him.

Terauchi looked from Endo to the major. Donnerty got his feet under him. Terauchi mashed him in the head with his rifle butt, and the major fell. Terauchi kicked him, but he didn't move.

"Lock up when you're finished." Terauchi followed the other guards.

They crashed through the underbrush until their uniforms dissolved among the leaves. I waited, arms limp at my sides. Their sounds drifted into the distance, dwindling, dimming. And gone, leaving only the booming, throbbing, unending roar of the ocean far below, howling revulsion at what I had done, at what I had become.

I stumbled to the edge. The bodies had already washed out to sea. I fell to my knees and sagged on my heels, clutching my arms, leaning over the edge. Bent in half, a warped fetal shape, mesmerized by the waves. I would never hear surf again without reliving this moment.

My shoulders started trembling. A sort of mewling came from somewhere. My hair fell forward over my head, and my hands tore at each other, fingernails gashing the skin. I crouched tighter, shivering, barely able to breathe.

As all the light in the world faded away.

A last convulsion, and the end of the sun. I rubbed my face, smearing blood from chin to temple. My jaw hardened, then moved, slowly, with the finality of a judge's sentence.

"Happy Birthday."

I crawled to the major's side. I tried to rouse him, but nothing worked. I removed his shackles and heaved him to the rim of the cliff, toward the right, above my ledge. He'd lost a lot of weight since I'd first seen him, or I'd never have managed. I slapped him, but it didn't help. He wouldn't stir. I took off his boots and laced them around his head—a crude helmet.

I pulled him further to the right, checked over the edge again, and put my hands on his shoulder and hip. I glanced at the sun. Only a sliver. No time left.

Major Donnerty's eyes flickered, but I didn't look at him again. I swallowed, and rolled him off.

He yelled. He'd woken up after all; maybe he could have climbed. He thumped onto the ledge with a flat, dull plop. I wheeled around on my belly and slid off, feet first. I went down fast and dropped the last few inches. I'd been on this ledge enough times I didn't need light.

I landed on the major, caught my balance, and squatted. His head bled and he was out cold. Again.

I dragged him into the cave and did what I could to stop the bleeding. He couldn't die now. Not now.

~~~~

I fought the back gate of the prison camp compound, forced it shut, and locked it. Shadows surrounded the world, broken only by wandering searchlights. I bent to pick up my assortment of chains.

Sakonju stopped me. "What took you so long?"

"Dark, Sergeant Sakonju. They leave me no light."

He grunted and marched off.

I stood and turned. A spotlight briefly flooded me. I could imagine what I looked like, face streaked with blood, eyes puffy, manacles dangling from one hand. The nails of my other dug deep into my palm.

One hour ago, I had been singing.
~~~~

Chapter 17

That night, most of the soldiers in the POW cave huddled around a pair of candles in wooden frames, blocking the light from the cave's northern crevices. They'd also propped up blankets over each of the crevices using their fishing poles. Blackout curtains, they called them.

Cards and poker chips had become the most popular of the games. Taffin knelt before a small boulder bearing his wooden cross. Brutus plucked feathers from a bird. He'd woven slender vines into a net and rigged it from a pair of crevices to supplement their food supply.

Anders and the corporal carried in Major Donnerty and laid him on a blanket in the light, breaking up one of the games. I followed, my face cleaned up, hands bandaged. Anders and Taffin had both shaved, but the others preferred the ragged image, so I hadn't tried to get another razor. Good thing. The hermit had been right, way back when. People watched what I did, especially now I had a reputation.

Why was I thinking about razors? They didn't signify. Not anymore. I had crossed the Rubicon, and the longer I thought about it, the more broken I became. The price for saving others had gone from risking my life to losing my soul. How could I continue? And what would happen to all these men if I couldn't?

I stood over the major. "Will he be all right?"

Anders felt the major's head. "He might be a bit grumpy."

"Why'd you hit him?" said the corporal.

No reason to let him bait me. The corporal knew better, it was just his way. The corporal wiped the major's bruises with a rag and water, and I went from man to man, unlocking their shackles with my new key.

"About time," said Zeiss.

Taffin held up his wrists. "Thanks, miss."

"Use the cream," I said, unlocking him. "You're infected."

"Got any more fish?" said the corporal.

"Not yet. I'll bring rice."

Bring rice? I was in automatic. I wanted to give up everything, slink into the deepest recess I could find, and never come out again. And I was talking like nothing had changed. As if these men would never find out what I had done.

Brutus groaned theatrically, then gave me a wink. He hated rice, and teased me about it, but I had no comeback today.

"You have enough water?" I said.

"Yeah," said Anders, "we're fine. We could use more cards, though."

I looked up and he wiggled an eyebrow like Groucho Marx. A joke. Why was everyone so friendly? They didn't understand. How could they? But they would, soon enough.

I turned away. "When he wakes—"

"Wait," said Anders.

The major moaned, and Anders and the corporal helped him sit up.

I closed my eyes. Already, it came. No more time to think. Just as well, get it over with. My family was gone, my honor nonexistent, my mission a joke. Maison would never return, the war would last for years, and I had not one redeeming quality left to my name. Let the religious be correct. Let there be a heaven, let there be a hell. Let there not be merely oblivion. For I had earned the unending torment of the damned.

I stepped over and crouched in front of the major. He gradually focused on my face.

And recognized me.

He roared and lunged, knocking me to the floor, choking me.

"You murderess! Greasy whoring butcher."

Brutus dove toward the major. Donnerty shoved him, and Brutus rolled across my knees. My trousers skimmed up my legs, exposing my knife, and the major grabbed for it.

Brutus kicked my leg aside and bent forward, blocking the major. The corporal and Anders hauled the major back.

"Let go," said Major Donnerty. "She threw Cooper and Whitmoore off a cliff."

"Major, you're delirious," said the corporal.

"She wouldn't kill anyone," said Anders.

"Damn you, I saw it."

Zeiss said, "She's our meal ticket."

"She's not even Japanese," said Taffin.

The major kept struggling and snarling. "She kicked them off the edge like they were garbage."

I hunched, coughing, clasping my throat. I couldn't believe Zeiss and the corporal were defending me. The only time they had shown the least sign of trust, and it was all so unbearably misplaced.

"Ask her," said Donnerty.

I shuddered and dropped my hand.

"Tell him, Kristy," said Anders. "He's got it wrong."

"Go on, butcher," said the major. "Tell them the truth."

Brutus touched my arm. I couldn't feel it. I stared at the major, the only person in the room who mattered.

The major glared back. "Gave the guards quite a show, didn't you, angel? Or is it goddess?"

My eyes took in the other men, and went back to the major.

"What's it feel like to put your foot on a man and roll him off a cliff?"

My face ached, drenched in acid and contorted into an ugly mask. I gazed at the major, lost in anguish.

"Your foot, on his chest. Did you feel the life, beating through your leg?"

My mouth moved, but nothing came out.

"What's wrong? Didn't I fall far enough? Or did these men stop you?"

I collapsed, crying quietly, and some of the soldiers distanced themselves, shunning me. I fumbled at my calf, removed my knife, and lifted it between my flattened hands, hilt away.

"Watch out," said Taffin. "She'll kill herself."

Brutus reached for the blade, but I stopped him with a tortured look. I got up and took the two steps to the major.

Major Donnerty thrashed again, but Anders and the corporal held him firm.

"Let go. You giving her another chance?"

I knelt and held out my hands like a tray, presenting the knife to the major, bowing deeply. Tears spotted the stones. Now it would come. Now it would happen. Now I would get what I had so long deserved. Even death would not salvage my honor, though. I was no samurai, I had no right to *seppuku*, no right for death to expurgate me. But the major, he had a right. To revenge.

"You think I won't use it?" said the major.

"Vengeance will slay us all," said Taffin.

"I know you will use it," I said. "But all you say is true."

Brutus looked forlorn.

"I have forsaken my parents, lain with the enemy, and now I am a murderer. What else is left?" And I was a traitor. Don't ever let go of that one. My mother had led me to treason. But somehow, I couldn't put voice to the ultimate sin. The crime I would take to my grave.

Yet if Dante were right, if treachery was the greatest evil, why did murder feel worse? Why did killing tear a deeper hole, leaving me shattered, unable to act? And how could I keep making the same mistake, thinking I was doing the right thing, and never believing it afterward?

"There were guards, weren't there?" said Anders. "You had no choice."

I shook my head. I'd given up on that excuse. Or outgrown it. It was far too convenient, and I'd used it all my life.

"There is always a choice." I held my hands out farther. "He is right. There are more important things than life, and I have betrayed them all."

The major spat again. "You fucking piece of shit."

I just proffered the knife. "Let him go."

The men blazoned anger, disbelief, detestation. More than I could bear. I bowed again, and the major stopped struggling.

"Please," I said.

The corporal relaxed his grip.

"Corporal!" said Anders. "Don't—"

The major ripped free of the corporal and grabbed the knife, slicing my hand clear through the bandage. He jabbed the blade toward Anders. Anders dodged and let go.

The major thrust fingers through my hair and spun me around, steel at my throat. "Freeze!"

Anders and the others backed off. I held still, eyes closed. Brutus danced on the balls of his feet, as near as he dared to the major, flexing his hands.

"Cooper was my best friend," said the major.

"Yes," I said.

"I knew him since grade school."

"Yes."

"And I have enough survival training to keep this bunch alive."

Oh, God. A ray of light. My punishment might not doom the others. I drooped against the blade, face softening. The major hesitated, and backed the knife away as I pressed into it.

"Thank you," I said. "Nearest water is half a mile north. Watch for tree snakes. And fish at new moon if you can. Full moon is better, but they have training patrols." Pointless to tell them about the submarine that would never come. And they shouldn't need the hermit, as if he'd even consider helping directly. "Oh, and the northeast beach is good for driftwood."

I stopped, waiting. Lifting my chin, stretching my neck.

Accepting. How much would it hurt? How long would it take me to die?

Nothing happened.

My eyes opened. "That's all I know. I swear."

The major acted uncertain, all of a sudden. Why? He studied the other men. They weren't looking at me, I realized. They were watching the major, in alarm, in repugnance, as he peered around the cave, taking in the blankets, the food, the games. I didn't understand. It made no sense.

He twisted my head until I faced him, and slid the point of the blade to the top of my throat. His brow knit. "Why didn't you kill me too? What happened to the soldiers?"

I frowned in confusion. "The guards left. I didn't have to . . . to kill . . . ."

My eyes shut, and I started crying again, silently.

The major slowly lowered the blade.

Brutus leapt forward and took the knife. Anders pulled the major away from me, and he didn't resist. Brutus knelt and held me while Taffin bound my bloody hand.

Why? Why wasn't I dead? Why hadn't the major finished it? Why did he make me suffer, refusing me the release of death? Did he truly hate me that much?

"She's the weirdest Jap I ever—" said Zeiss.

Taffin cut him off. "She's no Jap."

"Or she is," said the corporal, "and better at psych games than we figured."

"Corporal, get the others ready," said Anders. "It's a fishing night."

"Sergeant—"

"You are senior, Major. But I suggest until you learn the situation, you allow me to continue."

The major pursed his lips, nodded, and Anders signaled to the men.

Brutus replaced the knife in my sheath. That caught the major's attention, but he followed Anders out.

I stayed where I was, cradled by Brutus, until the others were gone. And then it came to me. I finally understood my punishment. Once again, despite what I had just said, I had no choice.

I had to carry on.

Chapter 18

I spent little time in the POW cave after that. I hesitated every time I entered, and never reacted to the eyes, the silences, the murmuring as I left. I tensed whenever the major came near. Sometimes I heard muffled arguments when I appeared, and wondered if they contemplated violence after all. Brutus waved a deck of cards at me once, as if I would actually join them again. I couldn't provide even a trace of a smile.

I hunted and fished, and found more ways to carry water. It numbed me, and needed doing. The hermit kept avoiding me, as he had since I'd shown him my medical sketches, and that, too, seemed as it should be.

The oddest thing was how I kept second-guessing every decision I'd ever made, recasting my memories in different molds. I was saving lives, and that had to be a good thing, didn't it? In spite of the cost? The idea defied every concept of honor I had learned, and yet, in another room of my mind, felt right. Was this rationality, or desperate rationalization, so I could live with myself? How could I trust my own thoughts if I couldn't even answer that question?

And still I packed away the grief every few days and returned to the POW camp to do my chores. To keep up my persona. To rescue another man, if the opportunity arose. It might be right, or honorable, or neither if there was no realistic chance to get them home. But I couldn't stop myself. Be it obsession or something else, it was who I was.

One black night a few weeks later, rain poured down my cheeks. Lightning filled my eyes; thunder, my ears. Waves pounded the beach higher than ever before, covering rocks up to the forest. There was so much rain I couldn't smell the pines, only the mold. I backed under a towering maple, my feet soaking wet.

A small light glinted to the south. The commandant wouldn't visit in the rain, but someone was there.

A faint piping, eerie and entrancing, came from my cave.

"No!" I raced toward the opening.

When I rushed in, Zeiss stopped playing his flute and jumped in front of me, arms out. I sidestepped and skidded to a halt. The corporal was feeding papers to my fire. My watercolors, the red of blood flashing as if it were fresh. I faltered when I saw the major crouching beside him, and rounded on the corporal.

"What are you doing?"

I darted forward and snatched a flaming sheet. The corporal grabbed it and dropped it on the fire. Zeiss' face was gloating. The corporal's, twisted scorn. But the major had the coldest lack of expression I'd ever seen.

"Get out of here," I said. "Someone's coming."

The major waved more papers at me. "Not likely. Why did you draw these? I won't leave you trophies."

"They're evidence." I shoved Zeiss toward the back of the cave. He threw me off.

The major pointed at a picture. "I never saw them do this."

"I did," said the corporal.

Zeiss pointed at another picture. "They did that to me."

"Get out! Corporal, you know better."

The major looked at the corporal.

The corporal smirked. "Girl's bedroom, you know."

I gawked at him.

The major snorted and dumped the rest of the drawings on

the fire. They flared up, bright as searchlights. "How many more secrets you got?"

Why was the fire so pretty? Disaster loomed, my records were ruined, and it was all so very cheery? I put my fists to my mouth and barely got the next words out, one at a time.

"Leave. Right. Now." A quiver ripped through me. "*Please.*"

They watched me a second longer, and Zeiss raised a hand, palm up. Maybe the major was satisfied they'd done enough damage, because he pointed to the rear tunnel and they left.

I bent down and shoveled scraps of paper into the fire, cleaning up. I couldn't save my work, but I could finish the job before whoever it was arrived. I'd better. The Japanese would not appreciate documentation of their tests.

A scraping came from the main entrance as the last remnant burst into flame. Sergeant Sakonju blocked the fissure, carrying an electric torch.

"You weren't around today." He flashed his light at dim recesses. "The commandant requests you be available when next it does not rain."

I stood and bowed to the appropriate angle, and Sakonju reentered the storm.

I slumped to the ground, my face roasting in the firelight.

The major reappeared in the tunnel. He stood there, considering me. I caught his eye, but had nothing left to say. After a long moment, he departed.

~~~~

The next time I visited the POW cave, the watercolor landscapes and bird pictures I had given the men in the past were propped against two of the walls of their cave. Not hidden among their personal treasures, not burned, but on open display. But only on two of the walls. The tale of the picture-burning must have spread, taking the prisoners beyond the murmuring stage, and splitting the room into factions—those who were suspicious, and those who hated me outright. I couldn't imagine other possibilities. So now I had another burden on my conscience. I had
~~~~

divided the men.

That day I entered with two new soldiers, bringing the total to a dozen. The major followed my every move, as always. I couldn't prevent myself from looking for him, and staying as far away as possible. I led the two half-dazed men to Anders, gave him a basket of tubers, and left.

Major Donnerty headed after me. Anders began to follow, until something passed between him and the major. I kept walking; the major could be going elsewhere.

But no. In the tunnel beyond the cave, the major quickly caught up. He closed until his breath warmed my neck. That stopped me.

"Do you have a plan? Or are you just accumulating bodies?"

It was the major asking. Somehow, that changed my mind. I could no longer keep their iffy future a secret. They deserved to know the worst, how little chance they had.

"I have a hope," I said.

"The war could last years. We'll go crazy."

"Prison camp is better?"

"If you offer no options, we'll make our own."

I faced him. "It is too far to sail anywhere except Russia. You would need a big boat. You don't have enough men for that."

"So what's your hope?"

Ten feet beyond his shoulder, Anders stood at the edge of the light. He'd followed anyway.

"I know a submariner," I said. "He may come."

"A U.S. sub? Bull. Here?"

"Perhaps."

"When?"

"At dark of moon. Or never."

He scrutinized me, digging for details I didn't have. I wanted to storm off, but I couldn't budge. I managed to turn away.

"Did you kill any more?"

"Not this time," I said, feet welded to the rock, unable to take a step until his words released me.

"How much blood have you taken?"

A tremor ran through every part of my body. It took a while to answer.

"Three lives have I destroyed," I said. "The two you know."

I looked back.

"And mine."

Chapter 19

A bird screeched in anger, fleeing from a larger one over restless whitecaps. Crab and mussel shells littered the narrow coastline, the reeking remains of a passing typhoon. The north face of the island's cliff glowed like fire in the waning sunlight. It would be in shadow at sunset within a few days. The sun was falling south, and autumn was upon us, with all its beautiful leaves and the promise of dormant life. How would it affect the food supply?

I sat on a boulder surrounded by waves near the base of the cliff, idling, musing, tossing pebbles at the churning greenish-grey water. I ought to be working. Making more snares, catching crickets for bait, weaving another sloppy reed basket. But I needed a rest. Even my dreams had gone into hiding, chased by nightmares, and my legs twitched with exhaustion every morning. Thankfully, I had no idea what I ran from in the fugue of the night.

Every time I tried to examine my feelings, it left me floundering. When I wasn't devastated at the destruction I had caused, that meant I was cruel and callous. When I let the anguish capture the smallest of footholds, I became a useless vessel of goo. The whole thing left me breathless. There would never be an answer, so all I could do was shovel my doubts into the Mariana Trench and get on with it.

So good it was to sit here, alone, inactive, forgetting the world, if only for an hour.

How many months had it been since I washed up on this isle of shame? Naive visions of espionage and redemption had evaporated so long ago they were hard to recall. The Japanese gossiped about the war, inspired by victories and the occasional boneheaded move by the Allies, like when an American admiral claimed 'when this war is over, the only place they speak Japanese will be in hell.' They got quite angry at other things, especially a Tokyo bombing and a Midway incident, but the Allies would know such information. Weapons, attack plans, defenses—I had learned nothing of value, nothing to compensate for my mother's actions. Nothing I could sneak away with, to buy my salvation. Instead, I could never leave this island, regardless what anyone thought of me. Not when it would mean abandoning my charges.

How many more could I rescue? I'd about reached the limit of how many I could feed, especially with fall coming. The doctor went on a rampage once, howling about snobs in a Unit-something not giving him a chance, and solved the problem for a while. He initiated a series of fake vaccinations and a minor epidemic in an attempt to collect data and impress his superiors. There were weeks with no surviving test subjects to dispose of, weeks when I had no one to save, weeks when the major accused me of giving up, or letting people die because I'd gotten lazy. Or worse, because I really was a Japanese agent, and already had enough victims for my 'little experiment.'

Damn it, why wouldn't my brain shut up?

Shots rang above, along the edge of the cliff. Had they found something? Were they shooting at me? I dropped to the water behind a rock.

Lieutenant Durban, the only Australian I'd seen in the POW camp, descended the side of the cliff. This could not happen. I'd never heard of a successful escape. There was nowhere to go. He was over halfway, scrambling like a mountain goat. Japanese guards appeared above, leaning over the cliff, some pointing, others firing. Bullets ricocheted past the Australian.

Durban neared the bottom, his nails clawing at the stone. A pair of rounds knocked chips off the rocks by his head. He clutched his chest and soared out over the rocks, landing in the open water. The guards fired a few more times, nattered between themselves, and left.

I poked up my head.

Durban erupted on the other side of the rock. I clapped hands over my mouth, cutting off a squawk, and slogged to shore.

Durban followed, dangling one arm. “Wait.” He banged his arm and grasped it. “Please, help me.” Blood trickled through his fingers.

I fell against an ancient oak and slid down the trunk, scraping my cheek along the bark. I pulled out my knife and murmured a hopeless prayer.

“Holy Mother, don’t give me another test.”

I slid a thumb across the tip of the blade, the wasp whose sting I could not accept. I had been given a penance, and had to carry on. But I could use the knife on another, if he threatened all I had done. I had to.

“‘What else is left?’ Why did I ask? Why did I have to . . . .” I closed my eyes.

Durban sloshed ashore, his feet smacking the mud towards me. “Damn, what’s with this girl? I should have learned Japanese.”

“Please,” I whispered. My hand tightened on the hilt.

“Please,” said Durban.

I turned. His eyes flickered from me to my knife to my face. In a flash, his look of entreaty faded to abhorrence.

“Snow Queen.”

My nickname spread fast. Even a new prisoner like this, fresh off the boat, had heard it.

I feinted, ducked, and got behind him, pinning his good arm and holding my knife in his back.

“The doctor taught me how to reach a man’s heart.”

“Didn’t the commandant do that?” He grunted when I lifted his arm higher. “Lousy accent. Where’d you pick up English, in the colonies?”

I grimaced. “Why didn’t you die?”

“I gather I’m the first to get out.”

“No, I mean, you held your chest.”

“A fake. They won’t look if they think I’m dead. Which I guess I will be.”

“You don’t know them. They will search until they find your corpse.”

“Why bother?”

“You are an insult,” I said. “You bested them.”

Durban laughed derisively. “Honor games. I guess you’d know.”

“Besides, they cannot be certain you are dead. If you are not found, they will comb this island until no secrets remain.”

Durban made his move. I’d been expecting that. I stuck him as lightly as I could.

He yelped and arched his back. “What are you waiting for?”

“Don’t you see? I cannot let them search the island.”

“Why? You running a black market?”

I bit my lip. Great, a smart-ass, too new to have the cockiness burned out of him. It should have been fresh air, not a shiver of icy wind down my spine. “I want you to understand. This place is riddled with caves.”

“Oh, you’re with National Geographic.”

“Shut up. I have over a dozen prisoners in hiding. The Japanese think I’ve killed them.”

“Japs? Damn, I thought you were German.”

I paused, hating his calm, his flippancy. His defiance. Qualities so very infuriating, and so utterly enviable. Someday, if I were caught, I would cry, and beg, and scream from the pain, for I had not an ounce of courage within me. The thought put an edge to my voice.

“Are you trying to make this easy for me?”

“Missy, I don’t know what the bloody blazes you’re talking about.”

“I’m explaining why you have to be found. And not alive, or you will tell them I let you go.”

"Why would I do that?"

"You couldn't help it. I've seen."

"I'm sure you have."

"Damn you," I said. "Don't you get it? You're dead. All you can do is kill the other soldiers."

"And you."

A blink. "Yes." How strangely irrelevant. "And me."

"You're so kind to enlighten me."

My shoulders would not hold still. "I've killed before. There's no other way to keep people alive."

"Then do it, witch."

My knife vibrated. "I'm sorry."

"Sure you are."

There was no part of me left that wasn't trembling. "I have to."

"Just don't miss."

"Please."

Durban's brow furrowed. The blade tilted down.

"Forgive me," I said.

"Not a chance."

My hand slowly fell. "I, I have to—"

Durban wrenched free, pivoted, and grabbed for the knife. He missed, and stared in shock at the reason. It lay on the ground.

I held my stomach and sank to my knees. Durban wound fingers in my hair and scooped up the knife.

A report echoed off distant rocks. A rifle. Durban glanced over his shoulder.

"I'm sorry," I said.

He looked back at me.

"I swear I tried."

He made a disgusted sound and let me go.

I wilted, boneless. "Now they will die."

"So what do you want me to do?" said Durban. "Kill myself?"

Another shot, and a distant yell.

"Crap." He knelt, dropped the knife, and slapped me. "Quit moping. You got any ideas? Either hide me, or get the hell out of here and I'll fight them on my own."

I rubbed my cheek. "That won't work. They'll take you alive."

"You're a real optimist."

My teeth chattered. Stupid nerves. Durban swiveled toward the woods, dog tags flying out of his shirt.

I gasped. "Wait. One chance. Not a good one."

I took the knife and elevated his sore arm. He sucked an oath.

"Don't move." I cut off his sleeve. "This will hurt."

I probed with the knife and dug out a bullet. He squinched his eyes and ground his teeth. I rubbed the blade with more blood, slipped it in its sheath, and tried to ignore Durban's panting as I bound his arm with the sleeve.

"Glad you're fast," he said.

"Sorry. Ricochet. Not a bad wound."

I drew him up and led him into the water along the base of the cliff. I sorted through vines until I found a crevice and shoved him in, arranging the leaves to cover the opening.

"Stay here. Give me your dog tags."

"What? Oh, right."

"Hurry."

He pulled them off. I slipped the chain over my head, flipped my hair over it, and slid the tags inside my shirt.

"I'll come back tonight. If I can."

I splashed out and climbed on a boulder amidst the breakers. I sat in lotus position, bowed my head briefly, and raised my hands on high, rubbing the bullet between my palms.

And then I chanted, reciting a poem of loss my mother had taught me.

I didn't have long to wait. Terauchi, Endo, Ijuin, and Sergeant Sakonju approached the rocks, bayoneted rifles at the ready. They stopped at the last bit of dry land near me and spread out, peering around. I kept chanting.

"You," said Sakonju. "Girl."

I twisted around. One hand zipped behind me and I bowed my head. "Hello, Sergeant."

"Come here."

I hesitated.

"Now!"

I stumbled over the rocks and waded toward the guards.

"Faster," said Sakonju.

I reached shore and edged toward them, keeping one hand behind my back. Kira, the naughty child. Maybe.

"You saw the Australian?" said Sakonju.

I looked down. He grabbed my free arm.

"Was he dead?"

"You not want him dead? Others on cliff you want dead."

Terauchi stepped toward me. "You finished him off?"

"Only a little." I tried to pull free, a half-hearted attempt I knew would fail. "He almost gone."

Endo laughed. I was beginning to wonder if he might be mental. He was always laughing. Sakonju and Ijuin, of course, didn't.

"How can we believe her?" said Sakonju.

Terauchi grabbed my other arm. He pried the bullet from my fingers and held it up.

~~~~

Little daylight was left, so the commandant held the bullet under his desk lamp. Sakonju and Terauchi gripped me by the elbows, holding me taut between them.

"This helps," said the commandant, dropping the bullet on his desk. "Bloody, and the right caliber."

The doctor entered, humming a march. "Where is my patient?"

"Dead, apparently," said the commandant. "And he ceased being your patient when he eluded your test."

The doctor turned to me. I kept my head down. He lifted my chin, noted the dog tags, and jerked them over my head.

"Mine," I said.

Sakonju poked my arm. "Settle down."

The doctor read the dog tags, showed them to the commandant, and jingled them in front of me.

"You know what these are?"
~~~~

"Necklace. Pretty."

Terauchi snickered.

"You stole this, didn't you?" said the doctor.

"He not need it anymore."

"How did you kill him?

I wagged my foot. "I do as you say. I not stick a bone."

The doctor grinned, pulled out my ankle knife, and caressed the dried blood. "I'll confirm blood type if you like, but I see no reason to doubt her."

The commandant picked at a brown spot on the slug. "Do so. Check this too." He tossed the slug to the doctor. "Kira, why was there no body?"

"Tide is strong. It cleans."

He chewed his lip, and nodded to the guards. They released me.

~~~~

In the POW cave much later, I stood between Zeiss and the corporal. They gripped my elbows, holding me taut. It seemed to be the order of the day. Brutus and Taffin bracketed Durban.

The major confronted us both. "It's so nice they believed you."

"I thought so," I said.

"Any of you ever see this person?"

The other men shook their heads.

"I just got dumped here two days ago," said Durban.

"Kristy," said Anders, "did you think about this at all?"

"You killed my friends," said the major, "but you couldn't kill this spy?"

"I'm no spy," said Durban.

"Everyone else here is a throw-away," said Anders.

"You're the only one to claim escape," said the major.

"Uninjured," Anders added.

"My arm?"

The major yelled. "You're a plant!"

"That's the dumbest—" Durban tried to take a step, but Brutus and Taffin held him.
~~~~

It was more than I could take. I started laughing. Wildly. Bitterly. I couldn't believe where this was heading, where these frightened, paranoid people wanted to go. I leaned on Zeiss. The corporal tightened his grip on my other arm. I struggled to speak, while everyone acted like I'd gone insane.

"I jeopard—" I tried again. "I jeopardize everything, because I am too weak to do what I should, and you want to kill him anyway?"

I sagged between Zeiss and the corporal.

"Are you all blind?" I yanked an arm free and leveled a finger at Durban. "He's a *round-eye!* What pride-struck Japanese is going to trust a round-eye?"

The men reared back, like the idea had never occurred to them. Like it was beyond their comprehension that anyone could be prejudiced against *them*.

"Thanks a lot," said Durban dryly.

"Don't mention it." Damn it, I could be as sarcastic as he was. "Besides, if they thought there was anything to spy on, they'd send in the army."

"Unless he's here to help you," said the major.

"Again, round-eye. Besides, if I'm that mysterious Jap trickster you keep worrying about, you're already out of luck."

That silenced the men for a second.

"Or," the major said slowly, "you are that trickster, and that explains the escape. It wasn't one. The Japs told you they'd let Durban go, and if he made it far enough, add him to the pile."

"Not a chance," said Durban.

That opinion wouldn't count for much. The major wouldn't expect Durban to believe he'd been duped. I dropped my head. What else was there to say?

Anders signed to the major and they went to the side of the cave, whispering together.

Durban chuckled, yet another of his inappropriate reactions. "Does everyone like you this much?"

"I'm a popular girl."

"Yes, you've quite a reputation in the camp."

I shuddered. “I’ve earned it.”

The major and Anders returned, one last hiss coming from the major.

“Let them go,” said Donnerty. He glared at me. “Like it or not, we’re stuck on your wagon. But if you leave the path, I’ll finish what I started. With your own knife.”

“You’ll have to get it from the doctor,” I said. “They’re testing the blood.”

“It’s mine,” said Durban.

Anders raised an eyebrow at me. So I raised one at him.

Chapter 20

A couple of weeks after 'the Durban affair,' I leaned my rake against a trash bin in the prison camp compound and headed for the long building that housed camp stores. The old woman emerged with a bag of rice, and stopped halfway down the stairs when she caught sight of me.

"Traitor. I should have thrown you back."

My steps trailed to a halt. I dared not reply to my elder. The commandant and his aide strolled around the edge of the building and slowed, watching.

"No true daughter of the Rising Sun could do as you have done," she said, cracking her words like whips.

I bowed my head until she stomped off, and entered the building. She hated this camp, hated the commandant, hated the government and the war they had sought, but I could never trust her with the truth of what I was doing. The poor old lady could never keep silent.

The commandant tugged one end of his new mustache. "Akiyama, you still have that inquiry regarding the girl?"

"Form 1732-kyo, for civilians," said his aide. "Yes, sir."

The commandant fiddled with his mustache, slowing further. He tugged again, shook his head, and picked up speed. The aide followed in his wake.

I peeked out the doorway. An inquiry about me, like the hermit had once mentioned. Never sent, and waiting in a drawer? The thought would be terrifying, if I let myself dwell on it. All I could do was hope the old woman's opinion about the character of Japanese girls would continue to carry little weight. After all this time, why should anything change?

I shied away from the weakness of that logic. Someday, someday, it would be nice to have a life that didn't rely on wishful thinking.

~~~~

The evening after I got my knife back from the doctor, Major Donnerty insisted on inspecting it. I stood before him in the POW cave, waiting. Possibly he wanted the power of making me hand it over now and again, proving my submission, or testing my loyalty. He held out the blade, and I slipped it in my sheath.

I gestured, Anders pointed, and fifteen men selected fishing gear for another night along the coastline. One soldier was missing a nose, another hobbled on one foot with a makeshift crutch.

"You're fortunate," said the major, watching the activity. "The new man confirmed your story. He was on the same transport ship as Durban."

He was talking about the boy I'd brought down yesterday, a kid with peach fuzz on his cheeks. He ought to be in ninth grade. I didn't reply, waiting for the major's dismissal.

"You sure it's clear this time?" said Donnerty.

"The commandant came last night. He's not that interested anymore."

"How sad for you."

My jaw clenched. "It's the last night of the old moon, and skies are cloudless. Tonight we should catch a lot."

He was back to studying my face. He'd perfected the way his eyes bored in, like he wanted to dissect my mind and find the acrid secrets that must be hidden within. I couldn't bear it, and couldn't stop it. A draining combination.
~~~~

"You don't know much about fishing, do you?"

That was a fact. Only what I'd picked up here. The men had finished gathering, so I led them out.

At the beach, I climbed on the tallest boulder, my favorite perch, and gazed out to sea. The major climbed up beside me. There had been no rain for a week, not a smidgen of wind for over a day, and the water was smooth as glass. A million stars crossed the horizon from above to below.

Neither I nor the major commented on the splendor of the night.

Two men fanned out north and south as lookouts. The others clambered onto rocks at water's edge and fastened fishing lines to sticks. There was no idle chatter, and the world grew peaceful.

An hour later, I stood alone on my boulder, watching the ocean. The major had joined the others, fishing on the rocks. Once he snorted in my direction. Something he thought was adequately expressed that way, evidently.

Another hour drifted past. Atop the boulder, my eyes snapped open and I recovered my balance. I wasn't supposed to sleep, I was on guard, for heaven's sake. I pinched myself and walked around in a tiny circle, getting the blood flowing, reciting the sequence of colorful layering in the stone beneath my feet. Uncertain I had it right. They were nothing but bands of silver and black in the dim starlight.

~~~~

Two hours more, and Major Donnerty met the corporal on the rocky beach. The corporal held a good-sized fish, as did several other men.

"That's enough," said Donnerty. "It's getting late. I don't see how you eat this stuff."

"Oh!" My hands flew to my face. A light. Flashing. At sea. My God, they'd come back. Maison had actually returned. I fell to my knees atop my rock and lit a match.

"Damnation." Donnerty dropped his fishing pole and sprinted for my boulder. The corporal flung his fish at Taffin and followed.
~~~~

I got my oil lamp alight and stood, cupping it and waving it back and forth. Donnerty vaulted up beside me, and I turned to give him the good news.

He snatched the lamp and blew it out. The corporal crushed my arms to my sides.

"What the hell are you doing?" said Donnerty.

"Signaling Japanese, obviously. After feeding you for six months and telling no one." I snarled like the bitch he thought I was. He'd ruin it all if he didn't let me signal. What the hell was wrong with him?

Donnerty lifted a hand to hit me.

"Sir. There's a light." The corporal jutted his chin to sea.

"Japanese patrols never give away their position," I said.

Anders mounted the rock. The other men congregated below.

"It's Morse," said Anders.

Donnerty stared from Anders to me to the light. "Can you read it?"

"No," I said.

"Yes," said Anders.

"Well?"

"*Barracuda,*" I said.

"What?" said the corporal.

Anders peered at the light. "*USS Barracuda*. She knew."

Donnerty motioned to the corporal. The corporal covered my mouth and dragged me off the rock.

"What are you doing?" said Anders.

"Take the lamp," Donnerty said. "Signal them."

"Why—"

"Use your shirt."

Anders ripped off his shirt and took the lamp. "But sir, Kristy is—"

"Follow orders, soldier."

For a second, Anders was the picture of mutiny, ready to take a swing.

Donnerty didn't back down. "She may be for real. But maybe not. A few prisoners would be a small price for trapping a U.S. sub, wouldn't you say?"

"No, sir, I could *not* say that."

"What if her next yell alerts the Japs?"

Had I really felt elation, for all of one split second? A smattering of joy, sloshing around in the bottom of the bucket? How fast it drained, replaced with resignation. I'd finally been proven right, and it mattered not at all. What should have been my exculpation was seen as nothing but evidence of a deeper, nastier plot.

"There's only one solution here. Now signal that boat." Donnerty jabbed toward the light.

Anders' shoulders drooped. He lit the lamp, shielded it with his shirt, and flashed it to sea in short bursts.

"Don't lose them. I'll be right back." Donnerty jumped down and grabbed my knife. He and the corporal hauled me toward the cave.

~~~~

A HALF HOUR AFTER the signaling had started, *Barracuda* lay in the darkness offshore, and Jeremy Maison's rubber dinghy approached the beach. Several men stood together, and flickers of lamplight revealed U.S. Army uniforms. There was no sign of Kristy Hara. One man flashed the lamp, and the senior chief in the back of the dinghy altered course toward it.

The dinghy slid to a stop in the shallows at the least rocky part of the beach. The nearly silent electric motor hummed at the gear change. Maison got out and waved at the chief, and the boat backed off as Maison splashed ashore.

An officer strode toward him, pointing at the dinghy. "Where is that going?" The other soldiers mustered together.

Maison drew himself up. "Lieutenant Commander Jeremy Maison, United States Navy. Commanding Officer, *USS Barracuda*. And you?"

"Major Anton Donnerty, United States Army, Philippines. Prisoner of war. Former. And this is Sergeant Anders. Now where is that—"
~~~~

"That boat will not return until I confirm this is not a trap. I will not risk my ship. Is that clear?"

"Certainly, but—"

"Where is your verification you are who you say you are?"

"Verification?"

"Yes. Your message said you were concerned about Japanese spies."

The major whirled on Anders.

"I told them the situation, sir," said Anders, "as I'm sure you wanted."

"You insubordinate—"

"It wouldn't matter what he said, Major. Your only verification is Kristy Hara, the girl we left here seven months ago."

The major spluttered. "You left? On purpose?"

"You don't think we'd send a submarine to a nowhere rock near Japan just on the off chance there might be POWs, do you?"

"But she's a . . . we thought she was a spy."

"She is. Ours."

The major and corporal traded looks. Behind them, Brutus and Taffin grinned.

Maison stepped back and drew his service automatic, aiming it upward.

"If this fires, you can forget any rescue. My men aren't about to wait around for one S.O.B. CO." He clicked off the safety. "Where's Kristy?"

"In the cave," said the major.

"I'll take you, sir," said Anders.

Maison lowered the gun. He waved the barrel at the major and corporal. "Stand aside."

They split apart, and the rest of the men made a corridor.

Anders held up his lamp and led Maison through. They headed beneath the red and yellow of maple trees in autumn, ideal for reflecting the flames of oil lamps. The beauty struck Maison as more than a little inapt. He clicked the safety and holstered his gun.

When Anders and Maison entered Kristy's cave, she lay bound

with fishing line and gagged with a shirt. Maison drew a knife and knelt beside her.

Her eyes flicked from the knife to Maison. She cringed.

Anders leapt forward. “Hey!”

Maison slit through a line.

“Ah. All right.” Anders removed her gag.

Maison cut again, and again. Kristy followed the blade. Every time the knife went toward another section of line, not toward her skin, Kristy gazed at Maison in wonder. He figured he kind of had that coming.

“Thank God,” said Anders. “I thought they’d killed you.”

“And you didn’t stop them?” said Maison.

“A fight out there would have killed us all. You’d have left without us.”

“I still might.”

“No!” Kristy wriggled out of the fishing line, bleeding in several spots.

“You okay?” said Maison.

“Can you walk?” said Anders.

~~~~

I staggered as they helped me up, and massaged my legs, flexing them. “Don’t you dare leave them behind.”

“Not even the major?” said Anders.

It felt like a slap. “That’s not funny.”

“Let’s go,” said Maison. “The chief won’t wait forever.”

They supported me and I hobbled out between them.

On the beach, the chief loaded half the men and backed the dinghy from shore. He turned and chugged toward the submarine.

I stood on the tallest boulder with Maison. I glanced south occasionally, making sure there were no lights, no signs of Japanese soldiers.

“You got all these men out of a POW camp?”

“I lost some.”

“I can’t believe you survived. I almost didn’t come back.”

“Yeah, well, I get pulled under. But I pop back up.”
~~~~

He let out a nervous laugh. "I've noticed. So what's the story with all the injuries? Most aren't combat wounds."

"They can tell you better than I. You should bomb this place."

"A POW camp?"

"It would be a blessing."

He gave me an odd look, and a silence took us for a while as the dinghy reached the submarine. There were so many things to say, to ask. But where to start?

Maison shifted his weight. "When we get you home, you'll be famous."

A scalding shame convulsed me, from the roots of my hair to the calluses on my feet. "No one wants to know me."

Maison crinkled his face, confused.

"Ask the major. I am a deserter, a whore, and a killer." I fingered my hair. "Besides, in war it is easier to hate."

"I know."

I nearly lost my footing. Was that guilt? "You were protecting your country."

Maison kicked a pebble off the boulder, shaking his head, and all at once I realized—he knew about my pictures. He knew about my mother. Yet here he stood, taking a position beside me, acting like he was the one in need. He wasn't aware of my other offenses, but he knew of my treason and came back anyway, saving me, granting me acceptance. Perhaps even absolution. Something in my breast began to warm.

"Your mother's in jail," he said after a moment. "She's lucky they tried her before people get any more bitter."

How was I supposed to respond to that? I hadn't expected clemency.

"They released your father to an internment camp. They moved all the Japanese-Americans away from the west coast, in case of invasion. Maybe they didn't want them shot by accident."

That was even more surprising. The releasing part, not so much the bit about internment camps. Isolation for their own safety? Possible, but he could be repeating an official line, or putting a Pollyanna face on it for my benefit. Who knew what the conditions were in such places?

"Your friend Maxine missed you at graduation."

I gasped. "You . . . thank you. Tell her I think of her."

Oh my, he knew Maxine. Of all the things I could ever imagine, that he would have been thinking of me all this time, checking up, learning about me—no, and no again. I could never have conceived of such an idea. And somehow, in some way, that released a frozen dam. Something in me relaxed, and something else emerged. A glow, a lightness, a grace I had forgotten I could feel. Maxine was well, and my men were going home. Life could flow again. Spring could enter my heart, even as winter came to the island.

I took a deep breath and let go my thoughts, relating what I had done since last I saw Maison. Condensing things, for sure. We had little time. Mostly things the others didn't know. Painful memories, yet liberating to admit. Whenever I needed to pause, Maison threw in a tidbit about what he'd been up to during all those new moons. As we finished, the chief approached with the empty dinghy.

A throat cleared behind us. "So," said the hermit in his golden Japanese, "do you want these pictures, or not?"

Maison and I spun around. The hermit held up a handful of drawings. Maison reached for his gun, but I dove for the holster, crouching, putting both hands over his.

"No," I said. "He's harmless."

"Harmless?" said the hermit in an English he could only have picked up from the universities of England. "Harmless? Well, dig me a hole and draw up a stone, I must be dead. I'm harmless."

He threw up the pictures and stamped away.

I slid down and gathered the pictures. Maison followed.

"Wait," I said. "Don't you want these?"

The hermit looked over his shoulder. "Not those. Those are that ugly evidence you wanted me to keep. Remember?"

"But you—how?"

"Snuck in, stole half. Good thing, the way the others burned."

He tromped off into the trees, and I called thanks after him.

"*Arigato.*" And then, more quietly, "*Sumimasen.*" The hermit waved a hand over his head but didn't reply, and I shivered. I had broken a promise. I hadn't let him have the last word.

I folded the pictures and handed them to Maison. "This is what goes on here."

Maison started to unfold the pictures, but I stopped him.

"No. Later."

He nodded, and led me toward the beach. The chief loaded the dinghy with the rest of the men.

"What did you miss most?" said Maison.

"I would give anything for some Shakespeare. Even a sonnet."

"The chief may have *Hamlet* in the ship."

I said nothing, and we neared the dinghy.

He indicated the stern. "Let's sit there. Smoother ride."

I went still. Time to tell him. Maison continued a step before noticing I was no longer beside him.

"I'll give you more in six months."

"More?" Maison gaped at me. "No! You've made your point." He waved at the island. "The Nips, I mean . . ."

I smiled sadly. "'Nips' isn't so bad. You should hear them talk about *gaijin*. Round-eyes." At his expression, I gave a helpless little shrug.

Maison raised a hand toward me, held it there, and dropped it. "I suppose I could force you."

"You think to keep me in the boat?"

"Yes, there is that."

The others were aboard, waiting. The chief fretted in the stern, revving the near-silent motor.

I rushed Maison to the dinghy. "Hurry. Patrols come soon." I pushed him into the boat.

He grabbed my wrist. "Please. Come with us."

I paused. I had to say this right. I had to make him see.

"I am not brave, or smart. I fell into this. But now I have a choice. And being here . . . has meaning." My eyes flickered over the men. None of them were staying to help free others. They could, but they had duties elsewhere. I could return as well. I'd never meant to stay forever.

And Maison had granted me the option. The gift he had given me was priceless, and I could not help fondling the words, immersing myself in the concept. "I have a choice."

Reality dampened my wonder, but only slightly. "Anyway, what could I go back to? An internment camp?"

"They wouldn't—"

"I am still Japanese."

"No," said Maison.

I looked at him quizzically.

"I think we all know who you are. Now."

I went blank. Now what? After all this, what was he—

Oh. Not an accusation. Merciful heavens, it was the farthest, most distant thing in the world. Slowly, slowly I smiled, letting it sprout, letting it flourish, until it blossomed all over my face.

"You understand." I put my free hand on Maison's shoulder and pressed him down. "You see *me*."

I stooped and kissed him once, quickly, chastely. He blinked a couple of times, fast. Shock? Or embarrassment again.

"Remember." I gently withdrew my hand, and signaled the chief.

The chief glanced at Maison for orders, but Maison kept staring at me, so the chief backed the dinghy.

Anders and Brutus waved, Taffin held up his wooden cross, and Durban tossed me a salute. I waved back.

Major Donnerty just watched me.

Maison mouthed silent words. "Six months."

I put my palms together and bowed. The dinghy turned and puttered away. After a while, it reached the sub.

I got back on my favorite boulder as the men went aboard. The chief slashed the boat, the fastest way to get rid of it, and shunted it aside to sink before following the soldiers down the hatch.

Maison was the last one down. He hesitated a long moment. I waved one more time, and Maison closed the hatch.

A few minutes later, the submarine descended.

I bowed my head, and looked back up. It wasn't a group of former POWs floating away out there. It was the future. Rebirth, for them, and redemption, for me. It was life.

The sliver of a rising old moon shone as clear below as above. Ripples from the descending submarine fanned out across the polished surface, widening, shimmering, and fading away. I kissed the fingertips of my right hand, touched my heart and forehead, and held my open palm toward the smooth, empty sea. My mind was quiet. Perhaps now the hermit would invite me for tea.

I climbed off the rock and headed inland, gathering up discarded fishing gear. In the distance, a lone bird chirped, anticipating the dawn.

Part 2: Home Islands

"If you're going through hell, keep going."

- various attributions

Chapter 1

I hummed as I gathered up discarded fishing gear and headed toward my cave. I couldn't help reliving the night, over and over. My men were safely aboard the submarine, and Maison had already expended his torpedoes. The boat's patrol was complete and they were heading home, the last hurdle behind them. I skipped a little, a dance step from my youth. I hadn't danced in years. After an hour and a half, humming morphed into soft, gentle singing.

Strange, what was that popping?

No, not pops. They sounded too deep for that. More like faint, drawn-out echoes of distant booms. Explosions, from the east.

I finished stowing all the rods, lines, and hooks in the abandoned POW cave. The men's catch, one largehead hairtail and four more-normal-looking fish, I'd already scaled and cleaned and left in my own cavern. I would be eating well for a change, even after making the hermit take a couple off my hands.

I went to one of the long vertical crevices in the outer wall of the POW cave, parted the vines, and tried to find the source of the noise. It took a while before I made out the distant blur of a destroyer, what with the glare of an enchanting sunrise. The surface sported baby waves now. A susurrant wind was returning, and the rarity of a glassy surface had passed.

Small eruptions of white burst up behind the ship, a whole string of them. And ten seconds later, another series of tiny roars. Ten seconds, two miles. Rows of short-lived fountains behind a turning, racing destroyer.

Depth charges. They hunted a submarine.

Maison should have been long gone by now. Surely he'd not have hung around taking pictures. There was nothing to see. Or had he, heaven forbid, had he waited to see if I would signal desperately from shore, having changed my mind, wanting to leave? Surely he'd not have done that. Would he?

Depth charges. There would never be two subs cruising the same hunting grounds. The U.S. didn't have enough to use them that way. Not like the Germans.

It had to be Maison. It had to be *Barracuda*. Nothing else could explain the presence of a submarine still lurking in these waters.

I sank to the stone floor and watched the miniature geysers sprout behind the destroyer. They couldn't hit the sub. They just couldn't. A small target, out of sight, and they had to set the charges to the right depth to do any harm. They couldn't possibly find the boat. Except submarines weren't totally quiet, and I'd heard about sonar, listening to things underwater. Did the Japanese have that? How else could they be tracking Maison? How else would they have any idea where he might be?

The attack went on another half hour. Then it stopped, and the ship stopped, and they let down a launch. It went out a short distance from the ship and circled, like it was checking out something.

Debris. It must be. Detritus from a sinking target. The hunt was over. The destroyer had won, and Maison's submarine, all my men . . . .

I sagged forward, trying to focus on blurring grains of sand strewn along the ground. They were lost. Everyone was lost, and it was my fault. Again I had made a wrong decision, and laid another mass of lead upon my soul. If I had gone with Maison, he'd not have idled around the island. He'd have been far away by now, and everyone would have been safe. Instead, my selfish bid for heroism had forced him to linger, to give me a second chance to depart, and everyone on the submarine had paid the price. My soldiers were dead. The crew of the sub. And everything I had worked for these past many months was a waste.

I was a waste. And now I could never be redeemed. No submarine would ever return to the island. For all I knew, Kristy Hara might still be a traitor in the eyes of the FBI. Maison may have lied. Maybe he had come to fetch me home, for trial, if he could trick me into it, and my only vindication was the POWs, who would never see America again.

I curled into a ball on the floor. Tragic failure, that's what Japanese history called it. Their most beloved figures were tragic failures. Never had I considered what it felt like to be one of them.

My chest hurt so much I could not force a breath into my lungs. An hour and a half. Ninety minutes. For so much time, I had been happy. For so much time, I thought I had made a difference. The most glorious moment of my life.

Now it was over. Time had passed, and the world had changed. Again.

~~~~

The sun blazed high to the south before I could move. A vast cavity opened up inside me. There was nothing left. Where once dwelt fear and hope, guilt and honor, self-loathing and love, now resided a great, gaping hollow.

I stumbled from the POW cave and crawled back down the dismal tunnels to my own cavern. Ten months since I ran away from home, ten months of war, and ten months of fooling myself into believing I could accomplish something useful.

Ten months, flushed away in blood.
~~~~

Chapter 2

"Kira Hara, are you in there?" A shout, followed by a mumble. "Foul bitch, how can she live like this?"

I roused, vaguely aware that three days had passed. I'd eaten nothing, and my mouth was dry as the Gobi in summer. Not sick, not physically, but weak. Awake, at least. Why?

"Kira Hara, come out now. I will not soil my uniform by entering that rank cesspit."

Sergeant Sakonju's voice. Rank? Oh, my fish, gutted and left in the open. Mark Twain really didn't like three-day-long guests if this was what he compared them to. I pushed myself to my feet and faltered to the entrance of my cave.

Sakonju backed away at my appearance. "The commandant should see you like this. He'll never miss you."

"Miss me?"

"Gather your things, if you have any. You're leaving the island."

"I, what? Why I leave? To where?"

"No questions. Hurry. Island's too dangerous for civilians now."

Sakonju gave me another disapproving once-over and marched off south. He remained visible longer than I expected.

The trees were shedding. What was it now, mid-October? His steps faded before the last of his cap disappeared. Moldy wet leaves killed sound. Their scent left a bitter taste in my mouth.

Too dangerous, he said. Finding a sub nearby made them want to evacuate civilians? Maybe. Or it could be an excuse, hiding a real reason. No matter. The army made its decisions, and gave its orders, and I must obey. I headed inside to bundle up my few decent clothes, some drawing supplies, and the spare knife the POWs had left behind. A comb I had carved from driftwood, a lump of grainy soap. Oil lamp? Too messy and fire-risky if they were shipping me out. Matches though, take those. Hooks and line, in case I could fish somewhere. Wrap it all in my best blanket. Burn my map, and anything else incriminating. Leave the fish. The aroma would keep them from exploring my cave for a while.

Oh, God, what had the hermit once said? He figured the army would expand the camp and explore the island more thoroughly someday. If they did, they'd find the POW cave. And then they'd track me down, wherever they were sending me now.

I needed to disappear. I had no idea where I was being sent, or why, or for how long, but I'd better come up with a plan.

Uh-huh, that made sense. Make a plan with no information to go on. Brilliant.

Though why I had a single solitary survival instinct left, I couldn't say.

A chill hit as I exited the crevice doorway for the last time. A home, of sorts, it had been. I'd never thought of it that way before, but now I was leaving, it had the vague hold of a thread, snapping behind me.

I shivered. Maybe I should be thankful they were shipping me off. This place might get bitter in winter, not like California.

I climbed down the rough stone entrance and trudged south along the path, through an eerie silence. The proverbial calm before the storm, maybe. Or the sergeant had scared off all the birds, and the temperature had sent the insects to sleep. One nice thing—Sakonju's passage had scoured the trail of spider webs, so I didn't have to pick threads off my nose every few steps like usual.

I peeked in the hermit's cave as I passed. Deserted. He'd left his stone statues, of course, but the tea service in the far corner was gone. If he was that far ahead of me, I'd probably get yelled at for dawdling. I hurried my steps.

And slowed again as I emerged from the forest north of the old woman's hut. Private Terauchi was berating the woman, trying to hurry her along, but refusing to carry any of the three unwieldy bundles the woman had fashioned with twine and old clothes. I was certain my assistance would be unwelcome. Tough. I would help anyway, and damn the consequences. I marched up and slid an arm through the strings on one of the bundles. I hefted it to a shoulder and grabbed a second bundle.

The old woman raised a finger at me, but it wavered. She dropped her hand, snatched the remaining bundle, and stalked south along the beach, toward the gate in the fence leading to the docks.

I followed. Terauchi checked inside the hut, came out empty, and headed north, perhaps on a routine patrol, perhaps to check out my cave and the hermit's. I hoped he choked on the putrid emanations from my own.

The docks were a maelstrom of activity surrounding a single ship, a small freighter unloading crates of various sizes and fifty-kilogram sacks of rice from mainland Korea. The process was complicated by a conglomeration of Japanese civilians jamming the deck, presumably all those removed from the western side of the island, the part blocked off from my side by the prison camp. I looked around for the hermit, but he was nowhere to be seen. No sign of the commandant, either. He had no interest in saying goodbye. I should have felt insulted, or better yet, grateful, but I was too numb. Nothing came through.

"Move it," said a soldier, directing the old woman and me toward a bow gangplank.

I followed the woman onboard. From there, it was all confusion. People jabbered at each other, asking where they were supposed to go. No one had received instructions for berthing spaces, someone claimed there were none and we were just packed topside for a ferry run to Fukuoka. Others disputed that; it was too far to expect us to stand the whole way. Near the far rail, two matrons contended for rights to lean against a binnacle.

The old woman dragged her bundle to a clear spot halfway down the deck and arranged herself on top of it. She pointed, and I stacked the other two bundles beside her. I hesitated, but she waved a stiff finger to the side. Away, away with you. She had never said a word. I took that as gratitude. I'd been expecting abuse. Or worse, more accusations, where everyone could hear.

I circled the deck, fighting through the press of humanity, watching the last of the crates get offloaded. Near the stern I found the hermit leaning on a railing.

"What have you heard?"

He shrugged. "Pretty much anything you can imagine. They are expanding the POW camp. They are cutting down the forest to plant rice; that one is a farce. They are short in the Home Islands because they cannot import from Korea and China, what with the military grabbing all the shipping. Growing more here would be pointless."

"So what's your theory?"

The hermit scanned the crowd. "My theory is you better decide if you are going to keep playing simple, or let people overhear you talking to me. Best you stay away."

That again. He really was going to continue ostracizing me. I thought after he'd given back my medical sketches, he'd forgiven me, and started believing what went on in that POW camp. From what I had been able to understand, overhearing people chatting about the Tokyo newspapers, the press had certainly leaked enough about savagery in China. That is, if you read between the lines of the military commentaries. Extensive 'punishment' of malcontents in Chinese cities. The hermit couldn't still be unaware of what his countrymen did, could he? Then again, he hadn't overheard the confirmation of such tales from POW chatter like I had.

"I have my own theory about why we are returning to Japan."

He did? Ah, maybe he was willing to talk after all. Just wanted me to be careful.

"This island was a haven for dissidents. I believe they want us in a camp where they can ensure we remain isolated, unable to communicate dissatisfaction to others. The war has taken a turn for the worse this year, and dissent must be more tightly controlled."

I nodded. That could be it, although the timing, right after finding the submarine, was suspicious. No children were present, so maybe all were self-exiles like him and the old woman. I had avoided incarceration in the U.S., and now I was headed for it here, if the hermit was right. Great. He twisted away and closed his eyes. To sleep, or pretend to. Either way, a dismissal.

I left my bundle beside him and wandered away, inspecting the ship.

I had a leisurely four hours before the ship got underway. Hurry up and wait, the all-time cliche. At one point I found a way below and located a restroom, wondering if they called them 'heads' like in the U.S. Navy. No, that was an inane thought. They'd not use such an obscure euphemism. Back on deck a bony man asked where I'd gone, and when I tried 'water closet' and 'toilet,' it started a mass exodus. Or stampede. It was going to be rough on older people who had to go more often, if one restroom was all that was available. I headed below at another ladder farther forward in search of more facilities. Later on I found a source of drinking water, which proved even more popular when I passed the word.

I received a few dubious looks, though. I wasn't sitting quietly like the others, awaiting orders. I was wandering around like an independent-minded Westerner. I slipped through a passage to the starboard side of the ship, losing myself among strangers.

Then the ship undocked. We'd not gotten halfway out of the harbor before the boat stank of vomit. Surprising what you never thought of, before it happened. A crewman drafted me to help clean the mess, me being both young and unaffected. I didn't mind. It gave me something to do.

But I didn't understand why he kept looking at my feet.

"Show-off," he muttered. "Wasteful, arrogant rich girl." He was barefoot. All the sailors were, as cold as the deck was.

"What do you mean?"

"Leather." He kept muttering as he went about his business.

Leather? The cast-offs the old woman had given me were considered luxury? What kind of state was Japan in? I returned to the stern and stuffed my shoes deep inside my blanket bundle. Some people watched me. Any kind of activity attracted attention. I sat on the bundle, worried someone might steal them, worried that was an American concern and Japanese were better than that, worried such thoughts were naive. The hermit snored softly beside me. I resolved to stay by my bundle until he awoke. Then I could safely leave it with him.

Hours trickled by. Watery soup was served, and small cups of rice. A short, overweight woman complained, but a sailor said they got the same. It had never occurred to me that my diet on the island would be opulent compared to the homeland. Anyway, I helped again, collecting empty bowls. The young and agile were responsible for civic duties like that.

I hoped everyone would get their sea legs soon, though. Cleanup duty continued.

Being helpful had one minor benefit. A stocky officer opened up enough to tell me the navy had been agitating for a base off the south coast of Korea for refueling short-range patrol boats. With the army already there for protection, it was the logical place to build one. Sighting an enemy submarine forced the issue, and the navy got their way. "And long past time," the ship's mate grumbled. "I've lost enough friends already."

On the second day, after a cold night huddled on deck, the ship made a sharp change in heading and bypassed Fukuoka. Another day we made two course changes, the second negating the first. Someone near the radio room started a rumor we were lost. Someone else called that nonsense, we were avoiding a submarine. After that panic died down came a new rumor, backing up the hermit's fears. We were not being sent to live with relatives for safety. Instead, the government was arguing over where to secrete us. Didn't want us exposed to the public on trains, so ship us to a port near a camp, even if shipping was tight and we were occupying a valuable asset. So the story went.

It didn't matter to me. I might have relatives, but none I knew of for certain, and no idea where to look. My parents had emigrated from near Tokyo in 1923, after the great Kanto earthquake. With a hundred forty thousand dead, I could have few relatives left, except maybe that ship-modeling cousin my mother talked about. If he was real.

The coastline of Japan slipped by, sometimes visible on one side, sometimes the other. We sailed northeast then east by the deck compass, passing between Honshu to the north and Kyushu, then Shikoku to the south, weaving between much smaller islands all the time. A final sharp turn to the north and our destination became clear at last. Kobe.

Not that far from Osaka, where I might have a cousin. Where I might be found out.

Chapter 3

Docking in Kobe took the rest of the morning. Idling in the harbor, pulling up to a pier, and being waved off since it was reserved for an overdue medical transport. Idling some more, and getting shunted off to a quay far to the west. Well past noon by the time all us passengers lined up on deck, clutching our belongings and eyeing a pair of buses surrounded by a half dozen policemen. Incarceration looked more and more likely.

My stomach growled. No sign of a meal on the boat as we were supposed to be off by now. And this late in the day, wherever we were going would expect we'd already been fed. "Typical bureaucracy," the hermit said.

I waited near the hermit as people shuffled down the gangplank, then remembered the old woman. I went forward and found her struggling to drag her burdens. I picked up the two I'd carried before and signaled my intent to follow. She sniffed and headed off the ship, swaying, readjusting to land.

The line of passengers filled the first bus. The rest, including the old woman and hermit, were directed toward the second. "You will work productively and with honor for the greater glory of Japan and the war effort," said the senior policeman, the one with the most decorations on his uniform. "You are not trusted in a munitions plant, but many young people have left farms to join the army or work in factories. You will take their place in the fields and rice paddies."

All right, that was better than a do-nothing camp, better than sitting around bored. I followed the old woman and, when it was our turn, lifted her bundles to the man tying them on the roof of the bus. I kept my own small package and headed for the door.

"Not her," said the old woman, pausing with a foot on the first step. She jabbed a finger in my face. "This one is no honorable dissident, merely a shipwreck victim, washed up on shore." She snarled at the closest officer. "She helped the army on the island. We do not want her."

The policeman hesitated. The hermit said, "She speaks truth. This rash chit of a girl helped the doctor in the POW camp. She has no place with the rest of us."

The policeman took my elbow and pulled me out of line. "They are correct?"

"*Hai*, commandant-sama."

The policeman scratched his cheek. "Hardly a commandant. Take your things. That's all you have? Well, get on into town. Follow that second road there to the hospital. They could use you."

"*Hai, omawari-san.*" Yes, mister policeman. I must be more careful with how I addressed people. Not go overboard.

"Halt." The senior policeman, addressing the other officer. "You do not take the word of dissidents. This girl could be one of them. They could be trying to sneak her out to cause trouble."

He turned to me.

"Who are you? Where did you come from before the island?"

"I Kira." I bowed. "From village Sake."

"Do you take me for a fool?"

I trembled. The old woman had accepted the lie, and distracted the commandant into dropping the issue. But this man? Would he arrest me if he didn't believe me? Try to beat some truth out of me? Once I drew notice like this, it was too late to hope they'd toss me on the bus and let me leave with the rest.

"Where do you claim this place is?"

"On the sea."

"Do not come insubordinate."

"Apologies. A fishing village. I have identification, yes?"

I dug out the card I had been issued so guards would let me enter the POW camp. Not that they didn't all know me by sight soon enough. I concentrated on my hand to keep it from shaking as I passed over the ID.

The senior policeman scowled at the card, but read it.

"All right, that part of your story holds up. But Sake? Are you sure?"

"Oh, yes," I said. "Father go all time, even when net need mending. Nice little tavern in village, he say. Mother complain. 'Your father in Sake again,' she say. 'Always he in Sake.'"

The junior policeman burst out laughing. The senior one stared at me. Through the window on the bus, the hermit shook his head and covered his mouth.

The senior officer raised a hand, but didn't hit me. He may have wondered if he was the butt of a joke. I kept looking innocent, the only defense I had. After locking eyes with me another moment, he dropped his arm and hustled the last of the evacuees onto the bus. Two policemen followed them on, the doors shut, and both buses ground gears as they gathered speed and headed away.

The hermit kept shaking his head at me. The old woman never looked back.

"Well, go on," said the head policeman. He and the others marched off.

I fingered my tiny bundle. Another close call. Others may have thought my story funny, but it didn't feel that way to me. But they'd let me go with no paperwork, no interrogation, no checking to see if I did as I was told. Or no checking for now. I took a few steps toward the hospital, until the police turned a corner and went out of sight.

My feet dragged to a halt. No food, no money. No job, unless I went to the hospital. No place to stay. Just abandoned to make my own way. Was this more cruelty on the part of the old woman?

But why would the hermit treat me so poorly? Perhaps it was not cruelty at all. Perhaps they expected miserable conditions where they were going, being among the very few Japanese who declined to support the war. The rarer the dissent, the harsher the reaction, or so they might fear.

In which case, the woman had done me a favor. A measure of mercy, seconded by the hermit. I couldn't be sure, but I wanted to believe the best in them. Could be another case of wishful thinking, but there it was.

I began walking toward the hospital again, slowly, looking around. People went about their business, sailors and dock workers, what looked like tradesmen with carts, a man operating a crane over on one pier. A few women hurried past, and children swept a street and collected trash in a barrel on wheels. No one paid me the least attention. And no one wore shoes. Wooden clogs or bare feet, despite the weather. No women in dresses or kimonos, either, all instead wearing ugly *monpe*, pantaloons of dull grey, black, or dark blue with matching jackets. I was glad I wore dusky yellow army garb, with my one blouse and skirt well hidden. They'd have been as bad as the shoes, an ostentatious display during the privations of war. It had never occurred to me those gifts from the old woman and the POW camp colonel were so valuable.

It was odd, though, strolling down the street, alone, free, ignored in the land of my nation's enemy.

My enemy. Weren't they? Was I so bereft of feeling I no longer belonged anywhere?

I wandered along the roads, narrower than those in Alameda, crammed with warehouses and shops and signs of domiciles on upper floors. Laundry on lines and an infant fussing near an open window. Open for ventilation? It wasn't very warm.

Interesting variations from home, where no one lived so near the docks. The buildings were wood, not brick or block, most with tin roofs. And congested, the streets filling with pedestrians and bicyclists leaving work at day's end. I'd not been surrounded by so many people since, well, I couldn't recall. I needed to get back that stiffness I'd had on the Korean island, that coldness, if I wanted to fit in. To not get caught.

What to do? Shelter and food, top priority, which meant money, which meant finding work. I had a reason I could not seek relatives for help—they had mostly died in the massive Kanto earthquake, and my immediate family died when a boat sank. I would stick with the shipwreck story, especially since the police had already heard it.

I headed for the hospital. The police might check on me, and if I disappeared right away they might become suspicious. But I'd not stay long. Someday the army would explore my cave back on that island. Someday they would figure out what I had been up to, and send police to arrest me. I no longer had the problem of sneaking away from wherever the dissidents were being sent, but I would have to abandon Kobe and leave no trail behind.

For now, how did one live in a Japanese city, especially in wartime? How was I supposed to fit in? My mother's stories were all nineteen years out of date. From what I had heard, life in Japan had evolved. Industrialization, emigration from farms to cities, and a growing force of puritanism forced on the population by the conservative government that attacked China and the U.S., the Dutch, the British. Even more rural to urban migration with the war effort, the policeman said. Well, I was another immigrant, obviously. Cities must be used to strangers.

I reached the second street and turned inland, climbing a gentle rise past a chandlery, a closed tavern with the door nailed shut, and cheap apartments. In spite of all the people, the town felt subdued, quieter than I remembered Alameda ever being, back in California. And duller, with no more color on buildings than on clothes. Harbor smells, dead fish and oil, faded with distance, helped by a growing off-shore breeze as the land cooled off.

A white building came into view on the right, fancier than others with its tile roof, and with a sign beside the front door. I thought it said hospital. I desperately needed to become more proficient at reading Japanese.

I would ask about getting identification documents. Learn

about salaries and costs. Figure how much money I needed before fleeing Kobe. It would be a process, but I could do this.

Shadows lengthened, my stomach rumbled again, and a chill set in. Time to get moving.

I headed up the steps and opened the hospital door.

Chapter 4

"Don't stand there. Come in and shut the door."

I dodged a hurrying doctor, wove my way between cots filled with injured soldiers, and waited for the nurse who'd spoken to finish with a bandage.

"What's wrong with you? You don't look ill."

I gave the nurse a quick bow. "Woman at front desk say to come help you."

She looked me up and down. "You don't sound like you'd be much help."

"I clean. Carry things. Work hard." I put on a hopeful expression. Sell it, girl. I was harmless. Eager to please.

The nurse moved to another patient and put a hand on his forehead. "Great. A charity case. Where are you from?"

"New in town. Off boat. Army took over my island."

She paused. "Relatives? You have a place to stay?"

"Woman out front say dormitory here, and cafeteria. I can stay if useful, she say."

"I see." The nurse trotted to another bed and yelled for the doctor to come help. "Get out of the way, for now. Go through that door over there. Unpack the baskets and put all the supplies on the right shelves. We'll see how you do."

I bowed, scurried out of the doctor's way for the second time in as many minutes, and went where I'd been directed. I slid the door shut behind me, blocking out almost none of the moans from the wounded.

Shelving lined the walls in the long, narrow room, peppered with bottles and boxes and, overall, way too few supplies for a major medical establishment. The army hospital on the island had been much better stocked. Baskets blocked access to shelves on the right. Most of the baskets had been opened, lids askew and haphazardly stacked. I opened one and removed a package. Syringes, with a label on the side. A name? No, those were numerals. A size. I walked along the shelves, looking for a match.

That would take forever, searching one location at a time. Be smarter. I took the time to walk along the walls, memorizing the layout as to what kind of thing went where. I couldn't read many of the labels. Despite my mother's emphasis on speaking Japanese, she'd spent little time teaching me to read. The forty-eight *hiragana* syllables were easy enough, but the *katakana* forms were harder to remember even though there weren't any more of them. And over two thousand *kanji* derived from Chinese? Children were supposed to be learning those from first grade. So find a schoolbook, then practice reading newspapers until it all flowed as smoothly as English. For now, I would have to rely on pattern matching.

The task was mesmerizing. It took me hours. Once I realized most of the labels were in *hiragana*, that helped. I unpacked one basket after another, piling up the empties, freeing up access to blocked rows and continuing the restocking until everything was finished. People entered the room to grab things and leave, some silently, some with a nod, but no one came to check on me. I finished the last of the supplies and left the baskets in a back corner, uncertain where to deliver them.

Then I looked around. Too many shelves were far too empty. A busy place like this should be refilling constantly, with plenty of margin for error in every type of bandage, medicine, or tool. They should be running their autoclave non-stop to sterilize syringes and scalpels for re-use, but even those seemed in short supply. A list, that's what I could do. Make a list of what they needed most.

No pencils sprang to view. No fountain pens. I found a small brush on a top ledge along with some paper and a bottle of ink. Someone's dusty, forgotten calligraphy materials. That would do. I shook the ink, uncapped it, and set to work, itemizing all the things the hospital was shortest on, the things they should order first. I didn't know half the stuff I was writing down, but I could copy symbols from the shelves for deficient merchandise. Another mind-drugging job, but I didn't care. It was what I needed. People continued to enter and take what they wanted, but I ignored them. When I finished marking down all their requirements in categories of urgent, second priority, and routine, I replaced the ink and brush, blew my paper dry, and opened the door.

"You're still here?"

The nurse from before. Good grief, there was sun streaming in the window.

"You've been here all night?" She pushed me aside and looked in the room. "Well, you're slow, but you seem to have done the trick."

I handed her the paper I'd filled out. "This what you need to order. I mark which you most fast need."

The nurse read through the list, tapped one of the items, and pinched her lip. She glanced at the stockroom, at the list, at me. "Something is wrong with you. No one can be as illiterate as you sound and as competent as you act. And your Tokyo accent is far too sophisticated. What are you playing at?" She folded the paper and handed me a few yen. "Go to the cafeteria. Get something to eat, then find the dormitory. I'll look you up after I check a few things."

The nurse started for the exit, but a doctor summoned her to assist with an urgent batch of war wounded docking at the main harbor.

I hurried out to ask directions to the cafeteria. The nurse was right—I had done too good a job, and made her distrustful. And the speech patterns my mother taught me stood out here? No one reacted to my broken patter back on the island, where soldiers from all over mixed up a dozen different dialects.

Major trouble. One lousy night and I had already blown my cover. I slithered from one mistake to another. If they didn't arrest me soon, for one reason or another, I'd have a nervous breakdown from worrying when they would. I needed a plan. And some food. I was starving.

But I couldn't eat in the hospital. That nurse might put the authorities onto me, or question me, and I could never survive a grilling. A huge yawn racked open my jaw, so wide it popped. I had to leave, now, not work and save up money and act like I was safe. I hurried to the front of the building. A different clerk was manning the desk this morning.

"May I have my bag, please?"

"This junk is yours? I wondered. Hey, where are you going?"

"Nurse is upset. I mess up."

"Nurses are always mad about something. You can work it out. We need the help."

"No, sorry. Cannot stay."

"Ah, come on."

I let the door slam behind me and hurried down the steps. I needed to be gone, lost in the early morning mob, before anyone started a search. If only I could find a place to lie down for a while. Zero prospects for that.

Was it out of character, running off like this? It was so hard, trying to remember every minute to act Japanese, or at least the way I thought they did, outside the military environment. On the island I had the excuse of being simple, not knowing any better when I acted improperly, but I was planning to cast off that persona and had better do things right.

No choice, not this time. Get away now, be it realistic or not.

I forced myself to head inland, turning corners at random, then following a gradually rising road that curved between warehouses and factories. Nowhere near as many mom-and-pop shops as I'd expected. Maybe the war was consolidating production into bigger industries.

Another dozen blocks and I came upon a line of people waiting outside a dining hall, the corner of what had once been a furniture store. I thought the sign said government something, so maybe it was cheap food, subsidized for underpaid workers. I drifted past the front of the building, confirmed my expectation, and got in line. Everyone was polite and silent, still half asleep. Like me. Poor time for reaching decisions, after pulling an all-nighter, but if I sat lost in a crowd and got something hot inside me, that would help.

Sweet potatoes, smashed and soupy. Not rice, not a speck of meat, and the tea was weak. The hermit was right, conditions were worse than pre-war. And this was still early in the conflict. What would happen when America got its ducks in a row? Maybe they were hoping the U.S. would be too busy fighting Nazis and give Japan free rein in the Pacific.

Useless speculation. I had my own problems to ponder.

I collected my food, using up half the yen the nurse had given me, and found a spot at the end of one table next to a wall where I could huddle and avoid being drawn into conversation.

So, this was it. Time to change my name, change my personality, and disappear. Was it really only seven days since my men had been alive, since I had been happy?

Concentrate. I'd thought up a Japanese name once, way back when, to justify using Kira instead. Keiko. Yes, I'd implied that was my birth name. Common enough it would be safe to use. A family name—what would they never expect? What about that one guard who always mistrusted me, who hated me more than any other? Terauchi. Right. So I would be Keiko Terauchi. That should throw any pursuit off the scent.

Huh. My bowl was empty, and newer customers were giving me dirty looks, searching for empty seats. I was still hungry, but on the bright side, that meant I had my appetite back. That was supposed to be healthy. I scrambled up, returned my bowl and cup to the collection bin for washing, and went to the door. No signs of police looking for suspicious characters. I'd probably been overreacting. No one would care about a dirty, disheveled outsider in the hurly-burly of so many others, mostly farmers seeking work in towns. I headed east, into the rising sun, figuring it might be fitting considering where I was.

A mournful whistle split the air. A train. That sound must be universal, one of the few things still uniting the world. And a way to travel. I just needed a destination. Tokyo would be logical, if I wanted to meld in. Seek out other immigrants and become immersed in the herd. Anonymity, that's what I needed. And the natural Japanese reticence to strike up conversations with strangers should work in my favor. I'd work somewhere, contribute to the war effort. Patriotism seemed to be a selling point around here, with all the signs posted by the Imperial Japanese Assistance Association, whatever that was.

I wandered the streets, circling around, listening for more whistles and hubbub. I seemed to be a bit of a standout. Few women wore their hair as long as mine, and my army clothes earned occasional scrutiny. Every so often an older matron, always of sour mien, stood on a corner or in the middle of the street studying women as they passed. They always gave me a once-over, but said nothing. Others weren't so lucky. One passerby was rebuked for wearing her hair in a permanent; Western decadence and disloyalty were the accusations, which the passerby ignored. Another woman was reprimanded for wearing a kimono, the same unpatriotic showing-off as my leather shoes. What strange inhibitions the populace embraced to show their support for the war. Yet nothing was outright illegal, apparently. No one was being harassed by the police, only by those self-appointed matrons.

A couple of hours and several miles later I found the train station. Farther than I was used to walking, but this flat land was easy compared to climbing around.

A schedule was posted outside the station entrance on a neat little board. There weren't many trains. A woman complained about the lack of fuel and civilians being second-rate, but she was quickly shushed by her traveling companion. Her complaints weren't what worried me. It was the prices, most crossed out at least twice and higher ones inked in. Inflation, and pretty bad if it changed so fast they didn't bother with a new sign. And way too expensive for me to even consider.

A man tapped one charge, rubbed the fresh paint on his fingertip, and muttered.

A policeman waved a truncheon. "Move along, get a second job if you can't afford it. Military plants can always use help. Make helmets, make canteens." He waved people off. "Travel is luxury, anyway. Wasteful."

I ducked my head and stayed at the edge of the group as it migrated away. Was I to be forced to stay in Kobe after all? At least until I earned something?

Someone hissed. A man beside me hesitated, then entered an alley on the left. A small, dark form moved out of the shadows and met the man. "I have vegetables today," said the bedraggled youth. "Fresh from the countryside. And a bit of barley. What can you trade?"

The man took out an old-fashioned pocket watch. "What can I get for this?"

The youth scoffed. "Those are common. A bag of beans is all it's worth."

"Throw in some sweet potatoes. They're easy to come by."

"All right. Two."

"Three."

"Done." The man handed over his watch, took his trade, and hurried back out of the alley. He didn't even glance at the policeman a block away.

Interesting. I hadn't thought about the likelihood of a black market. And for food, no less. The army base on the island had always seemed well supplied. But then, it had access to all the produce of Korea across a narrow straight, and the army had precedence for everything. Not so for civilians in the Home Islands, obviously. Even more surprising, illicit trading must be so common, even accepted, that they barely gave a thought to keeping their actions out of sight.

It could work to my advantage. I slipped into the alley and peered at the shadows. "Boy? Seller?"

The youth stuffed the man's watch in a canvas bag. "What you got?"

Yes, what did I have? What should I trade away for train fare? The shoes, for one thing, if leather was hard to come by these days. I couldn't keep them if they made me stand out. Didn't they raise cattle in Japan? So many differences from the U.S. that had never occurred to me.

I moved farther into the alley, set down my blanket-wrapped parcel and unknotted it. I laid out the shoes and the boy snatched them up before I let go.

"They're real, aren't they? Not that 'sea leather' from sharks?"

"Yes." I hoped so. I'd never heard of sea leather.

"Worn tops, a bit warped, and need resoling, but not bad. You want beets? Greens?"

"I need money. For the train."

The boy set the shoes back down. "I don't deal in cash. Too volatile."

My face must have betrayed me.

"Hey, calm down," said the boy. "Where you headed?"

"Um, Tokyo? Maybe?"

"Perfect. I know a guy, he drives a truck. Makes deliveries up and down the coast for an electronics company. Maybe we can do a three-way."

I retied my blanket. I'd keep the blouse and skirt for now, if the shoes were enough to tempt the lad. "You get the shoes, I get a ride, and he gets something?"

"A twenty-kilo bag of rice. I nabbed one the other day and he'll jump at it. Deal?"

Sure. Maybe the shoes were worth more, maybe not. Either way, I couldn't hang around Kobe learning trade rates. "Add in a sweet potato. For me."

He laughed. "You do look a little peckish." He reached behind him, pulled out a tuber smaller than the three he'd given his previous client, and tossed it to me.

I nodded. Good enough. I rubbed off the surface and took a bite.

That must have sealed the deal as far as the youth was concerned. He stashed the shoes, signaled me to follow, and led me through a warren of narrow streets, dirty alleys, and pass-throughs that wouldn't qualify for either. I kept seeing children running errands, carrying packages or sweeping or cleaning up the droppings of pets. Overall, the place seemed quite neat. But why weren't the children in school?

The boy introduced me to his driver friend, consummated his wheeling and dealing, and left me with the tall man. How singular—I would never have considered trusting such an arrangement back in California. Get in a truck with an unknown man and rely on him to do as promised? Unthinkable. Maybe my mother's tales had left a flavor that Japan was safer, or Japanese men more likely to be honorable. True or not, I was doing what I had to.

Although, in some indefinable way, it didn't seem all that important whether I succeeded or not.

I spent the rest of the morning nibbling my potato, watching the man unload one batch of crates, then start loading a different set from another bay in the back of a building. By the time I was done eating I was so bored I hopped off my barrel and helped the man with the larger and more unwieldy burdens. He nodded thanks when we finished, pointed at the passenger door, and climbed into the driver's side.

The truck bounced around worse than a wooden roller coaster. On top of that, it huffed and coughed like an asthmatic elephant. The exhaust pipe leaked, the floorboards had gaps, and fumes swirled through the cab with a combination of burnt flowers and sour seaweed. I opened a window to dilute the cloud.

"Are you sure your engine is okay?"

"It's this gasoline. Made from shale extractions and sardines."

"You're kidding."

"Nope. Serious. Shale and sardines."

That was the extent of our conversation. Hours later, in the middle of the night, after a layover in Nagoya for more loading, we reached Tokyo.

Chapter 5

The driver idled his truck a few blocks from the train station on the west side of Tokyo. "You'd better get out here."

"Yes?"

"What I'm carrying is headed for a navy installation. Doubt you want them checking your papers and making records of you."

"I don't have any papers."

"Damn, kid, where you been hiding? Even whores should have documentation by now."

"I'm not—"

"Yeah, sure. Whatever you say. Get out, or I'll turn you in myself."

I dismounted the truck, dragging my bundle. He was moving before I got the door shut.

And then it hit me. I was here, in the capital of the enemy, in the dark. Only one street lamp in four was lit, the regularity implying an energy-saving measure rather than burned-out bulbs. My initial goal was met. I had disappeared. When the army decided to track me down, they'd never find a nameless black-marketeer and connect a random customer to Kira Hara. Kira was gone, Kristy was gone, and Keiko Terauchi had arrived in Tokyo.

But papers. Documentation. I hadn't thought of what it would mean, lacking that. And the more I saw of this country, the more I realized how little I fit in. How out of date my mother's information was. Not just my weakness at writing, but my ignorance of changing laws and economic shortages and new demands on everyone's time. The truck driver had turned on a radio in his cab after Nagoya, to keep him awake, and listening to political commentaries, rants about patriotism, and war news all the way here had been eye-opening. When I could listen, that is. I slept for part of the trip. Incautious or not, I couldn't help it.

I headed up the street toward the lights, then turned east. The center of town would be that way. A few miles, no more than that. I passed through residential areas, narrow houses of Japanese spruce, *Hakone* mud plaster, and *Karawa* roof tile. Not that I could see them clearly, but I'd read about them. Rice paper walls inside and sliding *shoji* doors. A world as far from my Western home in Alameda as one could get.

Former home. I needed to stop using that word. I'd insisted to Maison that California was still my home, and look where it had gotten me.

Papers. They'd demand some kind of background story. Why in all the world's oceans had I ever thought I could infiltrate Japan, just because my mother came from here? I—

Oh. Oh my god, that was it. That was the realization I needed. Stop trying to blend in. Stop claiming I'd been born here. I'd come from somewhere else, someplace acceptable, non-threatening, but accounting for my being out of touch with the world, for lacking any resources. And, even better, explaining my knowledge of English—it would be tiring and risky to hide that ability for years to come. Obviously my pronunciation was wrong for any colonies held by Britain.

But the Philippines were perfect. A Japanese family could have moved there for business of some kind. Teaching locals a superior way to fish, perhaps. Claiming my mother was long dead felt appropriate. But if we'd lived in the south, excited when the Japanese invaded last December at the north end of the main island, that would explain hiding out in the hills from Philippine guerillas. Filipinos resisting the annexation of their homeland and killing any Japanese they could find. I'd say my father was shot a month ago as we tried to sneak out of the jungle to a Japanese base. I was rescued and sent home by the navy.

Multiple ships, I can't remember the names. A cargo ship to Formosa, a patrol craft on a run to Okinawa, another ship to the naval base at Yokosuka, or was it Yokohama? That truck driver's radio had talked about repatriating refugees, even while others were leaving Japan to colonize captured territories, so I wasn't unique. To finish, a ride up the coast in the back of a truck, arriving in Tokyo last night. An empty truck heading this way, no one saw me. No wonder I was so tired, underfed, and without any verification of what I said. Milk the story for sympathy, but don't overplay the hand. Show how hard I was willing to work, how grateful I was to the military for getting me out. How anxious to fit in.

An added advantage—it gave me an excuse to be depressed. Japanese may not typically stand around on street corners telling jokes, but everyone laughed on occasion. Humor was universal. Bringing myself to fake that would be impossible.

All right, I had a story. It should give me a chance. That was all I could hope for.

When I looked up, the rising sun outlined buildings directly in my path. Slightly southeast it rose. I'd walked into the middle of town, traveling at a goodly pace, and never being accosted or questioned. The advantage of being so distracted I appeared to know what I was doing.

I looked around. Perhaps the sun had been drawing me along before it ever came up. I was in some kind of entertainment district, with boarded-up restaurants and a bar with a sign showing it was now only open from five p.m. till midnight. One kabuki theater, a concert hall advertising performances with only German composers, and a single Italian opera. A sad replica of the glowing nightlife that must once have thrived here. But still upscale. Not the type of neighborhood for an indigent girl. I kept heading into the sun.

A couple of hours later I was surrounded by canals and bridges in the industrial eastern prefecture of Tokyo along the Sumida River. Docks and warehouses and cheap housing for tens of thousands of workers.

And my feet were sore. In fact, they were oozing blood. Not a lot, but they did ache. Barefoot on wooden planks was worse than cast-off shoes on dirt and rocks, at least after several hours. Or not worse, I just had to build up calluses in different places. Maybe I should get some clogs like so many others wore.

Now, time for something unlikely. I was still a spy, even if I lacked resources or the slightest chance to accomplish anything. Think misdirection. What would a spy never do?

How about walk into the nearest police station and ask for help?

I let out a snort. Sure, why not? Either it worked or it didn't. Either my journey ended, or I'd found a way to continue. What kind of alternatives did I have, after all?

I wandered a couple of blocks until I spotted another of those street corner busybodies reproaching overdressed women. This particular matron sniffed at my hair, then reached out and rubbed the sleeve of my jacket.

"Real cloth. Where did you get this?"

I frowned. What else would it be?

"Army issue, right?"

I nodded.

"I thought you looked like a whore, flaunting that long, loose hair. Soldiers aren't supposed to give away their uniforms."

"I am not a whore." Well, I was, but I was not about to admit it to this woman. "These clothes were a gift when they rescued me. Please, where is a police station? I need to find work, and a place to stay."

"Rescued you?"

I fed her the Philippine story, making her draw it out of me. Embarrassment, pain at my father's death, gratitude to the army and navy.

The matron sniffed again. I wasn't sure she was buying it.

Well, it was my first delivery, maybe I needed to polish the tale. It was rare in Japan for a person to have no relatives to lean on in a crisis, so that was a point of doubt right off. The 1923 earthquake was still my best excuse in that regard.

"Check the police stations," the matron said. "They post a listing of apartments. Doubt many are available thanks to the influx of rural workers."

"More people than are leaving for the war?"

"For sure. You should go to a textile factory. Stay in a dormitory for girls."

"Textile factory?" I said. "Because there's not enough real cloth?" What was the woman wearing, then?

She barked a laugh. "There's no cloth to be had because all the textile mills have been converted to munitions plants." She plucked her own *monpe*. "Once you're issued staple fiber like this, don't wash it unless you're desperate. It falls apart after two or three soakings."

"Staple . . . ?"

"Bark and wood pulp. A little cotton or wool to hold it together."

"I see. Why do you recommend an ammunition plant?"

"Good place for someone like you to contribute to the war effort. Now move along. See the police first to get documented, and make sure you check in with your neighborhood association after you get a place to stay."

She pointed down a side street, so I went that way, presuming it would lead to either a factory or a police station. The road curved, following the path of a canal. As soon as I was out of sight I sagged against a wall to rub my feet.

Ammunition. I couldn't spend the next few years making bullets to kill Americans. But the matron implied it would be unpatriotic not to seek a job supporting the military. While at the same time implying that it wasn't proper for girls to work at all. Talk about conflicting advice.

And how could I live in a dormitory with a whole slew of native Japanese girls, with all their modern slang and idioms my mother never taught me? Girls filled with years of government propaganda that I knew nothing about? Girls cradling childhood dreams unlike anything in my experience, and bemoaning the culture change that landed them in a factory?

No, I couldn't go to a textile plant. I needed something else.

I pushed off the wall and winced, looking down. Enough was enough. I knelt, felt around in my bundle, and swore. I hadn't brought my spare blanket. Wait, swearing? That wasn't how I'd been raised. Too much time around the POWs.

It crushed me. Again. All those men, dead. I had to suppress it, I wasn't safe yet. Maybe later I could think about them.

I ripped strips off my one blanket, tearing with more force than necessary, and bound my feet. A struggle to wrap my other possessions in the shrunken blanket, but with my shoes gone, the clothes and other things could be fit in. The matches in their greasy canvas pouch I slid in a pocket. It had always seemed a fire hazard, carrying matches that way, but that's how they sold them, to keep them dry.

The road led me in a half-circle, across a bridge, and back down a gradual slope toward the docks. A single-story police station squatted on a corner where my road crossed a main thoroughfare. All the other buildings were two or three stories, more shops with homes above, or former shops hastily converted into rooming houses. Some businesses were clearly not lasting. Markets and stores with nothing to sell. Small, inefficient workshops, their owners sent off to larger manufactories. With housing at a premium, the transformation made sense. One business was thriving, though. A cobbler, repairing shoes, making them last when replacements were so scarce. Nice that some people got to wear them, police and others higher up the totem pole than I.

I gritted my teeth, went over my cover story one more time, and entered the police station.

The paperwork nearly killed me. Figuratively, anyway. It wasn't like they didn't believe me, not exactly, but officers kept looking at me like they knew that old matron on the street was right. The government was closing the geisha houses and brothels, and driving cheaper whores out of business—a grand morality drive to some, but with so many men off to war, business was undoubtedly slow anyway—and the police ogled me like they knew right where I fit into that equation. But the push was for former prostitutes to enter the economy and do their patriotic duty, so they didn't give me a hard time. They just recorded where I said I'd been, what I claimed I'd done, and rolled their eyes. Then they stamped a series of documents, filed a bunch, and gave me some others. The process took hours. They ate lunch near the end, offering me nothing, and finally pointed toward the door.

"Come back and register your address when you find a place," said one.

I stopped by the bulletin board near the entrance. Sure enough, a few apartments were listed as available, not many, and at prices I had no idea how to judge. Inflated like the train fares, probably. I noted the cheapest after puzzling over some symbols I wasn't sure of, found the address on a wall map, and left.

Success, of a sort. I was official. I had infiltrated the enemy heartland and adopted my new role. A whisper of relief tickled my mind. On the flip side, I had no way to spy, now I was here. My mother's crime, my own crime, would remain unredeemed. Army bases were out of reach, and my days of plotting and scheming, sneaking and tempting fate, were over. I had tried, and failed, and that was the end of it.

An unintended consequence of penetrating the heartland, of course, was finding what it held. Decent people, a trifle wary of my past, but honest and nice, at least to their friends. Facts you didn't want to know about an enemy. People who were the complete opposite of what I'd seen in the POW camp.

The POWs. My men. God, I couldn't pry them out of my mind, and now I'd let my guard down. I'd dared to relax.

It had only been a few days since the submarine sank. It felt like weeks. It felt like hours, and it felt like months. The numbness had worn off, and I wanted it back. Moving, changing, adapting to a new world had kept me distracted, and common sense had tried to bury memories, but anger and misery came crashing back no matter how many times I banished them.

I staggered into an alley and sagged to the ground.

Chapter 6

"Watch it! You almost backed into that forklift."

"Sorry, Hyakutake-san." I struggled with three stacked cases of small-caliber ammunition. The forklift operator cast me a nasty look and steered around.

"And don't lift more than you can handle. Make more trips. We can't afford to lose good workers."

"*Hai.*" Better to be bawled out and thought a good worker than the alternative.

Stevedore, that's what I'd have called it in English. Had yet to hear the Japanese term. Not a bad job. Fresh air and I was getting a lot stronger. Best of all, it let me stay numb. Eat, sleep, and back to the piers. Late November already, and getting cold, but the work kept me warm enough, lading boats headed for the front lines.

I deposited my load on a pallet and stretched my back. All around me were scurrying men and a few other women, a yelling supervisor, trucks coming and going, and a ship's whistle blasting out who-knew-what kind of message. Cranes loomed overhead, sparring with the booms of ships, racing to unload trucks and fill holds. Smoke drifted from exhaust pipes, and sharp corners lurked at every turn, waiting to bite a careless worker. Usually me. No idea what was in the larger crates, but plenty of rice sacks and other small stuff for us to cart around. If you called a twenty-kilo rice sack 'small.'

"Get moving."

"Yes, sir." Mr. Hyakutake glanced at the supervisor. He did that most every time he chastised me. And then I figured it out, as the supervisor struck a blow with his bamboo cane, encouraging another worker to perform better. Hyakutake was protecting me. Keeping me in line before I came to the other man's attention. Next time I walked behind him, crossing to the other side of the pier, I made sure he heard my soft words. "Thank you."

Hyakutake harrumphed. I thought that meant 'you're welcome.'

Numb was fine, for a while, but I couldn't stay this way forever. Getting a reputation as a stable, reliable worker made sense, now I was surfacing and remembering what I was supposed to be doing—surviving, and finding a new way to atone for my mother. For myself. Not through classic spying, for I could not imagine a way to communicate with the outside world. But one thing occurred to me. There was a way to serve, an example set by partisans all through conquered Europe.

Sabotage.

That required total immersion in the Japanese culture, and total acceptance by those around me. That, I was accomplishing, even if it was through an involuntary blur of defeat. Sometimes it became overwhelming. I thought I'd been immersed on the Korean island, but there I could always withdraw into my cave, be alone sometimes, recover my equilibrium. Not here. Not in Tokyo.

I didn't want to hurt anybody. I'd seen enough of pain. How did one commit sabotage in a peaceful manner? Yet another of my contradictory, hopeless thoughts. But after a couple of months of drifting, ideas were filtering though the fog of my depression.

In the first place, stop calling it depression. Or mourning. It was nothing but self-pity. Give it the worst name I could think of and it would be easier to kick. Besides, if I stayed down here, wallowing in the pit, the warmongers in Japan had won. I had to get back into it, find a way to fight.

Easy to say. Hard to figure out. Tiny acts like punching holes in rice bags or dropping a case of ammo off the pier would get me severely punished or fired, and mean nothing crucial. Call it ego. I wanted to find something of substance. Or, more generously, call it practicality—no point taking risks unless the goal was worth it. Where I was now, on the docks, I had no place to start, no matter how much I wanted to.

Harder than I'd have expected, curbing my desire for action. Sooner or later an opportunity would arise. It might even rear up and smack me in the side of the head. I just had to keep my eyes open, my powder dry, and, well, some kind of sports analogy. Was there a Japanese saying for being open to opportunities?

Meanwhile, acknowledge my new situation. A life just as dangerous as on the island, but at a slower pace, whether I liked it or not, and I'd better adjust. More ominous, in some ways. Maybe even more eventful, for sabotage, if successful, might have significant value.

Bottom line, I needed to learn patience.

Chapter 7

The next evening I decided it was time to clean the fluff out of my mind. The fog of the past month. My Swiss-cheese brain had more mice crawling through it than a ship had rats, and those holes had better get plugged. After all, fitting in, proving my reliability, demanded awareness of what was going on around me.

I took one of my sketching papers from beneath the sleeping pallet where I'd hidden them. One thing had been clear the moment I left Kobe. I must abjure drawing if I didn't want to be tracked down. My style was too distinctive.

I sharpened a pencil and skimmed through the past. When I opened my mind, pinholes of crystalline memory pierced the murk.

~~~~

Mr. Hyakutake, he was my first friend on the docks. He helped me find an apartment on the top floor of a building near his family's place.

"Pretty meager," he said.

"It's cheap."

"No window, and rather musty."

"It's cheap."
~~~~

"Well, if you're satisfied."

Not that I was, but I'd live with it. The tin roof was in plain sight; noisy when it rained. All the perks of a prison cell, except I had to go downstairs and out back for toilet facilities. Only a short walk to the piers in the morning, though, along a series of canals and across a pair of bridges. And my salary on the docks was paltry.

I had dinner with his family one time. His wife kept staring at my long hair and giving her husband dirty looks, and a daughter my age imitated the woman. A silent sexual accusation that Mr. Hyakutake ignored, leaving me no choice but to smile pleasantly and try to ingratiate myself. By dinner's end, after I'd complimented every delicious course, Mrs. Hyakutake warmed enough to trade me a spare pair of clogs for my matches. I couldn't tell from the daughter's smirk if she disapproved or if she thought they'd pulled a fast one on me. What were matches worth?

Their ten-year-old son Hideki was a delight, though. A friend in five seconds, a bosom buddy in fifteen, and by the end of the meal I knew I'd have a hanger-on whenever I wanted one.

That was the night of my self-immolation. I sharpened my knife and sawed on my hair till it was as short as everyone else's. I probably received some strange looks the next day, but I didn't recall. I did remember scooping my fallen hair into a ball and thrusting it into a corner of the trunk in my room. Saving it. A reminder. I would burn it someday when I earned a release from my past. If I ever did.

Except for that meal with the Hyakutakes, I ate in government cafeterias at first. Easy enough to get a bowl of thin soup and a biscuit. Restaurants were closed for lack of food and staff, and I had no place to cook yet. I sat as far from others as possible, to avoid overhearing cracks about non-Japanese workers. What they said about Chinese and Koreans, about the indigenous Ainu or even the outcast Burakumin, would make an American redneck blush. Maybe this kind of thing was common all over the world. For all I knew, Eskimos thought they were the bee's knees.

~~~~

I paused in my scribbling memoir and scraped the last bit of rice from the bowl atop my hot plate. I'd traded for it after a few weeks, so I could cook a few things in my room, by the light of an open doorway. Rice and tea, when I hadn't run out. Mashed up sweet potatoes or pumpkins, more often.

~~~~

The most trouble I got into was when I complained about the fifty sen dues to the neighborhood association. Whole families only paid one yen.

"She's a troublemaker," said one woman.

Later that meeting, the woman paid me back for 'wasting their time.'

"Three hundred thirty grams of rice a day means a fourteen kilo sack should last forty-two days. But that is hard to keep track of. This troublemaker is small and female. Two bags every three months will be enough." The other families sided with her and voted to round down my rice ration.

After that not-so-subtle message, I allowed myself to be the odd one out whenever food rations were being distributed, like when the association received thirteen eggs to divide between fourteen households.

Amazing how much power the government gave these neighborhood associations, subject only to the larger community councils. And everyone had to join. I shook my head. Seriously, entire neighborhoods doing things together, like a team? Whether the people liked each other or not? My mother could have told me stories about Japan for a hundred years and I would never have absorbed the true feel of this place.

An egg now and then was one thing, but I fought for the luxuries. "You do not smoke," said my favorite antagonist. "You do not need cigarettes. We will divide up your share."

"They're mine to buy," I said. "To do with as I choose." You bought anything you could at the cheaper government rate, even when they cheated on their own price-fixing and let things inflate. It was far less than what things went for on the black market, and then you had trade goods. I won that argument when a young man supported my claim, even though his wife poked him in the ribs.

Maybe my neighbors didn't believe my Philippine story. Maybe they believed the former-whore rumor. They certainly seemed slow to warm to me.

~~~~

So many memories. Back to the important stuff.

~~~~

"Do you have a schoolbook I could borrow?" I asked Hideki one evening. "I never learned to read very well."

The rascal charged home and back in under a minute. "I'll teach you."

It seemed the highlight of his life, the next few weeks, forcing me to memorize every symbol he knew. Showing off how much smarter he was than a grown-up. Making me read the most boring documents in the universe, the 'Reader for Neighborhood Associations' and 'A Guidebook for Neighborhood Association Meetings.' Yuck. But oh, I sponged them up, if only to get through them faster.

I chuckled. "Grown-up? I'm only eighteen, for goodness sake."

"Nah. You're ancient."

The little scamp.

Sometimes he brought more interesting things. Or disturbing ones. History books, for example. One passage noted how Japan was lauded for its humane treatment of prisoners during the Russo-Japanese war. How could Japan have changed so much from 1905 to 1942?

Mrs. Hyakutake caught her son helping me read early one morning before work. She frowned, then seemed to think better of it, and dug out a copy of 'The Way of Subjects' for me. "It has excellent advice for avoiding individualism, liberalism, utilitarianism, and materialism," she said. "We must all be in touch with our deepest nature and in tune with the wonders of the Shinto sun goddess."

I thanked her. The hermit had warned me long before of the suppression of other religions, a case in point being when a man was jailed for claiming Christ to be superior to the emperor, who everyone knew was a deity himself. I would hardly make that mistake.

~~~~

I lit a new candle from the stub of the old one. I was wasting money, writing in the dark, but it was worth it for the occasional smile.

~~~~

I got stuck with several association duties no one else wanted. I delivered mail, which was the least onerous task, but I also got volunteered as the representative of my neighborhood association to the community council. What little free time I had got sucked into drilling with bamboo spears and learning the ways of a bucket relay for fire fighting, which I then had to pass along to those in the neighborhood at our monthly meetings.

"Remember, we no longer meet on the eighth of every month, Declaration of War Day," said the captain of the neighborhood association. "Now we meet later in the month after the community council session so we can distribute the next batch of rations."

Praying to the imperial palace, singing 'Going to the Sea,' planning patriotic ceremonies—it never ended. More singing, in honor of the national spiritual mobilization program, which was supposed to have ended back in 1940. Group prayer for the dead. Enrolling with the labor board, though women were never actually drafted for war duty. Registering with the Greater Japan Youth Association—yet more assigned tasks—and the guarantee that when I was twenty I must also join the Greater Japan Women's Association.

Whoopee.

One woman mumbled at one of our meetings. "Cleaning and

mail are the government's responsibility. They should lower our taxes."

An old gent leaned near me and said, "She's wasting her time. All they tell us is 'Do your part.'"

Taxes per se weren't the worst of it. They were on the rise, certainly, to support the war, but the kicker was that salaries were fixed. Worse, I was expected to save a significant portion of every paycheck by buying war bonds and savings stamps. I never figured out the difference, but both were rather like being forced to buy savings bonds in the U.S. With inflation gone rampant, a good twenty percent per year, money saved would gradually become money lost, essentially another form of taxation.

No matter. My goal was to fit in. I bought them.

~~~~

I lifted my pencil, felt the tip, and sharpened it with my knife. I'd written so much it was time for another sheet. But things were coming back to me. No major mistakes I could think of. Nothing to worry observers I was a security risk.

I fingered my ration coupons.

~~~~

Rationing didn't work all the time. I was allowed a little fish, but if none was provided to the neighborhood association, or not enough, that was that. And clothes? Well, I was catching up on those, when I could. Drab *monpe* pantaloons and jacket were first priority, and I remembered to not wash them, instead beating them gently when dirt built up.

Morale-building sessions. Don't miss those. Don't stand out.

Use my red stamp to sign off on community notifications like special meetings, blackout requirements, or building bomb shelters.

Oh, goodness. Their idea of a shelter was a hole in the ground. Everyone made their own. But everyone also had outhouses, and the ground wasn't far above the water level in the harbor, in the canals. Did the septic tanks leak? How bad was leakage into the harbor?

I traded away my fishing tackle the day after I heard about this. I'd never want to eat what came out of a canal. Besides, anything I caught would likely have to be turned over to the association anyway, to be shared around among fifty people.

Oh, right, the hooks and lines got me the hot plate. Some old guy I met was less finicky about food than I. And probably willing to hoard his own catch.

Entertainment. For my sort, a few theaters showing government-approved movies. Scattered bars serving 'sake' made from sweet potatoes or acorns. Art was limited to propaganda posters and a few scattered surrealists. Music was mostly restricted to Axis composers—jazz was not only banned, saxophones had been branded 'tools of the enemy.'

"If you sing," said a well-dressed man at one local meeting, "remember the notes of the scale now follow the Japanese syllabary. No more Do, Re, Mi."

I didn't have to worry about singing.

~~~~

I bounced my pencil off the new sheet of paper, already half filled. The most startling thought occurred to me. I found myself feeling sympathy for these people. None of them acted proud of the war, of their military's deeds. They just did as expected. The way most of them talked, the war's impact grew bigger in small enough increments that no one wanted to protest.

But what was I doing, letting empathy weasel into my brain? That wasn't supposed to happen in wartime. Was it?

I started to blow out my candle, then changed my mind. I was drained from the memory-pumping, but there was something I desperately needed more than sleep. Something they did much differently in Japan than America.

I headed down the street to the community baths. Despite all the shortfalls, they did spend fuel to heat the water.
~~~~

Chapter 8

Sort of a catharsis, realizing how much I'd learned since coming to the Home Islands. There was always something new. I read everything I could borrow to hone my reading skills, and realized one day I was skimming. A great sign. My speech had grown as rapid as that of native Japanese back during my time on the island, and I now picked up on idioms from children in the streets. Not many kids had gone inland from this neighborhood yet. Perhaps these people had no relatives to send them to, or weren't worried about Allied bombing. I pried a little, and got funny looks. "We're not separating from our children. Horrid idea. Unless the government makes it mandatory." Odd how my own parents had never given me that tightly-knit impression.

"Get to work."

"Yes, sir." I snatched up a couple more boxes of ammunition.

The supervisor smacked his bamboo cane against his leg, but he hadn't hit me with it. "You shouldn't be here, anyway. Women ought be married, not doing men's work."

I looked up. Right over his head, fluttering in the breeze, a bright orange, fringed ministry banner urged women to contribute to the war effort. All the austerity measures peppering the populace, and the government put fringe on their banners. I said nothing about the supervisor's perfect sense of timing and carted away my load.

I worked, I went home. I practiced air raid drills, and rescued a toddler who'd fallen into a pit dug alongside a sidewalk as a bomb shelter. People planted flowers around their shelters, and the child couldn't resist picking one.

I tried once to make a thousand-stitch belt to send to a soldier on the front lines. Women across Japan were doing this. Not lovers, not relatives, just anonymous women adorning obis for anonymous men, to improve morale. I took so long the head of the Youth Association said, "Never mind. Don't bother again."

I wrote a 'letter of encouragement' to a random front-line soldier, but after I got a vulgar reply I refused to repeat the experience.

I found a woman to trim my hair properly, to even up the mess I'd made of it. I told myself it wasn't vanity, but a necessity to avoid standing out. I almost believed it.

I made friends. Hideki, of course, was already a pal for life. Then I met Miku, a girl near my age, supposedly in training to teach mathematics, who lived on the floor below with her parents. She wasn't in training now, though. She worked on a production line cutting small-diameter pipes into short lengths and threading the ends. Airplane parts, she'd been told.

One day, right out of the blue, she asked me, "Are you menstruating?"

I backed into a chair, pushing to stay upright. "No. Not for months. But I swear I'm not pregnant."

"That's not what I mean. I don't either. A doctor said it's war stress and bad diet. I wondered if he lied."

I sagged in relief. "I thought something was wrong with me."

Miku looked as relieved as I. "Thank the spirits I'm not alone."

"For sure. You think diet could be affecting that woman we never see?"

"You mean the aunt next door? Don't you ask about her. Ever."

"But—"

"I mean it. No one's ever seen her. Everyone knows the family is cheating to get extra rations from the neighborhood association."

"And no one reports them?"

"Who to? The father works for the police."

I swallowed that tidbit. So much for 'honor.'

A few days later, in early December, curiosity drove me near the dock with segregated bands of contract workers imported from the Asian mainland. I'd not been watching long when a Korean laborer dropped a circuit breaker. The Japanese overseer in charge of the group beat the man with a stick while everyone else stood around and watched.

I tried to help. I picked up the ten-pound ship's circuit breaker, checked it over, and held it up.

"Please, sir, it's not broken."

Not one person reacted as I'd expected. The Koreans sneered like I was a simple-minded idiot butting into their business. The overseer barely restrained himself from turning his stick on me. The other Japanese viewed me like an outcast. When the overseer berated me for 'siding with scum,' I knew I'd made a grave mistake. I went back to work, ignoring the sounds of the continued punishment, and being ignored in turn by all the other laborers for the rest of the day. They wouldn't even meet my eyes.

On December 8, 1942, Hideki and Miku kidnapped me for a 'special event.' Every month on the eighth the nation celebrated the start of the Pacific War. I didn't burp on the date anymore. The first time—not the seventh?—oh, right, that International Date Line thing. Anyhow, today, on the one-year anniversary, someone had drawn a ginormous stars-and-stripes flag on *Ginza*, the busiest street in Tokyo. Everyone was flocking down to trample it, and my friends dragged me along.

Ginormous? I had definitely spent too much time around those POWs. At least I could remember them now without collapsing.

It turned out not everyone was doing the flag trampling. Many were shaking their heads at 'such foolishness.' I stood with those people while my friends joined the horde stomping across the pavement.

"Hey, girlfriend," Hideki said. "Why aren't you out here with Miku and me? You some kind of spy?"

"Girlfriend?"

Miku laughed. "No, a spy would jump right in to avoid attention, and never waste time working on the docks."

"Girlfriend? Really?"

Hideki pumped his fist.

It had not occurred to me that my neighbors might worry about my loyalty. No one had said anything about my unusual past. I should have expected paranoia, at least from some. I had done nothing out of the ordinary since my arrival, though, and as Miku said, it seemed enough to allay the concerns of most. At least my friends were enjoying the whole thing, as if the mere concept of duplicity were beyond belief.

The *Ginza* event served to confirm my earlier observation. The vast majority of people were onlookers, dour, doing their part like cogs in society's machine, but not cheering the situation their government had landed them in. Not even on this day of alleged celebration.

Two weeks later, Miku invited me to a different kind of ceremony, the funeral of her uncle. She wanted the support of a friendly face.

"This is Buddhist," I said, when I realized what was happening. "Aren't you Shinto?"

"Yes, but Shinto has no such service. We become Buddhist for the day."

Once again I had shown my ignorance. One of the million details my mother never taught me.

"By the way, you saw that woman with a gold ring?" said Miku.

"Yes."

"Risky. We're supposed to donate all our gold and jewels. They use diamonds in radios, I know that much. If you have anything special you don't want to turn in, better hide it."

"I don't—"

"Don't tell me. Just do it."

On January 1, 1943, I got another revelation. It was the biggest holiday of the year in Japan, and I received permission to watch a parade in Meiji Gaien stadium. Many women in the audience cast aside austerity for the day and wore dresses or kimonos. Even the government joined the New Year's spirit by issuing extra rations, including, wonder of wonders, sugar. Everyone baked up special treats. I didn't bake, myself, and my half cup of raw sugar didn't look too appetizing by itself, but Hideki's mother was more than happy to trade small cakes and some candy for it, which I used to treat the neighborhood children. It made me greatly popular for several days, and it was the first time Mrs. Hyakutake gave me a real smile.

With the new year came a further change. My acceptance by the children, my eager embracement of innumerable duties for the neighborhood association and community council and Youth Association, my continual surprise regarding things everyone else knew—no longer did anyone consider I might have been a prostitute before the war. No local could be so uninformed. My story about growing up in a backwater Philippine village became the only logical answer for my behavior, and I was now an object of amusement to the adults around me. Pleasant amusement; accepting, helpful amusement. My gaffe with the Koreans was forgotten.

People told me tin coins replaced aluminum since the latter was needed for airplanes. Don't eat the whale meat or seal sausages, they were a dreadful mistake by the government. Oh yes, that particular children's song is acceptable even though it is set to the music of Auld Lang Syne, since the tune had been judged 'nearly Japanese.'

Enough details to overload anyone's fuses, to make me wish I'd found a simpler place to live, like that cave on the island. I did try the sausages despite the warning. Talk about a quick way to clean out the digestive system. The perils of not following advice.

One cold spring morning I saw rows of children striding down the street carting heavy metal objects on poles. Stout horizontal branches with cast iron wood stoves suspended in the middle, two kids fore and two kids aft on each pole. On they tramped, singing Setoguchi Tokichi's 'Patriotic March.' I walked along beside them for a while, asking if they had received new stoves to heat their classrooms. The children laughed.

"Oh, no," said one. "These are old. We've not had anything to burn all year. Since we can no longer use them for heat, we are donating them as scrap metal. They will be part of a new destroyer for the navy."

"We also gave away a statue and our temple gong," said another, "since they need copper."

I could think of nothing to say. Clearly, more than one school was involved in the project, since both boys and girls were present. I kept pace a while longer, and noticed one little girl had bare feet, while most of the kids wore wooden clogs. The girl stumbled along, and was so short she had trouble holding up her section of the branch. I took off my own clogs and offered them to her.

The child's eyes grew large, and a boy on the same pole said, "Go ahead." The other three kids took the full weight, which may not have been a change. The girl ducked away, ran over to me, and put on the clogs. She dashed back into position, took up her share of the load, and flashed me a grin. I smiled back and moved to the side of the road, letting the parade pass by. As the tail end reached me an older woman, chaperone or teacher, paused and bowed to me before continuing on.

It made my day.

The only concern came when I turned away. A stern young man in a goatee had apparently witnessed the scene, and stared at me like he didn't know what to make of it. I suppressed a shudder, not knowing why a stranger should affect me like that, and hurried off.

On bare feet. All right, maybe I should have another concern, as well. When could I afford another pair of clogs, and would they be available when I had the ration credits to buy them?

I caught myself humming in my room that evening. For the

first time in six months, I was happy.

The thought sent me into silence. This was wrong, a betrayal of some kind. I had come to like this culture. I had accepted, and been accepted, in a way I never had in California.

Was I being turned? Was this the first step in rejecting the United States? How could I let that happen? How could I forget what Japanese soldiers did, back on that island, back in China?

How could I not be aware, clearly and forever, of what I myself had done?

The human mind was a dangerous thing. It dulled edges and blanketed memories of pain. It disremembered that which should never be forgotten. It failed its owner, time and again.

Night fell. It took me a long time to fall asleep.

Chapter 9

A new crane towered over the main pier where I worked. Shipping rates had grown as summer came. Guns and food and ammunition to replace losses in the Solomons, to beef up defenses on other islands. There was little talk of continued offensives. Officially, Japan had achieved its goals, and merely needed to wait out feeble attempts by the Western powers to recover that which was rightfully part of the Greater East Asia Co-Prosperity Sphere. Peace would come before long. No one I talked to could even conceive of any result other than victory. Japan had never lost a war.

Despite all my hours on the piers, I had yet to find a single way I could interfere. Slow things down, break something, throw gum in the works. Not without my being the obvious culprit. One day I skipped lunch and, when everyone else left to eat, tried to mount the side of the new crane to look around.

I made it halfway. Then I caught sight of an electrician watching me from the top of a pole he was rewiring. So much for no one being around. I gave a little wave and descended.

He met me on the ground when he finished his task. "What do you think you're up to?"

"I was curious," I said. "I've never seen the inside of one of those."

"You'd better hope nothing goes wrong with that thing in the next day or so. You'll be the prime suspect. You know what they do to saboteurs?"

I cowered. "I did nothing. I'm sorry."

"Yeah, well, like I said." He shook his head and loaded gear into his truck.

I chased off to join the other laborers at lunch. What idiocy had I been playing at? I would ruin every chance I might ever have to accomplish something useful if I got arrested when doing nothing at all.

That patience thing I was supposed to pick up? I'd better hurry and learn it faster.

Thankfully, the crane worked fine all week.

Turnover rates among dock workers remained high. Periodically a man received the dreaded red notice, the call-up to military service. A younger man sometimes replaced him, having received the white call-up to industrial service, but overall the workforce continued to shrink even as shipping increased. My calluses got thicker, my legs stronger, and those of us remaining took up the slack.

I joined the Patriotic Marine Transport Group, one of numerous labor groups meant to unite people in a common industry and spread the nationalistic spirit. It included everyone from management to peons as low as I, with lectures and rallies to drum up support for the war and make everyone feel part of a great endeavor. They even organized recreation for off times, and promised rewards of sake or rice for good performance. I never saw anyone getting rewards, and I had a sneaking notion that putting management and labor in the same group was just a way to prevent unions from forming. But I said nothing and went along. It was the thing to do.

I asked about other labor groups, and yes, there was one for artists.

"The Free Artists Association," one worker said. "My cousin is a member. Avant-garde and abstract nonsense, with no value for the war. I expect he'll be called up for military duty any time."

I ducked away and went to the other side of the dock to work, wondering what had possessed me to bring up the forbidden subject of art. Be more careful, damn it.

One day a new group approached the pier next to the one I was working on. The kind of people I had never expected to see again. Americans. Prisoners of war. Uniforms and insignia of army, navy, and in one case a patch with wings. Pilot or paratrooper or, no, I knew of no paratroopers who would have seen combat yet. Air crew, maybe. I thought the Japanese had controlled their groups of Chinese and Korean workers awfully tightly, but it was nothing compared to how they watched these Americans. Long slender chains linked them together, with rifles on all sides. The guards didn't have to shoo people away from the group as they marched them from buses to the pier. Civilians scowled and kept well back on their own.

I had once worried I was being disloyal, yet again the traitor, by even so slight an action as helping load ships with supplies for the front lines. But if it was acceptable to use prisoners for such labor, the same applied to me. I needed work, so much was certain, and until recently had not been able to read well enough to land a clerking job. Besides, one other woman who tried working in an office had been reproved for wanting a 'normal' job in wartime, and sent away, ending up at length in the same place I was. Nice to know there were a few like me who declined to make bullets in a munitions factory and instead chose the rougher outdoor service.

It took a while to set up wire fencing around a section of the pier next door, enclosing the prisoners and several trucks. A couple of guards unchained the men while a crane lowered an empty pallet to the dock, inside the enclosure and next to the transport ship my team had unloaded the day before. When all the preparations were complete, a dock supervisor shouted for the prisoners to unload crates from the trucks and stack them on the pallet, adding instructions about color codes on the crates.

Nothing happened. Good grief, had they not brought an

interpreter? Were all the competent planners with the combat units, not left behind to baby-sit POWs?

I gaped as guards beat some of the prisoners, pointing at the trucks, at the empty pallet. A couple of men tried to lift the pallet, as if they thought they were supposed to put it in the truck. They were knocked to the ground for their effort. The supervisor yelled his orders again, more loudly, which increased comprehension by the POWs not at all.

One prisoner pulled a crate off the truck and dumped it on a pallet. The supervisor nodded. A second prisoner added another crate. It didn't match the color directions, and the supervisor screamed at him. The guards got restless, gripping their rifles more tightly and glaring at their charges. A few fingers slipped inside the trigger guards.

I winced. Things could get ugly. I bowed to my supervisor. "Excuse me, sir, I believe I can help." I ran to the head of the pier and over to the fenced area. A guard swiveled and leveled his rifle at me.

I skidded to a stop, hands to my sides, empty, and called out in English. "They want you to take the crates from the trucks and pile them on the pallet. They're loading the ship. But look at the colors on the sides. They want them in rainbow sequence, purple first."

Someone sucked in a breath. Guards tightened grips on their rifles, prisoners shuffled, and a Japanese officer descended from one truck and stepped toward me. He had a distinctive goatee. The same man who'd seen me give clogs to a little girl.

The supervisor on this pier curled his lip. "Who are you? Is that English? You dare speak the enemy tongue? Where did you learn it?"

So what I'd heard was true. Schools no longer taught English, and anyone knowing it was treated with suspicion. Moronic. Were Americans this bad about Japanese? Did no one comprehend the basic rule of knowing your enemy?

"I'm sorry, sir. I can help," I said in Japanese.

"I should summon the police."

"No, please. I will explain for you." I switched to English. "You, soldiers, sailors, whatever you are. Get to work before they hurt you. They're serious, and they don't like Westerners. Load the pallet. Hurry."

The prisoners hesitated, but an older man with sergeant's stripes bellowed. "Smathers, Green, lead off. Get moving."

"But Sarge, helping Nips?"

"Can it, Wolverson. Manual labor is within the Geneva Convention. Do it."

The prisoners shuffled their way into some kind of organization, then began moving the crates. The sergeant climbed into the back of the truck with one other man, and they shifted boxes to the tailgate as others collected them.

The guards relaxed. The supervisor nodded satisfaction, but still didn't look pleased with me. I bowed to him anyway, and headed back toward my own pier.

"You. Girl."

I turned. "*Hai*?"

It was the army officer with the goatee, every bit as grim as the supervisor. He strode up to me, inspecting me like I was a peculiar bug. I locked my knees to keep them still. Would he call the police after all? I could never survive questioning.

"I've seen you around, haven't I?"

"*Hai*."

"How good is your English? You studied it more than a little?"

I gave him my Philippine story, abbreviated. Yes, I knew English quite well, reading and writing included. It had been necessary to communicate with Filipinos. "I did not mean to be disloyal with such knowledge. I apologize if I offend."

He unsnapped and resnapped his pistol cover a few times, then slapped it. "We have been instructed to report anyone with unusual ability in enemy languages. I do not know why. Don't worry, it was not the security ministry who made the request, not a witch hunt for disloyal elements. The order came from an admiral. You will come with me."

He signaled a guard to open a gap in the fence, took me over to my original pier, and told the supervisor he was taking me away. I didn't hear anything about paying me for what I'd done the past week, which was troubling. Money was tight.

Back we went to the prisoner pier. He had me give some instructions in English to the American sergeant, regarding other tasks they had planned, then told me to wait. He got on a radio and talked to three or four people, before nodding satisfaction and hanging up. By that time the prisoners had finished unloading the first truck and moved on to the second. The officer, who still had not told me his name, commandeered the empty truck, drove it through the fence line, and waved me to get in the passenger seat. Then he paused and studied me.

"You have told the truth? You will be in trouble if you have exaggerated your abilities."

"I have not exaggerated, captain-sama. I know English very well." What I didn't tell him was that my knowledge of modern Japanese remained suspect. I was still learning new Japanese terms resulting from the Government's 1937 anti-English campaign. Words my mother had never taught me. Like replacing the Anglo-derived *poketto* (pocket) with *monoire* ('put things in'), and *parasoru* (parasol) with *yohigasa* (Western style sun umbrella). Hundreds of changes, all silly, and ignored by many private citizens, including the guards back on my POW island. But here in Tokyo, radio stations and government-controlled outlets toed the line.

The policy even tried to make children stop using *mama* and *papa*, but that fell flat. Little Hideki thought it was hilarious.

"You are certain?" the captain said. "Written English and technical terms?"

"*Hai.*"

He growled something under his breath, then added, "Don't call me 'sama.' Makes me feel old. 'San' is good enough." The engine roared to life, and off we went, to God knew where.

Once again, my world was in turmoil. I was back in the thick of military affairs, swept up willy-nilly into who knew what kind of enterprise. How did I manage to do this to myself? I could have sworn it was not on purpose.

Chapter 10

Captain Omori, that was his name. Sentaro Omori, the same name as an admiral in the Imperial Japanese Navy, which seemed to make him proud even though he admitted he was no relation. I drew him out after we'd been driving half an hour through an outlying prefecture to the northeast, watching clouds mass above us.

"I taught art. So yes, I had to live with my parents until I got the promised promotion. Once the war heated up, the government closed such non-essential schools and the army sent me a notice. Now I get to oversee clerical work when I'm not on prisoner duty."

I decided to risk the expected response. "A shame about your academy."

"Short-sited bureaucrats and right-wing idiots." He swerved around a cart in the road. "Bad enough the army bought the election last year. Worse the government allowed the military to add a Pacific war on top of the China war. But the army controls the budget and does most anything they want. Like cutting every speck of culture from the life of Japan."

"Surely there must be something left."

He waived away my comment. "Banning books and music and movies from enemy nations is expected, but our own arts are suffocating from lack of funds and manpower."

I could tell him of my own love of drawing. Did I want to impress him, or try to befriend him? I knew nothing about him. He could be criticizing the government to test me, to see how I responded. So no, say nothing. Besides, I had given up that part of my life to obscure my trail, should anyone come looking for Kira Hara, and it would be foolhardy to lay a single crumb for someone to follow. In fact, I ought to throw my remaining art supplies in the nearest canal instead of hiding them under my pallet. Or use them up practicing all the new *kanji* characters I had learned.

A quiver raced through me when we reached his POW camp. That made no sense. It was nothing like the one on my former island. Tall double fences and guard posts, yes, but probably no medical experiments. The authorities would keep such things far from their civilians, wouldn't they?

The camp was not our real destination, anyway. Omori was returning the truck since he was one of the few qualified drivers, and they needed it for other purposes. He guided me to an old car to continue our journey, which, inefficiently, went back toward the city. Japan may be hurting for fuel, but they were also low on vehicles, Omori explained, and getting the truck back trumped petrol conservation.

Back in the outskirts north of Tokyo he took a side road, and a few minutes later we came to a fenced and lightly-guarded complex, six or seven buildings with navy insignia and other designations I didn't recognize. Omori parked and led me through a checkpoint. I pinned on a visitor's badge, took a seat in an outer office on the ground floor of the middle building, and waited. And waited. It was over an hour before Omori returned, in the company of a somber woman of middling years. I rose and gave a small bow.

She stopped in front of me. "Have you tested her?"

"No," said Omori. "I never picked up English. They stopped teaching it at my school in 1937 as part of the spiritual mobilization."

The woman grunted. "You should have studied it before that.

Or borrowed a text in high school. Too busy painting pictures."

"*Hai*, mother."

I started. Mother? That wasn't said as a term of respect. She must actually be his mother. Could be how he knew she was looking for translators. Or her boss was.

"The captain tells me you have been repatriated from the Philippines."

"*Hai.*"

"You are an orphan with no relatives."

"*Hai.*"

"So you have no need to contact anyone. No phone calls, particularly overseas."

"No." I ought to show respect, but I didn't know the woman's title or occupation to use the appropriate honorific. I could take a chance on the name. "No, Omori-san."

She pursed her lips. "Very well. You will not be given a security clearance. We have been instructed to be on the lookout for spies. Perhaps you have heard of our annual summer espionage awareness events."

"I am not—"

"I do not accuse. The point is that it would be too difficult to verify your story, and will be unnecessary if we put you to work on commercial literature. We have a backlog of technical journals from Britain and America that contain research results and describe projects under development, in areas we have not studied as much ourselves. More are received via neutral countries every month. We need to know what is happening in the world, to best apply it to our own efforts. Can you help us?"

I bit my lip. My mind had glossed over what translating for an admiral during wartime would mean. Helping in weapons development. Even if only on the periphery, it would still be of military value.

"I would like to say you have no choice. We need you, so you should help. But we have not been authorized to conscript women into the labor force like other countries. Very short-sighted. We register women but cannot call them up." Mrs. Omori made a disparaging sound.

Okay, military work, but on the other hand I would not be helping with anything specific. Journals were public information, published and given to the world. And maybe I could learn something of value, something to aid that goal of throwing a wrench in the works. Besides, refusing to help might raise questions.

"I would be honored to be of service." I bowed.

"Good. That's settled, then. Come with me."

I barely had time to bid the captain farewell.

"I hope to see you again," he said, bowing smartly. "Perhaps, er . . ."

"Yes?"

"Perhaps in a social setting?"

His mother made another rude sound. "Do you not have something to do?"

I flashed the captain a smile. I meant it as sympathy for her tactlessness, but the way his face lit up, I was afraid I'd accidentally agreed to a date of some kind. Heavens, I wasn't ready for that. No matter how much I was trying to fit in, no matter how long I had been in this country, healing from my prior failures, and actually making friends, I was definitely not interested in getting close to someone. Especially someone in the army.

Was I?

~~~~

One building over, one flight up, and two halls later, Mrs. Omori plunked me at a table in the corner of a small room, an office shared by two other young women. They were probably older than me, but they looked so young and guileless it made me feel aged. They nodded and continued reading magazines, one French and one Russian, making notes on small tablets.

"Wait here," said Mrs. Omori. Within ten minutes three silent clerks had entered and dumped, in succession, a fifteen-inch pile of American mechanical engineering journals, a British magazine about nuclear physics, and a Japanese typewriter—a monstrosity
~~~~

with a flat bed full of tiles with Japanese characters and a horizontal cylinder that held a piece of paper. The strangest thing I ever saw. No, that wasn't fair. Just because it didn't match what I was used to didn't make it weird. One clerk gave me a quick lesson, and I watched the contraption in awe. The drum with the paper rolled left and right, up and down over the bed of tiles, while an arm picked up the appropriate slug, stamped the paper, and returned the tile to its place.

"You'll get the hang of it," she said. "Just practice."

Mrs. Omori stopped by as I picked up the top journal and thumbed to an article.

"Do not try to expand or censor or explain. Do not pick what you think looks interesting. You do not know enough to make such decisions. Translate every article. Ignore advertisements and editorials."

I nodded understanding.

She paused at the door on her way out. I had thought she looked stern before, but now her face grew harder.

"Do not make the mistake of thinking yourself a suitable match for my son." And off she went.

How very intriguing. Nothing had brought home to me how much the war was changing all of society until I heard that simple statement. Women in the workplace, with rising independence and self-confidence, and men seeing them in such an environment. Men considering their own choices in meeting women, rather than accepting parental direction. And mothers resenting the loss of control, deeply perturbed about children making their own decisions, by definition the wrong ones without the guiding hand of their elders.

No, Mrs. Omori was not so much rigid as worried. Her world was crumbling and being rebuilt. Was that my true role in infiltrating Japan? To undermine not the military, but the social structure, and accelerate an evolution already underway?

It made me sad. Metamorphosis was painful, however beneficial the result.

In any event, why would I want to be a suitable match for the captain? His mother was right, I really would be a bad choice, what with my fisherman-father background, lack of money, and lack of education. For my own part, I didn't know him. He was the enemy. I was too young. I didn't deserve the kind of happiness a relationship would imply. And he had that stupid goatee, even if it did sit below a very nice smile.

I caught my breath. What did smiles have to do with it? He was the enemy.

Chapter 11

A new pattern grew to define my life. Every morning except the tenth, twentieth, and last of each month—the only days off in the government's new work schedule—I rose early and caught a gasoline-powered railcar six blocks from my apartment. It looked like a tram without wires. A bumpy ride of over forty minutes, or longer in bad weather, thanks to having only one line for both north and south traffic. There used to be another line, I heard, but spare tracks were taken up for the steel.

The railcar dumped me out a short walk from the research complex. I lined up at the gate, passed inspection, and headed over to my assigned space.

In a way, adjusting to a ten-day work week was one of the most disorienting changes in my life. While days in Japan were named in a seven-day cycle, no longer would I have a Sunday rest day. The reduction in time off was spreading, I was told, and would reach the docks before long. Partly another ministry rejection of Western influence, partly a necessity for more labor. But I was used to keeping track of things by day of the week, not number, and my days off kept shifting around.

My work went faster after the first few days, after I became proficient with the unexpected style of typewriter. Many Japanese characters were like a shorthand, so I could pound out meaningful sentences about as fast as with a Western typewriter back in high school.

Oh goodness, how long had it been since I thought of high school? Or California and Maxine and Rosita? Or the hermit, for that matter? I missed them.

God help me, I missed Sergeant Anders. And the Australian, Durban. Brutus, especially. Even the ones who despised me. At least then I had been trying. Doing something I thought would be useful. Not simply existing, frittering along day by day without a goal, without a purpose to my existence. Scoring coups was not the issue. Surely it couldn't be, since I had achieved nothing that resembled one. It was the striving, the attempt to make something useful of my life, that counted. Wasn't that what one of these Eastern religions taught?

Never mind. All that was past. Only the present mattered.

A long time passed, and Sentaro Omori didn't come around. He was undoubtedly as busy as everyone else, and I had no idea what kind of 'social setting' he would want to see me in. Restaurants were closed, and I had nothing to wear to any of the remaining evening entertainments. I'd managed to snag some underwear back when I traded away my army outfit, which was nice to have again, but nothing in the way of ladies' apparel was affordable by trade or purchase. I'd had a couple of dresses back home in Alameda, but . . . .

Since when did I think about finery?

More to the point, did I even want to see Sentaro? He could be a good source of information about army affairs, except I wasn't in the market for that anymore. I could not afford to get to know him, since that would mean letting him get to know me, and my cover story was too thin for that. So I really shouldn't see him at all, even if the occasion presented itself. No need for deceit, no need to feel dirty for misleading him about who I was, if I avoided the issue altogether. I could even blame it on being intimidated by his mother, if the subject ever arose. If I ever saw him again.

Why didn't he even try to come see me again?

His mother did. Mrs. Omori checked up on me pretty often at first, but as my documents gained kudos from the technical community, that tapered off.

I submerged myself in the work. I read, I translated, I typed. It was an old style typewriter they'd given me, printing characters from right to left, and a couple of the younger engineers complained my work was not in accordance with the new official guidance to print from left to right. But even newspapers printed headlines right to left half the time, mixing directions on the same page, and the older personnel preferred right to left, and it wasn't like I had any choice with the equipment they'd given me. The complaints stopped after a while.

The funny thing was, signs were often printed vertically. Who ever heard of a language you could write in any old direction you felt like? Then I remembered vertical signs in English, like for hotels. Odd how you never noticed something in your own world, yet it stood out in another.

I absorbed swatches of the material as the English passed through my eyes and the Japanese came out my fingers. The process grew automatic, yet astonishing tidbits glued themselves to my mind. Fluid dynamics and stress analysis, metallurgy and aerodynamic drag. Coefficients of one kind or another, and something called a Reynolds Number. Laminar versus turbulent flow, like smoke rising off the tip of a cigarette—smooth and straight at first, then speeding up and switching over to swirling turbulence. Fascinating material the more it sank in, the more I understood. I got permission to take a university text home to study on my own time, to better understand what I was translating, on the grounds that it could help me do a more accurate job. They bought my reasoning, though the truth was my desire to learn.

The nuclear physics was beyond me, but they stopped giving me that sort of material after a couple of months. A lieutenant dropped a hint that they were no longer working on any projects that needed it. Too expensive.

That kind of slip made me think security was lax. Possibly

everyone else had clearances and they forgot I'd not been given one. Researchers gossiped over lunch, and extolled the virtues of one development project over another while sitting at the same tables as me and my fellow *hon'yakusha*. I had never had a title before, but they called people by their job names in Japan, and mine meant 'translator.' Kind of fun. I tried to imagine people in America saying 'hello, miss teacher person,' or 'good day, mister auto mechanic,' and chuckled. A good idea that would never go over in the States.

Speaking of ideas . . . one began to percolate. What I was translating was engineering research. Structural issues. In some cases, metallurgy, tests with new combinations of elements, alloys of steel that included an amalgamation of different things mixed in. Nickel or copper, molybdenum or tungsten. You name it. Couple that with lax security, and what did you get?

Opportunity.

The point was, I didn't think they had enough translators to do everything twice and compare results. That would require an enormous commitment of scarce resources. So there were things I could do, if I doctored my translations in a most careful fashion. Things that could result in delays or dead-ends in Japan's weapons development. Microscopic things, 'accidental' mistranslations so the non-optimal alloy was chosen, and it wasn't as strong, or was less corrosion-resistant. Military hardware that wore out faster than it ought to, accelerated under the humid conditions in the South Pacific.

Problems need not be large. Bacteria was microscopic too. My interference need not be decisive. Anything that contributed to extra expense, to sub-optimal performance, was a benefit to Japan's enemies. After all, remember the bit about nails, horseshoes, horses, and lost battles.

I finally had my plan. Rust could rule the day. For now. Later, perhaps, I might find bigger chances.

Sabotage.

Chapter 12

My evenings were filled. Drilling with bamboo spears continued, or night-time fire patrols, or fire drills with sand buckets and water and ladders, for the Allied bombing they expected someday. On my days off I took my turn preparing community notice boards or any other service I was assigned.

In October I served as my neighborhood's representative witnessing a parade in Meiji Stadium. One hundred thirty thousand university students, virtually every young man not in the sciences or engineering, had been called up for war. Thousands were here, marching along and chanting, "Naturally we don't expect to return alive." At least it was solemn. I didn't think I could have taken it if they acted happy.

Rations were reduced again, and the government remained more concerned with providing sustainable calorie levels than assuring adequate dietary supplements. An old man who considered it dishonorable to use the black market grew sick from a vitamin shortage, and his daughter lied about her source of vegetables to get him to eat. Japan did have good mandarin orange crops, and some people found dandelions, which helped. I traded for the greens; kind of bitter, but I couldn't afford to get malnourished.

Then the rice allotment went back up a little, at the expense of the sweet potatoes. They'd converted golf courses and parks to rice paddies to increase production, and they diluted the rice with other grains to extend the supply. But the air force had learned they could ferment sweet potatoes to make aviation fuel, and that was key. Fine with me; I preferred rice.

I took Hideki to the zoo one off-day afternoon. I hadn't seen him in a while and wanted to be sure his family was okay. When we reached the entrance, the gates stood open and no other visitors were in sight.

"What's going on?" I asked.

"Something's wrong." Hideki led me toward the large-cat exhibit.

The only sound was a hum, growing louder and louder, transforming into a roaring buzz as we entered the building. A mound of flies swarmed in the shape of three dead lions. I grabbed Hideki's hand and hauled him back outside.

"The monkeys," said Hideki. "Check the monkeys."

"Wait, we probably shouldn't—"

Hideki pulled free and took off. I followed him past carcasses of giraffes, piles of dead birds in a giant cage, alligator corpses stacked beside a truck from a leatherworking shop. The aquarium section was empty. We didn't see another human until we found a couple of men butchering a cape buffalo alongside the slaughtered remains of gazelles and an ibex.

One of the men saw us and straightened up. "What are you doing here? Didn't you see the sign?"

"Sign?" I said.

"Huh. That storm this morning must have knocked it down. Well, the zoo is closed."

Hideki started crying louder.

I put a hand over his eyes. "Why are you doing this?"

"Ministry orders," said the other man. "These things could escape when bombing starts."

"Waste of food keeping them alive, anyway," said the first man. "Frivolous waste of manpower, for that matter."

I spent the evening trying to console Hideki. "You saw the bullet holes. At least the poor things didn't suffer."

"They could have sent them somewhere else."

"Not really. No city is certain to be safe. And they can hardly spare the effort to build a new facility in a rural area."

Nothing I said made Hideki feel any better. I could tell, because nothing I said made me feel any better, either.

~~~~

Despite my intentions, I ended up washing my *monpe* one time too many, and had to buy new at the December neighborhood association meeting.

"Hey, these are short-sleeved."

"That's all we have. Saves cloth."

"But it's winter."

"So buy a coat. You got an extra fifty points on your ticket allowance?"

"Out of one hundred total? No. I couldn't afford it, anyway."

"Just as well. The association didn't actually receive any this month. But here, have a sunflower."

"You're kidding."

"Not at all. The government is handing them out to improve morale."

~~~~

An island called Tarawa fell in the Pacific. New Years 1944 drew smaller celebratory ration supplements than the year before. I got no sugar. The last trace of heat disappeared from the building where I worked. The government blamed the shortages on the U.S., blasting them for having no honor, using their growing submarine force to sink merchant shipping instead of daring to attack warships. Never mind it was exactly what Germany had been doing with their U-boats for years. Mrs. Omori overheard me commenting about the inconsistency to a fellow translator.

"You pay too much attention to war news," she said. "It is not seemly for a girl your age. Leave such things to your elders."

"But—"

"And it is not your place to criticize the government."

Ouch. She had me there. The other translator shrank down in her seat, trying to avoid Omori's ire.

"*Hai*, Omori-san." I would certainly watch my tongue. But I couldn't help lapping up every drop of news I could find. My one connection to the outside world, and a lifeline to sanity.

An island called Kwajalein fell. American planes kept finding airfields closer to Japan. The government had repealed the twelve-hour work day limit in late 1943, and the national average climbed to eleven hours. I fit right in.

In February, I participated in a new registration of unmarried women for war duty, the Women's Volunteer Labor Corps. At the same time they pressured women to 'do their part,' they also told us to get married so we would be exempt. Insanity. Still no outright drafting of women, and when I described what I already did, the bureaucrats rushed me through the process so I could return to work.

And so I existed, lost in a haze of duty. Duty to the enemy, to people I liked more and more every day. People who succeeded in making me, God forgive me, laugh once in a while.

Work in the research complex came to a complete stop one day. I had always thought the second building over to the east was noisier than any of the others. By a lot. I heard it had wind tunnels for testing propellers and wing shapes, and a model basin for evaluating ship hulls. They were always pumping around air and water. But today came a different kind of sound that dwarfed the noisy building.

It was time to test new armor alloys for battleships, it turned out, and they were using a sixteen-foot-long rifled barrel to fire eighteen-inch diameter shells point-blank at two-meter squares of thick plate mounted in stands. Stands that could stop a freight train, they claimed. A blast, a crane lifting a new target into place, and another blast. Truly impressive, so long as I stayed well back and stuck my fingers in my ears. It rapidly became clear why there was a long, thin field of grain beyond the test stands. It was for the debris. Too bad they had to run their tests just now, though. It would have made more sense to harvest the grain first.

Didn't the neighbors complain about the din? It went on for hours. Fortunately, that was the only time they tested armor.

I saw the head of the facility once, but didn't get to meet him. Admiral Tokiyasu was said to have a larger budget than anyone, and ties to a Nazi wonder weapon. It sounded like hyperbole. A different admiral had a project I thought was amazing, though, in a scary way. A German 'milk-cow' had docked in Tokyo recently, not far from where I lived, and I ogled the enormous submarine on my off day. It wasn't used for combat. It carried spare fuel, ammunition, and torpedoes, and sailed around refueling armed merchant cruisers and normal-sized attack submarines.

When I admired the boat at lunch the following day, a bespectacled ship designer at the next table laughed. "If you think that's big, wait till you see what we've got planned. A submarine big enough to carry small aircraft. We're going to bomb the Panama Canal and disrupt America's naval flexibility."

I acted suitably awed. More hyperbole? Or real? That would be terrible, but there was nothing I could do about it.

That afternoon Mrs. Omori burst into my office. "Do you know German, also? The engineers like your work. I hope they're telling the truth, not merely flirting with you."

"*Hai*, Omori-san, I have also Deutsch." A speckling from junior high school, grammar and a limited vocabulary, but I'd not admit how little. Nazi information could be most interesting.

"Good. You will be transferred to Admiral Tokiyasu's personal sub-group. This is a great honor, and you had best reflect it." The Nazi 'milk-cow' had dropped off top-secret plans for a German invention, along with numerous publications and piles of supporting documentation, she explained. "You can forget about going home for supper. Your work hours are extended to thirteen hours a day, fourteen if you can handle it, and you will eat in the complex cafeteria." The admiral would take the German reports, enhance them, and develop his own project that would win the war. She sounded as proud as if the man were her own son.

Mrs. Omori didn't exactly imply the war could be lost without the admiral's new toy. Not one single person in Japan showed doubt about victory. But casualties were mounting, a negotiated peace seemed years away, and anything to accelerate the end would be a blessing.

So, learning German, after claiming I already knew it. Fast. Technical material, not the simple stuff. And not to speak, only to read. No instructor required, just the right kind of books. I headed over to the small complex library, but couldn't find what I needed. So I obtained permission to go off-base and took a bus to the nearest library.

Closed for lack of staff, said a sign on the locked doors. I asked around, but no one knew where to go to get a key and gain admission.

Back onto a different bus and south into town, to the Tokyo Imperial University. It was the first time I had had an excuse to visit one of the sites devastated by the Kanto earthquake, near where my parents had come from. I had lost so many relatives in that disaster. It wasn't just a story, my parents had barely survived.

I stood on the steps of the library, scanning the streets, trying and failing to picture what total destruction looked like. One hundred forty thousand people dead in that one natural disaster. Eerie to think how easily I might never have existed in the first place. How everything I had done might never have come to pass. And really, would it have made any difference, in the long run? Prisoners died, submarines sank. Maybe I wasn't to blame.

I couldn't get one single brain cell to buy into that logic.

I climbed the last three steps and entered the building, then wasted an hour and a half while a librarian and university administrator argued on the phone with someone back at the research complex, before they granted me access to the stacks. It took another call and another wait to allow me to check out basic German language texts when I found them, and have the university agree to transfer a pair of German-Japanese and Japanese-German dictionaries to the complex library.

I was getting used to dealing with bureaucrats. I'd expected it to take longer. I enjoyed the time by roaming through a glorious collection of Chinese and Indian art books and perusing a history of the local area.

Now, back to the complex, to study what I'd found and dig into the pile of new material. What would come to light from that Pandora's Box?

Chapter 13

I returned home that night to chaos. Every person in my apartment building was frantically packing, singing out to each other to gather up this or that, moaning about needing more time.

More time for what? What in heaven's name was going on?

Hideki popped out of the shadows and grabbed my hand. "Where have you been? You have to leave tomorrow."

"Why? Where are you going?"

"Not me, you. Everyone on this side of the street. They're tearing down your building."

"What?" I tried to disregard crying children and hear what the adults were saying. What to take, how to carry it. A call from one of the few public phones to a relative with a handcart. A shout not to forget a grandmother's good-luck scroll hanging on the wall.

"It's for a firebreak. They finished razing a line of buildings along the east of the naval warehouses, and moved on to this row of apartments on the north side."

"The government is doing this?"

"Of course. Have to protect industries and military bases." Hideki ran off at his father's call.

If the government was doing this, why was there not more advance notice? I trotted after Hideki and caught up with his father. “Hyakutake-san, are you being evicted as well?”

“Hello, haven’t seen you in a while. My family is lucky. The fire line just missed us.” He seemed in a hurry to get back home. Embarrassed at the others’ distress, perhaps.

“Where will everyone live? Apartments were tight before. What will become of the neighborhood association?”

“They will designate new neighborhood boundaries. As for housing, I cannot say.”

I was right. He didn’t like talking about it.

“If you are just starting to look, you are out of luck. Any openings nearby will be taken by now.”

People darted past me, bundles on their backs. “Isn’t the government helping?”

“No. When firebreaks are put in, the policy states it is the patriotic duty of the displaced to find their own new housing.”

“But—”

“I am sorry. I must go.”

He gripped Hideki’s hand and disappeared into the throng. A narrow two-wheeled cart rolled up the street pulled by a middle-aged couple, using bars off the front like it was intended for a burro. It stopped next door and people loaded furniture and bundles of linen, piling it high and looping ropes over the top.

I fought my way inside and up to my room. If we were being kicked out tomorrow, why such a hurry to get out tonight? It was late, I was exhausted from running around all day and working extra hours, and I had forgotten to eat.

I lay on my pallet and tried to read the one German primer I’d brought home. Shocking how much I’d forgotten, never using it. Not that I knew that much to begin with, I realized, thumbing through the index of the book. My candle stub sputtered and went out, so I lay the book aside and tried to sleep. The pounding of steps and the confused yelling continued below me, but I managed to tune it out.

~~~~

Thunder woke me the next morning. Crackling, crashing, and
~~~~

again the booming. I yanked on my *monpe* and raced down a flight to peer out a window. A bulldozer rammed into the building beside mine. Timbers cracked and the frame collapsed in a shower of dust. God, I had to get out. Now. I dashed back upstairs, stretched out my blanket atop the pallet, and piled my possessions in the middle. I hesitated, then even threw in the wadded ball of hair I had once hacked off. A souvenir.

Pounding came on my door. "Is anyone in there? The building should be clear."

"I'm coming."

The doorframe splintered and a boot poked through, followed by a curse.

"I said I'm coming." I unlatched the door and slid it open. A policeman stomped splinters off his boot. I stared at the uniform. Police. Angry. The one thing Hideki told me to avoid at all costs. You could never tell how they would react. "I apologize, sir. Honest. I didn't mean, I'll hurry, I'll . . . ."

"Get moving, girl."

I dove onto the pallet and tied up everything in the blanket. I never had gotten around to buying a suitcase. "I'm sorry. I thought we had until today. Please don't—"

Don't arrest me? Like asking would matter, if that's what he intended.

"You didn't see everyone leaving yesterday? You didn't read all the notices we have been posting?"

"My fault, sir. No excuse. I have been working so much it is too dark to read signs when I get home." I stuffed the bundle under one arm and snatched up my hotplate. "I should have tried harder."

The man made a disgusted sound and herded me down the steps and outside. Residents from across the street, in the safe zone, had come out in the early dawn light to watch the demolition.

"Relax, girl." The policeman gave me a polite smile, now we were safe. "A waste of wood, but we can burn the debris. Not enough manpower to deconstruct slowly and save the good material." He moved off, shooing children further back.

Oh. He was making sure buildings were empty, protecting the public. That's why he acted mad. He was worried.

My heart beat like all the snare drums in the band. I willed it to settle down.

Another pair of walls collapsed. I hugged my blanket-wrapped bundle, found a better grip on the hotplate, and walked east to see the finished firebreak. A block-wide swath of nothing, intended to minimize the damage when the U.S. began bombing them. America had already launched a 'nuisance raid' of a few planes shortly after the war began, off an aircraft carrier, but with the progress made in island-hopping across the Pacific, the ministries were looking ahead to the day Japan itself would be within range of land-based enemy air power. A rather defeatist precaution for a nation expecting to win, wasn't it? Nevertheless, probably good planning.

I could not imagine America ever gobbling up long stretches of much-needed resources like this. Of course, bricks and concrete and I-beams wouldn't burn as readily as the wooden architecture here, so maybe firebreaks wouldn't be as necessary, should the U.S. face heavy bombing.

It was still early, but I plodded the six blocks over to the railcar stop. May as well go to work. I had no idea where to look for a new place to live. I didn't want to leave the area despite the long commute, and despite my much higher salary at the research complex. I had friends here, or friendly acquaintances, and they didn't probe into my past. I knew the local black market, and where to inquire without arousing suspicion when unfamiliar with a custom or tradition. Risky and a waste of effort to acclimate myself in a different part of town. I would tell them at work what had happened, and ask for time off to find a place. They would be sympathetic.

Ten minutes after reaching my assigned space at the complex, I learned the fallacy of that notion.

"I told you you were being transferred. You no longer sit here," said Mrs. Omori. "Follow me."

The German literature was key, and urgent, and high priority. Omori-san had a whole string of synonyms she flung at me, to impress me with the importance of my assignment. If I had no place to live I could sleep on the floor of my office until I found a place. Which I could do on my own time. Of which I should have none, since I should donate my days off to the project. The diatribe continued until Omori deposited me in what was clearly my very own cubby-hole, a converted broom closet with a table, typewriter, and lamp. And a very uncomfortable-looking chair. To keep me awake.

I sat down to study. Eight more days until a day off, when I could look for a place to stay other than on the floor. At least I had a door to shut for privacy, and a lavatory down the hall. Not likely there would be an opportunity for a bath or laundry, though.

So it made perfect sense when, six days later, Sentaro Omori waylaid me on the way to the cafeteria for supper. Naturally, he would pick that time to pay a social call.

I ran fingers through my hair, trying to comb it out, and rubbed an inky finger on my *monpe*. The typewriter got messy sometimes. Sentaro gushed his greetings, so happy to see me again, and see I was well.

"You have been busy yourself, I am certain," I said. It had been months, after all.

Sentaro looked taken aback. "You have not received any of the messages I requested my mother pass along?"

It was my turn to blink. "Would I be insulting her if I said no?"

He let out a breath. "I swear she will never stop trying to run my life. Do you know, since I met you, she has sent me four times on errands so I could 'accidentally' run into some girl of her choosing. Four different girls. And not one of them with more on her mind than fulfilling the exhortations of Katsuko, the prime minister's wife: 'Having babies is fun!'"

I blushed. Talking about making babies. Had he no shame? Though if Tojo's wife had encouraged such talk, maybe it had become socially acceptable.

Sentaro warmed to his subject as we waited in line for our

food. He found the whole thing so amusing I couldn't resist grinning along with him.

"Step one, convince the world Japan is so crowded we need living space, hence the invasions of Manchuria and China. Step two, Japan owns so much land we are short-handed, so establish a marriage improvement movement ('motherhood is the national destiny') and a fertility campaign. Step three, outlaw birth control. Step four, make certain all military units are well supplied with condoms. No, no; no one sees anything antithetical in this."

I blushed again, and Sentaro seemed to realize discussing condoms was going too far.

"Anyway, did you know they even founded a school to train brides for Japanese men going to Southeast Asia? Can the customs be so different there?" He laughed again.

"All this will do little good if diets do not improve. Women are not—" I swallowed my words. I could not discuss such a thing with a man. Not one I barely knew. "I mean, some women would have trouble making babies with poor diets. And for those who can, I read that babies are smaller, less healthy than they used to be."

"Ah, yes, I see the problem." Sentaro had the good taste to look away and seek a table for us.

Conversation moved on to war news as we ate, but it lagged. Not an interesting topic. He began describing changes since his childhood, for good or ill. New construction, jobs created and lost, a friend who tried to establish a toy factory. He grew still. The friend had died recently.

I tried to draw him out. What were the best memories of his youth? Sentaro perked up and monopolized the rest of the conversation. Thank goodness. What had happened to my decision to avoid him? My fear of revealing too much about my past? I painted over the thought, hoping the pigment would stick. Talking with him was such a pleasant break from the most recent upheaval in my life.

"So," I said, carrying my empty tray to the return slot, "I gather you haven't been avoiding me, then."

"Nor you, me." He smiled again. He still had that stupid

goatee, but it fit him, in a way. Maybe it wasn't so stupid.

"Thank you for coming to visit. I have to get back to work now."

"At this time of evening?"

"I have nowhere else to go. In two days I can search for a new apartment."

He tried to get me to take the bus with him to the nearest public bathhouse, but that was too much, too soon. Maybe one day. I politely declined, gave him a bow, and hurried off to my room. My office, my bedroom, for now.

Oh, dear, I was going to have dreams tonight. Sentaro made me feel something I had never come close to before, certainly not anything that commandant on the POW island could engender. Something sweet, and in the midst of everything going on around me, pure.

But I was not unsullied. What would I do if I ever drew close to a man? What if I ever, spirits forfend, wanted to marry someday? I was tarnished. I was used. And any man would know it in the moment of truth.

I had to stay away from Sentaro. Except I had no slightest chance of staying away from Sentaro. I couldn't let him know my past, and I wanted so much to find someone I could tell everything. I needed to confess, and needed to keep silent forever. Resistance fighters in occupied countries had comrades. On the Korean island I'd had the hermit. How did they train spies to be alone all the time? How could I desperately want a chance to be happy once in a while, and drip with guilt whenever I was?

I was thoroughly, outstandingly, unforgivably messed up.

And Sentaro was still the enemy.

Chapter 14

Collaboration. That's what they called it. I figured it out in the middle of the night, waking from a dream about Sentaro. Flirting with the opposition, improving their morale, had no justification. My occupation was not manual labor like on the docks, like what that American soldier said was within the Geneva Convention for prisoners. Anything beyond that was aiding and abetting the enemy in wartime. It's what I had been doing for months, even if I did sneak in the trivial little piece of misdirection. I had to be helping the Japanese far more than I was helping my own side.

If all my work had been conscious infiltration with a valid ulterior motive, that would be one thing. A sacrifice for the greater gain. That may have been acceptable. But my little pinpricks of mischief, my baby inaccuracies that might, only might, lead to future problems, were likely inconsequential. For the most part, I had just limped along, doing as told, providing a valuable intellectual service for Japan. Once again, I had proven I was a traitor.

God, I was tired. Tired of sleeping on a wooden floor like a prisoner. Tired of not being able to do something positive, something to show my life had meaning. Tired of being so vapid I leapt at the chance to talk with Sentaro when he came to see me.

Tired of being weak. Of accomplishing nothing. Of being nobody. What would Sergeant Anders have thought, seeing me like this? I could imagine Major Donnerty's disdain. In what way would I be honoring the kindness of Brutus, the memory of Maison and all those other soldiers and sailors, if I let myself dissolve into oblivion?

I dragged myself onto my chair, cracked open a German treatise, and dug in. I would find something here. No longer was I translating public domain literature. They had put me to work on something special, and I must uncover that which I could make use of, to help the Allies, or hurt Japan. Something to redeem my latest treason.

I must.

Studying German for close to sixteen hours a day the past week had netted me the basics. The task went faster without learning to speak it. The language had already evolved from a confused mass of unpronounceable and ridiculously long words to a logical array of terms and meanings, and now I understood what I read with few delays for the dictionary. The technical stuff remained obscure at times, but it helped to go from German to English to Japanese. Inefficient. Better if I could cut out the middleman.

I surfaced for dinner, stomach growling, and gave thanks for every difficulty I had encountered in my toil. Anything to suppress my relentless depression. Such a useless state of mind. As bad as regret, squandering away my life. My moods had been bouncing around so much I'd have suspected pregnancy if that weren't an impossibility.

Damn it, that was the last time I was going to break down. It had to be. The absolute last time.

~~~~

My day off arrived. If my goal was to sow hiccups into Japan's weapons research, it would make no sense to speed things along by working on my off day. More importantly, I needed someplace more comfortable to sleep. I took my identification papers and
~~~~

some money for the black market, ignored Mrs. Omori's disapproving glare as I left the building, and caught the gasoline railcar to my old neighborhood in southeast Tokyo.

They'd made a lot of progress on demolition in the past several days. Thirteen or fourteen blocks were down, and the rubble was cleared where my house had stood. People were already planting pumpkin seeds and vegetables. Good space like that? Waste not, want not. Though filling a firebreak with vines and burnable beans didn't make much sense. I asked a policeman about it, but he shrugged.

"I need to find a new place to live. Do you know—"

"The station house has not a single listing left for vacant apartments. Don't bother looking."

I wandered around seeking familiar faces. No one was working the piers even though it was a Thursday, so they must have switched to the tenth-day-off schedule. The public cafeteria was open for lunch, with boiled and mashed acorns. Whoever thought this was a good idea for food was truly desperate. Oh, right, that was me. And everyone else in this country. Yet as bad as diets became, as much as people lost weight and ate weeds for vitamin supplements, the government balanced things enough to avoid starvation. Better than elsewhere in the world, if you could believe the newspapers.

Hideki found me after lunch. I figured a boy his age would have the low-down on everything of interest, so it was disappointing he knew of nothing for rent.

"But my sister is getting married. She's moving out. Maybe you could have her room."

The way Hyakutake avoided me the night of the evacuation, I wasn't sure about that. I followed Hideki home anyway. It was worth a shot, before trying other neighborhoods.

Hyakutake was out and his wife dithered about, mumbling uncertainties. It wasn't proper, they could use the rent money, she hated seeing a stranger in her daughter's room, she'd love to help Hideki's friend, she needed to think about it. In the end she said to come back next tenth-day. By then her daughter would be married and gone.

"Congratulations," I said. "That's marvelous news. Could I get her a present?"

"Oh, perhaps something sweet, if you can find anything. But in times like this, don't worry about it."

Mrs. Hyakutake fluttered about like a love-sick peacock. Pride and worry and all the trappings that went with the territory, like my next-door neighbor in Alameda planning nuptials a few centuries ago.

"It's silly, registering a marriage this soon," she said. "Nobody used to do that until they had a baby, until they were certain they were staying together."

"You know why, mother." Hideki grinned at me. "The government's marriage program has to show results."

"So nothing changes. Nothing meaningful. More numbers on paper so bureaucrats can pretend they did something."

I tugged an earlobe. "It sounds like—"

Oh my god, pay attention. I'd almost said 'like America.'

"Like what, dear?"

"Sorry, nothing."

"Well, come back, like I said. I'll arrange it. But it's a much nicer room than that hole they put you in across the street. The rent should be twice as much."

I calculated. Yes, I could handle it on my translator's salary, even with the taxes and savings deductions. What good was money, anyway, when I couldn't use my ration coupons for things like new clothes because little was available?

"I accept." I'd never seen the room, but what did that matter? It would be fine.

That left the rest of the day free, so I got permission to steal Hideki for the afternoon and treat him to a movie. They were replaying Leni Riefenstahl's 'Triumph of the Will,' and even if it sounded like Nazi propaganda, it made good theater. Hideki would love it. And I was smart enough to know the real reason his mother sent him off. Time to shop, using the government's special clothing allowance for wedding garb to rent a kimono for his sister. Girl stuff. Hideki would drive them crazy if he were around.

A part of me smarted, not being invited to accompany the shoppers, but only a tiny part. I'd never been close to either Hideki's mother or sister. They must have dropped their grudge, though, and realized there'd been nothing between me and Mr. Hyakutake. Otherwise, Hideki's mother would never have agreed to let me move in.

The following ten days went quickly. When I returned to the Hyakutakes' place with my things, there was a slight change. They'd moved Hideki to his sister's old room and put me in the smaller space. I didn't ask about changing the amount of rent. It would be more convenient, since it had access to the back hall and its exit to the alley, so I could come and go at all hours without bothering the family. Perfect, really. Hideki told me it was the best room in the house and he hadn't wanted to move. Of course, eleven-year-olds always preferred alleys with canals alongside, and didn't mind the smell of sewage, which had grown worse over the past months.

I wrinkled my nose.

"I know, I'm sorry," said Mr. Hyakutake. "After they empty septic tanks they're supposed to truck it all to the countryside for fertilizer. Or put it on 'filth trains.' But with manpower shortages and gasoline shortages, they're cutting corners more and more."

"It's fine."

"They said tides would flush it out when they dumped it in the canals, but don't you believe it."

"It won't bother me." Some lies were necessary.

So began the next phase of my existence. The commute was the same, except I avoided the block with the government matchmaking agency. One run-in with the marriage board was enough.

The neighborhood association was half new people, but the duties were the same. I tried to get out of paying association dues on the grounds I was now part of the Hyakutake household, but that didn't work. I ran into Miku once; her family had started looking for new apartments before everyone else, so they'd landed one not far away. She still worked at the factory for airplane parts, and had been promoted, but what made her most proud was the carpenter's awl she'd been issued.

"They're training us for urban warfare." Miku gushed, waving the awl like a sword. "Drilling once a week. Stab the enemy in the belly. Nowhere else, the belly, so they writhe in agony for their wicked invasion. No one is allowed to die until they have killed at least one American soldier."

I nearly recoiled. It took every fiber to smile and laugh and praise her enthusiasm, her samurai spirit.

It meant one thing, and one thing only. There were no longer any civilians in Japan. Not adult ones, and even high school girls were being issued awls according to Miku. War work went on in shops all over the city, and everyone who could hold a weapon had been labeled a combatant, expected to fight to the end and never give up. Which meant every single person, every block of land, was a military objective. When the inevitable bombing began, the strafing and invasion and killing, there would be no reason for America to hold back.

Everyone was a target.

I made an excuse about work I had been postponing and hurried away. It wasn't fair to judge Miku, she was merely doing her part. What the authorities said was her patriotic duty. But I couldn't stand the thought of Miku plunging her awl into a man's gut and sneering while he died, while she herself was shot. The image stalked my dreams that night.

A few days after that, my life took another turn. Sentaro stopped by my office and asked me out. For a date. Or what in Alameda would pass for one.

I was not in the mood for pleasure. I said yes anyway. It was necessary. I had to act like any other young woman in such a situation. It was too late to pretend I didn't like him. All part of the performance.

And the hard part was, I did like him. A part of me wanted to go strolling with him no matter how right or wrong the act. So the next off day I dug out my one good blouse and skirt. Tainted memories clung to them from the POW island—damn, I could still feel the commandant's hands on my body—but nothing else would do. I'd started saving for a kimono, but had no idea where I'd find one when I had the money.

The day turned into a winner. Sentaro brought fruit and salted fish and other treats he'd saved. I had seen so little meat lately it felt like a royal holiday.

"Wish I could have found some squid ink."

"Squid . . . ? What for?"

"So you could try it."

"For what? Drawing?" How did he know I liked to draw?

"No, silly. You eat it."

My face squinched up. Sentaro laughed. Was he serious? Did people really eat squid ink? No, it had to be a joke. Didn't it?

We took a tram to a park, apologized to the ducks for not feeding them, and visited a pagoda. That temple was a marvel. He led me around, describing the most elegant architectural trick I had ever heard of. Japan had many earthquakes, but of all the buildings that collapsed over the years, pagodas kept standing. It turned out they had a massive tree trunk suspended from the roof at the middle of the building, descending through holes in the middle of the floors of every story, and every story was sitting loose on top of the one under it. When the building shook, the floors shifted back and forth, rebounding off the tree trunk so they never got far out of position. Shock waves went up and down the building, floors took turns banging the pillar one way and the other, and the whole structure hung together. So clever.

Sentaro and I meandered for an hour, admiring the place. The adventure warranted a light hug, the first I'd given him.

In fact, it was the first hug I'd given anyone in nearly forever. I couldn't count the POW camp commandant. The last real time would have been Rosita, the night I left Alameda, over two years ago. So did I savor it more because it was Sentaro, or because I was desperate for affection? Pretty pathetic, if the latter.

That evening we took in a show at the last kabuki theater still open. Practically the last performance before its scheduled demise.

It was either that or the recently opened 'Decisive Aerial Warfare Ballet,' and neither of us could get excited about what that might entail.

Surprisingly, even the rich people walked to the theater.

"Well, sort of," said Sentaro, when I remarked on the democratic spirit of the well-to-do. "They have cars, and they get a gasoline ration, or charcoal for the cars using coal, but they park a few blocks away so they can be seen arriving on foot. Got to 'show the flag.'"

I laughed. Hypocrisy was universal. "Wait, they get coal for cars, but children's schools are unheated?"

"Cold is good for them. Makes them grasp the hardships facing our soldiers."

I nodded. It was the mentality here. I shouldn't let it bother me.

He almost kissed me at the end of the evening, but backed off at the last second. So polite. Did I want him to? Of course . . . not. Not, of course.

I grimaced and went inside.

And plopped onto my mat. Stifle it, girl. Dial it down. Tomorrow, back to work.

Chapter 15

I found it. This had to be it. It was right there, among the latest German documents. A weakness the Nazis had been struggling with. A key device that kept failing because it got too hot, but they had finally licked the problem. What kind of device? What were they building? Once I knew that, I could insert a mistranslation. A little thing, to keep Japan from using whatever weapon they wanted to copy from their ally.

I hadn't expected to stumble upon such an opportunity so quickly. And it—ah, that's what it was. A mysterious kind of engine, something new for airplanes. Something that could turn the tide of the war, and win it. A jet.

A weapon, an opportunity. It opened my mind like a flower bud. This was the answer, the thing I had been seeking since I left California. At last, at last, I could accomplish the impossible. I could actively contribute to America's war effort. I could achieve redemption for my mother, for myself.

The Germans had overheating problems, struggling to find the right metal alloy? Well, so would Japan. The Germans had solved it? Well, Japan wouldn't, not yet. I could do this. I could be a success for the first time in my life.

The cafeteria had rice for dinner that night, with a wedge of orange on top and a spray of greens around the edge. It looked positively festive. Must be the cook's birthday. Or she was getting married. Something had to account for the artistry. I asked the woman across the table, who said it was in honor of the dining hall supervisor's son being wounded in combat. That made little sense until the woman explained further. It meant the boy was coming home.

A happy ending. Someone had survived. And damn it, I didn't care if the lad was an enemy soldier, I didn't care what he had been doing to get wounded. Who he had been fighting against. He had been serving his country, doing what he thought was right.

And now, so was I.

Another thought pierced my soul. Perhaps I had been brooding for a year and a half, feeling sorry for myself, but a period of sorrow, a period of recovery, was not collaboration. I had done nothing different than if I were intentionally insinuating myself into the stronghold of my foe. I was trying. I had failed before, but not for lack of trying. How many people would fall in this war? How many would fail to come home, wounded or otherwise? How many would try their best to serve their side in the conflict, win or lose?

The woman across the table asked what was wrong, and I realized I was crying, for no reason at all, except I knew I wasn't useless. Was this what they called an epiphany? I was trying, and that gave me value, and maybe I wouldn't succeed, but none of that mattered. I had a job to do, and the chance to do it, and I would try. And so would the other side, for they had a job as well, and the honor to pursue it.

Lightning ripped down my spine. This was the moment, the sea change in my life. I had become Japanese. Or at least a warrior. I had seen much, endured much, yet could honor the enemy, admire the enemy, even like some of the enemy as human beings. Not the Japanese back on that Korean island, not the army leaders who started the war, but they were the extreme. Every country had bad eggs. Forget them. Focus on the majority. Japan was the enemy, and I could like every single person I met here. If

I succeeded in misdirecting the design of a weapon, my actions could result in the death of some of these people. If they caught me, I would be killed. Because that's what happened in war. But I would do what I must, and so would they, and I would like them and admire them to the grave.

What an odd feeling, to look at the world this way.

I wiped my eyes and clutched the hand of the woman across the table. "Thank you."

She didn't understand what for. And I could hardly explain.

I stood, bowed, and hurried back to my small office.

Chapter 16

I spread four-foot long sheets across my desk. Construction drawings and tabulated data. I could type German reports into Japanese, but small-print tables and pictures with annotated information had to be drawn by hand. A draftsman copied the jet engine design for me, and I filled in what was needed, including tables of alloy compositions for the various parts. The Germans had many such tables. The precise mixtures of nickel and magnesium and whatnot changed with the dates on the drawings, modified through trial and error.

Mrs. Omori burst in. I flipped over the top sheet. Why did I do that? Talk about shady behavior. I turned it back over.

“Apologies, Omori-san. I am infected with the secrecy of this place.”

She tapped a pen against her palm, but said nothing about my security paranoia. “I told you to stay away from my son.”

“He came to me, Omori-san.”

“That makes no matter.”

“Is he not an adult, able to make his own choices?”

She put a hand to her cheek, as if I had slapped her. “How dare you.”

How dare I what? Speak the truth?

"A mother and her son are no business of yours. You have no money, no pedigree, a very questionable past, and certainly no future with my boy. He will come to realize this. His great-grandfather was a samurai, and he deserves someone of his class. Save him, save yourself, the pain of taking this further."

Omori slid the door shut so hard it popped off its track. It took me the rest of the morning to figure out how to put it back.

Was Omori's outburst a valid excuse to stop seeing Sentaro? Did I want to stop seeing him? What would a real Japanese girl do? Defy authority for potential love, or knuckle under to threats? People couldn't all be the same, either choice might be realistic. But what should I do?

I knew what I really wanted. It involved Sentaro, and it most decidedly did not involve his mother or anything to do with the war. I slammed the thought in a glass jar and sealed the rim. I couldn't let it out, but it would be nice to look at now and again.

I returned to my tables of data, carefully changing the bismuth concentration in one place and a couple of other constituents for other items. That should do it. I took the original German table from an older design with overheating problems, the newer sheet I was supposed to have copied, and slid them in a pocket. I had a plan.

So did Sentaro. Have a plan. He burst in at dinnertime—nobody ever knocked on my door, I must not rate that kind of respect—and complained about his mother, how dare she intimidate me, it was high time she stopped trying to run his life. It sounded immature, but he had little experience directing his own destiny, from what I could gather. In any event, he insisted on accompanying me to supper, muttering about closed restaurants and not a lot available to impress a woman.

I smiled. He wanted to impress me.

Stop that. Stop smiling. I accepted his arm and let him guide me to the cafeteria.

Afterward he rode home with me. He tried to claim it was a particularly dark evening, which wasn't true at all this time of year. There could be a storm, and he had an umbrella. I looked up at the clear sky.

"All right, fine. I just want to do it."

I gave him another smile and took his arm again. This might work out fine. I had a plan, and he would do quite well to lend it credence if I could get him to clown around a little. Did Japanese men ever clown around?

Apparently so. Or sort of. Enough, anyway. As we neared my room, or rather the entrance at the back of the Hyakutakes' apartment building, I dropped his arm, tapped it, and said, "You're it." Children everywhere played tag, and I'd seen a version in the streets. I stepped near the canal.

Sentaro took the bait. "You minx." He darted toward me.

I twisted, pretended to slip, and fell into the canal, laughing all the way. As I went under I slipped a hand into my pocket, crumbled the two German drawings, and thrust them as deep as I could. Paper would not last long in these polluted waters. I kicked off the bottom and surfaced.

"Are you all right?" Sentaro rushed to the nearest steps to get down to my level and fish me out.

I kept laughing. "Don't worry, my fault, I'm fine."

He took a lot of convincing, but finally led me down the street to the public baths to get cleaned up. It was a first—this time, I let him accompany me inside.

When we got back, Hideki's mother stood at the door. She seemed impressed by Sentaro's rank and raised an eyebrow at me, as if to wonder how a girl like me could interest a man like him. What would my own mother think of Sentaro? Probably be thrilled. Mrs. Hyakutake guarded the portal until Sentaro left.

Altogether a most auspicious evening. The Japanese could never prove I had altered the German data. I had a solid reputation for accuracy. They would take my word I had made no errors. There would be later German data they hadn't seen yet, to fix the alloy problem, or my research team might figure it out themselves, but for now they would be stopped.

There was a price to pay. I got an eye infection.

Redness and swelling kicked in a day after my dip in the canal.

Four hours sitting in the public health clinic led to a short session with an elderly doctor.

"Why haven't you been here before?"

"I wasn't sick."

"Haven't you seen the circulars? Is your neighborhood association deficient?"

"No, they're fine." I massaged my eye. "I've been busy."

"Don't rub that. You're supposed to have a physical, get immunizations, and get your blood typed, just in case."

"Yes, sir."

"Stop rubbing. I know it itches, and I know what I'd like to give you, but we have few drugs left. They've promised us penicillin, but who knows when. Thank all the *kami* the nation has not had an epidemic. I don't know what we'd do."

I twitched on the stool.

"Sit still. What possessed you to go swimming in the first place?"

"I fell in."

"Sure you did. Fooling around, at your age. Well, I can spare a little ointment that should help. But no refills. You go getting yourself in trouble, it's on your head."

"Thank you."

"Certainly. Sorry you had to wait so long."

"You are busy. I appreciate whatever you can do."

"Which isn't much anymore." He opened a tube and spread a bit of lotion around my eye and on the lid. "I'm responsible for four times the number of patients I should be. In fact, I ought to be retired. You won't find a young doctor outside the military these days."

I held still and let him do his job. When he finished, I took the tube, thanked him again, and headed home.

I got no more time off for illness. Next day I was back in the office. I spent a month seeing mostly out of one eye.

The same day I removed my eye patch for the last time, an explosion ripped up the ground at the armor testing station. Everyone ran out to see what happened.

Admiral Tokiyasu stood with his lead design team in one group, backed by technicians and banks of monitoring equipment. They rounded a wall filled with small, four-inch thick bullet-proof glass windows that had shielded them from the site of the explosion. I joined the rest of the complex personnel.

"I thought you had the overheating problem licked," said Tokiyasu.

"We used the correct alloys. It must be a mechanical defect," said one engineer.

"Don't blame it on us. We did our job right," said another.

"Enough." Tokiyasu waved over some technicians. "Set up a tent. Treat it like a crime scene. I want to know what went wrong. Fast."

Technicians scattered to carry out his orders.

"She did it."

Everyone turned to see who spoke.

Mrs. Omori jabbed a finger at me. "Terauchi did it. She was responsible for the translations. She misled you all."

Silence greeted her remark. I didn't move. What an outrageous, unsupportable accusation. Even if it was true.

A voice came from the side. "Keiko Terauchi is seeing Omori-san's son. Omori is displeased with the arrangement."

Most everyone laughed, some more roughly than others. Omori turned red. Admiral Tokiyasu shook his head and waved his men to work.

I ducked away, uncertain if I was the butt of the joke as well. At least no one else suspected my role in the failure of the prototype engine, for clearly that was what had been on the test stand. But I had found an enemy in Sentaro's mother, and there was no solution in sight.

On the bright side, the Japanese would take that much longer to field a combat-worthy jet. My campaign was underway, and it wasn't microscopic anymore. This time, it was serious.

Sabotage.

Chapter 17

By June, all the jet blueprints had me in jitters at my self-imposed prohibition on drawing. Withdrawal symptoms, I called them. I took to sketching little scenes in the margins of scrap papers heading for the trash, then blacking them out before they were barely started. Larger and larger grew the images before I destroyed them. Was I safe yet? Dared I do this?

Then came the annual summer anti-espionage event. The concern was primarily all the foreign nationals in the country, mostly neutrals and Italians, some of which could be up to no good. But among the many slogans and a barrage of recycled dogma was a poster featuring one of my pictures from the POW island. The caption read, 'Have you seen this artist?' Contact information for one of the security services was listed beneath it.

The army had found my cave. They had figured out what I had done. And they may have put two and two together about their destroyer hunting a submarine off the coast.

I raced back to my office and tore through every loose paper I could find, especially those in the trash. I gathered up every tiniest scrap on which I had dared to release my innermost self, and smeared them with ink from the typewriter. Then I stuffed all the bits into a torn seam in my *monpe*, pinned it shut, and shivered the rest of the day, until I got the incriminating evidence home and drowned it in the canal.

How dare I risk my one indispensable goal? How dare I give in to weakness, indulging myself with the blissful act I had sworn could never be performed? I lay on my pallet, cringing. Yet another sleepless night.

One other poster stuck in my mind from the anti-espionage event. Wretched people planting a field under the watchful eyes of guards. 'Report Dissidents,' it read. 'They Can Still Be Useful.' The hermit and the old woman would be in a place like that. They really had done me a favor, kicking me off the bus. Had they seen the poster of my drawing? What would the old woman think of me now, wanted by the authorities? Would it get the hermit in trouble? I could only hope they'd be all right.

Summer of 1944 brought other news. The war was going so badly for Japan that in July Prime Minister Tojo was forced to step down. He had been in power since shortly before Pearl Harbor. My friend Hideki was most upset. He had the same given name as Tojo and considered it a personal insult. I consoled him by letting him tag along on my fire patrol that night. I didn't get to see him too often anymore. He had been forced into the student Volunteer Labor Corps and traveled into the country to weed fields most of the time. School lessons were sporadic, a few hours a week at best.

"And they're always yelling at us to spread out. Watch for planes. They might strafe us."

"How awful."

"I like the food, though. They're feeding us sparrows."

"Why?"

"It's a campaign to save the rice by trapping the birds. More meat than I've seen in months."

"How do they taste?"

"Kind of tough. They overcook them. Better eating when we catch snakes. I even got a frog once. But they're hard to find, and the sparrows are free."

"Can you bring me one?"

"Um, maybe. Not sure I could sneak one all the way home. I'm hungry all the time."

I laughed. "Growing boy syndrome."

It wasn't really funny. It wasn't just growing boys.

Come to think of it, I never heard birds in the city anymore. Desperate people with a spot of ingenuity may have found a way to trap pigeons, as well.

On July 26th, Germany introduced their Messerschmitt-262 jet fighter into combat. I recognized the picture in the newspaper. It was the plane serving as the model for Admiral Tokiyasu's development program. Disturbing news if it proved as effective as they said, and it would inspire Tokiyasu to push us all the harder.

At the end of the month, Admiral Tokiyasu called the entire research team together to read an article in the *Asahi* newspaper, which claimed that ten percent of all aircraft produced were rejected by the air force for being defective. "This facility represents the elite of the military. The plane we are designing will be the best in the world. Shoddy work will not come from our organization. Is that correct?" Cheers of confirmation greeted his words.

Astounding. Low morale and carelessness were so bad as to account for a ten percent failure rate?

Of far more personal importance, in mid-August I turned twenty and was required to join the Greater Japan Women's Association. I rebelled. "It's not fair. I already distribute toilet paper, repair umbrellas, and deliver mail for the neighborhood association. I drill with spears for the community council, drill for bucket brigades with the Youth Association, which I have to stick with until I'm twenty-five. Now this?"

The white-haired, pinch-faced clerk for the women's association scowled at me. "Oh, a lazy one, are you? Too proud to help us comfort the bereaved and visit injured soldiers?"

"It's not logical. How can I be a youth and adult at the same time?"

"You think you're the first to complain? That's just the way it is. You have to help out."

"That's fine for most women, but Admiral Tokiyasu has me

working over thirteen hours a day. Plus commuting time."

"Well, there you go. Relax during your commute. That should be enough time off for anyone. More than I get, I tell you."

I wasn't going to win this one. The old lady was right. If anyone had a prayer of avoiding being in two competing organizations at the same time, they'd have set a precedent I could follow. It hadn't happened. On the plus side of the ledger, I hadn't gotten in trouble for my outburst, since others complained as well.

Commuting time only. It wouldn't be enough to satisfy Sentaro, who wanted to see me more often. But he was getting busier himself, with an increasing load of prisoners to document, many of whom were getting cocky about their side winning, and harder to control. I'd just have to tell him I was no longer available except for minuscule fractions of my off days. Like today, which I had wasted registering for the women's association and being shown the basics of shooting a rifle. There was no way the government would have the resources to equip women with rifles to repel an invasion—the very reason the 'three million bamboo spears' movement got started—but bureaucracy demanded I spend half a day on the pointless training.

There might be one silver lining to all the things they had women doing these days: strides toward equality and women's rights from all the war work. One Shinto temple had even made the news for ordaining women priests for the first time in their eleven hundred year history, after the men volunteered for military duty or factory work. Good for them.

My mother would have been horrified if she knew I admired the Western suffragette movements.

And another thing—the well-to-do were being rationed the same as everyone. They had their own war losses and hardships. Even if they started with a large collection of luxury goods for the black market, the situation was leveling society to some extent.

Except. Except, except. The whole problem with silver linings was the black, malevolent cloud they had to sprout from.

Next day, I went back to the research complex. Reading the newspaper on the railcar always dumfounded me. There were few reports about the war in the European theater, but they appeared to be open and honest, despite censoring everything concerning the Pacific War. It was like the authorities didn't realize the loss of Italy and the reversal of Germany's fortunes could affect the morale of Japanese. But in the Pacific? We always heard about lost islands and casualties well after the fact. And no one had seen a weather report since Pearl Harbor Day, to keep such tidings from leaking to the Allies.

At the complex, I studied the latest picture of an Me-262 in flight. It reflected the failure of my most recent attempt to slow the project. When a plane flew that fast you needed to sweep the wings, not have them stick straight out to the sides. But you didn't have to sweep them back. They could have been swept forward. The German literature indicated they were toying with that design for a different airplane, and it had certain advantages, so I had tried to sell the Admiral's team on trying it. I had carefully lost the one document that indicated the advantages were outweighed by the difficulty of controlling flight. Ailerons were too sensitive on forward-swept wings.

Alas, the designers opted for the swept-back design like the Me-262. I had barely set them back a fortnight, pondering the alternative.

Oh, well. What next? Nothing too obvious. After Omori's accusation at the engine test, I had to keep well under the radar with whatever I tried.

Omori. A strange thought—Mrs. Omori was like my Major Donnerty in this place, an undying source of suspicion. There always seemed to be one of those around. The only difference was, her baseless accusations were actually accurate. Stretch the simile and this made Sentaro a sort of younger, more attractive Sergeant Anders, leery at first, then accepting. Mr. Hyakutake, a watered-down version of the hermit. And Hideki? Brutus, all the way. Trusting and supportive, without a single reason for it.

What kind of personality was I? Impossible question. No one ever saw themselves clearly.

Think. What to do? The engineers had figured out the

problem with the engine after a while, and run a bunch of metallurgy tests of their own, still seeking satisfactory high-melting-point alloys. Even when they figured that out, they needed more thrust, unless they dropped weight by removing the pilot seat armor plating and the self-sealing fuel tanks, like they did on other combat planes. No wonder their casualties were so high.

They argued over the exact wing angle a while longer, but resolved it, so now they were off to the races on control surface design. I had no idea how to impede that work.

Back in Tokyo a couple of nights later, I realized the 'dog days' were over. For a while, the dog population seemed to have grown, as streets filled with pets people could no longer feed. The animals didn't last long. Be they starved or eaten by the neighbors, the streets were free of the creatures now.

~~~~

In September, I began my obligatory once-a-month visits to hospitals to comfort the war wounded, as stipulated by the women's association. It wasn't that I didn't want to help, but as I'd told that bossy woman, I already had so many tasks.

The first soldier I talked with could barely speak, trembling non-stop. He'd lost both legs. The second had a manic laugh, telling me that out on the war front they knew things were bad, but were told the Home Islands were winning the war. Now he was back himself, he found out people knew how bad things were here, but were being told the troops out on the islands were winning the war. Classic double-talk.

Another of the wounded babbled. The first coherent thing he said was, "Don't tell my mother what I did."

I sat with that one a while, soothing his burned flesh with a damp cloth laid gently on the worst parts, and he began describing so many heinous acts the man in the next bed told him to shut up. Rapes of nurses in Hong Kong, random killings when resistance was suspected. He said he was never like that before. The army drilled brutality into enlisted and officers alike, perhaps thinking it necessary for a relatively small force to dominate a huge enemy
~~~~

population.

The man wanted forgiveness, but I could do no more than murmur soft words. He described things as bad as anything in the Korean island POW camp, and I had a sickening realization. I had been wrong. The POW guards were not the exception, they were the norm.

"If you think about it, there is a twisted logic," he said. "We are taught to have no respect for our own lives, since they belong to the emperor. If we have no expectation of survival, why not commit such abominations? Why not perform any number of unspeakable acts, when the unspeakable will be happening to us sooner or later?"

The poor man cried at this desecration of *Bushido*. His own army, his beloved people, had abandoned honor. It was too much for the soldier lying beside him. He called my patient a traitor and hollered for a doctor to get me out of there.

So, yeah, if I needed any more proof this war was about anything other than greed, pride, and evil, if I needed another shot in the ass to convince me I was doing the right thing on the jet, here it was.

~~~~

On October 15th the emperor declared a 'public victory holiday' to honor the miraculous sinking of all the American aircraft carriers in a single gigantic air raid. Some people actually believed it. The carrier *Enterprise* had been sunk about three or four times by now, I had lost count. Whoever gave Tokyo Rose input for her radio propaganda had a warped sense of humor.

After admitting the previous claims were in error, the Imperial Japanese Navy vowed to try again, to win a decisive victory or 'bloom as the flowers of death.' It was over by the end of the month. The Japanese Navy was crippled and America was back in the Philippines.

And then came November, and right in the middle of another railcar commute to work, right while I gazed out the window toward the eastern industrial zone, the world changed. Again. It
~~~~

was getting to be a bad habit with this demented world, even if the change had long been expected.

American B-29s made their appearance in the skies above Tokyo, and bombs began to fall.

In a way, the circle had turned, and it was appropriate. Sad, and inevitable. If only there were another way to end things.

There wouldn't be. It was Japan's turn to suffer, and the U.S. would not go easy.

In fact, if I thought about it, the circle was even bigger than 1941 or 1937. It went clear back to 1923, and the great Kanto earthquake that destroyed Yokohama and Tokyo. Yokohama, pearl of the Pacific, the centerpiece for liberal thought and Western influence in Japan. Relief poured in from around the world, led by the U.S., but many in Japan resented the help. The hotbed of individualism and democracy had been leveled by divine intervention, a common enough belief for natural disasters anywhere. So help from the decadent West was insulting. And idiotic pundits in America reviled Japan for 'not being grateful enough,' as if that were the only reason to send help.

The aftermath was a resurgence in the Japanese rejection of Western ways, and a rise in the power of the right wing, the 'Japanese fascists.' It all went downhill from there, until the incompetently-handled Marco Polo Bridge incident outside Peking in 1937 had grown into a Sino-Japanese war, which led to economic sanctions, which led to the Pacific War. A conflict that, as far as I could tell, had never had any clear end point, merely a desire to establish an economic empire of some arbitrary size.

Outside the window of my railcar, halfway through my commute, sprawled an imposing park filled with fountains and trees and songbirds. A pair of temples came next. The prettiest part of the ride. Why did it spark the darkest thoughts of the day?

Perhaps it was the irony. Beautiful, generous, wonderful Japan, full of culture, full of pride. Never before had an ostensibly democratic land allowed bigotry and overweening hubris to lead it from a minor, confused skirmish to a nation-destroying war.

Japanese planes had rained terror on China and Malaya and

wherever they went. What they had done at Pearl Harbor was negligible in comparison. The army's atrocities in conquered territories, against 'sub-human' locals, were disbelieved by every civilian I broached the subject with.

But whether Japanese conceded the truth of what their army had done, or denied it with their dying breath, the B-29s were paying them back.

If only the Japanese could acknowledge the mistakes their countrymen had made in the name of their empire, if only people could admit blame and regret and move on. Surrender? Why not? Profess mistakes and swallow the consequences.

Yet a mind-set that accepted ritual suicide, even expecting it for grievous wrongs, lent a certain logic to refusing to see one's failings. The Western tendency to admit mistakes, seek expiation, and shun suicide might be one thing Japan could consider, just as the West could learn much from Japan.

The still contemplation of a tea ceremony would be a start. My brain was in such a state.

Right, tea. Like that would happen. I knew only theory for those ceremonies. The number of hours during which I had achieved a quiet mind could be counted on one thumb. And after all, be honest. I felt suicidal way too often, myself.

Enough ruminating. My railcar had arrived at the complex. Another day, another translation. And mayhap, another delay on the jet.

Chapter 18

The bombing continued. The neighborhood association's response was to make everyone take vows of mutual aid, and parrot the government claim that 'it can't happen again.' Bombs could never fall in the same place twice. The odds of them landing where you happened to be were very low. It was all psychological fluff. Some people even claimed you could protect yourself by eating hard-to-find foods like pickled plums.

I decided the sand in the buckets wasn't for fighting fires. It was for sticking your head in.

Any precaution was better than none, though. I dug my own air raid shelter behind the apartment building. My pit went too deep the first time and water soaked in from the canal during high tide. My next one stayed shallow. It would protect me from horizontal flying debris, but that was it. I found a discarded sheet of roofing tin further down the alley, with only a few holes in it, and dragged it back to use as a cover for my shelter.

The pit soon became damp from rain, and moldy. It also collected bugs. I wished I weren't so squeamish about eating them, they would have been good protein.

"They're sweet," Hideki said, "but grasshoppers are better."

His own family had snagged a dryer shelter along the front of the building months before, and had no such visitors. Hideki showed it to me once, and I understood why they'd not invited me to use it now their daughter had moved away. It was hardly big enough for the other three of them.

I began storing my blouse and skirt at the office. The only time I could get together with Sentaro was after work on rare evenings. He had no time to ride into Tokyo and back anymore. One of our get-togethers was particularly fun. He tried to get me to drink a *bakudan*, cheap sake called a 'bomb' because it was so awful it exploded in your mouth. After he'd had a couple himself, he started explaining structural dynamics of bridges from the perspective of an artist, not an engineer.

"Think of the beams," he said, sketching on a napkin. "These connections are aesthetic constructions. One need not worry about stability considerations when beauty and grace are apparent."

I got him home safely.

God, I was falling for that guy. It hurt to think how much I liked one of the enemy. It was the sweetest, most delightful misery I had ever experienced. I couldn't fight it anymore. I dove into the torment every time I saw him.

His silly bridge description inspired me, though. Back at work, I dug into the jet drawings and found a way to cast doubt on the structural integrity of the wing mounts. Older German vibration calculations that implied the need for stiffening, so long as I 'lost' the later, revised numbers. Tokiyasu's team wasted weeks redesigning something that was fine the way it was.

I nearly got caught on that one, when one engineer started recalculating stresses from scratch, but he was very old and suffered a seizure. Brought on by poor diet, a doctor said.

It could have been brought on by thinking he'd found a case of treachery. I quivered in bed all night after the near miss. The air raid sirens went off as they so often did, but that one time I ignored them. As usual, the explosions stayed a few miles off, targeting munitions factories.

New Years Day 1945 warranted no celebration at all. People dried and ground stems, leaves, and acorns to stretch the flour supply. Rations kept shrinking and the in-city black market was having trouble filling in the gaps. Their rice cost almost fifty times the official price, the price set by the government for the little provided through neighborhood associations. People took trips to the countryside, close enough not to require special rail passes, just to buy vegetables and fish on the black markets out there, but we had to take durable goods and barter. Farmers no longer trusted cash.

Not just farmers. On February 3rd, Tokyo's fancy department store *Isetan* held a consumers' exchange. A chance for people to come and barter for clothes or anything else they needed. I couldn't believe the government permitted it. The whole thing reeked of a lack of confidence in the bureaucracy's ability to provide what people needed. The cigarette ration had dropped from six to three per day, and some people were reduced to smoking eggplant or corn silk, so I traded my hoarded collection of real tobacco and finally got a decent used coat. I could have squandered the trade on tickets to a rare Beethoven concert at Hibiya Public Hall, but only the rich did that kind of thing, and I had nothing to wear. And I could really use a coat.

The quality of sake went back up when they started making it with rice again, so more sweet potatoes could go into fermentation for aviation fuel. Not surprisingly, that was matched with another cut in the rice ration. Good for my black market sake trading, though.

Then the Hyakutakes invited me to a dinner party. Their firstborn son had finished flight training and been granted a one-day leave to visit his family. A few relatives and a couple of neighbors came over, bringing small jars of hoarded delicacies. I contributed what I had left of cigarettes and sake. The atmosphere tingled with a redolence we'd been missing for years.

Hideki made a point of introducing me to his courageous brother Susumu, prompting a joke from his father about a whirlwind romance, which made no sense at all until the meaning opened its jaws and gnawed out the last residue of my naivety. The flight school was not the normal kind. It was for Kamikazes.

I spent the rest of the meal in a trance. At one point the conversation between Mrs. Hyakutake and her eldest son became surreal, at least to my way of thinking.

"Did you enjoy learning to fly?"

"Oh, yes, mother, it is an extraordinary experience."

"When do you die?"

"In three days."

"Would you like more plum sauce?"

I said not another word. I smiled politely through the rest of the dinner, and took my leave.

A few days later, Mrs. Hyakutake tried to raise my rent, since rising costs were totally outstripping any increase in wages, but I insisted I lived with the same dilemma. And apartments were getting easier to find as some people moved in with relatives on farms to avoid bombing in the cities. Hyakutake dropped the issue. I headed off to the public baths, but they were closed that day due to lack of fuel to heat the water.

People were so short of money the government suckered them with a national lottery, lauding the 100,000 yen prize. But the winnings were in savings bonds, which couldn't be spent now and which inflation would deflate. People already strapped for money senselessly filled the war coffers by buying tickets. Not me.

The neighborhood association had not received a fuel allotment all winter. People scavenged bombed-out buildings for wood to cook with. Miku decided she'd had enough of the austerity measures and needed something to perk her up. She dragged me along to a hairdresser who was desperate enough to work on a holiday, and Miku got herself a permanent. She laughed at the tight curls smothering her head and tried to talk me into getting one, but with my high-profile job I didn't dare. I did get a light trim to neaten myself up, though. My hair had grown a lot since I'd hacked it off over two years ago, and I ought to look nice for Sentaro.

Ought to? Well, all right, wanted to.

The U.S. shifted to almost exclusive daylight bombing, which made sleeping easier. The planes were so high up they could rarely be touched by flak or the occasional Japanese fighter plane. But the altitude dispersed the bombs in shifting winds. I heard some people laugh at the bombers' ineffectiveness. Buildings here weren't brick and block, shattering with a single bomb and flinging debris to destroy an entire factory. Here they were wood, with roofs of tile or tin, and the force of explosions was not contained. Results were limited. Production continued.

Others didn't laugh. They cursed the American barbarians for bombing civilians, killing innocents. Once a plane got shot down on my off day, and two crewmen parachuted toward a spot not far from my neighborhood. Some people yelled about finding them and meting out justice. I raced back to my building and used the call box to alert Sentaro and the army. By the time the military showed up they could only take one airman into custody. The other had been lynched by the mob.

Nothing stopped the bombs. Nothing restrained the casualties. Pressure to get jets into production became overwhelming. Nothing else could go up against the heavily armed B-29s or their fast P-51 escorts. Germany was almost done for, but an encrypted radio message came in with more details on jet design improvements, so I kept busy with translations.

Over time, the U.S. figured out how ineffectual their conventional bombing was. Trains kept moving, ships kept sailing, and aerial pictures must reveal how Japan carried on, undeterred by the damage. So in February, they tried something new. They brought to Japan what had already been tried in Europe, by Germany on England, by Britain and America on Germany. They brought incendiaries. On January 27th, they dropped the first firebombs on Tokyo. A minor test, leading to more cocky optimism in the press. 'They'll never defeat us from the air.' One night in February, a couple of hundred bombers demolished a square mile of Tokyo.

It was only the beginning.

On March 9th, I worked late. I had discovered that control surfaces on a fast-moving jet could not be handled with wires like on older, slower planes. They used hydraulics. And to regulate the flow and improve the handling, the Germans had figured out how to fine-tune the pressure by putting an obstruction in the pipe that carried the fluid. But not just a simple orifice, with sharp edges and a lot of turbulent flow. No, they used a more expensive venturi, with gradual necking down and opening up on the far side of the flow path. But the word for orifice and the word for venturi could be switched. A simple mistranslation. Or better, the term venturi would simply not be used. I would put the orifice drawing in my translations, and none would be the wiser. And every control surface on the jet would be much more finicky. The whole plane would become hard to manage.

I stuck with it until I had my materials ready to hand in. The tenth would be my day off, and this was too important a piece of subterfuge to get wrong. Every document, every drawing, every annotated comment had to be consistent, so nothing would reveal my deceit. So that, once again, the papers that could prove what I had done could be snuck out and destroyed in the canal.

I caught the last railcar of the evening and headed south. As we passed through the northern districts of Tokyo a ruddiness grew on the horizon ahead. An orange-red thing, pulsing lightly, reflecting off clouds.

What clouds? There shouldn't be . . . oh. Smoke. Another firebombing.

But this time it was right in front of us, right where I was headed. The railcar continued into the city but stopped before the end of the line.

"Everyone out. Seek shelter." The driver shut off the engine and followed his own advice, hightailing it to the west.

Some passengers got off, others stayed sitting, none looking like they could decide what to do. I could only think of Hideki and Miku, of everyone I knew. I took off running toward the light.

A droning sound grew to a continuous roar. Hundreds of B-29s passed overhead at low altitude, circling around to drop from the north. Scattered fires spread in front of me, as far as I could see from left to right. The light brightened with every second. The bombers let go, and thousands of shimmering sticks floated down from their bellies, sparkling, reflecting the flames.

Slowly, slowly they dropped. I kept running. All around they fell now, shiny, pretty cylinders, everywhere I looked. Hundreds of planes kept growling above me, bringing more presents to the party, growing it to a storm.

Had anyone called the fire department? Never mind, they had to know, and I'd never find a telephone, so many lines had been ripped out to recover copper for brass shell casings.

Masses of people ran the other way, clogs snapping on the pavement like popcorn from hell. The cloth hoods we had been told to wear to protect us, 'air raid shrouds,' were worse than useless, catching sparks and flaring until people ripped them off. I stopped one man rushing by with a bundle of possessions on his back.

"It's on fire."

I pointed, but he didn't take in my words and ran on. Bicycles tried to fight through. One fell and the rider got trampled. I fought upstream, breaking free as the mass thinned and the next wave of miniature bombs reached the tops of buildings. No citizens were fighting the fires. Despite all the neighborhood drilling, not one person hung back to spread sand or water. And maybe that was smart.

The containers burst open. They ignited, some while still in the air. Hundreds of thousands of canisters, every one filled with a gooey mess that splattered dancing orange tongues across the ground. Roofs and walls and fences and gardens, wood and paper, and everywhere more wood and more paper, it all caught and burned and hissed and crackled. Baby fires ate, and gobbled, and grew up quickly, until they mated with others and spawned children of their own. Sparks became flames, and flames became blazes. And still the planes came, dropping more and more and more. All those firebreaks did nothing to limit the disaster.

The heat grew unbearable, but on I ran. I couldn't reach my neighborhood. It was too far ahead, in the heart of the industrial east of Tokyo, the center of the target zone. Not a prayer of reaching anyone I knew, yet still I tried. Why, I could not say. But

I struggled on as tongues of red shot across roads and falling buildings blocked alleys. As an official fire brigade abandoned their equipment and fled, one man's hair on fire. As a thousand scents assailed me, pungent oils from the bombs, wood smoke, the harrowing aroma of cooking meat, the stink of burning hair. I couldn't sort them out.

I ran, and stumbled, and faced a solid wall of fire a few blocks ahead. No longer any holes, any gaps to penetrate further. It had become a firestorm, sucking the oxygen, sucking everything inward as heated air rose. I sobbed, staring at figures within the glowing light. Some people still sputtered out of buildings and burst into flame, their skin turning them into human torches. They staggered a few steps until their feet sank into molten asphalt. Their bodies swayed like flags, until they blackened and fell. I could never have envisioned a holocaust like this, but I was seeing it now. Now, I was learning.

I lurched back, fighting a wind that wanted to blast me into the inferno. I couldn't help. I had to leave. I had to get out now, while I had a chance.

If I still did.

I dodged a crumbling building, found a path along an alley, and reached a canal. Water. That could save me. Two buildings across the way fell into the canal, hissing, turning water to steam. The canal was already filled with blackened debris, and something else. Bodies, boiled alive. Others had thought to save themselves down there, and failed. I turned away and ran.

Not many openings left. The conflagration spread like a rising tide, linking with other blocks of twisting, leaping tongues of yellow and red. My *monpe* caught fire and I ripped off pants, then jacket, running nude. I wasn't the only one. I grabbed a teenager standing in shock and dragged him along with me. He tripped and fell after a hundred yards. I couldn't go back. The fire was at my heels. I turned a corner and dashed alongside another canal, the only way left to go.

And stopped. The path to safety was gone. Nothing ahead but flames. Nothing on either side of the canal. I whirled around at a detonation, unidentifiable things collapsing behind me. So make a choice, burn alive or boil to death. Hiding under that concrete bridge would buy only a little time.

Wait, concrete? They rarely had such bridges over canals. A swirl of smoke parted and I realized it was bigger than a canal. It was a river, the Sumida. A real, flowing stream of fresh water coming from outside the fire zone. That would be cooler. Falling debris could never drive it as hot as the canals. I darted onto the bridge and leapt off the upstream side. As disoriented as I was, it was easy to tell which way the water flowed with all the drifting junk. I hit the water and clawed back to the surface through the debris. I shoved it aside. Strange, oddly shaped—

—not debris. Bodies. Burned and drowned, and all around me.

Oh, right, the river. I reached for my pocket to dig out the venturi papers and destroy them.

I had no pocket, I was nude. Where was my mind?

I swam to the bank at the mid-width of the bridge, protected by several feet of concrete on either side, and joined a few others already hiding there. Spots all over my body stung, burns exposed to whatever was in the water. I anchored my feet in the mud the way the others had, and we clutched arms, keeping each other from being swept away. This would work. I would be safe here. We all would. Maybe.

Cracking, rumbling, crashing sounds continued all night. Hundreds of corpses floated by, blackened and face down. Sometimes I couldn't tell if it was a timber or part of another body. I ducked under now and then to stay wet.

I managed to swim out and collect one old man, two women, and a child, to add to the collection under the bridge. A child. I ranted like a sailor until I got him safe. Parents were supposed to have shipped children to the interior. Too many were still around, including Hideki.

Where was Hideki tonight? I had no hope for him.

For a time we found it hard to breath, but it got better after a while. The old man slipped away before dawn.

It was almost noon on March 10th before the ashes cooled

enough to invite in rescue workers. I helped the others out of the water when someone came by to take care of them. I stayed in the river until someone donated *monpe* for me to put on. I declined other help, saying I was fine, they had more important work.

Then I walked.

Miles and miles I walked, exploring the ruins. Utter desolation, so complete the only things standing were a few telephone poles and stray, drunken chimneys, like eerie, tilted gravestones. Monuments to horror. Sixteen square miles of the city, gone in one night. Fires still raged in many places, and smoldered in others. No one tried to contain them. Water mains would be broken, and there could be no electricity to pump seawater from the canals.

I found bodies roasted in holes in the ground, the air raid shelters we had been told would help. Stacked bodies beside the shell of a theater, suffocated when the oxygen gave out. A glut of bodies cooked or drowned in the stagnant canals. Water was a natural instinct, and I had almost made the same mistake.

Huddled forms in the middle of the streets were charred wood, or tires, but some were the remains of people. I stopped trying to figure out which were which.

Miku was gone. Little Hideki. His helpful father, his distant mother. His married sister had only moved a few blocks away. There wouldn't be a single Hyakutake still alive.

One small medical center had been set up. I asked where the others were.

"We're it."

"This is all?"

"Nine doctors, eleven nurses. Tokyo's disaster relief medical unit."

He sounded so bitter I couldn't fault him. I left him to his work. Some Red Cross first aid teams were starting to show up, as well.

The screams. That's what I had been suppressing. Wailing panic, and shrieking agony that continued for so much longer than it should have, while people burned and ran and died. Now the memory came storming back. The howling pain of death by fire. The high-pitched screams most of all. The children.

Oh God, America had paid them back. Japan had done unimaginable things, had performed supremely loathsome acts, had been the ones to start this war.

But America had paid them back, and would do so again and again.

Merciful heaven, when would it end?

Chapter 19

I felt ill when I heard what else happened on March 10th. On the very morning I crawled from the river, nude and scorched, vomiting from the smell of seared flesh, Japan held a parade. In the very same city. Downtown Tokyo celebrated Armed Forces Day with trombones and drums and a crowd lining the streets, while I wandered a few blocks away, losing count of the corpses and reliving the sounds of the dying.

That night I moved into a dormitory at the research complex. I might have been able to find another apartment, but they were ripping up more railroad track to recover steel for weapons, telling people to walk or ride bicycles, and if they removed my line the commute would become impossible. Besides, they wanted me to work longer hours, and staying on-site relieved me of most association duties.

The dormitory was the most repellant place I had ever lived, being adjacent to the complex's power plant. The boilers used a fuel oil that gave off thick black smoke, leaving a greasy coating on every surface. The khaki *monpe* I'd been given when crawling out of the Sumida would never be comfortable. I'd have to go to my office if I wanted to dress up for Sentaro. I'd never bring my nice clothes to the dorm.

The other twenty-three girls never stopped whining about bombs waking them up day and night. They knew nothing of real air raids. The research complex only got hit by B-29s once, and strafed a few times by carrier-based fighters, judging from the silhouettes passed out by the military to help people identify airplanes. Most of the damage was targeted at nearly factories. But it was annoying eating government-issue dry biscuits outdoors until they repaired the facility's dining hall. Of all the places to waste a bomb . . . .

Mrs. Omori didn't like the dormitory move any more than I did—Sentaro came to see me more often. He speculated on what we might be doing after the war. A rather forward proposition, I thought. His mother went nonlinear when she heard him talking about 'a future.' She practically staked out my office to keep us apart. Even worse, I caught her rummaging through the translations one day after lunch, messing up the pages, searching for something.

I stopped in the doorway. "May I help you?"

She leapt several inches in the air and spun around. "What are you hiding?"

"Nothing. Why are you searching my things?"

"Why do you care, if you have nothing to hide?"

"You have no right to intrude on my work. I have gained stature here and am no longer your employee."

"You cannot speak to me that way. You sneak onto this site by tricking my son, but you cannot gull me. The Admiral should never have overruled me and given you access to restricted material. You are up to something or you would not be so defensive." Omori spat on the floor and pushed past me into the hall.

Was she right? Should I have let her pry? No, the woman hated me, and nothing would defuse her suspicions. It was clear what she was hoping to find. She wouldn't succeed, but I would be even more careful in the future, covering my tracks, just in case.

Reports of firebombings continued for months. One city after another was hit. Dozens. Scores. Japan got another new prime minister in April. As if that would help their situation. We heard

President Roosevelt had died on April 12th, but that had equally little bearing on the war, as far as I could tell.

More information came flooding in from Germany. A backlog developed, things they'd refused to share before. Why?

On May 8th we found out. Germany had fallen. Japan was alone, and America would be shifting troops to the Pacific. The Soviet Union might even pile on and take parts of Manchuria or some of the northern islands.

People kept saying it. Japan was alone. Yet not one whispered of ending the conflict. Japan had never lost a war. Something would save them.

More university students were pulled out of school and turned into Kamikazes. It was not the time for education, for long-term planning. The war was all. The Divine Wind would blow again.

Admiral Tokiyasu's team got a second translator, and I had no more opportunities to doctor my reports. Paper was so scarce, translations ran from one edge of the page to the other, and older reports were scavenged for blank spaces. I wished I still had the art paper from the Korean island. I could have made a good trade with it.

The last data from Germany identified the optimal alloys for engine construction, better even than what the team here had come up with, so the overheating problem was licked and they went into production.

A good ten months after Germany fielded their first Me-262.

Everyone on the team cheered. So did I. They had no idea my reason was different from their own. Twelve months would have been better, or twenty-four, but I took what I could get.

Sentaro kept trying to see me, and Mrs. Omori retaliated by making my life miserable with accusations of theft, immoral conduct, and insubordination. Did anyone start to believe her? Were they still laughing? People tended to believe what they heard a lot, regardless of what it was.

The government issued sweet potato seedlings all across the country, and I helped plant them along the edges of buildings and fences. Flowers got ripped out to make room. The intent was to harvest them in the fall for fuel production, but I didn't think a single one would make it that far. People were too hungry.

The newspapers lamented the death of two famous sumo wrestlers when a stadium was bombed out. The end of the last sport left in Japan, they called it. I scrambled to hide the newsprint under a drawing of the jet's tail section when Mrs. Omori entered my office. No need to give her another reason to complain.

Another major firebombing hit Tokyo on May 27th, on the northwest this time, so I joined others in making rice balls and rounding up any bedding people could spare for the survivors. When I tried to translate 'rounding up,' though, it earned me some wary looks. A cattle ranching expression, and it sounded too Western.

June. Okinawa fell. A Volunteer Fighting Corps comprised of high school girls serving as field hospital nurses, known as the Princess Lily Brigade, was wiped out. A good fraction of them by suicide. I had to leave the cafeteria to keep from screaming at all the people who considered this admirable.

Chatter in the dining hall centered around a new program to have students dig up pine stumps, where timber had long since been harvested. The resin would be used for aviation fuel, like sweet potatoes. Many thought it fantastical that a jet could be powered by tree stumps. I asked if they refined it like oil or fermented it like potatoes, but no one knew.

July. The crop outlook was dire, thanks to a lack of fuel for tractors and a loss of fertilizer production. Newspapers said farming techniques were back to the 1800s, and the weather was making it worse. Tremendous numbers of people had fled to the countryside after the firebombings began, ten million of them, nearly two thirds of the population in the largest cities. A few trickled back, needing the wages from war work to pay their taxes and get black market food from those sellers still accepting cash. The 'rice' that was available was half other stuff.

The authorities stopped pressuring women to work. Production was way down, in part due to loss of factories, but mostly due to lack of raw materials. Either way, there was no longer a worker shortage. Many former laborers were mobilized into the 'Final People's Movement,' digging entrenchments all over the place as defense against the inevitable invasion of the Home Islands. I thanked my fortuitous stars I was spared that task.

I overheard a drill press operator in the dining hall moaning that between inflation and stable wages, they could no longer afford even half what they could a few years earlier, at the rare times things were available to buy. And no increase in pay came with their longer working hours. His friends shushed him and hustled him out, but he kept on about taxes being three times higher, and another fifth of his money going to savings bonds. It was the first public criticism I had heard.

When a test component broke a week later, 'thought police' were brought in. They arrested the man and gave him a public flogging with three lengths of bamboo bound together. It may have been an accident, or it may have been something else. He may not have been involved at all. But his complaint had been reported. The lack of evidence might be what saved his life.

On July 26th, the Allies announced their Potsdam Declaration. Japan would never be allowed to negotiate a surrender. It must be unconditional. No one knew how to react to that news.

America started dropping leaflets telling people where the next air raids would occur. A humanitarian gesture to destroy infrastructure but save lives? Thumbing their noses at Japanese helplessness? Or trying to demonstrate it was useless to continue? Arguments raged over how to interpret the act.

Then came August, and the prototype jet was ready to fly. Built and checked out and polished and proud. Engineers put up pictures on walls all over the complex.

Come time for the test flight, I was invited to observe. The whole research team caught a train the day before and stayed in dorms at the airbase. We rose before dawn and hiked out to the field, munching on rations of crackers. Clothes sagged and those with leather belts had extra holes punched in them. I couldn't recall the last time I'd seen a fat person. As we jostled for position alongside the tarmac, a historian found a place near me, recording everything in a notebook.

I peered over his elbow. At the top of his page was the date, August 6, 1945. They would not waste fuel this day, said his notes. I got him talking easily enough.

"Ah, my dear, this is not merely a test flight, but also a combat mission. They mounted a 20-mm cannon in the nose of the plane."

"They're attacking something?"

"Our Admiral would never risk his prototype against a massed bomber formation with fighter escort, but America sends over lone B-29s for reconnaissance. They've learned we never expend effort to intercept them."

"So we know one is coming?"

"Absolutely. A bomber is heading for the Hiroshima area right now. It will get a surprise."

The jet accelerated down the runway and lifted off smoothly. The engines worked fine, the airframe was sound. The people around me expected no problems. Faster rose the plane.

The nose shot up. It couldn't climb at that steep of an angle, it didn't have the thrust. It stalled, at too low an altitude, no time to recover. The pilot tried anyway, caught a break on a gust of wind, and got the nose down. Too far. It dipped further and the plane dove.

Into the ground.

I couldn't breathe. A fireball roared into the sky, and my mind superimposed the grinning face of the pilot as he walked past on his way to the plane. I had done this. All the good pilots were in combat. They had put an inexperienced boy on the joystick and sent him up to test the prototype. So when the ailerons and elevators didn't respond right, orifices instead of venturis, he overcompensated. Twice. Up, then down. And he didn't have the intuition to eject.

I had killed another man.

I had thought about this once, long ago. I had decided I was a warrior, and there would be casualties. Others could die, and so could I. It was all quite logical. I had thought it through, and accepted the principle. Embraced it.

It was my final lie. My last delusion. I was no warrior, and never would be. I still couldn't breathe. A man was dead because of me. Again.

I had killed on the Korean island. I had been heartless and ruthless and frigid back then. But that had been to save others. I had no such justification this time to sustain me.

Mrs. Omori leveled a finger at my nose. "She did it! I said you couldn't trust her. Those weren't accidents before. Mistranslations or errors of oversight. She did this on purpose."

No longer could I defend myself. No longer could I think on my feet and concoct some plausible excuse. I stared at the fireball, shaking my head, silent.

"She did it. She doesn't even deny it."

Someone took my arm. I couldn't resist. I couldn't even try. I was empty. Numb.

"She's in shock," said one officer. "That doesn't mean—"

"She did it." Mrs. Omori could read my face. She could recognize guilt. "I am sure of it."

A colonel nodded. "See her to the train and keep an eye on her. We will return to Tokyo, confine her to her office, and confiscate her materials." He waited until I looked up and caught his eye. "We will investigate this claim."

I didn't absorb what came next, not for many hours. A blur of railcars back to Tokyo, a ditch full of mud while the train was being strafed. Some walking. My undersized room at the research complex, and soldiers gathering up all my papers. Someone brought food. Steamed pumpkin; they wouldn't waste rice on a suspect. They escorted me to the restroom when I asked, and stepped out in the hall when I wanted to sleep. I tried to avoid that. Dreams came.

Time passed. A day, maybe two. They moved me to a cell, the only one they had at the research complex. It had a mat on the floor, and I slept better. My appetite improved. A little. Guards whispered about some awful new bomb the Americans had dropped. One of them spat at me.

"You destroyed the jet that could have shot down their B-29. You didn't kill a single pilot. You killed a whole city."

It made no sense. One bomb couldn't destroy a city.

They brought in an interrogator at one point, a policeman from Tokyo. Which of the several security forces he represented, I never found out, as he wasn't in uniform. I lost a couple of fingernails and he broke one of my toes. He threatened a lot more pain, but never delivered. Thankfully, he only asked who my fellow conspirators were, who I was working with, and I could truthfully say I was alone. Had he asked, had he hurt me any more, I could never have resisted spilling the rank, sordid tale of my past.

Another wait, then they put me in cuffs and took me to a room for trial. Witnesses testified they'd found mistakes in a few key technical details of my translations, essential details, the kinds of things that led to the worst of their developmental problems. Including the orifice and venturi switch for the guidance hydraulics. They'd found a document I had failed to eliminate. My work was so exemplary in other areas that I condemned myself with my own quality. The research team had long since stopped having anyone overcheck my work.

Mrs. Omori positively effervesced while serving as a character witness against me, citing underhanded attempts to subvert her son and pump him for military information. Sentaro showed up briefly, said not a word, and left.

Then one engineer described the results at two cities America had hit with their new weapon, which he insisted on laying at my door. "If our plane had worked as designed, it would have saved eighty thousand at Hiroshima alone." I could have mentioned that an undertrained pilot in an unfamiliar plane with a single 20-mm cannon was not likely to achieve anything, but that would not have endeared me to the judge. Besides, the engineer claimed that without my impediments they'd have been flying far more, far better aircraft by now.

Well, that much was true. It made the rest more bearable.

The result was inevitable. They sentenced me and hauled me

back to my cell.

And so it ended. In a few short days, I would hang. A civilized custom—they gave people a little time to settle their minds, to accept the peace of death. I ought to be frightened. Terrified, in fact. I reached deep and came up with nothing. Relief, perhaps. A trace of regret that my parents would never know what came of me. A bit larger dollop of remorse that I had not done enough to honor the memory of Anders and Brutus and the other POWs. Or Maison and his crew.

Eighty thousand dead at Hiroshima. A hundred thousand killed in one night's Tokyo firebombing. One hundred forty thousand in the Kanto earthquake. In the face of such numbers, what was one more death? Why should I be special?

Two men thrown off a cliff on a lonely Korean island. A sunken submarine. A jet pilot.

Me.

What was one more death? Justice, long delayed and well deserved.

~~~~

They came for me. Had to get me out there in time for high noon, like in some silly old movie. What would they think if I told them this was the custom in westerns?

They brought my things so I could put on my blouse and skirt. One should depart this world in dignity, a private said, turning his back so I could change. Politeness when it no longer mattered. I'd heard of this—Churchill said something about it once—but I hadn't expected it here.

I put my last piece of newsprint on the pile with the rest. I wasn't sure if I'd been composing my story or composing myself, but it filled the time until this moment. Interesting how much I'd had to struggle to recall some English terms, after all those years of translating away from English, then moving on to German. The script was barely discernable over the top of the printed Japanese, and would be hard for anyone to read if they ever tried. If they did, and decided to piece together my story, I hoped they painted me
~~~~

at least a little brave.

That wouldn't happen. The authorities didn't care what I had to say. Dreams, regrets, or a confession, it was all the same. The purpose was to calm me, so I didn't humiliate myself as they led me away to the grand finale. No matter, it had accomplished what they wanted. I was ready.

They cuffed my hands behind my back and led me down a hall and outside into a warm summer day. Wednesday, August 15, they told me. They didn't realize it was my birthday. Twenty-one. I had made it to adulthood.

The courtyard between the buildings held most of the soldiers and research staff, here for the spectacle. They hadn't bothered with a proper scaffold, with a trap door and a long drop. Too much trouble and wood was in short supply, said one of the men gripping my elbows. He gloated that two posts and a crossbeam with a pulley would do for me. Where had they dug up that bright blue rope? It looked like sash cord for fancy drapes. Probably from some hotel that used to cater to Westerners.

A couple of soldiers set up a radio on a table in the center of the courtyard, running a wire back indoors to plug it in. Something unprecedented was about to happen. The emperor was going to address his people directly. It was nearly noon, they had to hurry, muttered one man.

Oh, the people were here for the emperor, not me. What an ego I had.

The major in charge of my execution detail signaled the two soldiers to drag me over to the gallows. They needn't have bothered. I was perfectly willing to walk.

"Perhaps the emperor will inform us of a glorious victory. No one seems to know. But you will serve as a fitting celebration, if so." The major gestured and one of the soldiers put the noose around my throat. He yanked it snug.

It was happening so fast. Years in coming, yet now it came so fast.

The major raised his arm. The rope went taut.

It was time.

Chapter 20

They hanged me.

My toes left the ground as the radio scratched to life. The emperor's speech began, and everyone turned to listen. The rope slid through the guards' fingers, my feet returned to earth, and tension slackened on the noose. I understood. They could not enjoy watching me die, and concentrate on the emperor's words, at the same time. It would be disrespectful.

The speech was difficult to follow at first, statical like a recording, and in a formal, old-fashioned kind of Japanese. Then I realized what I was hearing, what Hirohito was saying. The words rained down like spewing lava on the souls of his subjects. An announcer came on after he finished, clarifying the message for those who hadn't comprehended. People bent to the ground, groaning, weeping silently, as the meaning sank in. The emperor had accepted the terms of the joint declaration by the Allied powers. Nowhere did he use the word 'surrender.' He used words like 'the war situation has developed not necessarily to Japan's advantage, while the general trends of the world have all turned against her interest.'

The meaning was crystalline, and the follow-up announcer rammed it home. The war was over. Japan had lost. And the impact was pure uncertainty.

The major took a dozen steps when the broadcast ended. Someone switched off the radio. Engineers and clerks, my guards, the cooks and cleaning staff, everyone wandered around, or knelt, each alone amid the many, each lost in their personal bubble of grief. The terms of the Potsdam Declaration had been much debated in Japan since it had first been announced. What did unconditional surrender mean? What would happen to the emperor? Must they all become Christian? Would they be an American colony like the Philippines?

The anguish continued. The silence was eerie. The afternoon sun blazed on heads bowed toward the imperial palace.

No one paid the slightest attention to me.

After half an hour, the major pulled out his revolver and shot himself in the mouth. No one reacted. A few minutes later, another officer took his life. They could not bear the disgrace of defeat. The samurai code. *Seppuku*, modern style, in preference to being taken by the enemy.

After a time of being ignored, I looked at my rope. It dangled loose. I walked over to the shade, the rope passing through the pulley and trailing behind me.

A few people got up eventually and slogged indoors. No one looked at me. No one cared about my impact on the war any longer. Or not today. They might later. I went back to my cell and knelt on the floor. The newsprint I had covered with my chicken-scratches was gone, likely fodder for someone's stove. It was evening before a guard stopped by. He stared at me in silence, then said they had received orders to halt all actions in regard to prisoners. The occupying authorities would review all cases and administer their own justice. He removed my noose, unshackled me, and locked the cell door.

Next day they moved me to a jail in Tokyo. A few days after that, Americans arrived and took over. They didn't seem to care if I overheard them talking while they set up shop. Tales of Kamikazes circling a mile away from an Allied task force minutes after the emperor's declaration, clearly headed in to attack, but instead peeling off one by one and diving into the sea. Tales of total submission when the occupying troops had worried about guerilla warfare all over the islands, for years to come.

"They're like Robert E. Lee," said one. "After the Civil War some southerners wanted to hide out in the hills and keep fighting, but Lee said don't do it. He said they'd given it their best shot, and lost, and that was that."

"Thank God for honorable enemies," the other replied.

"You got that right. I tell you, man, it's embarrassing it took us this long to defeat a country in this bad a shape."

I asked them where they'd served. Nowhere, it turned out. America was sending in green troops as occupiers. They wanted no one who bore bitter memories of the fighting.

Remarkably compassionate. The issue hadn't occurred to me, but someone was thinking, and that someone deserved thanks.

They asked what I was in for, what the Japanese had intended. When I told them, they didn't seem to know how to react, and didn't say another word.

I was transferred twice more, the second time to a women's prison. Almost a month passed before it came my turn for judgment. I hoped they would move it along once they realized my conviction was legitimate.

I had waited long enough.

Chapter 21

"So, Keiko Terauchi, huh?"

I nodded, standing at attention. The colonel seated before me shuffled a few thin onion-skin carbon copies.

"I've read your file. Says you're a traitor. Not too many of those for a county this big. Damn few outright anti-military acts, even when you were losing. What made you different?"

I said nothing.

"You love the West? Hate your parents? Like to defy authority?"

I remained silent. I couldn't tell if he was naturally hostile or trying to get a rise out of me.

"Nothing to say? Well, treason is treason. I should probably give you back to the Japs and let 'em do their worst. We're supposed to patch up relations now the war's over, you know."

I could have told him who I really was, if my soldiers from the island had survived. But the submarine sank, and without that evidence I couldn't trust Maison's change of heart.

So this colonel was right, there was nothing to say. I had done what I had done. It was not my place to explain, or justify, or beg. It was this man's turn now, as America's representative, and he must make his own determinations.

He tapped his pen on the form in front of him, read a bit more, and looked up. "Screw that. You helped the U.S., and I'll be damned if I let the other Nips string you up for it. My brother faced one of those jets over Germany. Nasty things. Not only that, those A-bombs gave your emperor an excuse to break a tie in the Diet and end this madness, and this here says you helped on that too. Maybe. In any case, we were looking at a million casualties to get ashore on Honshu, and that's just Americans. God knows what would have happened to you people if we'd had to invade."

I bowed. He had made his decision. If he wished to justify his mercy, that was up to him. Why would he believe that engineer's claim at my trial, though? I had killed the jet pilot, yes, but I could no more take credit for helping end the war than I would accept blame for destroying an entire city. Germany had been annihilated before they gave up. The South in the American Civil War had been decimated before they threw in the towel. Russia had suffered incredible losses, yet resisted both Napoleon and Hitler. It was only years of fighting and losing, months of bombing and burning, and no chance to stop the enemy juggernaut, that could lead Japan to surrender. Sure, the final two monster bombs may have tipped the balance, but the nation had to be teetering before it could fall.

The colonel scribbled a note, stamped my file, and signed it. "That's it. Your record is clear. Sins wiped clean. Now go start a new life."

Guards removed my handcuffs, escorted me out of the building, and told me to be off. They slammed the door behind them.

And just like that, I was free.

Free. To do what? Japanese who knew me would have nothing to do with me after this.

Time for another fresh start. I must find somewhere to go. With no money, no possessions, no home, and no clue what to do next.

Business as usual.

And then I couldn't help it. I laughed. I laughed and I cried and I melted onto the steps and barely kept myself from floating away. The burdens of my life had been lifted by the casual swipe of the colonel's pen. The war was over, and I was emancipated.

I had once said I would burn the hair I had hacked off, my long lovely tresses, when I earned a release from my past. Well, my hair had burned in the great Tokyo firestorm last March, and now I had been liberated. My timing was only off by half a year. Close enough.

I laughed again. Oh, I had guilt. I had regrets, in plentiful supply. But I had been forgiven, by the official purveyor of justice in this time and place. As if he could possibly know what he was forgiving. So why did I feel exonerated? More likely it was relief. Maybe I really was glad to be alive. I could feel guilty again later. I would schedule a time for it.

Another chuckle escaped me. Hysterical, that was the word. Though perhaps I deserved a little hysteria today.

But what to do next, as a displaced American in occupied Japan?

Well, I could help the American occupiers, even if the thought did bring a faint longing for a past I could not reclaim. At least they were my people.

I stopped cold.

My people. God, were they? I could never return to America. The FBI's records would still have me down as a traitor for assisting my mother. They had my fingerprints from the house. I had committed myself to remaining in Japan for the rest of my life. So what else—

My jaw dropped, and it suddenly hit me. Of all the despicable, execrable things I had ever done, this one went deep and smashed me like a torpedo.

I had become my mother.

My mother had been injected, infected into a new country she had never intended to select.

That was me.

My mother had remained loyal to the land of her birth, despite overwhelming incentives to accept her new place of residence.

That was me.

My mother had hated her lack of options, then made her decisions. She had chosen what she considered the proper course of action, and borne the consequences. She had been criminal, and commendable, and honorable, and a traitor.

And that, more than anything, was me. A hopeless contradiction. A useless attempt to seek a proper path, something I could call virtuous, and becoming lost at every turn. For everything I did had been wrong, and right, and good, and evil.

Just thinking about it made me dizzy.

No more. Enough. I would not be my mother. I would make my way down a different path. No longer would I be Japanese-American, I would become American-Japanese. Cast off loyalty to the old and adopt the new, be that treason or fidelity. The same thing Japanese did when they moved to the States and committed to a life in their new home. What any immigrant did, leaving one land for another. I would embrace Japan, embrace my life here, and aspire to become worthy of being called Japanese.

I should change my name again, to hide from anyone bitter at my wartime deeds. Discard the old and . . . . No, wait. I could resume Kristy Hara. That was the one thing I could keep, to honor my father, my past. Western names would be tolerated soon, and it would not be so rare as to stand out. It would serve as closure, of a sort.

I wadded up my identification papers, the one thing in my pocket, and took off down the street. There were plenty of trash receptacles to choose from. And easy to obtain new papers, with fire and chaos to blame for the loss. I would lose all my years of savings bonds, but they had likely been confiscated upon my conviction. Even if I'd been able to recover them, they weren't worth much, what with the absurd late-war inflation rates.

I would frequent the soup kitchens being set up by the U.S. Army. People expected rations to become tighter before they improved, thanks to all the soldiers returning from occupied lands. I would hitchhike to Nagasaki, take a ferry, get as far from

Tokyo as I could, and help with the clean-up and rebuilding. I would slave and save and go to an art academy someday, when culture returned to Japan. I had not drawn in, goodness, nearly three years, except for those abortive twaddles in 1944 that almost gave me a heart attack. No wonder I had become a mental stress-bucket.

Sentaro had quite properly abandoned me. One should never forgive betrayal. Poor man, his mother would lord it over him. But perhaps I would meet somebody special someday, someone who could reconcile himself to my flawed condition, and help me raise a family. Perhaps.

I would seek a dull life. A nice life. I would not track down the POW camp commandant or the doctor. I had seen enough excitement, and the world had seen enough revenge. Let the authorities do what they thought best, and leave me out of it.

Tokyo Bay stretched out to the left. South to the Pacific, then east, far off, lay the world I had left behind. I kissed the fingertips of my right hand, touched my heart and forehead, and held my open palm toward the distant, fading past.

And then I turned west, toward my future.

Epilogue

"Grandmother, you have to see this."

"I don't like war stories." That was putting it mildly. I leaned on my walker and carefully lowered myself to the sofa. I had followed the aftermath of the Pacific War with surprise over the years, and sometimes anger. Surprise in the form of a book about the Nakano Spy School, an agency unlike anything else in the Imperial Japanese Army, training what were in effect modern ninjas. That is, authentic, historical, ethical agents, not the insulting latter-day fantasies about assassins, thieves, and over-the-top martial arts. Warriors with an emphasis not on blind military obedience, but rather creativity and empathy for one's enemies. More important than any other issue? Integrity. How else could one remain moral and upright while deceiving friends as well as foes? I could almost believe I had approached their lofty goals, except for one key deficiency. Ninjas were trained to survive. I had been too willing to die.

Speaking of fantasies and altered annals, that led to the anger side of my memories. I hated revisionist historians, pushing agendas and distorting perspectives, like that business with the atom bombs. They were more than appalling, but . . . America could send over one plane with a nuke, or more cheaply send three hundred planes with several hundred thousand incendiaries, yet no one talked about the horror of fire even though it was worse. Over three times the devastation and more killed, not one of them quickly. And total excess cancer deaths in all the decades since 1950, when studies began? Maybe a thousand. In the context of the war that was a drop in the bucket. And why was it so bad to live an extra thirty years before becoming a war casualty?

Okay, that was callous. Blame it on old age. To be fair, my experience in a firestorm could be coloring my judgment. Years after the war, excavators still uncovered charred bodies, people hiding in backyard bomb shelters while the city collapsed around them. U.S. schools taught little about what had been done to Japan. And yet—

—and yet, which was worse? American ignorance, or willful disbelief by Japanese of what their army had done, what their doctors had done, on behalf of their nation?

"Grandmother?"

"Yes? Sorry. You were saying?"

"Come on," said my grandson. "This movie is different. Everyone says so. It's supposed to be good, and the lead character has your name. It'll be fun."

"My name?"

"*Hai*, Kristy Hara. Come on."

Insanity, glorifying war in film, glorifying death. It seemed unfair I was still alive after all this time. But I let my grandson drag me off to the cinema. He only came to visit me in the nursing home once in a while. Men his age were so busy. When he came all excited like this, not out of duty, I could never refuse his request. He had always been a delightful boy, so unlike his mother.

Ah, his mother. I never regretted allowing myself to become a trophy wife to a man of respectability, an opposition leader released from prison after the war. I counted myself lucky to have done so. There were so few eligible men, and I wasn't about to marry an American GI like many girls did. I could never have pulled that off. And it was worth it, for the child I produced before he lost interest in me.

I missed little Kira, so unlike most of her generation. She adored her father, believed every report of Japan's atrocities, and rejected every adult who participated, including me. It wasn't like I could tell her the truth, not in the mentality of post-war Japan. But Kira was a brilliant, beautiful girl, even if she did leave home and never look back. Like mother, like daughter.

My grandson was the polar opposite, ignoring the past and visiting whenever he could. Like for today's movie. A qualm tripped through me. The character was 'Kristy Hara'? What were the odds?

He took me to a small place, what they used to call an 'art' theater in the U.S. The lights went down, the audience stilled.

And then I saw the movie.

I could barely catch my breath, watching some actress live out my months on the Korean POW island. Halfway through some words escaped me. "How could they . . . ? The hermit? He'd be long dead."

"Shh, Grandmother. It's just a movie."

I kept watching, gaping. So much they had right. Not everything, but so much. The hospital, the cave, the top of the cliff.

Me kicking men off the cliff.

By the time the submarine descended, leaving Kristy, leaving me, on the beach, my cheeks were wet. Then came the final scene.

The image of myself blurred away, replaced by sunlight glistening off fresh snow outside a two-story rest home. A young woman peered out the second-story window. Cut to an inside view. Behind the woman, an old man lay in his bed, eyes shut, exhausted.

"We got depth charged just off the island, Sarah. Hell of a thing, hearing explosions, feeling the boat shake. You can damn well bet we was praying and cursing so's to make the angels weep."

The young woman held a cup and helped him take a sip of water.

"We dove, wove, and idled. When he thought the time was right, Captain Maison fired some trash from one torpedo tube and released a bunch of oil."

"Why would he do that?"

"Made the Japs up top think they'd sunk us. After we got away, took us weeks to get home. We pooled experiences and pieced together Kristy's story. Maison had a yeoman take it down; that's those notes I gave you. By the time we fathomed most of it, we figured we were the biggest collection of asses in history."

"You couldn't—"

"*Barracuda* was sunk on her next patrol, four months later. Some undercover mission to Vladivostok. Navy didn't want to admit it, so they renamed a training sub *Barracuda* and scrapped it after the war."

Sarah set down the cup and returned to the window.

"Japanese defenses got tighter. The Navy never went back to the island. In October '45, they found it abandoned. Tracked down the commandant and doctor, though. The colonel was dead. The doctor got himself transferred into Unit 731 during the war, and was hidden away in a civilian hospital afterward. Still alive, last I heard. U.S. powers-that-be swept the whole thing under a reinforced concrete floor to keep Soviets from learning biological warfare secrets. They ordered us never to talk about it."

Sarah bit her lip. "And Kristy?"

The old man's eyes opened and slowly rolled toward her. He shook his head.

A nurse opened the door and stuck her nose in. "Time to rest, Major Donnerty."

The old man sank into his pillow.

"One more minute," said Sarah.

The nurse nodded and retreated. Sarah went to the bed and picked up a shopping bag. She drew out a Christmas card and laid it on the old man's waist.

"The Anders. A respected judge. Three children, seven grandchildren."

The scene shifted to a grainy old black-and-white home movie. A sunny day in a backyard, with an older Sergeant Anders holding a woman's waist. Three children played on swing set and teeter-totter.

Back to the rest home. Sarah laid a handful of Christmas and Hanukkah cards on the old man. "Saunders, a great mechanic. Taffin, ordained minister. Zeiss, music instructor."

Another grainy home movie. A reunion in a park, families talking, eating, laughing, with older versions of Zeiss, Taffin, and the corporal. Two kids clung to Zeiss' legs while he reeled around waving his arms.

A newer, better quality clip. A much older Sergeant Anders, Brutus, and others grinning at a horseshoe pit, arguing about whose turn it was. Beyond them, dozens of adults, and some forty grandchildren running, shouting, frolicking.

Sarah's voice overlaid the picture. "The Fenwicks, Broadmans, Rockovs, Teppanis. All told, fifty-one children, over a hundred grandchildren, and the next generation well underway. Two doctors, five teachers, and a senator. That is what you should be remembering. Scientists and dancers, technicians and rock bands."

The scene cut back to the rest home. Sarah added the last of the cards to the pile on the old man and set down the bag.

"So don't you tell me Kristy Hara was never seen again."

She kissed her fingertips and pressed them to the old man's forehead.

"We see her—" She went to the door. "—every day."

She missed the knob on the first try, got it open, and left.

The old man lay motionless, until one hand crept from beneath the sheets and rubbed the corner of a card. The movie credits began to roll as the picture dissolved back to a scene of me, standing alone on the shore of the island.

"Well, Grandmother, what did you think?"

I stared at the credits. The director, the producer. And then I saw it. The writer. A woman named Sarah Donnerty. I hadn't misheard the nurse in the film. The major, of all people, had leaked the story.

"I can't, I mean, they really survived. It didn't sink."

"What? Oh, yeah, the Americans. I'm surprised they killed off Kristy, though."

"All these years, I thought . . . ."

It broke me. Foolishness, getting all emotional at my age. Why hadn't I ever suspected? *USS Enterprise* had been reported sunk numerous times in the Japanese press. Mistakes like that were common.

But no, I could never have believed my men got away. My powers of wishful thinking would never have stretched so far.

"Um, I guess you liked it." He handed me a handkerchief.

I snatched it and rubbed my face. Others around us shuffled down rows and up aisles toward the doors, murmuring amidst a miasma of popcorn stench and inappropriately uplifting background music.

I couldn't move.

"Grandmother? Are you all right?"

I composed myself, swiveled in my seat, and watched him. Comprehension came slowly. He was usually more agile on the uptake. Then he backed in his seat, staring. I couldn't tell if it was shock, or pride, or revulsion.

"There's more," I said. "There's more to the story."

~~~~

On a cold spring day, months later, I descended from an airplane in San Francisco. A jet. I had never before flown in a jet. I didn't trust them, but it was the only practical way to get across the ocean.

A woman in passport control acted astonished. "Are you—" Then she colored slightly and waved me through. "Sorry. Never mind."

My grandson rented a car, put my walker in the trunk with the luggage, and drove me to Alameda. Nothing was left of the old neighborhood. We had searched, but found no record of my friends Maxine and Rosita.

My grandson had gotten ahold of Sarah Donnerty, though, after his original letter temporarily disappeared in a blitz of fan mail. She hadn't believed him, at first. She thought it was a prank, and not the only one she'd heard. But somehow, in a later round
~~~~

of emails, he got her attention. That would explain all the probing he had put me through, digging for details about Major Donnerty and the POW camp. When Sarah finally accepted that he knew the real Kristy Hara, she had insisted he drag me across the Pacific.

Sarah had wanted to pick us up at the airport and escort us around, but I wasn't ready for that. I needed to take things more slowly, to adjust to my return to these shores. To reacknowledge the land of my birth. To breathe in the smells and learn the flavor of this newer America.

Our schedule gave me little time for acclimation. That very evening, without a rest and with barely time to change, my grandson took me to a party on the second floor of our hotel. Something Sarah Donnerty had arranged, he said. Sarah met us in the lobby first and led us in. It gave me qualms to think this pleasant young woman was the granddaughter of a man I had almost killed. A man who had almost killed me.

The conference center was jammed. Ripples fanned out as the crowd saw me, backing in rings to make room. Someone clapped, so of course they all had to, and praise and thanks washed over me. None of my men were still alive. Major Donnerty was last and had passed away the previous year. He'd not likely have wanted to see me again, anyway. And they told me Maison was a war casualty. But the room was packed with children and grandchildren, and I wanted to meet every one of them. I wanted all their names, all their histories. Well over a hundred, including spouses, and there were certain to be more who couldn't make it. A southern drawl, and I'd found Sergeant Anders' offspring. I tried to recognize other characteristics from my men, but people were too different. One of Taffin's grandchildren still had a picture I had drawn of him, and begged me to sign it. No trace of his Brooklyn accent. Durban hadn't had any kids, but I searched until I found a daughter of Brutus; she was the chattiest person there. It was drinking from a fire-hose and I was lucky to remember one name in twenty.

Sarah must have spent every penny she earned from her story to fly in so many people. It had to be a kind of resolution, to help them appreciate their past and honor the memory of their ancestors. So much pomp could not possibly all be for me.

The hardest thing was their acceptance of my murders. My actions had, in essence, been no different from Nazi concentration camp inmates who helped their captors kill fellow prisoners. It was help, or die yourself. Everyone had a right to make it through, any way they could. But it still didn't feel right, and that was an insult to those in the camps, and that wasn't right, either. It was all so confusing.

The party also included a few silly souls with cameras and microphones. They acted like I was some sort of hero. Ridiculous. Heroes solved their own problems. I muddled along, drifting on the currents of war, making tiny waves when I could, and getting rescued by others. Not the stuff of legend. All I wanted was to revel in the confirmation that my soldiers had survived, and gone home, and made lives for themselves. Knowing this, I could die happy.

My grandson and Sarah saw me trapped by the reporters. They teamed up, ran interference, and broke me free. Impressive that strangers from different cultures could work together so well. But if I caught either of those two making eyes at the other, I'd set them to rights in short order. There was only so much sugar I could take.

I nodded thanks and got back to meeting the descendants. One older man shook my hand like a politician seeking a vote. A little girl presented me with a violet. A pair of teens wondered if they could name their choir the 'Hara Harmonizers.' Fortunately, they got distracted by hors d'oeuvres and I moved on before I had to answer.

Someone had a small dog in a bag. The fourth 'Kristy' in their family. It had become a tradition. Other people were more serious, grasping my fingertips or kissing my cheek with mumbled words. I tried to thank them back, but none of them understood why. Maybe I didn't understand, myself.

They'd set up what they probably thought was a Japanese tea service along one wall, for those not wanting alcohol. I took a cup, smiled, and kept on mingling, clasping one hand after another.

These people didn't know the half of what I had done after their fathers left the island, but I had told my grandson, and it would all come out soon enough. That could well revise their opinion of me. Even more, it could change how everyone back in Japan saw me. They might not want me to return.

But none of that mattered. What anyone thought of Kristy Hara had never been the issue. These people were alive, and well, and I . . .

. . . yes. Oh, yes.

My mind is quiet.

The End

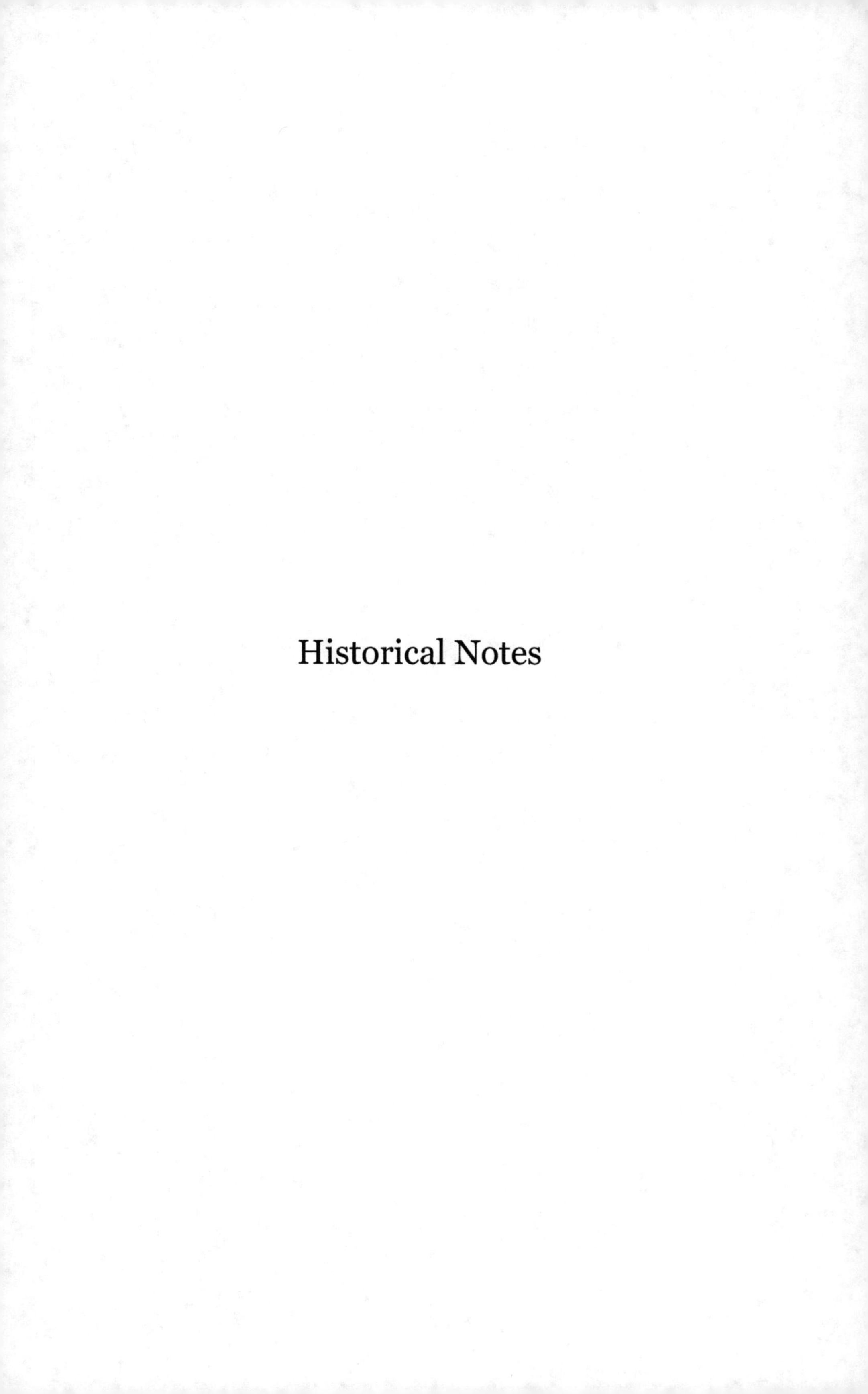

Historical Notes

Historical Notes

1. An excellent reference work regarding civilian life in World War II Japan is "Valley of Darkness" by Thomas R. H. Havens (University Press of America, 1986; originally published by Norton, 1978). It includes several interesting photographs, including one of the imperial army band marching down a street in Tokyo the morning after the March 9-10, 1945 firestorm, with refugees fleeing in the foreground.

2. John Man published two books that provide perspective on some aspects of Japanese cultural history—"Samurai: The Last Warrior," and "Ninja: 1,000 Years of the Shadow Warrior." Many other references address the same topics.

3. The semi-autobiographical novel "A Boy Called H" by Kappa Senoh contains much detail regarding one young teenager's life during the war. "Cherry Blossoms in Twilight" is a short memoir of a young girl's experiences, by Yaeko Sugama Weldon and Linda E. Austin. And "The Gods of Heavenly Punishment" by Jennifer Cody Epstein provides another fictional civilian perspective of the war years.

4. Some things can't be made up. Like the dinner party for a Kamikaze. A Japanese-American beta-reader, born in Tokyo in 1938, described a scene between his aunt and his cousin, and their conversation is reproduced here. The pilot in this story is named after that cousin.

5. Otherwise, the novel is fiction, except for historical figures and events such as the names of the emperor and prime minister of Japan, and the admiral in charge of the jet development program. In addition, most all of the incidents depicted in Part 2 actually happened, like people tromping over a giant American flag painted on *Ginza* Avenue, and children carting off their school stoves for recycling. I remain curious about the choreography of the "Decisive Aerial Warfare Ballet."

6. The names of other Japanese characters in the story are derived from combinations of given names and family names of Japanese generals and admirals who served during the war. Most especially, there was a Japanese admiral known as "King Kong Hara," both for his size and his love of American horror films. This combination of Japan and America seemed appropriate for Kristy.

7. Numerous sources are available on the military history of the period, documenting Japanese atrocities in occupied lands and their treatment of prisoners of war. Other sources, declassified long after the war, discuss testing on human subjects, particularly biological warfare tests by Japan's "Unit 731." Again, the specific characters and acts in this book are fiction.

8. Military operations and dates are portrayed as accurately as possible, even when information would have often been delayed or suppressed inside Japan. Even the problems with American torpedoes being duds early in the war were real, thanks to extraordinarily poor designs and a "cost-saving" decision not to test prior to deploying the weapons.

9. Regarding casualty figures, the book uses revised estimates published decades after the events; i.e., those which appear to be the most accurate. (This was a judgment call. Both higher and lower estimates exist.) This was done in preference to using the guesses being tossed around at the time, which varied considerably.

10. Kristy's damage comparison between Hiroshima and Tokyo is correct (about 4.7 square miles obliterated at Hiroshima, and near 16 in the Tokyo raid depicted herein; both events left survivors who were physically and mentally scarred). Her opinions are based on her own experiences and the technology of the era. (Obviously, nuclear weapons later became much more powerful.) But the shock value of the atom bombs, despite the fact that firebombing had been causing far more damage, was cited as a basis for surrender in the emperor's speech.

11. After the war, a series of committees were established in the U.S. to study the "Biological Effects of Ionizing Radiation," and they have issued BEIR reports every few years since then. They address excess cancer deaths from the atom bombs (approximately 20 percent of all people die of cancer; that number is rising as other health risks drop). Kristy's post-war estimate is based on their studies. An interesting article regarding the first such report (BEAR I at the time, for "Atomic") is at http://atomicinsights.com/shaping-public-perceptions-radiation-risk.

12. Finally, on a personal note, my father was the U.S. Army Air Corps meteorologist on Tinian during the war. B-29 raids on Japan originated from Tinian, Saipan, and Guam in the Mariana Islands, and he gave the weather reports for them, which determined primary and secondary targets. After the war he suffered from PTSD, in large part from seeing the Strategic Bombing Survey reports of the damage inflicted on Japan, and knowing his part in it.

About the Author

Charley Pearson retired after a career with the U.S. Naval Nuclear Propulsion Program (a.k.a. Naval Reactors), overseeing chemical and radiological environmental remediation at closing facilities following the end of the Cold War, releasing them for unrestricted future use with EPA and state agreement.

Other deeds included creating a lay-up protocol for ships going into extended maintenance periods that saved the Navy tens of millions of dollars in later rust-removal efforts. Upon retirement, awarded the National Nuclear Security Administration silver medal, the Navy's Superior Public Service Medal, and what insiders jokingly refer to as "the vaunted NR plaque."

Charley can be found at charleypearson.com (includes contact information). And if you know of anyone having a mind to write something themselves, that site includes a "Writer Aids" page with many suggestions and links to the advice of others. Hope it helps!

www.ingramcontent.com/pod-product-compliance
Lightning Source LLC
Chambersburg PA
CBHW060547310726
48982CB00007B/1038
* 9 7 8 0 9 9 7 2 9 9 3 5 9 *